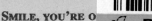

Amid the gunfire and growing racket, someone else screamed: "It's coming back!"

An instant later, the huge airplane roared over once again, this time even lower and trailing even more of an ear-splitting noise behind it. Everyone could see it this time. It was big and black. And yes, they all saw the cameras this time too. Not only a huge lens in a bubble located on the belly of the plane, but people in black uniforms were aboard the plane, hanging out open windows, taking pictures with hand cameras!

The Chief started screaming at his men again to shoot at the airplane. But it was already too late. The plane was gone, heading back from where it came, the mountains to the north.

Suddenly everything was quiet again. People were just standing around, dazed, in shock. Nothing like this had ever happened in Khrash before. Even though they were Al Qaeda, they were protected here. Or at least they thought they were.

And as the Chief and Saheeb the Syrian watched in horror, Jabal finally lost it.

"Allah, have mercy on my soul," the terrorist gasped. "The Crazy Americans . . . They are coming to get me!"

"Maloney's page-turning plots are what everyone would like to see in real life: direct, decisive action against the Al Qaeda killers, without ceremony or pretense. Maloney has his finger on the pulse of the nation. As he sends his Superhawk heroes into the global fight against terrorism, his grasp of modern technical detail combines with the most authentic presentation of terrorist forces, making this the top action series in the market place."

—Walter Boyne, author of *Operation Iraqi Freedom: What Went Right, What Went Wrong, and Why*

"Mack Maloney has created a team of realistic characters that pulse with patriotic fervor . . . Maloney hasn't just crafted a great war story, he has set a new standard for action-packed thrillers."

—Robert Doherty, bestselling author of AREA 51 series

SUPERHAWKS

★ ★ ★

STRIKE FORCE DELTA

Mack Maloney

St. Martin's Paperbacks

SUPERHAWKS: STRIKE FORCE DELTA

Copyright © 2005 by Mack Maloney.

ISBN: 0-312-93822-5
EAN: 9780312-93822-2

Printed in the United States of America

St. Martin's Paperbacks edition / December 2005

St. Martin's Paperbacks are published by St. Martin's Press, 175 Fifth Avenue, New York, NY 10010.

10 9 8 7 6 5 4 3 2 1

PART ONE
Saving Thunder

Chapter 1

There was enough plutonium in the suitcase to blow up half of West Africa.

The suitcase was locked in the trunk of the old battered Land Rover, wrapped in lead blankets and duct-taped over and over, more than a hundred times. At the moment, it was leaking only a small amount of radiation.

Six men were riding in the Land Rover. They were all carrying AK-47 assault rifles and machetes. They were members of the Angolan Popular Front, hardened veterans of insurgency and jungle warfare fought over the past few decades against a variety of enemies, including the armed forces of South Africa.

There was another Land Rover driving in front of this one. It was painted white with huge red crosses on its hood and doors—but this vehicle had nothing to do with the International Red Cross. It, too, was filled with armed men. They were mercenaries, many of them ex-members of the British SAS.

The third vehicle in this strange parade was a doubly

armored Humvee. Eight men were jammed inside this tanklike truck. They were members of Delta Force, America's premier Special Forces team. They were the most heavily armed group of the three.

It was midnight. It was raining hard. The three vehicles were speeding along a muddy winding mountain road very close to the border of Nigeria and Cameroon.

The three disparate groups were not compadres—far from it. They were three parts of an exchange team. The plutonium, partially enriched and near weapons grade, was being swapped for 16 pounds of uncut diamonds worth $70 million. Russian-made and in the possession of the Angolans via a very circuitous route, the nuclear material would be disposed of at sea once the insurgents were paid. The diamonds were being provided by Central Bank of Paris; the United Nations had purchased them via a secret bank account. The British mercs had arranged the transaction; they were in for 10 percent. The muscle, needed as insurance that the deal actually got done, was being provided by Delta Force.

The plan was simple, this after months of intense negotiations. The plutonium and its caretakers would drive to a point just over the border into Nigeria where officials from the United Nations' Non-Proliferation Group would be waiting. They had the diamonds, plus bags full of cash. The Brits would be paid their $7 million, then sent on their way. The plutonium would be surrendered to the UN group and the diamonds would be handed over. Then the Angolans, too, would be allowed to disappear.

From there the material would be taken aboard a French Army helicopter for its trip two hundred miles out to sea to be dropped to its watery grave. The UN group would then combine with the Delta escort and together they would drive to the port city of Oran, where a U.S. Navy cruiser was waiting offshore to take them aboard.

The three vehicles were right on schedule, crossing into Nigeria just a few minutes after midnight. The meeting point was at a border station next to the Okewa Bridge, a place conveniently abandoned by Nigerian troops for the evening. The tiny convoy pulled up to find the UN group already there. Four men wearing blue windbreakers with the letters *UN* emblazoned on the back were waiting on the porch of a tiny cement block building. They had a strongbox containing the diamonds; they also had the $7 million in cash for the mercs. A French Army Alouette copter was parked nearby, its rotors spinning, its crew looking out on the proceedings anxiously.

The rain had stopped by now and the full moon was coating everything in a pale silver light. Some passwords were successfully exchanged, shouted over the rumbling of the copter's engines, this as the plainclothes Delta soldiers set up a defense line in front of the border station. The mercs got their payoff first. Ripping the fake Red Cross symbols from their truck, they promptly left, driving back across the bridge and into Cameroon. The Angolans then took the lead suitcase from their trunk and, ever on guard, walked it over to the UN group.

One of the UN representatives was a nuclear physicist. He tore open the duct tape, cut away one layer of the lead blankets, and then took a long, noisy sniff of the suitcase. Like a connoisseur testing his favorite Bordeaux, he gave a dramatic thumbs-up. The Angolan fighters relaxed. The diamonds' strongbox was turned over to them; they jumped back in their Land Rover and were quickly across the border, too. The UN scientists then put the suitcase aboard the helicopter, and with little ceremony, the aircraft prepared to take off.

That's when the Al Qaeda fighters showed up.

They came out of the jungle directly behind the helicopter, dressed in black and carrying German assault rifles. Using the copter as cover, they'd been lying in wait, hidden under mats made of flora, sticks, and branches. The first thing they did was brutally gun down the four members of the UN team, shooting each man many times in the head. Then they shot out the engines of the two remaining vehicles, rendering them inoperable. All this happened in a matter of seconds.

A firefight instantly broke out between the Delta soldiers and the Muslim fighters. Their backs to the Okewa River, the Americans pushed their disabled Humvee over on its side and took up firing positions behind it. Though they were heavily armed, it was clear from the start the Delta crew was vastly outnumbered, as more than three dozen Muslim fighters had emerged from the jungle.

Nevertheless, the Americans began spraying the terrorists with M-60 machine-gun fire, grenade launchers, and M16s. Two of the Delta guys were armed with enormous Mossberg shotguns; each time their triggers were pulled the night would light up as bright as day. But by this illumination the Americans could see even *more* Muslim fighters materializing from the forest. The Americans were mowing them down in the most methodical fashion, but like a horror movie, every time a terrorist went down, two more would take his place. Soon their bodies were piling up in front of the over-turned Humvee like cordwood.

The terrorists' strategy was clear. These guys weren't really assault soldiers, nor were they Al Qaeda's version of a special ops team. They were just suicidal mooks with guns, fodder, to be cut down for one reason only: to cause the Americans to run out of ammunition by shooting at them.

It was a steep cliff down to the river; there was no way the Americans could go that way safely. They were cut off from the bridge and were too far from the thick jungle to make a strategic retreat into the overgrowth.

In other words, they were trapped.

The eight men took down more than 50 of the raiders—but finally ran out of ammunition. A vicious close-quarters fight ensued with knives and bayonets, but again the sheer numbers overwhelmed the Americans and soon they had no choice but to give up. Curiously, the terrorists did not kill them—in fact, they took great pains *not* to kill the Americans. *They* were the prize, not the plutonium. All eight were quickly taken prisoner.

While all this was going on, the crew of the French Army copter simply watched, offering no help even though their aircraft was heavily armed.

The Americans had their hands tied with electrical wire and were led off into jungle.

Only then did the French military helicopter take off and slowly fly away.

Chapter 2

It was called the Extraterrestrial Highway.

It ran for miles into the Nevada desert, north of Las Vegas, up toward the mysterious towns of Tonopah and Rachael—mysterious because they were relatively close to Groom Lake, the top-secret U.S. military base also known as Area 51.

There was a stretch of this lonely roadway known as the Straight Snake. It ran for nearly 40 miles with barely a curve. At night, cars could be seen pulled over to the side of this road, their occupants looking up into the sky, hoping to spot a UFO or a top-secret U.S. military airplane. Sometimes they saw both.

It was late afternoon now, and a very earthly activity was taking place. Twelve men wearing sun-bright orange jumpsuits and armed with extremely sharp sticks were picking up litter along the road. They were prisoners, inmates of the Las Vegas County Jail performing community service for the state.

The trash along the highway was a predictable mix of beer cans, soda bottles, condoms, and fast-food wrappers. A stretch van had carried the prisoners here; most were awaiting the outcomes of their trials or trying to raise bail. Four county deputies sat inside the air-conditioned vehicle, watching their charges in comfort, protected from the 100-plus-degree temperatures outside.

The dozen prisoners went about their duty slowly, trying to stay as cool as possible in the stifling dry heat. At some point a plain Ford four-door sedan came ambling along, smoke pouring out from under its hood. It rolled to a stop across from where the deputies' van was parked, the only other vehicle on the straight-as-hell stretch of highway.

At just about the same moment, the air around the prisoners and the deputies began to shake. It was a strange sensation. The sky was clear; visibility was 100 percent—yet it seemed like everything around them was moving. Everything except the ground below.

This was not an earthquake.

It was something else. . . .

All work picking up litter stopped. The deputies shut off the AC unit, thinking it was the source of the strange vibration. But it wasn't. The shaking only increased. It was now rocking the van violently from side to side.

Then just as suddenly, the sun seemed to blink out. A shadow fell across the prisoners, the deputies' van, and the disabled car. That's when everyone just looked up. What they saw at first appeared like a huge bird of prey coming down at them. In the next instant, it looked more like one of the alien spacecraft the highway was famous for. In the moment after that, these two visions combined to make something else: a very top-secret aircraft. It was called a V-32CX Super-Osprey. An aircraft the size of a small airliner, with the ability to land vertically, it was all black and sinister looking. An almost-ghostly beautiful Asian woman could be seen peering down from the aircraft's open side door.

Five of the prisoners looked up at the bizarre aircraft and immediately threw down their litter pickers. One of them yelled over the commotion: "Our ride is here!"

They began running across the desert toward the strange aircraft, which was now landing about one hundred feet away. The deputies were stunned—so were the other prisoners. They couldn't fathom what was happening. It took the lawmen a few precious seconds to get their asses in gear, and by that time it was too late to stop the fleeing prisoners. The deputies burst out of the van, but all they could do was restrain the rest of the litter crew from running out to the strange aircraft as well.

One deputy finally got on his radio—but that's when the two passengers from the disabled car suddenly appeared in their midst. They were not simple civilians, now that the deputies had their first good look at them. They were large individuals, muscular, tight jawed, with piercing eyes, casually dressed. Government types—the deputies could tell.

One of the two men fanned out a wad of cash. Thousand-dollar bills. Twenty of them. He passed half the bills to the four deputies, while his comrade passed the rest to the prisoners, this as the strange aircraft, having taken in the five prisoners, left quickly, going straight up, turning, then disappearing at astonishing speed over the eastern horizon.

"Government business," one of the men said to the deputies calmly. "No one here saw a thing."

The strange aircraft flew into the night, heading east, in radio silence, its cross section showing up on radar screens below as nothing more than a bird, if at all.

It was refueled in flight twice, once over Colorado, again over Illinois, both times by Air Force KC-10 Extenders. The weather grew worse as it flew on, first rain and then thick fog. By the time it reached the East Coast, nothing else was flying. Big or small, every airport along the Atlantic seaboard was socked in.

The aircraft's destination was a very isolated cliff located several hundred feet above the ocean, surrounded by nothing but beach and thick forests. The nearest road, the nearest house, the nearest living soul to this place were many miles away.

There was a single airstrip up here. On one side of this runway were five huge aircraft hangars, all in severe disrepair and abandoned long ago. On the other side were the cliff and then the sea beyond. This place was once a bustling Coast Guard air station; in years past large maritime patrol craft would land here to be serviced. But the base had been decommissioned for nearly two decades, and the weeds and the corrosive salt air had overtaken it since.

It was at this desolate location, appropriately called Cape Lonely, that the futuristic aircraft finally landed.

There was a one-man welcoming committee on hand waiting for it.

He was Eddie Finch. An ex–Coast Guard NCO now in his sixties, he'd been assigned to Cape Lonely Air Station during his active career. Now he was like a ghost here, still haunting what might very well be a haunted place.

He was out on the runway pulling weeds when the strange aircraft arrived. He'd been told, by a close friend, that the airstrip, little used in the past decade, would be needed tonight, that a single aircraft would be coming in to land.

Like those before him, Finch felt the strange airplane's arrival before he heard it, then heard it before he saw it. The air around him started moving; his ears started ringing. Then the most god-awful-looking thing came straight down, out of the thick fog, landing like something from outer space. It took Finch a moment, but then he knew exactly what it was and who it was carrying. But still he was upset.

"If I knew it could land like that," he grumbled, "I wouldn't have been out here all night, pulling these damn weeds."

The weird airplane never turned off its engines. Its side door opened and the five men in orange prisoner suits tumbled out.

They greeted Finch warmly. He looked like a thin Santa Claus and was a grandfatherly type. The five men held great respect for him. They crowded around him.

"How much time do we have?" one of them asked the elderly man. "Enough for a cup of coffee?"

The old man just shook his head. "Not this time. You're moving again right away."

He motioned over to the edge of the cliff. A smile came to his wrinkled snow-bearded face.

"Want to see something?" he asked them.

At that, the thick fog miraculously parted—suddenly they could see beyond the edge of the cliff to the coastline and the ocean below. Floating about five hundred feet offshore was an extremely rusty containership.

The five men let out a hoot. For them, this might have been the most beautiful sight in the world.

No sooner were the words out of Finch's mouth when another sound enveloped the cliff. This racket was a little more familiar. Horizontal rotor blades turning in the mist and wind. Powerful engines on another powerful machine. It came out of the fog a moment later.

It was a helicopter. But again, not an ordinary one.

It looked mostly like a UH-60 Blackhawk, the mainstay of the U.S. military's helicopter forces. It was dull black, charcoal almost. This was because it was layered in Stealth paint.

It was about one-third bigger than the typical Blackhawk, though, and it was very wide. It could carry nearly a dozen more people than a standard UH-60 and many more weapons, too. This one was festooned with heavy machine guns, Gatling guns, grenade launchers, missile launchers, the works. In many ways, it was a flying tank.

Add in its sound-dampened engines, its suites of high-tech navigation and communications gear, its night-flying capabilities, and the fact that, again, it was covered in the technology of Stealth, no surprise its nickname was the Superhawk.

"It's only because that thing," the old man was telling them, pointing back to the futuristic transport, "is too big to land on the ship that they had to send this up for you. But I understand you'll appreciate the ride itself. For sentimental reasons."

"Amen to that," one of the five men replied.

As the five ex-prisoners quickly made their way to the copter, its side door opened and three men stepped out. Two were crewmen of the aircraft; the third man looked sick. His eyes were downcast, his hands shaking slightly. He'd been a darkly handsome individual at one time—but his face had fallen, his eyes had sunken in, and his lips seemed permanently sealed by worry and anxiety. The five men tried to talk to him, but he was oblivious to their presence.

Finch took the ailing man by the arm and led him away from the copter. "Take good care of him," one of the guys in the orange suits said. "He's important to us."

His new charge now standing a safe distance away, Finch returned to the helicopter and handed the prisoners a bag he'd been keeping under his jacket. It contained a dozen doughnuts. The men looked in the bag and laughed. It was an inside joke.

They all shook hands and the prisoners climbed into the helicopter. But suddenly they heard a voice calling out over the twin noises being made by the futuristic transport and the Superhawk.

"There's one more!"

That's when a sixth person stepped out of the top-secret VTOL aircraft. Dressed all in white, long black hair blowing behind her like some Asian goddess, she was beyond beautiful.

Her name was Mary Li Cho.

Everything just stopped. All the noise and the wind and the sound of the sea below. Just stopped . . . as she seemed to glide across the field separating the two aircraft, the futuristic plane taking off behind her. Finch focused in on her and whispered to the five men in orange: "Is *that* her?"

They all nodded.

"That's *her*," they confirmed.

They made way for her and she climbed aboard the Superhawk first, followed by the five men and their doughnuts. They all turned and saluted Finch, even the Asian beauty. He saluted back.

The copter gunned its engines, causing a huge downwash of air and exhaust. Finch stepped back, his hat flying off into the breeze—but he didn't care. This was more exciting than anything he'd experienced in his twenty-five-plus years with the Coast Guard.

It pays to have friends in high places, he thought.

He watched as the helicopter seemed to fall right off the side of the cliff, descending to the rusty ship below. The copter landed on the ship's middeck not a minute later—and promptly disappeared, another trick in its arsenal.

The ship was already moving when the helicopter set down. It had pulled anchor and was now halfway into a 180-degree turn, pointing its stern east, out to sea.

Back up on the cliff, Finch watched as the containership completed its turn and then, with a roar of power that sounded like a handful of jet engines, which was not far from the truth, the ship soon shot ahead at incredible speed, nearly 40 knots in just two minutes, and quickly disappeared over the darkened horizon.

Finch stood there for a long time, the downcast man silently joining him at his side.

Finally, Finch whispered to himself: "Good luck, guys—I'll keep the coffee warm for you."

Chapter 3

The containership's name was the *Ocean Voyager*. Eight hundred feet long, 105 feet wide, and 60 feet from the top of the mast to the bottom of its cargo bay, it weighed thirty-thousand tons empty. It was square and rusty and at least a dozen paint jobs behind the curve. When it was originally built back in the early 1980s, on a good day it could barely make 15 knots.

The ship was ugly—and that might have been its best asset. Its deck was a jungle of tie-offs and ropes and winches and chains and a million other things to trip over. The deck was also crowded with containers, in some places stacked three or four high. Most of them were as rusty as the ship. Lashed together with creaky bars and hinges, they looked like a bunch of railroad cars that had somehow become lost at sea. In other words, the vessel appeared no different from any other of the hundreds of containerships plying the world's oceans.

But the *Ocean Voyager* was not really a containership. It was a warship, powerful and unlike any other.

If it had an official description, it would be Air-Land Assault Ship/Special. But no one privy to its existence ever called it that. It was based on a British concept, born of low defense budgets back in the 1970s, in which the Royal Navy would deploy the Harrier jump jets on converted containerships, thus negating the need to build new, expensive aircraft carriers.

The *Ocean Voyager* was that dream come true in spades. It began with two elevators that had been installed just forward of the ship's recessed deckhouse. The same size and type used on the U.S. Navy's supercarriers, they were powerful enough to lift forty-thousand pounds from the bowels of the ship up to the deck. These elevators served as movable launch and recovery pads for aircraft flying from the vessel. And they were well hidden. When they weren't in use, six containers were slid on top of the elevators, preventing them from being seen from above.

The elevators served the small airborne strike force that was hidden below decks. The first time this very secret undercover vessel saw action was a year before, in the Mediterranean and then in the Persian Gulf. For that, its maiden voyage as a combat vessel, it had carried two of the supersecret Superhawk helicopters and a pair of AV-8s, the U.S. Marine version of the famous Harrier jump jet.

Now, there were four Superhawks on the ship, in addition to one surviving jump jet. The helicopters were all new, just off the assembly line. A platoon of Marine Corps air mechanics serviced these aircraft in the ship's crowded belowdecks hangar. Spare parts and ammunition for the aircraft were stored nearby in—what else?—seaborne containers. Just about everything the ship needed to stay at sea and do its thing was hidden in plain sight inside the containers lashed to its deck.

But the ship's assets only began with the planes of its tiny air force and the highly trained special ops troops who flew them. There was a section toward the front of the ship, on the bottom level, that was crammed with five white oversize containers. Inside these nearly antiseptic compartments could be found some of the most sophisticated spy equipment known to man.

Nicknamed the White Rooms, these containers held tons of eavesdropping and satellite tracking gear. The people who worked in these containers—the Spooks— could tap into Echelon, the National Security Agency's ultrasecret satellite system. This meant that just like several dozen NSA sites around the world, the ship could intercept just about any phone call made, E-mail sent, fax transmitted, anywhere on earth, then read, copy, and even alter it without the sender or receiver ever knowing a thing.

The white containers also housed dirty tricks sections where just about anything needed in the spy game could be produced, duplicated, or counterfeited. Weapons could also be made down here—anything from a germ bomb to a small nuclear device.

So the *Ocean Voyager* packed a punch. High-tech aircraft, a small army of high-tech warriors, a huge snooping capability—and its own weapons factory—it was all powered by four gas turbine engines, the very same powerplants that drove the F-14 Tomcat fighter jet. The *Ocean Voyager* could move through the water like nothing else its size.

But whose ship was this? Who built it? Paid for it? Who was able to get all these weapons and spy gear, air-

planes, and people on board—to sail off and do what
was considered the dirtiest work in all of the dark world
of secret operations?

There was no easy answer to any of those questions
except the first one. The ship did not belong to the U.S.
Navy or the Marines or any branch of the U.S. military.
Nor the Central Intelligence Agency, National Security
Agency, or any other U.S. intelligence Agency. The
most accurate answer was that it belonged to the people
of the United States of America. The crew served the
country's citizens directly.

Its purpose? To track down anyone involved in the
planning, funding, or implementation of the attacks of
September 11th and punish them severely. Simple as
that. Invading countries? Regime building? Humanitarian missions? These weren't on the minds of the people
who ran the ship. Its reason for being was to haunt Al
Qaeda, to use the terrorists' tactics on the terrorists
themselves, to fight down and dirty, no holds barred
against the Islamic fanatics—and God help anyone who
got in the way.

The people on board were already well-known in the
underworld of the Middle East, in that nether region
where the terrorists made their money, sold their drugs,
and plotted their missions of mass murder. These killers
for Allah considered the regular U.S. military to be big
and lumbering, a giant easily heard from thousands of
miles away, long before it made any move against them.
But these same terrorists knew the people on *Ocean
Voyager* to be something quite different. To the terrorists, they were bad spirits, the bane of their existence,
demons who slipped in with the night, a razor blade
knife in hand. They'd already killed a number of Al

Qaeda's shadowy leadership, and they'd already disrupted several major Al Qaeda operations. Just the speaking their name was enough to send chills up the spine of any Al Qaeda member, assuming such vermin *had* spines.

For those in the United States who knew of them, the people who crewed this ship were usually referred to as The Ghosts. To the Muslim terrorists who feared them so much, they were known as the Crazy Americans.

And at the moment, just about all of them were drunk.

The most impressive place on the *Ocean Voyager* was the Captain's Room. Located at the top of the stern-mounted control house, it was a large multiwindowed cabin, done smartly in mahogany and steel. It featured a library, a wet bar, a galley, and a very ornate wooden table, which allowed those sitting at it to look out, with an unobstructed view, to the ocean beyond.

The room also contained many high-tech items. Huge TV screens, satellite readouts, radar-imaging systems. Just like the Spooks' rooms downstairs, it looked more like something out of NASA than something out at sea.

In this room now, just an hour after the ship's hasty departure from Cape Lonely, the members of the mysterious special ops group had gathered. There was plenty of cold beer and liquor to be had and plenty to eat. Out the window were the softly rolling sea and a bright full moon. Overhead, the stars glowed like jewels.

This was a reunion of sorts. The Ghosts were an assorted cast of characters. They numbered more than 100 now; when the unit first sailed a year ago, the number was barely more than half that. This was another strange thing about them: other special ops groups who'd come into contact with the Ghosts along the way, some even sent out to track them down and arrest them, had wound up joining them instead.

The original team—or at least the officers—all had one thing in common: Each had lost a family member or a loved one on September 11th or to some previous terrorist act. They were all veterans of special operations, too, but with this extra incentive: These secret warriors became the type of operatives whose skills were complemented by a deep-seated desire for revenge, a way to pay back Al Qaeda for bringing so much misery and destruction to their lives and the country that day.

The core of the original group had been made up of about two dozen Delta Force soldiers, two fighter pilots, and several copter drivers. Their extended family included the guy who actually sailed the ship—a veteran Navy captain named Wayne Bingham known to everyone as Bingo—and his crew of 35. Since that time the Ghosts had been joined by a dozen or so members of the very hush-hush State Department Security unit, nearly a dozen SEALs—again a team that was originally sent out to apprehend the Ghosts—and three members of the Defense Security Agency, another deep-secret Pentagon unit, which, among other things, specialized in rooting out terrorists within the ranks of the U.S. military.

Almost everyone here now in the Captain's Room was wearing an orange prison suit, another part of the odd chapter of where the unit members had been in the past few weeks. The five men who'd been picked up in

Las Vegas were on hand; they'd been arrested for tres-
passing on government property, ironically after preventing a terrorist attack on nearby Nellis Air Force
Base. But many of the others were attired in bright
prison wear as well. Up until 24 hours ago, they'd been
prisoners, too. Their jail was the holding facility at
Guantánamo Bay, the place where the U.S. military kept
prisoners captured in the various wars against Islam. All
of the Ghosts were Americans, though, and the secret
unit's activities had been heroic and had saved tens of
thousands of innocent lives. But the truth was, they'd
also rubbed so many in D.C. the wrong way that at one
point the *entire* unit had been secretly locked up at
Gitmo.

But now they were all free again; that's why it was a
kind of class reunion. Some of these guys hadn't seen
one another in a long time. So the beer flowed and there
was laughter and handshakes. A baseball team, reunit-
ing in spring training after winning the World Series in
the fall, was like this.

Most of these men were chiseled, huge, and muscular, especially those of the group who were ex–Delta
Force. The SEALs and the SDS guys, too, were all
pumped—shaved heads, tattoos, and sunglasses at
night. They all looked the part—in fact, they looked like
extras for a movie being made about special operations.
Even the beautiful Asian girl, Li, seemed right out of
central casting.

The unlikely-looking host of the party was sitting at
the far end of the table, speaking with a few of the senior members of the unit, drinking Jack Daniel's
straight. He was a little man, barely five-four, sixtyish,

with a completely ordinary face, red complexion, and enormous jug-handle ears.

His name was Bobby Murphy. He was the brains behind the outfit.

The story of Bobby Murphy actually began with a terrorist incident back in 1972. The Summer Olympics were held in Munich that year. Midway through the competition, Palestinian terrorists kidnapped a dozen Israeli athletes, held them hostage, and eventually killed them all. German authorities allowed most of the terrorists to escape. About two dozen in all, they scattered themselves to the four corners of the earth.

Shortly afterward, the Israeli government created a secret unit whose sole aim was to hunt down and kill every one of these terrorists. It took them more than 15 years, but the secret unit eventually got every one of the Munich Massacre killers, shooting each one between the eyes, but not before telling him who they were and why he was being whacked. It was crude, it was immoral, and it was highly illegal. But it sent a message to the Palestinian terrorists: If you screw with Israel, we're going to get you, no matter how long it takes. You will never spend another peaceful night. You will always be looking over your shoulder. Eventually, we will find you, and we'll kill you, and it won't be pretty.

That's what Bobby Murphy wanted to do for America after September 11th. He wanted to send a message to Al Qaeda: You have done this to us and you have succeeded. You might try something as big or even bigger on us and succeed again as well. But whatever the case, we're coming to get you. No matter how long it takes, we'll hunt you down, we'll find you, we'll kill you, and it won't be pretty. Considering the mass murder that had happened on 9/11, Murphy didn't think anything less than this sort of campaign would do. And eventually he found a few people along the way who agreed.

But *who* was *he* to have such grand designs? His own past was so shady, even Murphy himself wasn't sure of every twist and turn he'd made.

He was a spy—that everyone was sure of. He'd worked for every intelligence Agency in the United States—CIA, DIA, NSA, NRO—his career of 20 years had been an alphabet soup of bag jobs and undercover missions.

Or at least, that was his story. No one in the special unit knew for sure, and at this point there was no real need for asking. Murphy was such a regular guy and an authentic patriot, anyone in the group would take a bullet for him. And one thing was for certain: Murphy knew a lot of people in the U.S. intelligence community. But as he'd told all the team on more than one occasion, this was not the same thing as having a lot of friends there.

Shortly after 9/11, Murphy approached the highest officials of the CIA with his bold concept. He felt that the country needed a boost, a shot in the arm to get out of the gloom and depression that had followed the events that dark day. He reminded the CIA of the Doolittle Raid on Tokyo shortly after Pearl Harbor, when a handful of small bombers dumped a small amount of bombs on Tokyo. The damage was slight, but the propaganda and morale victory was enormous. Murphy wanted to do the same thing—reach out and put the hurt on someone, *anyone,* connected with 9/11 and do it right away, to alleviate the hopelessness that seemed to have seeped into the country after the attacks.

The CIA turned down his idea. Too dangerous, they said. Too much career risk if things went wrong. No matter what the mission, the Agency would not get on board. Undeterred, Murphy went to all the military's intelligence services—the DIA, Army Intelligence, Air Force Intelligence, Naval Intelligence. All of them turned him down, too, for the same reason: too much risk to their own asses. But, Murphy had asked them: Isn't the fact that three thousand Americans were murdered in cold blood enough to justify any risk? Apparently not, was the answer he got everywhere.

But he did not give up, this funny little man with the thick Texas drawl. Two years, three, of knocking on doors, trying to get meetings. Then finally somehow he got an audience with the President himself. Again, as the story went, at the end of that meeting, with the President reportedly in tears, Murphy was given $1 billion—that's *billion*—to do his thing. He was also given assurances of no interference, from anyone. Politicians, the military, *no one*. He was given *carte blanche* to take the fight back to the terrorists by playing by the terrorists' own rules—underhanded, no mercy, no guilt. Very unpleasant stuff.

The *Ocean Voyager* came from all that—it was the unit's first base of operations. They'd traveled to the Middle East in it the previous year, hunting down Al Qaeda members like dogs and dispatching them in some of the most painful ways possible. In that time they'd saved the supercarrier USS *Abraham Lincoln* from a suicide attack, rescued several hundred Americans from certain death atop a high-rise in Singapore taken over by Al Qaeda–linked terrorists—*and* they'd prevented a team of terrorists that had infiltrated the United States with a load of Stinger missiles (with help from people in Washington) from wreaking havoc in America's skies.

The team's true-life adventures were things of pulp novels—their accomplishments, their bravery, their ruthlessness. But again, they were also considered by many in D.C. who knew about them to be a rogue team—and this, too, did not sit well with those in power.

And to be fair, not one man in this room could claim to be an angel, to be free of sin. They'd been down in the mud with the terrorists for more than a year now, and it was a dirty place to be. In many ways, the Ghosts *were* crazy. Some would say they were actually *America's* terrorists. But they'd also killed many more Al Qaeda types than the entire U.S. military combined.

Bottom line, the Ghosts got the job done and were getting the job done, and if they ruffled a few feathers— or tons of feathers—along the way it didn't make any difference. They were people stuck in the grieving process; they refused to accept the fact that their loved ones were really gone for no good reason. They'd also lost team members; good friends had been killed in pursuit of this. This made for a very strong fusing of resentment, revenge, and ruthlessness. Translation: If you were a resident of any Muslim country and you were peaceful and good and not intent on killing every American you could see, fine, the team had no business with you. But if you were a Muslim extremist or a financier of terror or trafficked with Al Qaeda types, even for a nanosecond, you had big reason to be worried.

Just like the Israeli assassins with the Munich terrorists, eventually the Crazy Americans were going to get you.

So their first year had been filled with ups as high as the Himalayas and downs as deep as the Mindanao Trench—these had been Murphy's very words to them to start this beer fest. But here they were, back together again, freed by his almost scary manipulations of both the Las Vegas court system and the U.S. military.

But their freedom had not come without a price. . . .

Murphy called the meeting together and now addressed the whole group for the first time. He was no great orator. He was by nature very shy. (He looked more like a teacher or an insurance salesman than a spy.) But it was the way he said the words that got to them. When Murphy spoke, he always had a rapt audience.

Yes, he began, they were all finally free. He was able to get them all off, for the time being, with the powers that be in D.C. Though these things could come back to haunt them as the world turned at the Pentagon, officially now they had all been released—from Cuba, from Vegas—on personal recognizance and into Murphy's custody, for which Murphy paid a huge bail.

"Let's put it this way," the diminutive spy said. "Where we once had a boatload of enemies in Washington, now we have just a few. And while we used to have very few friends there, now we have more than a handful. We are in a better place."

He took a moment to let this sink in.

"Now, that said," he went on, "I want to emphasize that just like before, we are not inside their command structure. We don't take orders from them, and I'll be damned if we ever will—not after the way they treated us while we were saving their asses at Hormuz and Singapore."

He paused for a moment. "All that being said," he began again, "something has come up. . . ."

A silence descended on the room. The festive, beery atmosphere changed to one of dead seriousness. Again, when Murphy spoke like this, the unit's members knew it was wise to listen.

"Our 'new friends' at the Pentagon have a problem," Murphy said soberly. "And they would like us to get them off the hook."

A murmur of discontent went through the room. No one liked the sound of this. The idea of helping the people who were trying to chase the team down just a few weeks ago did not sit well with them.

Murphy sensed this tremor right away. He held up his hand and quieted the grumbling. "I know exactly how you feel," he said. "But I think we have to help them out, for one simple reason: Because we are still Americans, and some of our brothers are in trouble. Big trouble."

Murphy hit a button and one wall of the room disappeared, to be replaced by a huge projection screen. It was showing a close-in satellite photo of a clearing in a very dense jungle, a bridge nearby, and a small cement building. Two vehicles were aflame; smoke was obscuring one-third of the image. There were shot-up bodies lying everywhere.

"This picture was taken about a week ago," Murphy began. "That river is in West Africa; it separates Nigeria and Cameroon. This was the scene of an exchange of enriched plutonium for money involving some British mercs, the UN, and the French military."

Another groan went through the room. The unit had

no love for the French; in fact, they had very strong evidence that the French Secret Services were helping Al Qaeda in their quest against American interests. The bastards. . . .

"It's a long story," Murphy went on, "but the exchange was being chaperoned by a unit from Delta Force. A special team called Delta Thunder."

Murphy looked around the room and saw a few confused faces. More than a few of those present were past members of Delta Force, America's premier special ops unit.

"Never heard of 'Delta Thunder?'" he asked them. "No surprise. It's a very secret unit *within* Delta. It's so classified that even the rest of Delta doesn't know about it."

A few people just shook their heads and sipped their beers at this. Black on black, secret upon secret—just how deep did America's deep operations go? Did anyone really know?

"Because no one knows about these guys is the very reason that we've been asked to help them out," Murphy explained. "They were kidnapped, after this gunfight, by a local Al Qaeda cell. These mooks are undoubtedly torturing them—and we know they have plans for their demise. But because very few people know about these Thunder guys, there's really no one deep enough to go in after them without blowing their cover."

He waited a beat, then said: "And that's why we're the perfect people to rescue them. Because very few people know about us, either."

Colonel Ryder Long just sat back in his chair and popped another beer. He could feel the ship moving at tremendous speed beneath him—when those aircraft engines were firing like they were on afterburner, the huge ship rode the waves like a speedboat. But moving fast wasn't the same as moving smooth. Ryder was an Air Force guy; he was the team's resident fighter pilot. When he wasn't flying, he preferred his feet on solid ground.

He'd flown the unit's first Harrier. (Later he was joined by a second pilot, Gerry Phelan, flying a second Harrier. Phelan was killed during the battle above Hormuz.) Ryder was also the senior officer in the unit, though military protocol was all but dispensed with when it came to everyday life around the Ghosts. He was north of 45 years old, had been a test pilot before this and a kind of special ops fighter pilot before that, with extensive flying in and out of Area 51 in Nevada and the vast stretches of top-secret ranges beyond.

The day of 9/11, he was asleep on his couch in his home in Las Vegas when the first plane hit the first tower in New York. His wife, his beautiful wife, was on that plane, flying back from Boston after an assignment for her news station. She was among the first victims of the Al Qaeda attack. Ryder's life changed that day. He could fly any plane put in front of him; he was probably one of the best pilots ever and had been involved in many exciting and very deep op missions in his career. But he was nothing without her. She *was* his life and he just couldn't comprehend living without her.

He went into a massive funk, alternating between draining bottles and praying. Finally he found himself at rock bottom, in a filthy motel room, looking down the wrong end of his hunting rifle. That's when the phone rang. It was an old friend from the intelligence biz offering Ryder a chance to get back at the people who had killed his wife. A new unit was starting up to do just that, and did he want to join? Ryder put the gun aside and replied: "Just tell me when and where."

The other officers of the original team were from the same situation. Red Curry, one of the original copter pilots, had a brother killed that day, a fireman rescuing people in the first tower. Martinez, the unit's original operations officer, had a daughter killed in the first tower. The leader of the original team's Delta contingent, a huge monster of a guy named Dave Hunn, had a sister killed in the second tower. She was there on a job interview, one of the youngest victims of the attack. On and on, misery and loss. . . .

Again, this was their motivation, and *this* was the genius of Bobby Murphy. Getting them together, getting the money, and bringing the fight right back to the terrorists' doorstep.

And now, they were getting another mission.

Murphy changed images on the huge screen. Now they were looking at a port city, obviously still somewhere in Africa, a computer-generated image that looked extremely real.

This was Loki Soto. Shoehorned between the already crowded border of Guinea and Sierra Leone, it was an accident of ninetieth-century country making, a leftover forgotten on many maps back then and even some today. It was a port city but a very run-down one, a ramshackle place taking up barely two miles of West Africa's Atlantic coastline. The harbor facilities were dreadful. Only the rustiest tubs, scows, and tramps came here.

That's why it was such a strange place for a castle.

Its name was *Casa Diablo,* literally Devil House, and actually it was an old Portuguese prison shaped like a medieval castle. The jail cells within were made of thick stone; the walls were very high. Murphy explained that during the slave-trade years the place was famous for its torture chambers, a way of getting the unruly human exports in line. That reputation for cruelty was still alive and well there today.

Casa Diablo was about the size of a city block, and there were only two means of access: a huge front door and a smaller one out back. The back door was called Door of Death, because prisoners who were murdered inside the prison were just dumped out back to be disposed of by local animals. The front door came complete with a large wooden gate, a drawbridge, and a moat. Whenever either door was opened, it was heavily guarded.

Murphy showed the team a photo of the prison's roof. It was crowded with both troops and weapons. And unlike the surroundings, these weapons were very modern. The top of the fortress was crammed with high-tech antiaircraft guns, Chinese made, most of them. A number of two-man SAM teams were also on hand to watch for threats from above. For targets on the ground, high-caliber machine guns covered every corner of the ramparts, giving fields of fire on all the streets surrounding the prison. There was even an artillery piece up here, with a range long enough to reach ships in the harbor, about a half-mile away. In the old days, this would have been called a shore battery.

"This place has the reputation for being impossible to get into," Murphy told them. "With all the guards, every entrance covered, and all that hardware on top. The whole city and even the port are covered. One wrong move by anybody and these guys start throwing lead. Bush pilots in the area know better than to fly anywhere near this place—someone from here even took a SAM shot at a Boeing 727 cargo plane a couple years ago, just missing it.

"It's a poorly kept secret that Al Qaeda took over this place just about the same time, two years ago. Loki Soto is an anchor in their so-called 'Arabs in Africa' movement. It's a strange little place where they can sell and buy, ship and take shipment of just about anything, be it weapons, drugs, money, human beings. You name it. There is no big government to come down on them; there's hardly any government there at all. And certainly none of the surrounding countries want to get on the bad side of the mooks these days. They can't get their own populations in line, never mind worrying about these Islamic assholes giving them trouble."

Murphy looked back at those gathered, just shook his head, and said: "This is where the guys from Delta Thunder are being held."

More murmuring around the room.

Murphy switched images and suddenly they were all looking at a live broadcast of the prison—from a satellite. (He had just tapped into one of the National Security Agency's most classified more advanced satellites, another talent of his.) They could clearly see many people moving around the roof of the castle. They could also see the weapons, the radars, the radio antennae. And they could see something else, too. A huge concave dish—this was a satellite receiver, a TV linkup, part of a system that could broadcast events happening inside the prison worldwide.

"These guys are equipped like a mini-CNN," Murphy told them all. "It's all new gear, just set up. The Al Qaeda bigwigs sent them all this TV stuff for one reason."

He paused a moment and then said: "They plan to kill the Delta guys . . . on live TV. They're going to claim that they've been interfering in local African affairs, and thus are being executed for their crimes. They are going to broadcast their executions around to the world, via that new upstart Arab network Al-Qazzaza TV. This will be Al Qaeda's way of announcing to the world that the *jihad* is in Africa to stay."

"Who the hell is behind this?" someone in the group asked. "This is a pretty elaborate setup for the mooks. And we all know that Al Qaeda doesn't exactly throw its money around. That all looks like expensive stuff. The guns, the TV stuff."

"It is," Murphy replied. "And whenever we talk about big-ticket Al Qaeda items, we're talking Saudi involvement. The Saudi Royal Family. The Saudi religious police. The Saudi National Guard. Everyone in here is smart enough to know—especially after what we've all gone through—that Al Qaeda does nothing big unless it has the backing of those assholes who run Saudi Arabia, no matter what lengths they go to deny it. And I'm sure I am not alone in saying, for about the millionth time, that those numbskulls in Washington invaded the wrong country a few years ago. Instead of going north out of Kuwait, they should have gone south, and taken care of those ungrateful backstabbing pricks once and for all—but no. Not with all that oil in the ground. And so we are left with this. And things *like* this."

He took a moment to calm down. The subject of the duplicitous Saudi Royal Family was always a tough one for Murphy to address. He'd put this group together of members of the armed forces who had lost loved ones that day of 9/11. The Saudis had helped finance the carnage that day. Therefore, the Saudis were his enemies. Simple as that.

"That's why we have to help these Delta Thunder guys," Murphy finally went on. "They aren't *just* like us. They *are* us. Battling right down there in the dirt and mud and blood, while the brains back in D.C. dine on caviar and crackers for lunch. Again, I know it sounds crazy, but these Thunder guys are *so* classified, the few people who know about them just couldn't figure out who they could send to attempt a rescue—if anyone could figure out how to do one, that is. Between this and the fact that the Thunder guys have a charter of total disavowal by Higher Authority, well . . . I can tell you right now, if we don't go in and get them, no one will."

He went to another image. "Now to answer your question specifically," he continued. "There is one person in particular who is pulling the strings here. He is the head of Al Qaeda's newest African cells."

The new image on the screen showed a man who was obviously high up in the Saudi Royal Family, in full turban and robes, leaning against an Aston Martin sports car. Unlike most of the Saudi Royal Family, he was somewhat handsome, more Western looking than a typical Muslim mook. On the driver's side door of the car was an image emblazoned into the silver paint. It was a diamond.

"He is Al-Jabazz Saud Ben-Wabi," Murphy said of the forty-ish man. "Also known as the Diamond Prince. He is a cousin to the guy we sent into the Pan Arabic Oil building the day of Hormuz—but really, they're *all* related somehow somewhere over there. Like most of them, he gets a huge allowance from the Royal Family—billions, in fact. It is clear, though, that like his departed cousin, he spent a lot of money before 9/11 and gave a lot of support to Mohammed Atta and the hijackers who attacked our country that day."

"Beside this wealth, he also has interests in diamond mines throughout Africa. There are many diamond mines on the continent, and many wars have been fought over them, over who owns them and who gets control of what comes out of the ground."

Murphy went on: "It is the Diamond Prince's people who managed to kidnap the Delta guys. It is his people who plan to kill them on live TV.

"But here's a complication: The people who live in that port town are ordinary Africans. They are innocent villagers who, in a way, are being held hostage by the mooks, too. By plopping themselves down in the midst of this population, the African Al Qaedas have added another layer to their defense: They know it would be very hard for someone like a U.S. special ops package to go in there and fuck them up without fucking up all the innocent people surrounding the place, too.

"So these mooks aren't just prison guards; they're occupiers here, too, with a local militia backing them up. This is something that we have to keep in mind."

Another image. It showed the Diamond Prince, this

time dressed completely in Western-style clothes. No robes, no headdress.

"Meanwhile, the 'DP' himself is on vacation in Belgium," Murphy went on. "Buying racehorses to run in the Kentucky Derby, and again, no one is doing anything to stop him, because he is so connected to the Saudi Royal Family and they're connected to the people who really don't like us very well in Washington. So, welcome to the twenty-first century, gentlemen and lady. Where this country's enemies are so close to us they have a hard time getting their knives into our backs."

He returned to the still image of the prison; this time it was photographed in infrared.

"Those Portuguese really knew how to build these things," he said. "A small A-bomb might not be enough to put a crack in some of those walls. But it gets worse."

He pointed to areas of the prison that were now showing up in dark red.

"In addition to everything else," he went on, "these guys in the prison are sitting on top of a mountain of explosives. There are tons of TNT stored inside the place, we are told. Why? Because they know this will make their little clubhouse even less of a target. One bomb, one bullet, one match that lights up the wrong part of that place, it will go up and that whole shantytown around it will go up, too—and kill everyone, mooks and innocents alike. Who wants a PR problem like that? Killing innocent Africans, even though Africans have no problem killing each other at wholesale prices. If the U.S. did it, we'd be screwed in the court of public opinion. So, as you can see, with the thick stone walls, only two means of access, the weapons everywhere, innocent people surrounding him, and a shitload of high explosives, this asshole Diamond Prince thinks he's got every base covered when it comes to making this place impregnable. And you know what? He probably does."

"So how are we going to go in and get Delta Thunder then?" someone else asked.

Murphy drained his drink. "How are we going to do it, you ask?" he said, revealing a rare smile. "Just like this. . . ."

Ryder headed below as soon as the meeting in the Captain's Room wrapped up. There were things down here he had to attend to.

He took the stairs, all six levels, a steep descent to the ship's so-called service deck. It was a dank, cavernous place, illuminated mostly by blue halogen lights to cut down on any heat spikes that might leak to the decks above. Such things could tip a spy satellite or maritime recon plane that all was not kosher in the containership's cargo hold.

It seemed like years, and not just a couple months, since Ryder had been down here in the belly of the beast. He was always surprised how cramped it was. The *Ocean Voyager* was a huge vessel, but its cargo bay was permanently crammed with the necessities of its strange mission. Potable water, dry food, fuel, bombs, a million other things that couldn't be kept safely in containers up on top would end up down here. The White Rooms also took up space, as did the engine suite, which had to be big enough to fit the four jet-engine turbines and all the gear needed to turn the ship's quartet of propulsion screws. Add to this all the clutter that just came along with the interior of a containership: overhead beams, webs of wires, bulkheads, ladders, and pipes everywhere. It was as crowded down here as it was up on deck.

Ryder made his way through this maze now, heading to the hangar section. It was located about two-thirds of the way down the hold, next to the pair of powerful aircraft elevators. This was probably the most crowded place on the ship. As it was, the team's two original Superhawk helicopters barely fit inside this allotted area. Now they had *four* of the exotic choppers, and the new pumped-up version had an extra-long tail, a bulbous nose, and, again, was as wide as a truck. Finally reaching the hangar area, Ryder was amazed at how skillfully the Marine air mechanics had jammed the four copters into their postage stamp–size space.

But shoehorned in between the new helicopters was another unusual aircraft. Droopy wings, strange nose, high tail, very weird exhaust tubes. It was an AV-8 Harrier, Ryder's jump jet, the American version of the famous British VTOL fighter.

Trouble was, his Harrier was a mess. It hadn't flown since the hellish battle above Hormuz. In fact, Ryder had crash-landed it aboard the containership at the conclusion of the deadly melee. At one time, this Harrier had been a very cool aircraft. Its engine was extremely powerful, and its wings were longer and stronger, meaning they could carry more and heavier bombs. The gun pod attached to the fuselage was not the typical 30mm weapon but a monstrous 50mm cannon. But now, due to the extensive battle damage he had incurred at Hormuz, the jump jet looked like nothing more than a pair of wings hanging off a bucket of bolts.

It was close to midnight. They were traveling so fast,

they would be close to the coast of Africa in just two days, an incredibly swift voyage. The team would be going into action soon after that, and Ryder hadn't even *sat* in the battered jet since his crash landing, never mind taking it airborne. It was important that he check it out now and get to be one with his airplane again.

He rubbed his hand along its fuselage like an owner stroking his ill thoroughbred. The small army of Marine mechanics was working feverishly on the copters nearby, getting them ready for the rescue mission. The Marine sergeant spotted Ryder and walked over. The Marine explained that as soon as they were allowed back on the ship his guys had done their best to put the Harrier back together. It had been close to a total wreck, so there was only so much they could do. The airframe and engine were sound and the electronic guts had been stitched back together, so the plane *was* flyable. But how long it would stay that way the gunny couldn't say.

Ryder thanked him and climbed into the cockpit. The view up here was only worse. There were so many weld patches on the upper wings and frame, they almost formed a weird kind of camouflage design. There were also hundreds of dents everywhere, big and small, plus the canopy was cracked in several places. He wondered if the plane would look any better up top in the sunlight, instead of in the gloomy blue light down here below. But then, quite possibly, it might look worse.

Ryder spent the next 10 minutes doing diagnostic checks on his cockpit gear. The jarheads were right. All indications were that the primary systems needed for flight—engine, control surfaces, landing gear, flight computers, life support, and so on—could still perform.

But to what capacity he would only know once he was airborne. He hoped everything would last at least long enough for him to fly the upcoming mission.

Suddenly it got very quiet in the hangar area. All noise stopped; the rivet guns, the oil pumps, the external power generators, everything fell silent. Ryder could not see through the forest of copters, but it was obvious the Marine air mechanics had been distracted and all work had come to a halt. Ryder had a hunch why.

Li Cho walked into the hangar area a moment later.

She was dressed entirely in green camo, baseball cap included. Everything was tied back, everything was buttoned down, but she still looked stunning. Ryder had never seen camos worn quite like this. He couldn't imagine her ever going into combat. Yet . . .

He and she hadn't really talked much since he'd been sprung from his litter-picking duties in Nevada the day before. The flight east in the Osprey had been whirlwind, as was their transfer over to the spy ship. In those few times they did speak, it had been cordial, all business.

But they had a history. Two months before, when it was learned that the Al Qaeda missile team had stolen into the United States, a handful of Ghosts had made a spectacular escape from their prison in Gitmo and were soon on the trail of the terrorists. This group included Ryder, plus Li's colleagues from the Defense Security Agency, the guys named Ozzi and Fox. The escapees needed a place of operations in the D.C. area and they needed a place to hide. As Li was the third member of the tiny DSA unit, they wound up hiding in her house just over the border in Virginia.

During this time, she and Ryder had had an occasion

to be alone, and in a sweet and unexpected moment she almost got him to talk about his deceased wife, something even his closest friends would never attempt to do. Awkward though it was, it had been a turning point of sorts for him. It was the first time since his wife's death that he'd let his guard down and opened up, if just a little. He felt like a bit of sunlight had finally broken through to warm his ice-cold heart, at least for a little while. And it was all thanks to Li.

That's when she started creeping into his everyday thoughts, popping up at the most unusual times. This, too, was a big change for him. Not only had he pined for his wife every day since her death; he'd *dreamed* about her almost every night as well, sometimes for hours, sometimes just a few minutes. But now, in his always-troubled dreams, when in the past his wife would make an ethereal appearance, tapping him on the shoulder or calling out to him from a distance, Ryder would turn to find it was Li instead.

Along with her colleagues Fox and Ozzi, she'd jumped over to Murphy's team from the Defense Security Agency, essentially going AWOL for the greater good. And besides being drop-dead gorgeous, she was a brilliant military analyst, educated at Georgetown in counterterrorism. She was also very friendly with the rest of the Ghosts. She made for an unlikely one of the boys, yet she never had any problems conversing with any of them—all except for Ryder. With him she was always a bit cautious and shy, while still aware of the connection they'd made at her house that night. He took her reticence as a good thing. It meant she was *thinking* about him and that's why she was so on guard. He knew this because he was the same way with her—awkward and nervous, simply because he was *always* thinking about her.

But, of course, Li was *so* beautiful, he was sure everyone else on the boat was thinking about her, too.

She didn't just walk by the hangar area. Instead she turned and started walking toward his plane. *Jesuzz . . . ,* he thought. *Here she comes. . . .*

Ryder was out of the cockpit quicker than if he'd hit the ejection seat. He landed on the deck, feetfirst, right in front of her.

"Colonel? Am I disturbing you?" she asked with a nervous smile.

He tried to stay cool. "Not at all. . . ."

She was carrying a large plastic bag. "You didn't get your new uniform yet, did you?"

Ryder was still in his prison garb. "Not unless orange is the new color this year."

She handed the bag to him. "Mr. Murphy asked if I could bring this down to you. He thought it was a good way for me to start finding my way around the ship."

All right, Bobby, Ryder thought. He dug into the bag and came out with a new flight suit. It was all black, with many utility pockets, places for ammo, radios, thing like that. It had the team's patch on its right shoulder. It showed the Twin Towers, with an American flag billowing behind them and the letters *NYPD* and *FDNY* floating in the background. Below was the team's motto: *We Will Never Forget.* Ryder always felt a lump in his throat when he looked at the patch.

"Nice threads," he said. "But where's yours?"

She shrugged. "He never mentioned one for me. And I'm not even sure I should wear one. Being so new here."

"Well, I don't know if there is a hard and fast rule . . . ," he said, sputtering, running out of gas.

Suddenly she was out of things to say—and so was he. But he didn't want her to leave.

"What do you think of my ride?" he asked in some desperation.

She turned to the Harrier. "Is this the McDonnell Douglas version?" she asked. "Or is it the Brit-built?"

Ryder felt a zing go through him. A girl who knew the difference between a GR-8 and an AV-8? Now, *that* was sexy. . . .

"It's a little bit of both," he explained. "Murphy had someone put it together, slapped a lot of Stealth paint on it. Boosted the engine a bit. Flew good—at one time."

She studied the plane's battered condition. "It's a real disaster now, isn't it? Can it still fly?" she asked, innocently running her hand along the wing.

"I guess we're going to find out," Ryder replied.

Another silence. The Marines had gone back to work. The boat was rocking wildly. She looked around the deck and half-sighed.

"I'd heard a lot about this ship before I came aboard," she said. "But never did I think I'd actually ride on it someday. It was more like something from a sci-fi book. I just wish I knew where everything was."

Ryder saw his opening and pounced. "You mean you haven't been given the tour yet?" he asked her.

She smiled and shook her head. "Is that an invitation?"

Another zing.

"You bet," he replied.

They started at the back of the ship. Ryder showed her the stern-mounted helipad where he'd crashed his jump jet months before. He brought her up to the wheelhouse deck where during their first voyage Bingo's guys would make pancake breakfasts for the crew on the huge, very low-tech grill located here.

Next stop was the ship's bridge, where Bingo's guys ran the bizarre high-speed container vessel. Navigation, propulsion, steering, the gear up here was on par with that on the U.S. Navy's most advanced warships— Bobby Murphy had made it so. Then they visited the Combat Room, the windowless compartment behind the bridge. As well, much of the equipment here—the air defensive suite, the myriad radar trackers, the satellite com gear—was of the same type as that found aboard the Navy's supercarriers.

He brought her below to the engine room where the four GE-404 turbines were spinning with the noise and power of a quartet of jet fighters. Then they went to the White Rooms, where the Spooks lorded over hundreds of flat-screen monitors, banks of radio receivers, and computer screens, all in order to tap into Echelon, the NSA supersecret satellite network that was the ultimate in twenty-first-century eavesdropping.

Throughout it all, Li, being Li, asked dozens of questions. How, why, when, who. Ryder did his best to answer as many as he could, and for those he didn't know the answer to he simply made things up, thinking it might be fun to apologize to her later.

Finally they arrived in the ship's mess; both needed coffee. It was a huge compartment, painted black for some reason, with all its portholes blocked with canvas, also painted black. Though it was past one in the morning, many tables had people at them. All conversation stopped when Li walked in of course. Ryder steered her toward the coffee station, passing a table where Curry, the unit's other senior pilot, was sitting with some of the Spooks. At this point, Ryder's boots were barely touching the deck. As he and Li exchanged greetings with them and kept on going, Ryder heard Curry stage-whisper: *"You lucky bastard. . . ."* Ryder gave him a covert thumbs-up in reply.

Ryder and Li got two coffees to go and walked up to the bow of the ship. Here it really was like sitting on the front of a speedboat. The ship was moving so fast, through high seas, it was throwing up large amounts of a spray while leaving a gigantic wake behind. Yet the full moon was up and the stars were out and it was an amazingly clear night above.

They sat on a chain locker box and watched the show.

"Can I ask you a question, colonel?" she said after a few minutes. "Another one, I mean. . . ."

"Absolutely. . . ."

"That poor man they took off at Cape Lonely. Who was he?"

Martinez. The original unit's operations officer. An Army colonel and a member of Delta Force, he'd been a genius at getting the unit's aircraft, soldiers, and intelligence people moving in sync. His was a sad case, though. Shortly before the attack on Hormuz, the Ghosts had tracked down a group of terrorists who were planning to hijack up to 10 airliners as part of a bigger plan. The Ghosts knew when the terrorists were showing up at the airport; they knew when the terrorists were going to board their flights. They just didn't know where the terrorists were all going next.

At the time, it was thought the terrorists were flying on

to Europe, where they would take connecting flights to America—and it would be *these* airplanes they would hijack and use to crash into targets inside the United States. Theorizing the terrorists had confederates waiting for them at European airports and wanting to catch them too, Martinez made the decision to follow the terrorists instead of taking them down immediately. The titanic battle at Hormuz was the result, as the target all along was the Navy's supercarrier the USS *Abraham Lincoln,* entering the Persian Gulf that very morning, and the airplanes used were the ones the terrorists first boarded. Luckily, none of the hijacked aircraft reached the intended target—but hundreds still died. Martinez was never the same after that.

Ryder told Li the story as concisely as he could. She stared up at him throughout, her face very serious, drinking in every word.

"Martinez was a good guy," Ryder concluded. "But there's no way he could go on this mission. I just hope they get him back to his family, before it's really too late."

Li thought about this for a while, then just smiled again. "Thanks," she said. "I'd heard of him—and I know you all respected him. But I wasn't sure what the full story was, and I didn't know anyone I could ask, without making a fool of myself. Well, except you." She laughed because her words had come out so funny.

He smiled, too. "Is there a compliment in there, somewhere?" he asked her.

Here they sat, dodging the spray and looking up at the moon and stars. The minutes turned into an hour. And as always, she was full of questions. It took some prodding, but Ryder finally told her about his adventures as a top-secret test pilot years before he joined the Ghosts. Flying missions deep inside Area 51, participating in bizarre war games, doing things so way-out, even he didn't believe some of them had happened.

He regaled her with tales of the team's exploits not just at Hormuz but in the Philippines, too—those heroic days before they wound up hiding in the attic of her house. He spoke sincerely of how the twin foundations of the team were its patriotism and the shared loss of loved ones. He told her how cool it was that the team was not affiliated with any of the country's military services, that they served the people of the United States directly, and that despite his career in the Air Force he wouldn't have it any other way now.

On these subjects, Li mostly listened, enthralled and, strangely, a bit envious. She had helped the Ghosts immensely in ending the threat of the Al Qaeda missile teams inside the United States—and she had done so at great personal risk. But it was obvious that she still didn't consider herself a member of the team. Not yet anyway. . . .

They wound up talking about many things, except the upcoming mission and Murphy's plan to assault the impregnable fortress of *Casa Diablo*. It was all pleasant and comfortable and exciting. And so, *so* different for him.

During all this, they were consciously inching closer to each other. At times Li would tap his knee to make a point. His body would reverberate at her touch. Ryder felt like he was back in high school, on a date with the most beautiful girl in math class. Again, this was a monumental step for him. His heart still felt like a stone, the same cruel weight he'd carried around since the day his wife died. But now, with this gorgeous girl so close, it was like he was in another place, on another world, where the gravity wasn't so bad. When a particularly huge wave of spray came up over the bow, she went right up against him to escape getting doused—and this time, she stayed.

"I had something else I wanted to ask you," she said, her hand suddenly touching his.

Ryder went numb, but in a good way. "Sure, anything," he blurted out.

She opened her mouth—she was about to say the words—when suddenly every bell and whistle—and Klaxon and siren—on the ship went off at once.

Captain Bingo's deep voice came over the intercom. "Condition Blue. All hands to battle stations. Unidentified aircraft incoming. . . ."

Ryder and Li were stunned.

"Battle stations?" she gasped. "Where the heck is *my* battle station?"

It was a helicopter. It popped up on the Combat Room's air defense screen at exactly 0200 hours. Just 20 miles out, it was flying low and fast, coming out of the northeast and heading right for the ship.

This was very strange. At the moment, the *Ocean Voyager* was almost in the mid-Atlantic. The nearest land, in either direction, was hundreds of miles away. So where had this helicopter come from? It had to be from another ship. But it didn't seem lost. To the contrary, on first spotting the blip Bingham had altered the ship's course, going to a due south heading—and the incoming aircraft adjusted its flight path as well. There was little doubt that whatever this thing was, it was intent on coming right at them.

So the bigger question was: How did anyone know the *Ocean Voyager* was even out here?

Within a minute of the alarm being sounded, the top deck of the containership was crawling with armed crewmen. They'd drilled for such things in the past. Each man was carrying either an M16 rifle or an M-60 machine gun. The members of the primary strike team—the Delta guys, the SDS, and the SEALs—took up key positions around the ship, including the helipad and at the highest part of the wheelhouse. The ship's crew, the sailors who actually made the vessel run, then scattered themselves among the jungle of containers on the open cargo deck. They, too, were armed with M16s.

But their weapons were mere popguns compared to what the *Ocean Voyager* was really packing.

There were two red containers on the port side of the ship, two more along starboard. Another was located up on the bow, a sixth down at the stern. These containers were specially built to drop their sides at the touch of a button. Inside each were two CIWS guns—high-tech Gatling guns that were able to spit out an incredible six hundred rounds *a second.* Their function was to fill the sky with thousands of lead projectiles on the idea that at least some of them would hit anything coming in at the ship. To get caught in the barrage of one of these guns was to face a nasty death by perforation.

And the crew had been through this sort of thing before. During the ship's first cruise, a helicopter suddenly appeared, landed on the ship—and the people onboard took Murphy away, in handcuffs, under arrest, throwing the team into chaos. Just how their diminutive leader was able to get out of that tight jam he never told them. But the Ghosts really didn't want it to happen again. Nor did they want this helicopter to be an attack helicopter, as some were known to carry very deadly long-range antiship missiles. It wouldn't take more than one or two of this type to put the *Ocean Voyager* on the bottom, with all hands going down with it.

So everyone involved was very anxious as they hunkered down at their positions, weapons ready, waiting. A few tense minutes went by—then, suddenly, another announcement was made over the ship's PA system. This one was as surprising as the first. In his deep booming tones, Bingham told the crew that the helicopter had contacted the ship and that it was displaying no hostile intent.

In fact, the people in the ship's Combat Room had picked up the copter's IFF signal and from it determined that not only did the copter not belong to a potential enemy, but it was actually a part of the *Servizio Pontificio Aereo*—the Vatican City's Papal Air Service.

This news went through the ship like wildfire.

The Pope was coming to see Murphy. . . .

The copter came in a few minutes later, and much to the disappointment of the ship's crew, it was not *Il Papa* dropping in to hear confession. The copter was an all-black Bell Textron, a military version, with no visible national markings, and certainly too sinister for anyone from Vatican City to be flying in.

The copter's IFF signal had been a clever fake to get close to the ship without being blown out of the sky. This could mean only one thing: The aircraft's true owner was the CIA.

It set down on the rickety helipad hanging off the ass end of the ship. Two men in civilian clothes climbed out, leaving the pilot with the motor running.

Murphy was on the landing platform, waiting for them. Having already had a brief radio conversation with them, he knew who they were. There were no handshakes, though. Murphy simply gave Bingham a signal up on the bridge and the ship's whistle was blown three times. The dozens of armed men hidden around the upper decks showed themselves and were told to stand easy at their stations. Again, while not friends exactly, the visitors weren't enemies. Not typical ones, anyway.

Murphy wordlessly escorted the pair up toward the Captain's Room. No one who saw him pass liked the look on his face.

Faster than the speed of light, another rumor went through the ship: These people were here either to stop the rescue mission or to take Murphy away.

Or both.

Murphy fought to stay cordial. It was hard to do.

He led the two men into the Captain's Room and invited them to sit at the big table. One agent was older, midfifties, red faced, with coal-black eyes, a real veteran of the Agency. The other was midtwenties, moussed hair, wide-rim glasses. An egghead.

Murphy offered them coffee, beer, or a drink of something stronger. They declined. Taking a beer himself, Murphy settled into a chair across from them. The big room suddenly seemed empty with just the three of them in it.

The two had a matter of importance to discuss with Murphy, they said. As a preamble, they tossed out various code words and names of high-placed CIA officials to convince Murphy they were who they said they were. There was no doubt, either, that they were well aware of the Ghost Team and what they had done in the past year. The two men were able to recite details of some of the team's more famous exploits, spitting out information that only someone deep on the inside would know.

Still there was tension in the room. Murphy despised the CIA. Didn't trust them, didn't respect them. Because of their ineffectiveness and bumbling in the days leading up to the attacks of 9/11, Murphy blamed them almost as much as he blamed Al Qaeda for what happened.

Furthermore, he was extremely pissed that the Agency found him way out here in the first place. But more out of curiosity than anything, he wanted to hear what they had to say.

"We know you guys are going after Delta Thunder," the younger of the two agents began. "And we know that Delta Thunder is being held by guys loyal to the Diamond Prince."

Murphy just sipped his beer. "Go on. . . ."

"And we see much wisdom in this," the young agent continued. "But we've got another operation going a parallel mission, if you like, only bigger. Smacking his guys around in Africa is one thing. But we want to go after the Diamond Prince himself. We know there's no way he's shacking up in that prison. We can't imagine him ever dirtying himself by stepping foot for very long on the Dark Continent.

"In fact, at the moment, he's in Brussels. And he will soon fly down to the Riviera. From there he is going to Cairo—and then he is going home, back to Saudi Arabia. He's traveling with a small army of bodyguards right now—but when he gets back on his own turf, he lets down a bit. It will be a delicate operation. But we think there's a good chance we can get him when this happens."

Murphy was still doing his best to keep his temper in check. He smelled a rat here.

"Well, you boys seem to have all the bases covered," he said in his thick drawl. "You know where he is. You know where he's going. You know when he'll get there. Why did you come all the way out here, in the middle of the night, just to tell me what you've been up to?"

"Because we need your help in corralling this guy," Agent Mousse Hair said. "Your people can do special things. Things other people can't or won't do. We'd like to tap into that expertise."

Murphy smiled darkly. "Oh? You want us to bomb his ass?" he asked them. "You want us to go in and tear his palace apart—and take him out piece by piece? Because that's the sort of thing that we do. We are not subtle. We are not delicate. You're smart guys—you've proved that. But you guys should know our methods of operation."

The younger agent almost laughed. "When we say we need your help," he replied, "we don't mean that we need you and your entire little army. We just need someone who's traveling with you, the perfect person to pull off what we have in mind."

Murphy looked at them both. This was a curveball. He thought these guys were here to co-op the Ghost Team and incorporate them into their operation—leaving Delta Thunder to hang. But that didn't seem to be the case.

"So, you're not here to put the *kibosh* on our rescue mission?" he asked them.

"Not at all," the young agent said. "Those Thunder

guys are valuable people. And again, we're all for bloodying the Diamond Prince's nose and losing those assholes in that prison—if you can figure out a way to get in there and do it. But what we got in mind will take him out of the picture completely."

Murphy couldn't argue with their intentions. It was dealing with the Agency—the people who'd turned him down years before. That's what was turning his stomach into knots.

"Sounds promising—but I'd rather keep my team together," Murphy finally replied. It was his way of telling them no. "We're pretty tight here. Don't want to upset that chemistry. I hope you understand."

Murphy then stood up, indicating the meeting was over. But both agents remained seated. The mood suddenly turned dark.

The older agent spoke for the first time. "We don't have much time," he began, his voice rough from years of cigarettes and booze. He was obviously the Bad Cop of the pair. "So I'll put it to you this way: Either deal with us, or we blow the whistle on you. The rescue mission—and your whole little traveling circus."

Murphy felt his face flush. "You guys must be misinformed," he replied evenly. "I've got everything you see here signed off by everyone including the Joint Chiefs. Closed books. *Carte blanche*."

The older agent began to growl. "You might have made a deal with *the Pentagon* to get your people released from their various incarcerations," he said through gritted teeth. "But no such deal has been made with us. And you know how things are these days. Intelligence trumps the military brass. And that means all your asses could still be in the fire with one word from us."

Murphy almost went over the table at them. "You flew a long way out here to threaten me," he spit back at them.

The younger agent just removed his glasses and shifted uncomfortably in his seat. "Look, just make a deal with us," he said.

To which the older guy boomed: "Or we blow the whistle on you—and you're *all* back in jail. . . ."

Murphy was furious. But he was smart enough to keep his cool. He took a beat and calmed down. Maybe he was approaching this from the wrong direction.

He asked: "Who is it that you need?"

As he said this, Murphy was sure he knew the answer: These guys were here to ask for Ryder. His flying skills were well-known throughout the black ops community.

But the CIA agents had a surprise for him.

"The person we want," the young agent said, "is Mary Li Cho."

It was Bingo who told all this to Ryder. He found the fighter pilot still at his battle station, next to the port-side CIWS container, part of a crew that would activate the awesome weapon should it be needed.

Bingo pulled Ryder aside, told him what the CIA guys wanted, and also told him that Murphy had passed the request on to Li. The bad news was, she'd agreed to go along with it.

Ryder was furious. He rushed back to where the CIA copter was still waiting. By this time, Li was already packed and on the helipad.

She was standing on the edge of the landing platform, the black helicopter's downwash making her long hair flow wildly behind her. The noise from the copter was deafening. Murphy was at her side, in a very animated conversation with her. Fox and Ozzi, her two fellow DSA agents, were also there.

Ryder went right up to Murphy. "Please tell me what's happening," he shouted over the roar of the copter.

Murphy gave it to him straight. The agents' request—and their threat to fold up the strike team if they didn't play along.

"I thought they wanted *you,*" Murphy told the pilot. "When they asked for Li, I was sure we'd be able to wiggle our way out of it. They might want her, but they could never take her against her will. They would sleep with the fishes if they did."

"So what happened then?" Ryder demanded to know.

Murphy just shook his head. "She *wants* to go. They won't tell us what their plan is exactly, but she feels it's her duty to help them. Plus, she knows it will preserve the team. And no one can talk her out of it."

But that didn't mean Ryder wasn't going to try.

Fox and Ozzi saw him coming and backed off the helipad, hoping Ryder could succeed where they had obviously failed.

Now it was just Ryder and Li on the helipad, yelling over the noise of the helicopter.

"This is a *very bad* idea," Ryder said to her while the two CIA agents waited anxiously inside the copter. "This Diamond Prince guy is dangerous. He controls a lot of armed people. He has access to lots of weapons and deals with his enemies without mercy."

"I know all that," she replied.

"And these guys?" Ryder said, pointing to the pair of waiting CIA agents. "They're as bad as the mooks. Murphy doesn't trust them. I don't trust them. *No one* trusts them."

Li just shook her head. "I know that, too," she said. "And everything about it seems wrong. But how can I say no? This is my job, as a citizen of my country. I can neutralize one of the big fish of Al Qaeda. One of the people who was instrumental in pulling off 9/11. Plus the team will be allowed to stay together. Isn't that what we were just talking about? How important all this is?"

Ryder couldn't believe this was happening. It was like a bad dream come true. Not an hour ago, they'd been sitting on the nose of the ship, getting wet and falling for each other. Now she was standing here, bags packed, getting ready to leave him.

He looked deep into her eyes and she was looking right back at him. Tears were forming. "Besides," she said. "This way I can earn my stripes. To get my uniform. My patch."

She reached over and touched the side of his face for a moment. Her hand was cold and trembling.

Then she climbed aboard the copter and it took off, just like that.

The last Ryder saw of her, she was looking out the side window, waving good-bye.

Chapter 4

The prison ran on gasoline. Two generators, powered by a pair of old Ford truck engines, provided electricity for the old fort. These engines ran 24 hours a day and were notoriously inefficient. Spark plugs were always fouling, gaskets blowing, oil leaking. Two prison guards were assigned around-the-clock just to keep them going. The surrounding city of Loki Soto had no infrastructure, no power grid. Without the engines turning, there would be no electricity to light the lights, warm the ovens, or run the torture devices.

The Ford engines were incredible gas-guzzlers. They had to have their fuel tanks refilled every two days. This meant four hundred gallons of gasoline had to be delivered to the prison, by tank truck, every 48 hours.

This was a downside for the terrorist named Shaheen Faheeb. He was the commandant of the prison, a close associate of the Diamond Prince, and an experienced jihadist. Osama bin Laden himself had approved Faheeb for the prison job.

Born poor in Saudi Arabia and just 30 years old, Faheeb was one of Al Qaeda's top operatives in West Africa. No surprise, he was a ruthless, sadistic individual, someone who had directed suicide bombings in Pakistan, Afghanistan, and post-Saddam Iraq and had gleefully blown up women and children on his own, all in the name of Allah, of course. Faheeb was also an expert at security, with an eye to perception. He knew that this prison ran as much on its reputation for being impregnable as it did on its 12-foot-thick walls. Impossible to break into. Impossible to break out of. Impossible to bomb. It was his job to maintain that reputation.

Trouble was, Faheeb hated the smell of gasoline. He'd grown up near the great refining fields in northeast Saudi Arabia, and when he was a child his nose was always filled with the stink of gas. That was one reason he liked it here in Africa. All he could smell here was the jungle and the fish and the sea.

Except every other day when the fuel truck rumbled up to the prison's front gate and he had to supervise its scheduled delivery of a couple hundred gallons of gas.

And today was a delivery day.

Faheeb had awoken late this morning, hungover after drinking too much elephant wine the night before. As he stumbled out of his quarters into the bright hot African sun, he imagined he could already smell the odor of gasoline even though the truck was probably still down on the docks getting filled for the trip up to the prison.

He made his way down to the guards' meal hall, where a huge kettle of tea was steaming away as usual. There was no food available yet; the food delivery would be concurrent with the fuel's arrival. But Faheeb wasn't hungry anyway, not yet. What he headed for was the hookah pipe that sat next to the teakettle and, like it, was always smoking away.

There was a mixture of tobacco and hashish in its bowl and Faheeb took two deep gulps, enough to chase his hangover away. Feeling better, he stepped over two guards who were lying in the middle of the kitchen floor, praying in the general direction of Mecca, and headed downstairs.

He found his way to the bottom level of the five-story prison, soon arriving at his master sergeant's post. The man jumped to his feet and greeted Faheeb with a deep bow. Faheeb replied with a hard slap to the man's face. This was his way of asking the sergeant a question: How are our guests? The Delta soldiers? Are they still alive?

The sergeant covered his head and began yipping. "*Yes! Yes!*" They had survived the night, despite the repeated torture sessions.

"And everything is on videotape?" Faheeb bellowed.

"Recorded in color," the sergeant replied in Arabic.

Faheeb slapped him again, but this time less hard, almost affectionately.

"Good dog," Faheeb told him. "You get to eat and sleep and breathe, for at least one more day."

Faheeb started off again for the front entrance, and this time his nostrils did detect the faint stink of gasoline.

The fuel truck was near.

The front of the prison was just 20 feet from the edge of the town. The local Africans were wise enough to stay clear of the area at this time, on this day—everyone knew when the gasoline truck made its delivery. The prison's guards were known to drink heavily while on duty. They also had itchy trigger fingers. The tension that could arise when the fuel truck arrived made these two things a bad combination. So every other day when the gas truck arrived from the docks a half-mile away, the streets were usually empty.

It got a bit tricky security-wise on delivery day. This was really the only instance when outsiders were allowed into the otherwise impregnable fortress; that's why Faheeb always had two days' worth of food delivered at the same time. It was also why he made a habit of intimidating the fuel-truck drivers whenever they appeared. Inside these walls should be last place anyone would want to be. Faheeb also insisted that the same drivers never appear twice. He didn't want anyone getting too good a look around in here. Especially with the eight new "inmates" the prison had taken in recently.

There was also a safety issue involved: Even though there was a rudimentary fire-suppression system in place, the prison was literally a powder keg of TNT—its most radical defense against an outside attack. But now they were allowing a truck filled with four-hundred gallons of gasoline to drive in the front gate. One spark—from an improperly tuned car engine or the flick of a cigarette—and the prison and at least half of Loki Soto would be blown sky-high, long before any water sprinkler system kicked in. So Faheeb had to make sure that not only were the people driving the truck on their toes, but the men who would be watching over the operation were alert as well.

He reached the main door to find the officer of the personal guard waiting for him. This man was in charge of the 10 extra fighters who, along with the prison's normal contingent of guards, provided the muscle for this place. These extra gunmen were the hard-core Al Qaeda members inside the fort. They were like Faheeb's Praetorian Guard; where he went, they went. This morning they would be stationed on the ramparts just above the main door, ready to blast away at anything that even hinted of hostile intent.

Faheeb slapped this man as well, but very gently. The officer reported his people were in position and ready. Faheeb glanced up the wooden stairway to the left of the door, and indeed he could see half of his bodyguards already leaning over the west-facing wall, their AK-47 assault rifles up and loaded. Two huge Chinese machine guns were also in the mix. Anyone making a wrong move out on the street, in the nearby buildings, anywhere, would be facing a virtual wall of gunfire.

It was now 10:00 A.M., delivery time. The officer of the guard called down from the next floor that the truck was indeed approaching the gate. Faheeb drew up his own rifle and then nodded to the man sitting next to the gate controls. He punched a button that activated a chain pulley assembly, and slowly, like something from medieval times, the huge wooden door began to draw open.

The twin smells of the morning's tide and the stinking gasoline hit Faheeb at once. It was another day in Loki Soto. Beyond was the slummy downtown and, beyond that, the port itself, as usual full of coastal tankers, dilapidated fishing boats, and rusty containerships.

Faheeb pulled a kerchief over his nose and mouth, a thin barrier against the stench. The old four-wheel tanker truck was waiting right where it always was, about ten feet from the edge of the bridge that crossed the moat and led to the prison's front door. Per procedure, the truck would wait here until receiving directions from Faheeb himself.

It idled while Faheeb did his own look around. He scanned the street in back of the truck, the moat, and the roofs of the buildings beyond. Everything seemed clear. The food delivery kids had arrived at the same time. Faheeb brusquely waved them in; they scampered across the bridge with baskets of sugar rolls, pita bread, and raw lamb. Then he pointed in a sinister way at the driver of the fuel truck and indicated he, too, should come forth.

The man hit the accelerator a bit too hard, causing the truck to backfire and nearly giving everyone involved a heart attack. The tension became as thick as the stink in the air. The truck rumbled uncertainly across the old bridge, its driver hidden by the early-morning shadows. Faheeb watched its approach like a hawk. Was it going a little slower than usual? Was this even the right truck? He raised his weapon a notch. Was something wrong here? Or was his paranoia just getting the best of him?

Faheeb stayed frozen in the open doorway as the gas truck lurched through the main gate and finally stopped. He immediately yanked the driver from the cab. Faheeb was a big man, and the driver was a slight black teenager. Or at least that's what he appeared to be.

Faheeb began slapping the driver viciously, this as his guards closed in on the driver's assistant in the passenger seat.

"What do you know?" Faheeb screamed at the driver. "Who sent you here to do this?"

But the driver could only cover up from the blows and shake his head. "It is my job!" he began screaming back. "Just my job!"

Faheeb finally stopped striking the man and pushed

him back toward the tanker's hose. "If it is your job, then get your lazy ass to work!" he shouted at the man.

Meanwhile, the bodyguards allowed the passenger to get out of the fuel truck and together he and the driver dragged the delivery hose across the room. Here a four-hundred-gallon tank sat, taking up one end of the vault-like enclosure. This was where the fort's lifeblood gasoline was stored.

The driver nervously attached the hose to the tank and started pumping. Half of the bodyguards came down from the ramparts, their weapons turned toward the driver and his helper. Faheeb knew the two African youths would have made perfect suicide bombers, igniting the truck and destroying the fort and everything in it. Luckily, the enemies of the people Faheeb worked for didn't operate like that. At least, he didn't think they did.

The refueling went unmercifully slow as always. Once the gas was flowing it didn't seem like it would take all that long for the four hundred gallons to go from truck to tank, but at this point Faheeb imagined the gas moving in slow-motion dribs, drabs, and drops. There should have been a larger storage tank here; everyone involved knew this would have made more sense. Then these three-times-a-week sessions could be reduced to something more manageable, like once a week. But that would be against the financial wishes of Faheeb's superiors. Al Qaeda was much too cheap to buy a large, safer tank.

The tension grew almost unbearable. Faheeb's stomach was in knots. He was sure that at any minute the back of the tank truck would burst open and some country's special ops forces would come tumbling out and then they'd all be on their way to a fiery end.

But no . . .

That did not happen.

The tank truck finally ran dry. The driver and his assistant quickly jumped back inside and backed out of the fort. The doors were closed, and the stink of gas left Faheeb's nostrils. The tension eased. Faheeb took his Arab-style skullcap and wiped the sweat from his brow. At least *that* was over.

He called to his remaining bodyguards up on the roof. It was time for breakfast. Faheeb retreated back to the kitchen, the weight of Allah off his shoulders once again. A cup of tea was waiting for him; so was a fresh sugar roll. His bodyguards arrived moments later. As they were his best fighters, they always dined with him.

Faheeb took his seat at the head of the old wooden table. His bodyguards sat around him and waited—only Faheeb could start the meal. He faked a prayer and, now ravenous, took a huge bite of his sugar roll. His men did the same a second later.

A second after that, Faheeb went over in his chair, his head hitting the floor with a loud, bloody crack. White foam spewed from his mouth. He shook once, violently—and then he was dead. The 10 men around him all hit the table a moment later, following their leader into the black hole of death. All of them victims of the sweet pastries that today were covered with fast-acting highly toxic curare poison made to *look* like sugar.

Just like that, nearly half the prison's hard-core gunmen were eliminated.

The first Superhawk helicopter crashed onto the prison's roof a moment later.

Captain Johnny Jackson was dreaming that Boy Scouts had rescued him when he heard the mighty crash. He was chained, by hands and feet, in the lowest jail cell at the bottom of the notorious Diablo fortress. The cell was just six feet by six, big enough for him and his torturers— three if they all squeezed in. Just big enough to reel back with a whip or a piece of electrical cord or a rubber hose. That's what his tormentors had been using on him, 12 times a day, 24 hours a day, for the past six days. The bottom of his cell was covered with his own blood.

It was the worst kind of torture. His kidnappers did not want to kill him; nor did they want to get information out of him. That would have meant the beatings and whippings had a point to them. No—they were doing it to him, these Al Qaeda people, simply because they liked it, got a rush from it, found it satisfied their ingrained long-repressed sexual urgings, twisted from eons of wandering in the desert and stepping in camel shit. They did it because they were *all* sadists deep inside—all terrorists were; he knew this much from his Delta Thunder training. They did it simply because they could.

Jackson was the team leader of the captured Thunder squad. He hadn't seen any of his men since they'd been overwhelmed at the border crossing, after the murderous lopsided gunfight. His last visions of that night were the pile of bodies in front of their makeshift barricade, the storm of tracers going in both directions, and the French Army helicopter waiting nearby, doing nothing to help.

He and his men had been betrayed. That much was clear. But who exactly had stabbed them in the back? Who'd revealed that they would be accompanying the plutonium shipment? The British mercs? The United Nations? The Angolan fighters? The French?

It really didn't make any difference now. They'd been

caught and they were in a place that was impregnable, and because of Thunder team's supersecret status he knew a rescue attempt was highly unlikely. Thunder was the "Mission Impossible" element of Delta—if they were caught, the President would disavow any knowledge of them . . . blah . . . blah . . . blah.

Africa was Delta Thunder's beat. Riding shotgun that night was just their sort of job—though many times they would go right into target cities before doing a mission and become one with the population. They were experts at blending in. That was another reason for their deep-secret status: Everyone in the Thunder unit was black.

It was almost an inside joke, this rap on the United States' special ops units that seemed to hold water. There were many special warriors fighting for the Stars and Stripes—but most of them were white. Why? Were America's Special Forces racist? Discriminatory? At least in the case of Delta Force, the answer was no. In fact, in the past few years Higher Authority had secretly selected the most qualified black candidates for units such as Delta Thunder, one of six operating in Africa, sometimes hiding their advancement by pretending to wash them out. This had been kept so quiet, most people in Delta Force itself did not know. But the black warriors were out there, fighting just as hard for America and her ideals as their white brethren.

And sometimes they died doing it. And this was certainly going to happen to Thunder squad. Jackson knew it because their kidnappers had already told them they were going to be beheaded, one by one, on videotape, which would then be broadcast to the world on Al-Qazzaza. So they were all going to die, and soon. In a way, Jackson at peace with this—some of the time anyway. But the other times, when he thought about how it was actually going to happen, it was just awful.

That's why it was so strange that in between the beatings—which would go on for exactly 30 minutes—Jackson would fall asleep. Sleep soundly and deeply and have vivid dreams of his home and family back in Brooklyn, of helping his wife with her term papers and bringing their son to Boy Scouts meetings, and how those Boy Scouts had all jumped on a plane at Kennedy, flown over to wherever the hell he was, and were breaking him out of this hell.

And that's what he was dreaming about when he heard the mighty crash on the roof.

He woke up thinking: *The Boy Scouts are here . . .*

And he was close.

The first Ghost Team helicopter crashed atop the prison roof at exactly 1015 hours—precisely the moment Murphy had planned it to.

The pilot was Red Curry, one of the original team members. He'd flown full throttle at treetop level for 20 miles, sneaking up from the south. He'd counted down the seconds on the mad dash in, hoping that the curare-sugar concoction conjured up at the bottom of the *Ocean Voyager* and placed inside the prison's pastries by the local bakers for a hundred-dollar bill would work as quickly as the Spooks said it would. If so, he knew it would make this job a lot easier. If not, well . . .

Curry also knew about all the antiaircraft weapons on the prison's roof. He knew their locations backward and forward after studying Murphy's meticulously drawn sketches of what their objective looked like. He knew the portable SAM teams were stationed at each corner of the square-topped building—four teams, probably a total of 20 missiles. Placed in between were the large-caliber guns, twice as many as the missile teams, eight in all, plus the 88mm artillery piece. These were all extremely formidable obstacles.

That's why it was decided to crash one of the new copters onto the roof—sacrificing it for the mission. True, landing normally would have taken mere seconds. But with all the firepower up top, seconds were hours, the difference between life and death, success and failure.

Besides, intentionally crashing a copter was easy. You just slammed it down, with no worries about particulars, like breaking rotors or landing gear or tail flaps. Make a lot of noise, cause a lot of confusion, and drop a lot of smoke. And always come in firing.

Curry was the only one at the controls. His crew of four was on the aircraft's quartet of massive M-60 machine guns, blazing away. The plan was to bang in on the east corner of the fort, take out the missile team and the gunners on either side of them. If Curry was able to do this—in about six seconds—then a second copter, coming out of the north, again at treetop level, could hit the south side of the fortress, KO the remaining machine guns, artillery pieces, and missile teams, then set down next to the crashed copter. This would allow copters three and four to come in and deposit on the roof the Ghost Team's shock troops, who would then attempt the actual rescue.

And this is exactly how it happened. Curry's copter came down with such violence, it cracked the stone roof of the prison. The copter was intentionally low on gas, preventing the chance of a fiery disaster. However, Murphy had attached a dozen cans of lubricating oil to its airframe, which did catch fire on impact, immediately causing a huge cloud of smoke. The second copter came in just a second or two early, nearly landing in Curry's line of fire. Its gunners nailed everything on the west side of the building's roof, though, including the forest of TV antennae. As planned, the billowing smoke hid the approach of copters three and four. They swooped down on the remaining guards so quickly, their guns blazing, barely a shot was fired in return.

It was all over in 12 seconds—again exactly the time Murphy thought it would take. Suddenly there were 24 strike force members on the roof and in control of its weapons—and they'd received nothing but a few scratches in return.

So much for the easy part.

They had to get down into the prison itself—and again, they really hoped the poison had done its job. Two Delta guys had stolen into the town the night before; they'd made the deal with the very willing bakers and seen the cakes poisoned right before their eyes. But did the mooks eat breakfast at the same time every day as Murphy had somehow determined? They were going to find out.

Murphy had also figured there were about 36 guards in the prison in all, both hard-core Al Qaeda members and local thugs. This was almost twice the number of American shock troops. And only 12 of the Americans would be going below. The rest would stay atop the roof and keep it secured while the rescue operation was ongoing.

But, if the poison had done its work, then there would only be about a dozen or so guys down below they had

to kill. If the poison hadn't worked, a small army would
be waiting for them.

The so-called Inside Men prepared to make their way
down into the prison, this as the troopers staying on the
roof tossed all the dead mooks over the wall to the moat
below. The Inside Men finished checking their equipment and declared themselves ready. But there was one
more piece of the plan that had to happen first. They
waited—but just a few seconds. Then they saw it coming: Ryder's Harrier. Trailing smoke, wings a bit wob-
bly, rocketing just a hundred feet above the harbor. It
was on time and moving incredibly fast.

The jump jet went over the roof a moment later. It
barely cleared the top of the wrecked number-one helicopter; that's how low it was flying. The noise was incredible, its shock wave like thunder. It shook the
thick-walled prison and all the buildings all around it.
This was the cue the shock troops were waiting for. The
strike team headed down the stairs.

There was none of the hand-holding six-guys-
grouped-together-going-as-slowly-as-possible thing here.
There was just no time for that. Instead, the strike guys
went down the stairwell at full speed, two abreast, the
first two wearing almost total body armor and carrying
powerful Mossberg shotguns. The next two were armed
with M-60s, and they, too, were like sci-fi monsters, so
thick was their armor. Behind them everyone else was
carrying their standard M16 cut stock with extra-long
magazines. This was not a silent entry. Crashing the
copter on top of the fort had made that impossible. This
was all about surprise and confusion and speed. Going
against convention, the idea was to make as much noise
as they could.

It took them 10 seconds to reach their first objective: the prison kitchen. The true tale would be told here.

They burst in to find 10 dead men, heads on the table, white foam bubbling out of their mouths. An eleventh body was on the floor, twisted into a grotesque position, white foam mixing with blood from its fractured skull. One of the troopers snapped a photo of this body— making sure they could ID it as Shaheen Faheeb. Then he spit on the corpse, and the other troopers let out a grim cheer. The poison had worked, on time and as advertised. Still, the troopers sprayed the room with gunfire, making sure the dead really *were* dead.

Outside, the jump jet screamed by again, rocking the old fort to its foundation a second time. The strike team formed up again and continued their descent.

They ran into the first real opposition on the third floor. Two fighters somehow revived from deep below were coming up the stairs as the shock troops were coming down. The Muslim fighters got the first shots off in the winding stairwell—their bullets bounced off the first two team members, one of them ricocheting back into the neck of one of the fighters. The second mook was cut in half by twin blasts from the Mossberg shotguns.

The strike team didn't slow up a bit. They trampled the dying bodies and just kept on going.

They reached the second floor and here the team split into two. One squad broke off and headed for the prison's engineering room; the others continued the descent. Team One came upon the engineering room just down the hall. It was little more than a broom closet, but inside the troopers found just what they were looking for: the controls for the prison's crude fire-prevention system. Pipes of all shapes and sizes ran through the prison's floors, ready to burst at the hint of a spark or smoke. Inside the engineering room were three big pumps and three big handles, the guts of the system. Everything smelled of salt and brine, and for good reason—the pipes were full of water, pumped in from the ocean nearby.

The jump jet roared by again, shaking everyone and everything a third time. The troopers began opening the valves.

Meanwhile, Two Squad had reached the first level and was still going down. Five terrorists were waiting at the bottom of a stairwell one floor up from the prison's dungeon cells. Undecided and frightened, they had no desire to advance toward the commotion above but would shoot anyone who came down the stairwell.

That's why a couple grenades came down first. They were short-fused blockbusters, and there was nowhere to turn for the mooks. The two bombs went off one-two and literally splattered the five terrorists all over the walls of the stairwell.

The shock troops came rumbling down just seconds later, again not stopping to inspect the goo, just charging on, the sound of rushing water in their ears, finally to the bottom level of the prison: the place where the jail cells were located.

Here the battle began for real.

The Harrier's panel clock was not working, so Ryder brought an egg timer with him. It was counting backward, telling him the time he needed to be over the harbor, over the piers, then over the prison for the first time.

That's how split-second Murphy's plan was. So far, it was going like clockwork.

Just a minute before, while the copters were sneaking in from the north and south, Ryder put the Harrier into a circle, just 20 miles off the coast of Loki Soto, over the horizon, out of sight on the crystal-clear day. Once the egg timer had counted down to 60 seconds, he booted throttles and headed in.

His head was still spinning from the events not two days before. Li's hasty departure and the circumstances surrounding it still burned a hole in his stomach. But he had to push that painful aspect aside for now. File it temporarily somewhere, in the back in his brain, so he could concentrate on the task at hand. Still he was uneasy and in bad spirits. Curiously, it was like part of his body was missing.

He arrived over the tiny port town seconds after turning east, flying very low and creating such a racket, anyone below had no choice but to duck and cover. Ryder went over the prison an instant later, at full throttle, nearly hitting one of the helicopters and creating a tidal wave of earsplitting noise. The tiny port was instantly in chaos. Knowing the prison was filled with high explosives, the townspeople started fleeing for their lives. No one wanted to be around when the castle cooked off.

After his first pass, Ryder looped around and came back over, this just as the raiders were in the kitchen laying the coup de grâce on the poisoned terrorists they'd found. He went over twice as fast and even lower this time, creating even more confusion. Murphy didn't want any civilians killed in the raid—that was very important. Ryder couldn't guarantee, however, that there wouldn't be more than a few broken eardrums by the time he was through.

He went out over the water and turned toward the prison a third time. Half the team members on the roof were loading terrorists' weapons into the copters; the others were nervously watching the streets below. The town did have a well-armed street militia, more thugs in the employ of Al Qaeda. It would be unhelpful if they started turning up.

Ryder went over the town a third time. On this pass he managed to break just about every window in the neighborhood surrounding the prison, those he hadn't broken already, that is. This was just about the time the raiders were turning the water valves to open and were rushing down to the bottom level where the cells were located.

This was when Ryder ran into his first bit of trouble. He streaked over the castle, then turned north, over what was really the heart of the town. Here he was surprised to discover a trail of tracer fire coming up at him. He quickly banked out of the way and found on the street below indeed a small army was gathering. It was the town's Al Qaeda–supplied militia. Murphy had predicted they would probably try to aid their comrades inside the fort.

Ryder continued his bank to the left, performing a very tight 180-degree turn. He did this so swiftly, the gunmen below couldn't keep track of him. He lined up the nose of the Harrier on the street below and pushed the panel button to activate his gun pod. He was sure the noise alone would cause those below to scatter for their lives. He engaged his trigger—but nothing happened. The gun jammed.

He pulled up and out quickly, hoping this was just the fire-control computer and that he could override it. But he started punching buttons and looking for answers and came to the conclusion that it wasn't the computer at all, but the old battered gun had malfunctioned, choking on all its own ammunition.

This was not good.

But he didn't have time to think about it. The egg timer went off. He had to be someplace else. He flipped over and rocketed back toward the fort again.

Hanging beneath Ryder's left wing was a GBU-10E/B Paveway Mk 82 laser-guided bomb. A weapon usually found on A-10 Thunderbolts in years past, it was a rarity these days. But while not the most modern of weapons, at five-hundred pounds it still packed a punch, which was important now. Again, the Mk 82 was laser guided, meaning it would home in on a laser beam being bounced off the target. The same two Ghost Team members who'd poisoned the sugar rolls were now in the building across the street from the prison, holding a laser designator.

Sticking to the same tight timetable as Ryder and everyone else, they began illuminating the northwest corner of the castle, a place Murphy had somehow determined was the weakest point on the fortress. When Ryder banked over the harbor and turned east once more, his weapon system computer immediately picked up the laser designation. It seemed to be burning a hole in the lower right-hand corner of the castle.

Ryder armed the weapon; then, with the corner of the prison still dead in his sights, he let the smart bomb go. . . .

• • •

Captain Johnny Jackson knew by now that these were not the Boy Scouts making all the ruckus above. He was still awake, still chained to the wall of his cell, but just by fate he could look out the tiny slit in his cell door to see the small war going on just outside in the hall.

The lead was flying, tracers bouncing all over, balls of flames blowing by the door. The noise was horrendous. At first, in those few sleepy moments after waking up, he thought this was an earthquake, that the fort was coming down on top of him, and that this tiny cell indeed was where he would die, not at the hands of his captors but in spite of them.

Then the water came. In drips and drabs at first, from the pipes in the ceiling to the top of his head. But then the drops became a trickle, the trickle a small waterfall. In seconds it was a torrent. Salt water, pouring out of the ceiling. . . .

My God, Jackson thought. *I'm going to drown. . . .*

Never would he have guessed that drowning would be how he would leave this hellish place. Fire, yes; beaten to death, maybe—without his head, most likely. But underwater? *God must be having a laugh somewhere,* Jackson thought.

But then came the noise of more explosions and more of the unmistakable racket of gunfire. It was so close now, he could smell the gunpowder. Someone was trading shots with the guards right outside Jackson's cell door.

It went on for what seemed like forever. There was no way he could tell who was winning or even who was fighting against whom. Finally there was one last huge explosion—and then everything was still, except for the gushing water.

Then the cell door opened, and in the next second two soldiers stumbled in. Jackson had no idea who they were. All he knew was that the water was coming down on them as well . . .

Then Jackson saw the patch on their shoulders. A symbol of the Twin Towers and the stars and stripes and the initials NYPD and FDNY, and the motto "We Will Never Forget."

That's when it hit him. These were not fellow Delta soldiers. These were the infamous Ghosts—the mysterious special ops unit that had saved the world at Hormuz, and then at Singapore, and again in stopping terrorists recently from shooting down scores of airliners in the U.S.

Now they were here to save him.

The two soldiers saw him, saluted, then released him from his chains by firing directly at the locks.

Jackson collapsed immediately. He couldn't speak, couldn't stand. One of the soldiers injected him with something. Jackson felt like he was suddenly lifted off the ground. *Morphine* . . . he could feel it coursing through his veins. In an instant, he felt on top of the world.

The soldiers then picked him up and carried him out into the hall. The water was nearly two feet deep out here, and in it Jackson could see the bodies of his torturers, some shot and bloody, some clearly drowned. What had been a waterfall in his cell had turned into a tsunami out here. Surprised by both the deluge and the assault troops, the mooks had paid the price.

His rescuers carried him down the hall, sloshing through the still-rising water, kicking bodies aside. Many had been shot in the head; others had been skewered by bayonets, as well as drowned. Releasing the water had served two purposes: It had dampened the tons of explosives inside the prison and, by sheer surprise, had killed as many of the terrorists as the strike team had with their weapons. Even in his battered condition, Jackson had to admire the ingenuity of it all.

Just before they reached the end of the flooded hallway, the two soldiers stopped, pressed him against the wall, and covered his body with their own. A second after that, the northwest corner of the prison was blown to pieces.

Next thing he knew, Jackson was looking out onto the street that bordered the prison. Townspeople were running by, fleeing from the commotion around them. A rush of water was following them down the street, emptying into the harbor beyond.

In front of him was a helicopter—big, fat, and bristling with weapons. Sitting in this copter surrounded by more soldiers in outrageous combat suits were Jackson's men, the rest of Thunder. All of them were wounded and bloody, but they were still alive and breathing. They'd been carried out by the mystery soldiers, too.

That's when Johnson's rescuers picked him up again and carried him to the helicopter. More gunfire could be heard. A jet fighter roared overhead. The castle seemed to be on the verge of collapse.

Above the chaos, one soldier yelled to Jackson: "Time to go home. . . ."

Chapter 5

The casino was built in the shape of a Bedouin tent. It was a grand, futuristic facade, polished white, with red flags billowing from its top. It had two main floors. The first level, expansive and square, held a huge overly ornate casino, baccarat and roulette being the featured games. Women in short tunics, plunging necklines, and high heels flitted through the crowd dispensing Egyptian beer and cheap Russian vodka. Many other women were drifting through the casino as well. Young, well-dressed, and Eastern European mostly, they were prostitutes, plying their wares.

There were many private rooms located around the periphery of the casino floor. Originally built for private games of chance, this was where the more connected clientele went to consume drugs in private. Amphetamines and barbiturates, occasionally cocaine, and sometimes even pure opium would make an appearance here.

Women, gambling, liquor, and drugs . . . this was not the French Riviera. The casino was in Bahrain, a deeply

Muslim country that nevertheless offered the sins of Gomorrah to the right people for the right price. The "right people" meant the members of the Saudi Royal Family, whose homeland was just a short plane ride across the Gulf.

The casino was located in an isolated part of the island nation. There was a private airstrip here, and that's how most of the Saudi princes arrived at this place. The runway had been built long enough to accommodate not only private planes but also fighter jets, such as the American-built F-15, a model flown extensively by the Royal Saudi Air Force. Why would jet fighters ever land here? Because the royal princes who flew over here from Saudi Arabia many times requested armed fighter escorts for their short hop across the water. A matter of prestige more than security, many times these supersonic escorts would be told to wait—either in the air or with their engines running parked on the taxiway—until the escorted Prince was ready to go back home. On busy nights, toward the end of the week, there might be up to two dozen F-15s either flying around above Bahrain, making for a very crowded sky, or jammed up on the tarmac below.

Tonight was a busy night.

The man named Al-Jabazz Saud Ben-Wabi, aka the Diamond Prince, landed at the airstrip just after nine in the evening. His new Gulfstream jet set down just ahead of its two-ship Royal Saudi F-15 escort. The DP was known to get so drunk at the casino, it would take him hours to get his feet back under him. Like a limo driver on call for a drugged-out rock star, the F-15 pilots would have to wait it out until the megarich Prince decided it was time to leave. Either airborne or parked, they were in for a long night.

The DP had 3 bodyguards with him—reduced from the usual 12 or more he carried when he was abroad. He was wearing so many diamonds—on his fingers, in his ears, around his neck—that one guard was on hand simply to protect the jewelry. They didn't call Ben-Wabi the Diamond Prince for nothing. Two somewhat distant cousins were also with him. Middle-aged identical twins, both were named Gebeeb. Bringing the cousins to the casino was a request from their mother, a less well off aunt of the DP. Though he had made a vague promise to them to hook up later on, he was planning to rid himself of them as soon as he reached the casino.

He would leave them on the first floor of the club—this was where the less beautiful of the Beautiful People spent their evenings. Only the top of the pops got up to the secretive second level. This floor was, of course, where the DP would always go. He would never think of trafficking with the unwashed people below.

Like any other night of the DP's choosing, tonight would be filled with food, drink, and then rough sex. Just who would be the recipient of this last activity was yet to be determined, but the DP rarely had trouble finding a victim or two over here in racy Bahrain. Any age, either sex, any hair color, shape, or body he wanted would be made available to him by the casino owner, a kind of favorite-guest service. For the DP, after that it was just a question of letting the games begin.

A limo was waiting for the DP's entourage as they deplaned from the Gulfstream. It carried them the stone's throw distance to the casino, this as the DP's F-15 escorts took their places along the already crowded aircraft ready area. The whine of nearly a dozen waiting F-15s would provide the background music for what was about to happen here tonight.

The limo arrived and, as planned, the two Gebeebs were shuffled off to the tables of the first level, this as the DP's bodyguards took up positions outside the front door. The DP himself was escorted to the second floor, and here a virtual paradise awaited him. Or at least what someone of his DNA would consider paradise. The second level consisted of an immense ballroom. Ninety percent of its floor was covered with fur rugs and silk pillows. The lights, hanging low from the gold-leafed ceiling, looked like lanterns from a Chinese junk. There were gently gurgling fountains and lots of ferns and vines, and ice tubs containing the best champagne, the best wines. Equal parts lavish and tasteless, it was right out of *Aladdin*—the cartoon version.

A trio of managers appeared as soon as the DP walked in; they commenced bowing and scraping right away. Was his guest here? he asked them. They replied yes, a thousand times yes. He was waiting deeper inside.

And the girls, were they here? Again the answer was yes. Twenty-two of them, in fact.

And what of the local police? The managers assured him that two patrol cars were parked out back as usual and that their officers had been "bonused." Translation: They had been paid off and would not be a factor tonight.

Only then did the DP smile, twisting the largest diamond ring on his left hand. "My two cousins, downstairs," he told the managers, "make sure they win at the tables."

Then the DP indicated the conversation was over and

the managers disappeared. He walked deeper into the low-lit, gaudy romper room.

He found his guest soon enough. He was Jabal Ben-Wabi, his older, uglier brother. Just slightly less rich than the DP, Jabal was a lot less glamorous and very unrefined. Due to a childhood illness, he was missing his left eye. Because he wore a covering over this empty socket, his nickname was *Qacba,* Arabic for "Patch."

He was as grubby and gnarled as the DP was polished and clean. While he was in the favor of the Saudi Royal Court, Jabal was not as well liked as the DP. Jabal was worth about $1 billion, the DP ten times that. And where the DP was usually dressed in white robes or Western-style clothes, Jabal wore the attire of a peasant, robes of reds, blues, black. There were 32 brothers and sisters in their family; Jabal and the DP were actually more unalike than having much in common. The DP thought of himself as being much more cosmopolitan.

They did share one bond, though: Both were thick in the underground world of Islamic terrorism. The DP was a financier and dreamed of starting his own empire in West Africa; Jabal was frontline hard-core Al Qaeda.

Just like the DP, Jabal had had a hand in the attacks of 9/11. He'd worked with bin Laden himself on the overall plan and was the middleman in arranging for passports for more than half the 19 hijackers and their handlers. Without him, many would have never been able to get into the United States in the first place.

When the United States invaded Afghanistan a month later and crushed the Taliban, Jabal escaped to Iran, as did many of the Al Qaeda bigwigs. Since then, he'd been moving back and forth over the border between

Afghanistan and Iran, directing many of the terrorist operations in Pakistan and Kashmir and recruiting new members to fight in Iraq. More chilling, though, he was also known as one of bin Laden's chief executioners.

Jabal had come here at the invitation of the DP, who had yet to hear about the attack on the prison at Loki Soto and needed some more warm bodies for his grand designs in West Africa. Jabal was in the business of providing warm bodies. The DP was hoping they could make a deal, but only after a night of entertainment.

They greeted each other warmly. They hadn't seen each other in months. The DP bid Jabal to join him atop a particular high pile of pillows. Two bowls of yogurt and warm lamb guts were waiting for them. The Patch settled in beside his brother, and by custom they shared a date palm. Then a servant poured a glass of champagne for each of them. Their night had officially begun.

Jabal had one thing worrying him, though. He'd only been to this casino a few times before; by contrast, the DP usually flew out here twice a week if he was in town. Jabal had heard this place had recently gained a reputation for bad luck after an incident involving their close cousin Prince Ali Muhammad. He'd killed a girl here during rough sex about a half-year before. The murder wasn't what was bothering Jabal; that sort of thing went on here all the time. It was that shortly after the incident their cousin Ali had met a very gruesome, if mysterious, end himself. His chartered jet somehow went off-course and slammed into a place called the Pan Arabic Oil Exchange, a business he owned. The word in the casbah was that their cousin's untimely death had something to do with the incident that had happened in this very place just days before.

The DP knew of his brother's fears and quickly sought to put them to rest.

"It had *nothing* to do with that," the DP told him, again nervously twisting the huge diamond ring on his left hand. "What was bad luck about it? Did our cousin get found out? Did the police charge him? Did the employees here inform on him? No, none of these things happened—because it was just status quo here. His death was unrelated."

But Jabal was not yet at ease. "We have all heard the Crazy Americans were behind his death, as revenge for this murder thing," he said.

Again the DP just waved his concerns away. "They are *not* related," he said a bit sternly. "He had many issues with the Crazy Americans. The death of the girl he'd taken here was a very minor incident in comparison."

Jabal listened and sipped his drink, but with a little less gusto.

Truth was, Jabal was terrified of the Crazy Americans. Terrified that his name was on their hit list and when they reached it his days would be numbered. Just like cousin Ali Muhammad. Just like so many of top jihadists over the past year. These American Ghosts didn't just kill you—they made you feel it before you died. Long, slow, and sacrilegious. Despite what his brother was saying, Jabal believed that once the Crazy Americans got under your skin, there was no way you could ever get them out. You drove yourself crazy with worry—until they caught you and tortured you and then buried you alive in a shallow grave along with a pig whose throat had been cut. Jabal could not bear the thought of dying that way.

The DP saw the wheels turning in his brother's head.

He poured him another glass of champagne. "Please, my brother, put these things out of your mind," the DP told him. "Just for tonight. Be like me. I do not share your fear of these Crazy Americans. I think they are a myth. Propaganda, rustled up in desperation by their intelligence people. Besides, we are safe here. My bodyguards are stationed at the front door. The police are in our pay and they watch this place like hawks. No one can reach us here. Be logical about it, and believe me your fears will disappear."

Jabal thought about all this for a moment. He didn't feel completely at ease but then drained his champagne and finally smiled. He had terrible teeth.

"All right then, let us revel," he said. "And let Allah sort everything else out."

The evening began in earnest with their favorite food being served atop the pillows. Brought in on one huge silver platter covered and steaming, it was essentially a pile of grilled-cheese sandwiches and a couple quarts of Chinese takeout. This was followed by German ice cream and cookies. The brothers consumed a bottle of champagne each and had made two toasts with *sake* in memory of their dearly departed cousin, Ali. His problem, they decided over dinner, was that he got caught. He'd left a trail in his *jihad* activities—he was running money to Al Qaeda cells right out of his office building. Hundreds of people were involved, and they all died along with him that day his plane crashed into his own building. A half-blind man could have found out Ali.

The DP and brother Jabal were smarter than that. They were experts at leaving no trails. They cleaned up their messes or had trusted people do it for them. More important, they were even higher up in the Saudi royal structure than Ali, and the closer they were to the top, the more protection they knew they had from the inconveniences of life. So, for a while, Jabal actually did relax.

Once the meal was dispensed with and the dishes were cleared away, two young boys bathed the brothers with hot cloths. Then the girls were brought out.

There were 22 of them as promised. The DP and Jabal could have all of them or none of them. The girls were from all over the world; indeed, the DP's handlers were approached all the time by managers of young women or the young women themselves, asking to be made part of DP's harem, as they knew as much as a million dollars or more could be made if they were selected. That was the case with the more sophisticated ones anyway. Others had simply been sold to the DP's minions as sex slaves. Sophisticated or not, none of them had the faintest idea what could be in store for them on the second floor of the casino. They were all beautiful, but they were all disposable, too. Just the way the DP and Jabal liked them.

A kind of game ensued as the two brothers pretended to compete for the pick of the litter by flipping dice. This ended presently, though, as Jabal's Viagra started kicking in. He selected three blondes—they could have been triplets—and hurried into one of the luxurious private rooms that ringed the ballroom.

The DP let Jabal go, more convinced than ever that he had less class, less style, than he. There was only one woman to be selected here. She was at the very end of the line. Absolutely gorgeous. Perfect body, wrapped in a tight leather pseudo S and M outfit, held together by little more than spikes the size of knitting needles, she was a black-haired vision, looking very vulnerable.

Best of all, she was Asian.

The DP would have her tonight.

The Diamond Prince was almost too handsome to kill.

Li hadn't expected this. He was tall and dark, with the looks of a male model, at least in the low light of the second-floor ballroom. His dark eyes radiated a certain air of intelligence. He had an attractive smile. His physique wasn't too shabby, either.

But she knew all about the DP by now. Her CIA handlers had made sure of that. His extensive connection to 9/11. The billions he'd made selling weapons in Africa. His involvement in the ongoing genocide in the Sudan. The girls he'd murdered, during rough sex, right in this very building. Dashing or not, he was a very bad guy. And he had to go.

But Li was scared stiff. She'd never trained to be an assassin. The furthest she got was a self-defense course at FBI Quantico. But as her Agency handlers had told her, this was war and what she had to do was no different from shooting an enemy general on the field of battle. By her one act, many future terrorist attacks could be prevented. Many lives might be saved. She had to see it through.

She was carrying just the weapon to do it with, too—thanks to no small piece of brilliance on the part of the CIA, considering she'd gone through more security to get into this place than someone coming to see the President of the United States. It all started when her handlers made arrangements with a Bulgarian slave trader to insert her into his cache of young females earmarked for Bahrain this weekend; getting to the Arab country was the easy part. Once on the ground, though, she'd been taken to a building attached to the casino, strip-searched twice, questioned by the DP's security people, and then strip-searched again—and only then were she and the other girls allowed into the casino itself. Once in, they were frisked, every hour on the hour, until the DP finally showed up and the vulgar chorus line assembled. Bottom line, it would have been impossible to sneak a gun or a bomb or even a knife inside here.

But still, Li was packing a murder weapon, hiding it on her body, in plain sight.

The Diamond Prince had selected her first, from the line of attractive young women. But she was not the only girl that he fancied. He also separated a young blond girl from the others. Barely 17, she was from Slovakia and thrilled she'd been selected, too.

Dismissing the rest of the girls, the DP turned to Li, who was now standing beside him next to the mountain of pillows, and whispered in her ear: "I'll bet you like the clams as well as the oysters." It was a line from the movie *Spartacus*. Translation: "I hope you go both ways."

Li rubbed up against him and cooed: "I like it all."

The DP led them both to one of the nearby bedrooms, making a big production out of taking Li by the arm like a gentleman, while practically pushing the giggling young blonde ahead of him, like a lamb to slaughter.

The bedroom was done in the same bad taste as the pillow-happy ballroom. Lots of flashy silk and cheap-looking Chinese lanterns. The DP forced the young girl onto the bed; she was still laughing, but a little nervously now. Then with a gush of charm, he poured Li a glass of champagne. She watched him carefully, making sure he didn't slip anything into the flute, like a roofie or worse. Only after she saw him take a sip from his own glass, poured from the same bottle, did she pretend to sip hers as well.

The bed was equipped with leather restraints. The DP drained his champagne and then without another word tied the blond girl to the bed, first by the ankles, then by the wrists. Then he ripped the tiny negligee from her body. When the girl somewhat playfully complained the DP was being too rough, he slapped her hard across the face. It was only then that the young girl realized something was not right here.

Li knew what was going to happen next—her CIA handlers were well aware of the DP's *modus operandi*. Once the young girl was restrained, the Prince would wrap a silk scarf around her neck. Then, while fondling her, he would begin to draw the silk tighter, slowly choking her, up to the brink of asphyxiation. Then he would have sex with her near-lifeless body and, once depleted, would finish the job with his diamond-encrusted fists. Li was surprised, though, that it was all happening so fast. In a weird way, she'd been expecting a little more foreplay.

The DP stripped down to his shorts and refilled his champagne glass. He ran his hands up and down's Li's body, this as the girl on the bed started to cry. Her weeping only served to further stimulate the DP. He drained his second glass, then moved back toward the bed, silk scarf in hand. The girl began begging for her life, but again, this only increased the DP's excitement.

He put the scarf around her throat. The young girl screamed—but it was no use. The bedrooms here were virtually soundproof. Besides, no one in the casino would ever come to her aid, even if they'd heard her cries. Again, this sort of thing went on here all the time. As the CIA men had described it, it was the casino's *kink du jour.*

Hovering over the young girl now, the DP looked over his shoulder at Li and winked. She blew him a kiss of approval. He smiled and pulled the scarf tight. The girl began gasping for air. A little tighter. She tried to let out another scream—but this time nothing came out. The DP removed his shorts and started to climb on top of her. That's when Li walked over and tapped him lightly on the shoulder. He turned back to her, certain she wanted to get in on the action. Instead, he saw in her hand one of the spikes that had been holding her outfit together. It was long and sharp and shiny. Without hesitation, Li plunged it into his left eye.

There was surprisingly little resistance going in. The spike was nine inches long but was essentially a carpenter's nail. It went through the pupil, then the entire eyeball, and then into the DP's brain as easily as if it were going through butter. There was very little blood, too, and only the slightest sucking sound. Li gave the spike one last thrust, pushing it all the way in, and then let it go. The DP just stared back at her—his remaining pupil going wide—baffled by her sudden betrayal. He reached out, not to grab her but just to hold on to something, anything. Li just took a step back. He fell to the floor with a thud.

Then the words just tumbled out of her mouth: "Now you'll need a patch, too—just like your brother."

The girl on the bed tried to scream again. But Li immediately put her fingers to her lips, even as she was loosening the scarf.

"Just stay quiet," she hissed at the girl. "You can still get out of this alive."

Still, the girl begged Li to untie her—but Li knew better. If the girl stayed tied, then the DP's minions could never accuse *her* of killing their boss, at least that's what she hoped.

So Li just followed the plan. She left the girl as she was, calmly fixed herself up, straightened her costume, and went out the door, closing it tightly behind her.

The only people in the ballroom were the servants. Li walked by them summoning up the best imperial air she could muster.

"They want to be . . . *alone*," she said to one, in passing.

The servant simply nodded. He considered Li lucky. The DP rarely left witnesses to his indiscretions.

She walked across the ballroom to the private elevator. As she was getting on, two middle-aged men, twins, were getting off. They both looked dim-witted and drunk. They were also giggling like schoolgirls. She hit the down button and went to the first floor. Crossing the crowded casino, she slipped out the side entrance, where she knew a carousel of limousines awaited.

She climbed into the nearest one—the driver asked her no questions. He immediately turned the car around and headed for the airstrip just down the road. From here the plan was simple. The same CIA-owned Gulfstream that had brought her and the rest of the Bulgarian cache to Bahrain would be landing here again. In fact, it should be touching down right about now. It wouldn't even shut off its engines. Li would climb aboard and they would be halfway to Ramstein

Air Base in Germany before anyone discovered the DP's body.

She leaned back against the limo seat and let out a long breath. Maybe then it would hit her, she thought. Maybe once she was out of this horrible place and back in the arms of civilization she would break down and shed tears over what she'd just done. There was a distinct horror in taking another person's life, she was sure. But the feeling hadn't arrived yet. At the moment, she was still rock hard and steel willed.

The limo arrived at the airstrip—but this was not the same place Li had first seen this afternoon. Back then, it looked like nothing more than a patch of asphalt in the middle of a field of sand. Now it looked like a military base. She counted more than a dozen F-15 fighters parked along the runway. Each plane was brightly lit and had mechanics nursing it. Not only were these people here, but there were also soldiers—or at least heavily armed men in uniforms—guarding the jet airplanes.

The driver pulled in about halfway up to the airstrip. There was a small gate here where most people boarded their private planes. Li lowered her window and miraculously heard above the whine of the idling military jets the sound of a Gulfstream's smaller, higher-pitched engines. She looked up to see the familiar green and white aircraft pass overhead, turning for a landing. This was the CIA transit plane. *Thank God,* she thought.

The limo driver turned to ask her if this was where she wanted to go—but stopped before he could say anything. His eyes suddenly went wide. Li stared at him for a moment, then looked out the back window of the limo. There was a line of vehicles with flashing lights coming up behind them. *Police cars. . . .*

Her heart sank. These cars belonged to the Bahraini cops. Several were always parked in the casino's back lot. At least a half-dozen of them were surrounding the limo now, the flashing lights creating weird shadows everywhere.

A small army of armed men jumped from the police vehicles and ran up to the limo. Some were in uniform; others were obviously plainclothes bodyguards. They all had their guns drawn and were pointing them right at her.

At the same moment, Li realized the CIA Gulfstream had landed. It taxied up to the small gate, not 20 feet away. She could see through the limo's windshield to the plane's cockpit, making out the face of the pilot plus one of her handlers. She almost cried out to them—but it wouldn't have done her any good. They sized up the situation with Li and her limo—and kept right on going. Back out to the airstrip, where, engines screaming, they immediately took off again.

Leaving her behind.

Suddenly the door beside her opened and two men stuck their heads in. They immediately started yipping and pointing at her. She recognized them. They were the twin idiots she'd passed on the elevator. The Gebeebs, the DP's dim-witted cousins. They were the ones who'd found the DP dead.

Suddenly someone pushed them out of the way and took their place in the door.

It was Jabal Ben-Wabi, the Patch. Smelly, drunk, ugly. He was holding Li's bloody spike in his hand.

"You bitch!" he screamed at her. *"You American bitch!"*

He launched himself into the back of the limousine, grabbing her arm and twisting it. Instinctively she started to fight him off. But he began slapping her and then punching her—hard. Then he put his face right up to hers.

"I'm going to kill you," he hissed at her. "And when I do, the whole world will be watching. . . ."

Chapter 6

Ryder was freezing in the desert. He saw sand dunes and scorpions and even a few palm trees off in the distance. Yet, his hands were covered with ice and his feet were encased in snow. It was like he was standing at the North Pole *and* in the middle of the Sahara. As for his late wife, she was nowhere in sight. That's why he wasn't sure if this was a dream or not.

Then, from behind, a voice beckoned to him: *"Get up. We've got a problem."*

Ryder opened his eyes to find Red Curry, the team's other senior pilot, shaking him awake.

"And it's a *big* problem," Curry was saying to him. "Get up to Murphy's cabin right away. . . ."

With that, Curry left, allowing Ryder to crawl out of bed with some dignity. It was hard to do, though. His legs were stiff; his arms were aching; his head was ready to burst. He'd just slept for nearly 24 hours, yet he was still bone-tired.

He'd been the last one to land back on the ship following the raid on Loki Soto. It was only a 35-mile trip, as the *Ocean Voyager* had been waiting for them just over the horizon, 10 minutes away. But a few miles out from the African coast, the Harrier's engine started coughing. At the same moment, all of his oil pressure gauges began blinking red. Then most of his primary power went out. One look at his fuel gauge told him he was pissing gas by the gallon. The jump jet was falling apart around him.

It came down to having one of the three remaining Superhawk helicopters turn back and ride nursemaid for him for the last few miles of the return trip. His plane's engine was backfiring and smoking heavily by this time. The guys in the copter had signaled that they'd counted more than two dozen holes in his fuselage and on the tail of the plane. Some of those militia rounds had hit him after all, or maybe people had been shooting at him all along as he was buzzing the town and he just hadn't realized it. Either way, according to the copter guys, his airframe looked like Swiss cheese.

Aware that his return might be messy, those on the ship got all the copters and occupants safely down below before they told Ryder to come in. As it turned out, his landing wasn't so much of a crash as it was a spine-crushing bounce. The sound was sickening, especially after he came down the second time, cracking his landing gear and ripping his tail section in two. A fire broke out under his wings. The engine began tearing itself apart. Even the controls on his flight panel began sizzling.

The ship's crash crew immediately covered the airplane in fire-suppression foam, quickly snuffing out the flames. Ryder didn't even bother to climb out. He just slumped farther into the pilot's seat. The last time he'd pranged the Harrier on the ship, after the Hormuz battle, it had been resurrected to fly again. But at that moment, he knew the jump jet had made its last flight.

Following the moving of the Delta Thunder guys to the sick bay, the Ghosts went up to Murphy's quarters to celebrate their successful operation. All except Ryder. As he usually did after a heavy mission, he took a six-pack back to his quarters alone, drank one beer after another, then lay down to get his first real sleep in what seemed like centuries.

But now he was awake again.

And something was wrong.

He ran up to Murphy's quarters, taking the steps two at a time. Reaching the grand wooden door of the Captain's Room, Ryder didn't stop to knock. He burst in, expecting to see the whole team assembled. But he was surprised. The room was empty, except for Murphy. The diminutive Texan was sitting at the far end of the long table. He looked devastated.

He waved Ryder in. The pilot took a seat right next to him. Ryder knew the world was about to fall on his head.

"I'll just give it to you straight," Murphy began. "Because there's no other way to do it. . . ."

Ryder just stared back at him for a moment. Then it hit him.

Li . . .

"What's happened to her?"

"She's dead," Murphy told him starkly. "The mooks got her. Executed her."

Ryder went numb. He couldn't feel his fingers. He couldn't feel his boots on the deck. The room began spinning 360 degrees, yet he remained still. He opened his mouth to say something, but nothing would come out at first.

Finally he was able to croak: "How . . . ?"

Murphy shook his head. "The Agency sent her into that freak show casino over in Bahrain. Her mission was to ice the Diamond Prince—and she actually did it. But then something went wrong. She was supposed to fly out as soon as the DP was toast, but the DP's guys caught her at the airstrip seconds before she could get on the escape plane."

Again, Ryder just stared at him in disbelief. If the mooks caught her just seconds before she was to get on the escape plane, that meant the CIA guys must have been there to witness her capture—and didn't step in to help.

"You mean they left her behind?" he asked Murphy, anger growing.

Murphy nodded slowly. He was almost in tears. "We left her in the hands of those assholes," he said. "And they chickened out on her. They might as well as have put the gun to her head themselves."

Now Ryder was shaking; his brain was just not accepting what he was hearing. He'd begged her not to go. They all did. But she'd become convinced that it was the best way to serve her country—and become a real member of the Ghost Team. The result was now a nightmare.

Murphy poured Ryder a drink. He downed it without even knowing what it was.

"The guy they saw pulling her out of the limo was the DP's brother—Jabal Ben-Wabi," Murphy explained. "They call him the Patch. He's one of Al Qaeda's chief executioners. He already beheaded at least six American hostages on TV, people Al Qaeda snatched in Iraq.

When someone falls into his hands, it's just a matter of getting the execution videotape to Al-Qazzaza TV. Daniel Pearl. Nick Berg. Jack Hensley. Eugene Armstrong. You know their names. You know how they met their end. In every case, Jabal Ben-Wabi was there, front and center, hiding behind a mask."

"Yes, but, maybe—" Ryder whispered.

Murphy stopped him from saying any more. "We intercepted a call before you got up here," he went on. "A line we got into Al-Qazzaza's news desk. The caller told them to expect a new execution tape very soon—that it was being made with a girl and two guys from the Philippines and that he was watching them getting . . . well, beheaded . . . at that very moment. This Patch guy works fast. That's his trademark, the bastard."

Ryder put his head in his hands. Murphy patted his shoulder, trying to comfort him. "As soon as Li left the ship, I told our friends down in the White Rooms to start eavesdropping on the CIA's black ops communications net, as a way of following her on her mission. I heard their phone calls when things started to go wrong. That's how I know what happened. I knew it even before the guys at CIA headquarters back in Virginia did.

"The only upside of all that," Murphy continued slowly, "is we'll know where she is as soon as the CIA does. The body usually turns up, you know, just before the beheading video airs."

Ryder just couldn't believe it. *She was dead.* It was beginning to overwhelm him. The time they'd just spent together. Drinking the awful coffee. Dodging the spray. His filling her head with the Stars and Stripes. The question she was going to ask him before the whole world changed.

He closed his eyes tight, as if in darkness there would be some light. But no such luck. Instead, he was startled to see an image of his old hunting rifle staring him in the face again. He tried to shake the vision away, but it refused to go. He sank deeper into the abyss. First he lost his wife; now he'd lost Li. What kind of life was he living here? Why was God piling on him? What long-forgotten sin had got him in all this trouble?

He'd worked very hard to keep his act together after his wife died. At the time, he didn't believe it was possible. He just couldn't imagine life without her—that's what put him on the wrong end of his hunting rifle the first time, *so close* to blowing his brains out just on the chance that there was an afterlife and he'd be with her again.

Then came the Ghost Team and he was able to get his second life, one dedicated to hunting down his wife's killers and the people who so cowardly attacked the United States on 9/11. And he'd whacked a lot of them since then. Dear, sweet revenge.

But now this. The unthinkable. Pushed back to square one. The mooks had killed another person dear to him. How could this happen to someone twice in a lifetime? Certainly the love affairs were different. With his wife, it had lasted a dozen years. With Li, counting all the time they'd actually spent together, maybe a dozen hours. But it was love all the same, wasn't it? The hole left in his heart was just as deep. Just as dark.

Eyes still closed, he knew he had two ways to go here. One was to go find a real rifle someplace and blow his head off once and for all.

Or . . .

"I've got to quit the team," he told Murphy suddenly. "I hate to leave you hanging, but I've got to go. . . ."

He let his voice drift off.

Murphy asked him: "Where are you going?"

"I don't know," Ryder replied. "But I've got to find this Patch guy. Hunt him down. I don't care if he's in a cave, in a mansion, or floating on a boat down the Nile. I don't care if he has twenty grandkids around him. I don't care if he's stumbled on the Road to Damascus and has suddenly turned into Mother Teresa. I'm going to find him and I'm going to beat him to death with my own hands. What he did on 9/11 was bad enough. But now, for what he's done to Li? He's a dead man—or I'll die trying to make him that way."

He knew this all sounded too dramatic, but he meant it.

"And after I grease him," he went on, "I'm going looking for those two CIA assholes who left her behind. And I'm going to do the same to them."

"You're going to do all this by yourself?" Murphy asked him.

"I have to, Murph," Ryder replied, finally taking his head out of his hands. "If I ever want to sleep again, that is. Damn, I hardly sleep now. But there's no way I can let them get away with this. I just can't. . . ."

Murphy smiled sadly. Then he just nodded toward the big picture window at the other end of the huge cabin.

"Go take a look," he said.

Ryder got up and made his way to the window. Down below, the big aircraft elevators were bringing up the three remaining Superhawk helicopters. Members of the strike team were moving all over the top deck as well Gear packed, weapons in hand. They were getting ready to launch. . . .

But where were they going?

"They're going with you," Murphy told him from across the room. "Because they believe as you do. Li was one of us, even though she never thought of it that way. They took her from us and now they have to pay. That's how we work. That's what we do."

Ryder was speechless. No words could express what he was thinking.

Murphy joined him at the window. "It will mean the end of the team, of course," he said. "They're expecting us back in the U.S. in three days and they'll pull the plug on us for sure if we don't show up. I mean, we'll *really* be unauthorized this time. But I don't care. I'm with you one thousand percent. Even if it's the *last* thing we do, we can't leave it any other way. Not for us. Not for Li's family."

But Ryder was suddenly not so sure. "But I don't want *everyone* to walk into the jaws of death with me. This is something I have to do my way. On my terms. As bad as that sounds."

Murphy shrugged. "You're the senior officer of the team," he said. "You've *always* been the senior officer. Just like with Martinez before you, these guys will follow you anywhere. They *want* to go. And frankly, if you had a change of heart, I believe they'd go without you."

Ryder looked over at him. "Really?"

"Don't you see?" Murphy asked him. "They *all* loved her. Everyone on the goddamn boat—even the guys who'd only known her for a short while. That's just how she was."

Ryder looked down at the team again. Again he tried to say something, but the words got caught in his throat. He was proud and devastated at the same time. For some reason, the way the afternoon ocean sun was hitting the deck, the patch each man wore on his right shoulder seemed to be gleaming, almost sparkling with electricity. It was a very strange moment for Ryder.

Finally, he was able to speak again.

"But where the hell do we start? Where do we go looking for this Patch guy?"

"At least I can help on that," Murphy replied. He cranked up his handheld electronic notebook. It was tapped into everything the Spooks were doing below. "We tracked the Patch's last phone call to a city called Khrash. Turns out it's a snake pit of Al Qaeda types, a haven for them. In fact, it's where their fighters go for what amounts to R and R. The NSC actually believes that at least some of the most notorious beheading videos of the past couple years were filmed there—and not in Iraq at all."

"But if it's not in Iraq," Ryder asked, "where the hell is it?"

"In a place some people think is worse," Murphy told him.

"Afghanistan?" Ryder guessed right away.

"Right on the western edge." Murphy nodded. "So close that if you sneeze hard enough you're in Iran. A very nasty part of the world."

Ryder just shook his head. His brain had finally shifted into gear.

"Nasty?" he said darkly. "They don't know what 'nasty' is."

• • •

The ship turned 180 degrees and was now heading toward the Mediterranean Sea. It was moving at incredible speed, its four jet engines firing in afterburner mode. Ryder soon joined the activity on the deck. The trio of helicopters was in position, rotors turning. Some of those team members who were going—Delta guys, SEALs, SDS, 36 in all—were wearing uniforms still dirty from the mission to Loki Soto. It made no difference to them, though. Their shoulder patches were clean.

The copters were loaded up with little ceremony. As always, most of the troopers were carrying short-stock M16s with extended magazines. But some were also carrying backup weapons such as Mossberg shotguns or grenade launchers. Each man also had his razor-sharp bayonet attached to his first weapon of choice. This was a trademark of the team.

The mood was grim but determined. Murphy had been right. Romantic subplots aside, they'd all thought of Li as one of them—just as much as the SEALs who'd defected or the SDS guys or the original Delta operators. They *had* to go avenge her death. Had to find her killers and had to make them pay. Or at least die trying.

The question, though, was *how* were they going to do it?

Usually they were very well prepared before leaving on a mission. Everything planned to the last detail by Murphy, backed up by intelligence from the Spooks. Just like the recent attack on the Loki Soto prison. Noodled down to the second, never complex, always beautifully timed. And never without enough equipment, weapons, and fuel.

But this? This was different. They didn't even know where they were going. Only that they were heading deep into Al Qaeda territory. That is, if they could even get that far. But again, that was the whole idea. Successful or not, they had to try. They would just have to pick up stuff they needed along the way.

There were some last-minute additions to the strike force. Team members could be seen throwing such items as extra ammo, flares, and American flags onto the waiting copters. One of the Delta guys called a sailor over and made a quick request of him. The sailor disappeared only to reappear a minute later bearing the man's hollow-body guitar. The Delta guy took his knife from his belt, quickly snipped the strings from the instrument, and took them with him. The sailor casually threw the de-stringed guitar over the side of the ship.

Murphy soon joined Ryder on the deck. He was carrying two things he had to give to the pilot. One was a simple black box; inside was a yellow cell phone. Ryder studied the device for a moment. It was video-capable, so they would be able to receive pictures through it. It also had a scramble feature, meaning it would be almost impervious to eavesdropping.

"This is the most secure phone in the world," Murphy told him. "So be careful how and when you use it. And protect it with your life. We don't want it falling into the wrong hands."

The second item was a small duffel bag. Murphy put it firmly in Ryder's hands and then indicated he should look in it. Ryder undid the top string and peered inside. The bag was full of money.

"Goddamn," he swore. "How much is in here?"

"Two million dollars," Murphy replied casually. "It's all I brought with me."

"But what's it for?" Ryder asked.

"You're going to Afghanistan," Murphy told him. "*Everything* is for sale there. This might come in handy on your way. It might also help out once you get back on the ground."

Murphy then told Ryder he and the Spooks were already working on a way to, at least, get the team to their destination intact and with some of the equipment they might need when they got there. But it was definitely going to be a shoestring thing, with nothing guaranteed along the way.

"Any help you can give us will be appreciated," Ryder told him.

Finally the copters were ready to take off. They only had enough fuel to reach the tip of Africa or maybe southwestern Europe, still several hundred miles away. They would have to feel their way across the Med and to the Middle East from there. It was a daunting task for any special ops group—but the Ghosts were different. They were good at finding their way in the dark.

The copters were just about to get the go sign from Bingo standing up on the flying deck when there was some movement down by the stern.

Eight men had marched in close formation to the deck just above where the copters were ready to leave.

It was Delta Team Thunder. Still in bandages all of them, still weak and marked from their beatings, they'd come out nonetheless to see the strike force off. They stood at attention and on their commander's call went into a rigid salute.

Ryder was standing next to the lead copter. He looked up at the Delta guys and felt that lump in his throat again.

Damn. . . .

He finally climbed aboard his copter. Bingo gave the go sign and up they went, all three Blackhawks, one right after another. It was only seconds before they were all airborne.

They formed up and immediately turned toward land. As Ryder settled into the copilot's seat of the lead copter, psyching himself for what lay ahead, the red cell phone rang.

It was Johnny Johnson, the CO of Delta Thunder.

"I appreciate your sendoff," Ryder told him. "It means a lot to us."

"It means a lot to us as well," Johnson replied, his voice strong and determined. "Especially after what you guys did for us. And we know what you're going through. So let me promise you this: No matter where it is you're heading, or how you get there, my men and I will join you as soon as we can. . . ."

PART TWO
East to the Qimruz

Chapter 7

It was another long night above Afghanistan.

The strange-looking airplane had been airborne for six hours and 32 minutes. In that time, it had endlessly circled a small target area over the western part of the country, going nowhere fast. The seven-man crew was already drained. It had been a bumpy night, with turbulence shaking them ever since takeoff. Still, they had six more hours of flying to go before they could even think about landing. And even then, after a little food and a little sleep they'd be back up here again, circling, circling, circling . . . like some monstrous mythical bird unable to find its way home.

The aircraft's official name was EC-130H2/P. It most resembled the American-built C-130 Hercules cargo plane; indeed, stripped down to the bare essentials the EC-130H2/P was a typical 130. But there was nothing typical about it in its current form. In fact, it was probably one of the weirdest airplanes ever built.

Most noticeable was its elongated nose; it stuck out

nine feet from the front of the cockpit. Looking out over it were a multitude of oversize cockpit windows, tinted black and resembling bugs' eyes. There were wires strung from these cockpit windows back to the aircraft's tail fin, and on these wires hung mysterious-looking gray spools. The tail wings themselves were hideously distorted; there were four instead of just two, and each of these four winglets had a small forest of antennae sprouting from it.

The aircraft carried no country markings or insignia. The fuselage and main wings were extra thick, giving the overall impression that the plane had muscles. Plexiglas blisters ran up and down the airframe. More strange protrusions grew behind the four overly large turboprop engines. The plane itself was painted crystal-camouflage black to mimic the stars at night. This only added to its bizarre, sinister appearance.

On the airplane's underbelly was the strangest thing of all. It was an igloo-shaped compartment that could be raised and lowered from the body of the aircraft. Called the Snowball by the crew, it was one of the most closely guarded secrets in the U.S. military.

This strange bird was not built for combat. It carried no weapons, or not the typical ones anyway. It was a psych-ops plane, an aircraft jammed with electronic gear whose purpose was to influence the hearts and minds of the people it was flying over, in this case the wild hill tribes of northwest Afghanistan. Predictably nicknamed *Psyclops,* the plane could bend minds, shape opinions; "get under the skull" in psych-ops lingo, of anyone within its reach. It could do this in several ways, all of them highly classified.

The plane was flown by the 31st Special Operations

Group. Its call sign was Commando Solo—*commando* meaning "special operations" and *solo* meaning what they did they did alone. But its crew wasn't black warriors or deep-ops types. In fact, of the seven onboard, two were cops, two were volunteer firemen, one was a high school teacher, one was a banker, and one was a paramedic.

And maybe the strangest thing of all was that these men didn't belong to the CIA or the DIA, AFIA, NSA, NRO, or any of the short list of America's deep-secret operations like Ruby Fruit, Seabreeze, and Team 99.

They were actually part-time soldiers. Members of the Pennsylvania Air National Guard.

Civilians, in uniform.

It was now 0100 hours.

For most of the night the *Psyclops* airplane had been orbiting above a province near the Afghani-Iranian border called Badghis. Staying steady at fifteen-thousand feet and 140 knots, they performed one 360-degree turn every 20 minutes. This meant the airplane was always just a little bit tipped to the side, making it impossible to set anything down—a clipboard, a coffee cup, the latest *Playboy*—without having it slide away.

Captain J. C. Dow was the pilot of this weird airplane. Fifty-one years old with close-cropped hair, he was chief of police in the small Pennsylvania town of Indiantown Gap. His copilot, Clancy Cook, was also 51, also a cop. He served on the PD of Harrisburg, the city that the 31st SOG called home. Dow and Cook had been members of the Pennsylvania Air National Guard for more than 20 years.

The other five members of the crew were the DJs, as in *disc jockeys*. The most innocuous thing the aircraft did was broadcast its own radio programming. Every night, like some massive overnight shift, the DJs sent out news and music to the Afghan people below. "To all you young lovers out there . . . ," as their crew chief used to say. The music was a mix of ethnic Afghani, Euro-beat, and Elvis, around-the-clock, with no commercial breaks.

But this was just one of the airplane's abilities. It could also broadcast its own TV programs, which, like the radio shows, were filled with American propaganda. When the conditions were right, the DJs could break in on regular TV programming below, overwhelming the local signal and barging in with one of their own. The airplane also had the ability to flood the Internet with messages of its own creation, this by carrying an extremely powerful mobile version of a WiFi. The plane even had a TV band on board that could be used only by the President of the United States, should he want to address the Afghani people directly.

Psyclops could also broadcast announcements through its wing-mounted loudspeakers directly to the ground below, using an electronic voice that was designed to sound authoritarian and godlike. Sometimes it could be heard up to 40 miles away.

The plane had photorecon ability, could drop leaflets and even send out electromagnetic jamming pulses.

And then they had the Snowball. . . .

Again, while the mission of the *Psyclops* was to basically screw with the average Afghani head, on the books at least the plane was on a humanitarian mission. In the first Gulf War, due to psych-ops, mostly leaflet drops, one hundred thousand Iraqi soldiers surrendered or de-

serted. How many would have died if they'd gone on
fighting?

This was what the crew was doing above Badghis territory this night. Bombarding those below with messages
from America, some subtle, some not so. And there was
no heavy lifting involved. Much of what rained down
from the *Psyclops* plane was preprogrammed, written,
and recorded in dark rooms by men high up on the security chain. For the *Psyclops* crew, most times it was just a
matter of pushing the right buttons.

In a way, that made what they did even more curious.

These days, if they flew high enough, Captain Dow
imagined he could look right over the top of Iran and
see the fires and smoke of the real war still raging in
Iraq. Strange, but it was almost a lonely feeling, this
yearning for distant thunder. It wasn't like he and the
others *wanted* to be over there—they just wanted people
to know that *they* were over *here*. Contributing. Trying
to win one war, with about one-tenth the manpower, as
their comrades to the west were trying to win another.

They just didn't carry much juice. Sure, the *Psyclops*
was a top-secret aircraft, but not like a Stealth bomber
or the Aurora spy plane. They were never in the middle
of the action. They flew the fringes of combat, always at
night, always just beyond the glow.

And they'd been doing it like this for many, many
months now. Unheralded by necessity. Out of touch
with their families due to the strict security. Unnoticed
and uncounted, by even the higher-ups. It was easy to
think that they'd been forgotten as well.

It was strange then that on this flight, which was just
like all the others, Captain Dow was feeling a bit odd.

He was a man of hunches—poker, the state lottery, the racetrack. And he had a good record of guessing right. Sometimes he was not sure where these premonitions came from; sometimes they made little sense. But the ones that seemed the most unlikely, the most out of left field, usually proved to be the ones that came true. . . .

And tonight, this hunch for some reason was telling him that these long uneventful flights that they were so resigned to doing were about to change.

That somehow, someway, they'd be seeing action soon.

Chapter 8

Southern Italy

The place was called Reggio di Brizzi. It was located on the southernmost tip of Italy, at the very end of the boot.

There was a small U.S. support base here called LORDS. Pentagon-speak for Long Range Distribution System, it was a logistics center, run by the U.S. Navy but serving all branches of the U.S. military.

There weren't any supplies here. This place was all about the latest military buzzword: *megaflow*. The facilities at LORDS did nothing less than keep track of all U.S. combat equipment, from bullets to bombs, used by the American military in operations in the Middle East and Southwest Asia. Located inside a plain concrete building not far from a cliff overlooking the Med, the centerpiece of LORDS was its pair of huge Gray supercomputers, machines that could do trillions of calculations a second. At a cool $3 billion each, they had more brainpower than a division of supply clerks.

Still, it was a daunting task to keep tabs on an institu-

tion that consumed 1 billion dollars' worth of supplies
every day, day after day. Thus the need for *two* supercomputers. But the system actually worked pretty well.
Despite all the artificial gray matter, LORDS was a
model of simplicity. Almost everything used by the U.S.
armed forces these days was bar-coded. The Grays kept
track of all those bar codes—where they were going,
who was getting what, when they were getting there—
and broke everything down into two lists: what was
available and what was needed to refill the supply.

If a combat unit in Kuwait or Kabul or Karbala
needed a new machine gun for its Hummer, a track for its
M1 tank, or armor plating for its helicopters, somehow,
someway, that request would transit through LORDS. If
the wanted item was in the inventory—a lot of which was
spread out all over the Mediterranean—then, in most
cases, it was on its way to its destination in a matter of
days, sometimes hours. If not, the needed piece of equipment was ordered from supply points back in the United
States.

Again, the Grays did most of the work; that's why on
this dark night, thunder booming, wind blowing like
crazy outside, only Ensign Gary Olsen was atop "Reggie
Breeze," manning LORDS's so-called Forward Office.

This was the pits of graveyard duty: 2300 hours to
0900 hours the next day. Sitting in a room with nothing
else but the two huge computers, Olsen had been stationed here for 18 months. It was lonely, and the instal-
lation, being so isolated and hanging out over the Med,
could be creepy. But it was sure a lot better than getting
his ass shot off in Baghdad.

He spent most of his time tonight at his desk, reading

comic books, checking the two Gray lists only once in a while. When something went off-kilter—like a naval gun gone missing, some ammunition unaccounted for, or even a load of food or water not arriving at its appointed destination—the Grays would sound a simple electronic alarm: One beep meant there'd been an incident, but nothing serious. Two beeps meant an event worth looking into. Three beeps indicated something big was up.

It was now 0230 hours. Olsen had just finished the latest *Superman* when the Grays started spitting out a series of single beeps. No big deal: These low-level warnings would happen an average of twice a hour. Still, Olsen rolled his chair over to the main readout screen and looked to see what the fuss was about.

A pallet of ammunition was missing from the U.S. Navy base at Folobra in Sardinia. They were .50-calber rounds, several thousand in all. While at first look this might have merited something more than a one-beep warning, Olsen knew that usually in these cases the lost article was not stolen but had simply fallen through the cracks somewhere, stored away in the wrong part of the warehouse, something along those lines. He made a notation of it in his log and rolled back across the room, ready to begin his new *Fantastic Four.*

He was halfway across the floor when the computer began emitting single beeps again. Olsen stopped in midroll and was quickly back in front of the readout screen. Fifteen hundred gallons of helicopter fuel was missing from a U.S. Navy base in Sicily. Again, another routine incident. Olsen made the notation in his log and started across the room again.

But then the Grays started bleating again, and this time they were beeping twice. Olsen had already reached the other side of the room. He had to launch himself back once more.

Four Hellfire missiles could not be accounted for at the U.S. Army base in Sbreka, Bosnia, just a few hundred miles east of Olsen's current location. This was why the second-degree alarm had gone off. Hellfire missiles were state-of-the-art air-launched weapons that could be highly destructive in the wrong hands.

He studied the readout screen and then his log. Three lines in red—three incidents, two minor, one *mezzametz,* all in less than five minutes. In all his time working at Reggie Breeze, Olsen had never had more than two alarms of any kind in an hour's time.

As he was contemplating what this might mean, the beeps went off again, and this time it was a third-degree alarm.

"Jesuzz Christ . . . ," he moaned.

Two giant two-thousand-pound bombs were missing from a U.S. base in Turkey, along with something called an M-31/EAS, which was a portable arresting gear setup allowing jet fighters to land on runways built too short to normally handle such aircraft.

This was getting serious now. Olsen immediately instructed the Grays to look for any pattern in the incidents, as this might indicate something along the lines of organized theft. On the other hand, no pattern would indicate these things were just random, which was what Olsen was praying for. Because if this *wasn't* a random thing, then guaranteed, a large amount of shit was about to hit a very big fan.

The Grays were superfast, and before Olsen could

say the first three words of a Hail Mary, the readout screen started blinking the words: *Alert Security Officer*.

The supercomputers had found something.

Olsen immediately put in a call to his CO, buzzing his pager, which he knew the senior officer always kept on his person, even when he was asleep. Then Olsen read the Grays' preliminary report: These events weren't just cases of missed inventory or things falling through the cracks. These *were* thefts. They had all happened over the past eight hours and indicated whoever was stealing these things was moving east, across the Med, apparently stopping at every U.S. base they could find, in a more or less straight line.

What's more, the Grays were now telling Olsen, reports of security breaches were turning up from these very same installations. In each case, unauthorized personnel had been reported skulking around the base before the thefts were discovered. Then the Grays spit out one last piece of information: Again, in each case, it was being reported that at least one unauthorized helicopter had been spotted in the area.

Olsen scratched his head. Unauthorized personnel? Unauthorized helicopters?

What the hell was going on?

At that moment, his CO arrived. The usually gruff security officer seemed different somehow. Normally he'd be pissed at being woken in the middle of the night. But at the moment, he seemed almost too cheery to be upset, like a man holding a secret.

Olsen read him the Grays' report, as he was supposed to do. The thefts, the reports of unauthorized personnel, the unauthorized copters, the missing weapons, ammo, equipment, and fuel. Olsen's conclusion: A terrorist group had somehow gotten ahold of at least one helicopter and was going on a well-planned stealing spree. If true, it could be disastrous for U.S. interests in the area.

The CO listened but then shook his head at the Grays' recommendation that an all-points alert be put out across the Med. "That won't be necessary," the CO told Olsen.

Olsen was puzzled. "But, sir—these people have already stolen several million dollars' worth of combat gear. Dangerous stuff."

"Higher Authority's got a handle on it," the CO replied, calmly lighting a cigarette.

"Higher Authority, sir?"

The CO smiled—a rarity. "Higher Authority doesn't necessarily mean Navy High Command, Ensign."

Olsen had to think a moment. "Are you saying a special ops unit is taking these things?"

The CO just shrugged. "Maybe. . . ."

But Olsen wasn't going to settle for that—besides, it looked as if the CO *wanted* to tell him. "If some special ops group wanted all this stuff," he began, "then why didn't they just requisition it through proper channels? Those guys do that all the time—with the right authorization, that is."

Again the CO shrugged. "Maybe they're not an authorized special ops group."

This took a few more moments to sink in, but finally it dawned on Olsen what was *really* going on here.

"The Ghost Team?" he asked in a whisper.

The CO let out a long stream of smoke and nodded. "But remember, I never said that. . . ."

Both men had heard about the Ghost Team, of

course. They were a very mysterious special ops outfit that might very well be operating without government approval—or at least beyond the control of the Pentagon. That's what made them so cool, though. Their exploits at Hormuz, Singapore, and right inside the United States had made them folk heroes. Like characters from a comic book, these near-mythical figures seemed to be the only people actually fighting the perpetrators of 9/11.

"I talked to someone just a few minutes ago," the CO finally confided in Olsen. "Someone with a Level six security rating, which he proved to me was legit. He asked that we just turn a blind eye to this, said that it would end shortly."

"All this stuff must be for something important," Olsen said, in a million years never thinking he would be involved with the Ghost Team someday, however tangentially. "Something to tell my kids, I guess."

The CO nodded, then joked: "But only if your kids have a Level Six security rating."

Then almost as an afterthought, Olsen asked him: "If I might be so bold sir, this guy you talked to—what was he? An admiral? A general? CIA?"

The CO just shook his head. "He didn't say. He just gave me his security level and the day's passwords." He thought a moment, then added: "Funny, though. He did give me his name—Mullen, or Murphy, something Irish. But he sounded like he was right out of the middle of Texas. . . ."

Chapter 9

Colonel Armeni Barji was asleep at his desk. Again. . . .

He was commander in chief of Iranian Revolutionary Air Force Base #3, here at Hakpit, in the extreme western portion of Iran, a place near the vast southern marshes that led right into nearby Iraq.

Commander in chief of an entire air base might have sounded like a big job, with lots of authority and political pull, but in this case, the opposite was true. Base #3 wasn't a combat facility. It was a graveyard.

And what was buried here?

Fighter planes. Old ones.

Base #3 was where the bulk of Iran's F-14s had come to die. Not to be refurnished or made ready to fly again. But to be entombed.

Iran was the only country the U.S. Navy's premier F-14 was exported to—this back in the days of the Shah, a pig by another name, but a pig who had many high-level friends in the White House at the time. The sale had taken place more than 30 years before, and because Iran had been turned upside down by Islamic radicals in the intervening years, for a while the Tomcats wound up being flown by one of America's staunchest enemies. That situation didn't last long, though. Lack of spare parts started humbling the Iranian F-14 fleet after just a few years. These days, hardly any of the exported Tomcats were flying regularly.

Eighteen of the F-14s were now here at Base #3. Officially, only four of them were airworthy, and them just barely. Could those four actually go into combat? Could they ever hope to fire the weapon the Tomcat was built for—the very dangerous over-the-horizon Phoenix missile? No way. These planes were used mostly for training purposes by the Iranian Air Force or, on occasion, for aerial flyby displays made during military holidays.

This was no place to be then, and Colonel Barji was bitter. Now almost 60 years old and at one time a general, he'd flown in the IAF since the war against Iraq back in the late seventies. He'd carried out strafing missions on rebellious villages inside Iran and the occasional sneak attack on Sunni Muslims living just over the border in Iraq. That had been the extent of his military career— shooting at unarmed people. But just by longevity alone he was somewhat of a hero inside the Persian air corps.

Or he used to be anyway. A dispute over lack of flying time with his old F-14 unit located just outside Tehran led to a fight with his CO. Barji was reprimanded, disciplined, reduced in pay and rank, and sent here. That had been two months ago. One of Iran's most seasoned, most veteran pilots was now a nonperson, out in the marshes, at the country's aerial cemetery.

So, yes, he was bitter.

But he was also looking forward to getting his revenge.

Barji had been working a scam since the day he arrived at Base #3. In his first week, he'd submitted a false report to IAF headquarters stating that one of the flyable F-14s had been destroyed by a hangar fire. It was a lie, but no one in Tehran ever came down to check it out. So not two weeks into his stint here, Barji had one of the workable F-14s in his back pocket.

Then he had his men—they too were black sheep and exiles—steal as many parts as possible from the 15 or so inoperable F-14s, covering their tracks this time with false repair reports. By doing this, they were able to essentially construct an entirely new F-14. One that could fly and carry bombs and fire a nose gun, but was a complete phantom, a plane that could not be found anywhere on the books.

At the same time, Barji let it be known, through a network of relatives he had spread out over the Middle East and southern Europe, that he had two F-14 Tomcats for sale.

He wasn't so stupid that he would think a legitimate government would buy them to use in their air forces. What he was hoping for was some country—China, Russia, maybe India, would buy them and secretly have their pilots train *against* them just as U.S. pilots trained against simulated and real MiGs at places like Top Gun and Red Star in the American desert. In that regard, the planes could be regarded as very valuable.

His asking price: a bargain basement $1 million each.

If he ever got it, he would defect immediately and live the rest of his life in very non-Revolutionary style in South America.

Or at least that was the plan.

The planes had been for sale for nearly a month now, and Barji had yet to get any takers. No feelers. No nibbles. Nothing. Again, he was not naive. He knew this thing was fraught with danger. Though Iranian officers had been selling off pieces of the armed forces for years to places like Pakistan, Uzbekistan and other countries, he realized that with each passing day he was closer to being caught by his superiors. Only a very grisly execution would result.

He was asleep at his desk because there was no phone in his living quarters and he wanted to be on hand should a prospective buyer call. So it was strange then that while dreaming of a phone ringing underwater he thought he heard a knock at his door instead. Or was that thunder?

He opened his eyes, expecting to see out the window that yet another lightning storm was making its way across the marshes. What he saw instead was a man, calmly sitting in the chair across the desk from him, holding what looked like a stack of dollar bills in his hand.

This person was dressed all in black, including a black ski mask tucked under his oversize battle helmet. He had his feet up on Barji's desk and was smoking a cigarette.

Barji wiped his eyes. He was so sure he was still asleep, he actually smiled at the phantom, then put his head back down to resume his slumber.

That's when the man slammed his boot down on Barji's desk again, resulting in a loud *thump!*

Barji was wide awake now. The man was real.

"What is this?" Barji began blustering in Farsi. "Who are you?"

The man sat up straight. "I'm here to buy your airplanes."

"What the hell?" Barji coughed, this time in English. "You can't come in here and—"

The man held up his hand and interrupted Barji. "Are they for sale or not?"

Barji's vision cleared to the point where he could now see the patch on the man's right shoulder. Barji recognized it right away. A picture of the Twin Towers with an American flag flying behind, the letters *NYPD* and *FDNY* floating above, and below the words *We Will Never Forget.*

Barji thought his heart would stop right then and there.

The infamous American Ghost Team was here? At Base #3? How was that possible?

At that point, Barji looked out his window again and saw all his men being marched past the headquarters building. Hands in the air, they were being herded along by more gigantic soldiers in ski masks and battle helmets.

Barji turned back to the ghostly figure. He knew well the reputation of these bloodthirsty Americans. They supposedly slaughtered any Muslim who crossed their path.

"You are here . . . to *buy* the airplanes?" he mumbled again.

"That's right. . . ."

Barji was very confused. "But . . . you're the American military."

The masked man just shrugged. "We're Americans," he corrected Barji. "Let's just leave it at that. Now, do you want to deal or not? We're in a hurry."

Barji was still baffled. He didn't know what to say.

"Look, I'm here to make a purchase," the man insisted. "What do you care who you sell them to?"

But still Barji was having a hard time taking all this in. All he had to do was pick up his phone, hit the red transmit button, and an emergency call that something was wrong at Base #3 would be flashed to Tehran. He might not live for very long after taking such an action, though.

And in reality, the phantom was right. What difference did it make who bought the planes? Russian, Chinese, Indian . . . that's just who Barji had been expecting. But an American's money would be just as good. Better, in fact . . .

But it was still *so weird.*

"And that?" Barji said, pointing to the stack of bills in the man's hand. "Why pay? Why not just take the airplanes?"

The man smiled, his teeth visible through the ski mask. "It's easier to have you cooperate," he replied simply. "Quieter, too."

That's when Barji got a sly look in his eye. He had a pistol in his desk drawer. "So what's to prevent me from keeping the money, keeping the airplanes, and shooting you right now?"

The man just shrugged again—then pointed to something over Barji's shoulder. The Iranian officer turned to see five men standing ramrod still and in unearthly silence, not two feet behind him. Each one had an M16 rifle with a bayonet attached pointed at the back of his head. They, too, were wearing the Twin Towers patch.

Barji almost wet his pants. Had they really been back there all along?

These people **are** *ghosts,* he thought to himself in terror.

At that, the man in the chair leaned forward and put his hands on Barji's desk. "Now please," he said, with some exasperation. "Can we get this show on the road?"

Barji could almost feel the sharpened edges of the bayonets touching his skin.

He gulped and then croaked in thick English: "By all means." The man in the chair relaxed, then stood up. "OK, that's better," he said, putting the stack back inside his pocket for safekeeping. Then he added: "And, oh yeah, we need some bombs, too."

Base #3 was a sprawling place. It stretched out over 16 square miles, though a lot of it was underwater most of the time.

There was, however, an auxiliary runway located at the far end of the base, the part closest to the Iraq border. It was almost never used.

This was where Barji and his mysterious visitors were now. The two phantom F-14s had been brought here, by his own men, still under the guns of the strange Americans, pulled with the base's pair of two-ton trucks. Two more trucks were filled with five-hundred-pound bombs. Also on hand were two portable ignition units, equipment necessary to start the planes' engines.

Both of the F-14s were horribly stripped down. Most of their avionics were gone. Certainly all the gizmos associated with the Phoenix missile system were missing. All of the long-range tracking and radar suites—gone. Even their rear seats, where the planes' radar officers would usually sit, had been ripped out. Their cockpits were as bare-bones as a modern jet fighter could get.

The engines weren't exactly up to snuff, either. Many of the turbine blades had cracks in them, and the compressors were leaking something all over the ground. But when the ignition units were attached, both planes did turn over, and more important, they stayed turning. It took a few minutes, but they finally reached the minimum number of rpms needed for them to get off the ground.

Parked nearby was the trio of very unusual helicopters used by the Americans. There were many soldiers in black moving around now. Some were unloading bombs from the trucks and putting them into the copters' spacious cargo bays. Others were keeping an eye on Barji and his men. Just about all of these soldiers were carrying huge rifles, topped by the razor-sharp bayonets.

This was not how Barji had anticipated his deal would go. But money was money. If he survived this strange transaction, he couldn't imagine himself not being rich, even after paying off his men.

As soon as the F-14s' engines were warmed, a couple figures emerged from the helicopters. They were dressed in black pilot suits but were also carrying sidearms. They walked over to the big fighter planes and checked to make sure both still had their arresting hooks attached. Then they climbed in and, after a few minutes of studying the cockpit instruments, began taxiing for takeoff. Barji crossed his fingers, praying to Allah that the damn airplanes got off the ground.

The two jets moved smartly and, despite the darkness and the bumpy runway, screamed away into the night.

With a little goose from their pilots, they leaped into the air, one right after the other, climbing for altitude.

They went wide out over the marshes and performed a series of loops and spins, barely seen in the waning dark but at extremely low altitude. This display went on for a few minutes before both planes suddenly turned as one and roared over the small group gathered on the auxiliary runway.

But instead of slowing down to land, they kept on going, flying off to the south.

Barji looked back at his buyers, confused again. He was expecting a bullet to his head by this time. Instead, the man who'd originally spoken to him handed him the packet of bills held together by many rubber bands.

"I still don't understand all this," Barji said. "Why pay us? Why didn't you just shoot us all—and simply take the airplanes?"

Suddenly the American got right in his face. "Listen, asshole," he growled. "When we start a war with you guys, you'll know it."

With that, all of the men in black walked back to their helicopters, climbed aboard, and took off. They, too, flew south.

Barji's men all collapsed to the ground and started wailing in prayer, so relieved that the American Ghosts had not butchered them. Only after Barji saw the silhouettes of the helicopters disappear over the horizon did he undo the rubber bands on the stack and start peeling off the bills. There certainly seemed to be enough to add up to $2 million. Would he be a rich man yet? The first thousand-dollar bill looked real . . . but to Barji's dismay, the rest of the pack were fakes, hundreds of pieces of a green-ink Italian newspaper, cut precisely to look like dollar bills. They blew out of his hands, one at a time, and soon covered the runway.

Then Barji looked closely at the first bill, the only authentic note in the pack. Or so he thought. It, too, was fake, a very clear, photocopy of the front of a real thousand-dollar bill.

The reverse side was blank white paper. On it, written in thick black pen, was one word: *Sucker.* . . .

Chapter 10

Abdul Harbosi was having a bad day. He was a low-level Taliban operative, middle forties, unmarried of course, the eleventh son of what once was a prominent Afghani family. He lived in a place called Qimruz Gorge, an almost-forgotten region of western Afghanistan. Made up of tall mountains and barren valleys, the Qimruz straddled the far eastern border of Iran. Only a few mountain passes separated it from the Persian state, and the traffic, such as it was, flowed both ways. Over the years, the tribal inhabitants of the Qimruz considered themselves as much Iranian as they were Afghani. That's how close they were.

Back when the Taliban ran Afghanistan—before the Americans threw them out—Islamic terrorists from all over the region came to the Qimruz because of its proximity to Iran. Supply lines for weapons and money were easy to find here. As it was also a place from which someone being pursued could get inside Iran in a matter of minutes, it was the perfect place for Taliban and Al

Qaeda fighters to come to hide. No surprise, most of the twenty thousand people who lived here were bin Laden sympathizers.

Afghanistan was changing. It was becoming more modern, more democratic, in many of its regions, ever since the Americans arrived. Not so in the Qimruz, though. The old rules still applied here. Women were still required to wear coverings head to toe or risk being stoned to death. The population still had to pay almost 100 percent of their meager incomes in mullah taxes or risk having their homes demolished by the notorious religious police. Anyone caught singing had his or her throat cut. Anyone reading a Western-style book had his or her eyes gouged out. Get caught flying a kite, playing with a toy, or wearing more than three bright colors at once, and you'd find yourself hanging at the wrong end of a noose. No matter what your age was, man or woman, child or elderly, if you stepped out of line and defied the religious authorities, you felt the wrath of Allah big-time.

These harsh rules didn't apply to everyone, though. Those Taliban and Al Qaeda types who'd relocated to the region had the run of the place. They stole the people's food; they raped their daughters. They drank alcohol, smoked cigarettes, and were gluttons. They engaged in perverted sex, alone and with others, and they murdered on a whim. They did anything they wanted, and that meant just about everything that was forbidden for the civilian population to do.

There was no real government here. The Qimruz was ruled by a brutal warlord named Kundez Sharif. A veteran mujahideen and essentially a *de facto* king, Sharif was also a multimillionaire, amassing a great fortune simply because he was sitting astride one of the oldest smuggling routes in the world. Gunrunners, heroin trafficker, or white slaver, everyone paid a price to pass through. Anyone resisting could expect nothing less than a slow, painful death.

Because Sharif was so feared in Kabul and also because his fiefdom was so close to volatile Iran, it was widely assumed that the U.S. military would not come here, at least not anytime soon, to clean out the rat hole. Much work still had to be done in the more populous eastern part of the country. Plus a political A-bomb might result should any fighting between the Americans and Sharif's forces spill over into Iran.

So this was the Qimruz. Protected and patronized, 330 square miles, insulated from the real world, and where a brutal and barbaric religious theocracy still held sway. Cold and rainy almost all the time, it was one of the most unappealing, uncivilized places on earth.

And it held only one real city. Its capital, of sorts.

The name of this city was Khrash.

Even as a low-level Taliban, Abdul Harbosi had enjoyed some of the fruits of what was going on within the Qimruz, especially inside Khrash. He'd raped. He'd killed. He'd stolen. He'd made life miserable for those people not so connected to the mullahs as he.

But he was also a *kardiss,* Afghani slang for flunky. His boss was the chief of police of Khrash, a very powerful man and a lieutenant for the supreme warlord Kundez Sharif himself. When the Chief wanted something, the shit ran downhill. Many times it landed on Harbosi's head.

It was for this reason that Harbosi was now out in the

wilds of the Qimruz, unprotected against the rain and cold, riding a very humpbacked horse, looking for a videotape.

Why did the Chief need a videotape? Harbosi had no idea. Khrash's location out on the fringe was both a blessing and a curse. A blessing in that the men who ran the place were left alone by the central government and thereby the U.S. military. But it was a curse, too, because despite Khrash's being right next to a major trading route with Iran, not everything was available when and where you wanted it. Cigarettes and tobacco were always in short supply, as were wine and hashish. Batteries, lightbulbs, CDs, things easily bought in just about every other city in Afghanistan, were always hard to come by in the Qimruz and especially in Khrash. This applied to videotapes, too. At the moment, not a single one, new or used, could be found in the entire city.

So Harbosi had been sent out to find a videotape. Either a new one or one that could be taped over. At the moment, nothing seemed more important to his boss, the Chief.

Most of the villages scattered about the Qimruz were within 20 miles of Khrash. These places had local rulers, too, subwarlords who were subservient to the all-powerful Sharif. These subwarlords were usually the wealthiest people in their village; owning a TV, a VCR, or even a satellite dish was nothing to them. And with Afghanis being such great hoarders, sometimes these subwarlords had a surplus of items that people in the capital of Khrash found themselves in lack of. Harbosi's quest this cold night was to see if any of these subwarlords might be willing to give up a blank videotape or two for the Chief.

Harbosi had been at it since late that afternoon; that was more than eight hours on the same miserable horse. He'd visited six homes of minor warlords in that time. These people were all polite to him. They took him in for tea and cake, the ritual hospitality famous all over Afghanistan. But when it came time for Harbosi to make his request, his hosts invariably clammed up. They had nothing to spare except for dates and nuts and great praise for Allah. Harbosi was sure at least a few of the subwarlords had had a videotape or two hidden away but were withholding them, strictly for selfish reasons. Again, this was no surprise. Harbosi was a *kardiss*—he knew no one paid any attention to him. Had someone a little higher on the food chain been sent on this mission, it might have had a better chance of success.

But his was not to question why. So he clopped along, his back aching, his fingers turned black from holding the reins for so long. He was heading for the house of a man named Goshi, his last to visit in this part of the Qimruz. It had been raining earlier, but now overhead the clouds parted and the stars came out. It had suddenly become a crystal-clear night. Yet strangely, on a couple occasions Harbosi could have sworn he heard the crash of thunder, somewhere distant.

He reached Goshi's house, a one-story structure made from mud and gravity, located on the northern edge of a very sleepy village. A gray TV satellite dish sticking out of the flat roof offered a hint that Harbosi's search might end here. Both he and the horse relieved themselves in Goshi's front yard, and then Harbosi knocked on the front door.

There was no reply.

Harbosi knocked again. While it was almost 1:00

A.M. and Goshi might be asleep, certainly someone in his security entourage should be awake, standing watch. But still, there was no answer.

This was so odd, Harbosi toed the door open and looked inside. The one-story house was empty, even though some candles were still lit and a pot of tea still emitting steam was on the dinner mat nearby.

Harbosi was baffled. He knew Goshi a bit. The sub-warlord was a particularly brutal man who once slaughtered an entire family—22 of them—simply because he'd heard that some were not removing their shoes at prayer time. Just as the top warlord, Sharif, ruled the Qimruz with an iron fist clutching a Koran, so, too, did Goshi run his tiny domain.

But Goshi was also a very superstitious man and paranoid as well. Always surrounded by bodyguards, he rarely left his house in the daytime. And never, *ever* did he venture out at night. He was famous for this.

Harbosi looked around the empty quarters and thought a moment.

There was only one other place Goshi and his bodyguards could be.

Few people in the world, including just about the entire U.S. intelligence community, knew that the Al Qaeda network had its own air base.

The airfield was located inside the Qimruz, on a ridge called the Obo. It was a small, flat piece of land, hidden by mountains on three sides and a steep cliff on the other. Hard against the same peak that separated this part of Afghanistan from Iran, Khrash was about twenty miles to the south.

Obo Field held just one runway, about thirty-five

hundred feet in length, plus three support buildings and
a small fuel tank. This place had been built originally by
the Russians during their occupation of Afghanistan; it
was used as an emergency base for damaged aircraft to
land. This was why the runway was only so long and the
base support buildings large but spare. After the Russian withdrawal and the Taliban takeover of Afghanistan,
the Great Mullah himself gave the airfield to bin Laden
as a gift.

No warplanes could be found here—Al Qaeda didn't
have an air force. But it did operate a small fleet of
leased cargo planes, all registered to fake companies in
Nigeria. Most of them two-engine French-built trans-
ports these airplanes picked up supplies from places
such as Damascus and Tehran and landed them here.
The typical cargo—guns, money, explosives—was then
dispersed among Al Qaeda sympathizers on both sides
of the border. On rare occasions, very sensitive cargo
also flew into Obo Field. WMD materials. Captured
U.S. smart weapons. Hostages. . . .

The small airstrip was activated only when a supply
flight was scheduled to sneak in, maybe once every two
months. The base lay dormant the rest of the time,
which was probably why it had escaped the gaze of U.S.
spies—or most of them anyway. But as it was, the field
just happened to lie within Goshi's territory; in fact it
was just a half-mile up the road from his house. This
was the only other place Harbosi could imagine Goshi
might be this time of night.

Leaving the horse behind, Harbosi started out again
and soon reached the ledge that overlooked the Obo
ridge and the tiny airfield beyond. Harbosi was about to

start down the trail leading to the base when he heard a
series of very loud *bangs!* Three explosions, one right
after the other, somewhere nearby.

Harbosi stopped in his tracks. What was this? Three
more explosions went off. He hit the ground. He had to
be smart here and avoid trouble. He hesitated a moment,
but then, instead of going down the trail, he crawled to
the ledge and peeked over the other side.

He couldn't believe what he saw.

The tiny base was under attack. Helicopters were flying all over the place, weapons blazing. Tracer bullets
were bouncing off the runway, the fuel tank, even the
walls of the mountain nearby. Flames were everywhere.
It was like the ground had opened up and a little piece of
hell had been allowed to escape. Harbosi had never seen
anything so violent.

He quickly realized that running for their lives below
were Goshi and his men. Scattered all over the small airfield, the helicopters weren't just shooting at them; they
were hunting the men down, one by one, and blasting
them to bits with their enormous aerial guns.

Now, as Harbosi watched, horrified, one of the helicopters swooped down and let of a dozen or so soldiers
jump off. These men were as big as monsters and they
were dressed all in black. They chased the remaining
bodyguards to ground, firing their huge weapons and
herding them into one spot directly below Harbosi. It
was down there, at the base of the ridge, that Harbosi
saw the final stage of this one-sided gun battle. The soldiers in black cornered the last of Goshi's bodyguards
against the rocks and shot them down, each man going
with a bloodcurdling scream. Then Harbosi saw the sol-

diers walk among the bodies, firing into them, making sure all were dead.

Harbosi was too stunned to move. He could only imagine that Goshi and his men must have been tricked into coming down here in the middle of the night. For a man such as Goshi, who was afraid to go out even in the daytime, it must have been quiet an enticement, or a major order, to lure him out to his death in this dark, miserable place.

The three helicopters abruptly landed. The soldiers in black started unloading equipment from them and were in a great hurry to do so. But exactly what kind of equipment was this? And why would anyone want to attack this lonely area in the first place?

Once the copters were unloaded, the mystery men began scrambling around the smoking air base. One of the helicopters took off again and disappeared over the other side of the mountain; it returned just moments later carrying a large object from wires swinging below its belly. About the size of a small car, this thing was a piece of heavy machinery on wheels. Whether the copter had dropped this load on the other side of the mountain so it could go into battle unencumbered Harbosi didn't know. In any case, once the copter had set the load down, it disappeared again, over the mountain, returning again in no time at all, carrying the same kind of cargo.

The men in black began working on the two wheeled machines. They pushed both devices to a point halfway down the runway. They seemed very determined to get these things to stay in place, removing the wheels and securing them with counterweights, chains, and wires.

Once set, the men pulled a very thick cable out of one of the embedded machines, stretched it across the runway, and attached it to the locked-down device on the other side. Then a couple dozen of the soldiers yanked on the cable, assuring that it was tight.

That's when Harbosi heard the thunder again. And this time it wasn't so fleeting or distant. It was loud and earsplitting.

And it wasn't real thunder.

But it was close. . . .

The tremendous roar was coming from two huge fighter jets that had materialized out of the clear night sky. They passed right over Harbosi, hideous dark gray shapes, with sharp noses and flames coming from the back. They looked like monsters with wings. Harbosi was a simple religious thug. But he knew a thing or two about warplanes, having dodged bullets and bombs with his Taliban friends when the Americans first arrived. These were fighter jets. American built, this much he could tell. And it was obvious they were going to attempt to land at the small airstrip where the men had stretched out the cable.

But here's where Harbosi got very confused. Their planes were wearing the markings of the ROI—the Republic of Iran, the big Islamic brother next door. Why would their friends the Iranians attack Goshi's airstrip?

The two planes circled the base once, going right over him a second time. One suddenly broke off, set down its landing gear, and went in for a landing. Harbosi saw a large hook lower from the rear end of this jet. Much faster than he could figure out what was going on, the jet slammed onto the runway, its hook catching the thick cable, yanking the plane to a screeching halt. All this was so loud, Harbosi swore that his eardrums were going to burst.

The jet was enveloped in sparks and smoke, a fiery cloud of its own creation. The soldiers ran out to the plane, engines still whining, and pushed it off the runway and to the side of the little airstrip. No sooner was this done when the second jet fell out of the sky and it, too, slammed down with a shriek, its hook catching the cable and yanking it to a violent noisy stop.

Again, Harbosi was not a smart man—eating, sleeping, walking, talking, that was just about the extent of his intellectual prowess. But he thought he knew what was going on here. The runway was too short for such powerful warplanes as these. They needed help in stopping, like planes landing on aircraft carriers.

But if that is true, Harbosi found himself thinking, *won't they have trouble taking off, too?*

Now came the strangest part. Most of the fires had gone out around the airfield; those that hadn't were quickly extinguished by the soldiers. Meanwhile, the rest of the men in black opened up the three support buildings, pushed all their aircraft inside, and sealed them up. Then all was quiet again.

Just like that, it was as if nothing had happened. . . .

That's when Harbosi felt something very cold touch the back of his neck. He looked over his shoulder to find four of the enormous soldiers standing over him. They were all wearing black ski masks, had huge knives sticking out of their belts and bayonets on the ends of their weapons. One of these bayonets was now resting on the side of Harbosi's cheek.

Harbosi threw up his hands in surrender. The soldiers hauled him to his feet. He started babbling, telling them that he was a servant of the Chief, who himself was a servant of the warlord Sharif, who praised the Great Mullah and al Zawhari and the sheikh bin Laden himself.

"My friends from Persia," Harbosi was crying now, "we all praise Allah. You have your own reasons for attacking this tiny piece of my very large country. But I am like you. I am like a brother to Iran."

That's when one of the huge soldiers pulled off his ski mask. Beneath was a very Caucasian face with steel-cold eyes and fire coming from his mouth. A name was written on the collar of this man's uniform. It said: *Hunn*. He looked absolutely ferocious.

He grabbed Harbosi by the neck and yanked his face to within inches of his own.

"Do I look Iranian to you?" he growled.

Chapter 11

It was the middle of the second night when the *Ocean Voyager* had reached the Suez Canal. It had traveled at high speed over the past 48 hours, keeping its four jet engines on the naval equivalent of afterburner whenever possible. They'd tried to be careful. A huge container-ship moving at the same speed as a racing boat would tend to drawn attention. Bad weather across the Mediterranean had helped; it allowed the *Ocean Voyager* to rush its way through rain showers and fog, cutting down on the number of potential witnesses. Still, they left more than a few fishermen along the coasts of Italy and Greece scratching their heads and asking the same question: How could something so big and so ugly move so fast?

Bobby Murphy had been living on coffee since the strike team left. Not sleeping, not even leaving the Captain's Room. Instead he'd used much of the time on his sat phone talking to old friends, calling in favors, threatening, cajoling, bluffing, and breaking at least a dozen national security laws, all to get the Ghosts as much help as he could.

It was a ball-busting two days, but with Murphy's help the Ghosts had finally reached Obo. But that's when it got serious. Now that the strike team had boots on the ground, real thought had to be given as to what they should do next.

In their previous missions, Murphy had always been the brains, with Ryder and the team providing the hammer. This always worked out because the team members really didn't *want* to think about how it was going to be done. They just wanted to kill mooks.

This time it was different. Sometime during the mad dash across the Mediterranean, Ryder had become part of the brains, too. True, Murphy had dredged up much of the intelligence, but it was Ryder who had put it to grand use. He'd orchestrated the equipment raids across the Med; he'd dreamed up the juvenile stunt to get the F-14s out of Iran. When Murphy located the Obo on some obscure NSA sat photos, Ryder figured how they could use its smallish runway. Either taking Murphy's suggestions or coming up with ones of his own, this time Ryder was *involved*. No longer just a cog in the Ghosts' killing machine, the former test pilot was running at full rpm. Committed. Out for final revenge. And unlike the shit-box Tomcats, he was showing no signs of slowing down.

But again, *now* it got serious. As in most special operations, getting there was usually half the battle. But the strike team was in place, and by all indications few people knew they were there.

So, the question was: What should they do next, in this, their last mission?

. . .

To this end, Murphy's fabulous cabin had been turned into a war room.

Scattered across his ornate table were mountains of books, some as high as the peaks around the Obo ridge, or so it seemed. Murphy was almost lost under them. They covered a number of topics. One book was devoted to the art of kidnapping. Another appropriately subtitled *A Cold Hell on Earth,* detailed the nineteenth-century history of Afghanistan. Still another book contained a collection of secret reports resulting from U.S. actions in Somalia back in 1993, specifically October 3rd. The day that would always be remembered by two just words: *Blackhawk Down.*

Another book detailed the vicious World War Two battle of Iwo Jima. The famous picture of the handful of Marines raising the flag atop Mount Suribachi graced its cover. Still another book was called simply *Unsuccessful Coups in Africa.*

This was research. Between making all those phone calls and breaking all those national security laws, Murphy had been reading, knowing they needed at least a ghost of a plan if the strike team ever did make it to their destination. He was looking for something, anything, that could help them if they ever got to phase two.

And at this moment, just as they were beginning their transit of the Suez Canal, heading for the Persian Gulf, that search for a little piece of magic was still continuing. Frustratingly so.

Not that Murphy's resolve was faltering. If anything, he was just as inflamed about avenging Li's death as was Ryder. And their journey across the Med, stealing the things they needed along the way, had been nothing short of brilliant—and blessed by good luck. But now that they were in place, more than once Murphy had considered the situation and caught himself murmuring, *"What the hell have we gotten ourselves into."*

The purpose of the mission was simple: to kill Jabal Ben-Wabi, aka the Patch. The problem was, Jabal Ben-Wabi was in Khrash and there were about fifteen thousand Al Qaeda and Taliban fighters in there with him. While these people, all of them hard-core terrorists, were not there at his service exactly—after all, they were there on R and R—they would no doubt come to his aid en masse should the Patch need them to.

So how were the Ghosts going to get him?

After all his reading and meditating and consulting with Bingo and the Spooks and even Johnny Jackson of Delta Thunder, Murphy had, at least, come to one conclusion: If they wanted to first find, then kill Jabal Ben-Wabi, there were only three options available to them. The trouble was, two of them were impossible.

Option one was to have someone inside the city kidnap Ben-Wabi and deliver him to them. Murphy dismissed this idea right away. Kidnapping was a cottage industry in Afghanistan and had been for hundreds, if not thousands, of years. And a real pro could probably do the job. But Murphy had worked the spy game for years—or at least he told people he had. Any arranged kidnapping meant first getting to the top of the Patch's security ring and then finding the right person to not only bribe but also trust enough to actually do the job. Thievery was also big in Afghanistan. It was just as likely that anyone they engaged to snatch the Patch would take the money and run as it was that he'd complete the job. Besides, grooming reliable confederates would take weeks, if not months. The team didn't have that kind of the time.

Then option two: the smash-and-grab. Sending in the strike team in the dead of night and snatching Jabal themselves. Ironically, the way the team was made up, i.e., chopper-borne special ops guys, this was a mission that would have seemed right up their alley. They'd even done a few since they started terrorizing the Muslim world.

The problem here was that over a place like Khrash such a plan could quickly turn into Blackhawk Down, the Sequel. What they were facing was not rousting some chump from his family's home in the middle of the desert. This was trying to grab someone in a city hosting a convention of mooks, each one carrying either an AK-47 or a rocket-propelled grenade launcher. Flying over Khrash would be as dangerous as flying over Detroit on New Year's Eve—or Baghdad in January of 1991. If they were spotted, guaranteed there would be a lot of fire and lead coming up to meet them.

Add to this what they would actually have to do. No matter how good you were at airborne special operations, something remained constant: Helicopters always had to slow down to let their troops off. And when copters weren't moving, they were very vulnerable. What made Mogadishu such a disaster was that the Skinnies discovered RPGs could take down helicopters, something simple gunfire couldn't always do. Kill the copters and whoever they'd just dropped off was surrounded and trapped. End of story. End of sequel.

Besides, the Ghosts had no idea where the Patch was and, again, knew no one inside the city who could give them a clue. And it wasn't like they could go rooftop to rooftop or door to door looking for him. So while a lightning strike operation was actually the team's forte, in this case it had potential disaster written all over it.

There was only one last alternative to consider then. The third option. The *final* option. But it was so outlandish and, frankly, suicidal that on this dark night, heading into the Suez Canal, Murphy didn't want to even whisper its name, never mind write it down. His psyche couldn't take it.

Besides, three things had to be done before he could even *think* about developing a real plan based on this final idea: The Ghosts would have to get some solid recon, down-and-dirty stuff they just couldn't glean by stealing NSA satellite photos. They would also have to make some new friends quick—or maybe contact some old ones—in hopes that they might buy into the cause.

But for a plan based on the final option to have any chance of working, the first thing they had to do was the strangest thing of all.

They had to let the mooks in Khrash know that the Crazy Americans were coming and just pray that at least some of them were afraid of Ghosts.

One hour later
Over northwest Afghanistan

The weird airplane known as *Psyclops* was preparing to head back to base when everything changed.

It was 0530 hours, the typical end to a typical mission. The sun was coming up; the crew was exhausted,

the big airplane almost low on gas. Because the light inside *Psyclops* was so eerily subdued, shades of red and
blue emanating from the dozens of VDT screens being
the only illumination, the crew felt caught inside an endless night, even in the daytime. Nothing was bright inside the *Psyclops*—except the so-called White Screen.
This little-used piece of equipment was located at the
far end of the cabin. When it came on, the interior of the
plane lit up like high noon.

And that's what happened just as the big plane began
its turn off mission orbit. One moment, the cabin was
dark; the next, a bright white light washed through it.
The large TV monitor at the rear of the plane had suddenly come alive.

This was highly unusual. The airplane carried dozens
of radios, set to dozens of wave lengths. AM, FM, Ultra-
FM, Ultra-AM, shortwave, long wave, burst wave,
scramble wave—it was a Marconi wet dream with
wings. It also contained what amounted to a small TV
studio, capable of receiving and transmitting broadcasts
on UHF and VHF and via satellite.

But the White Screen was something entirely different. It was a highly secret first-tier broadcast channel that had the ability to block out *every other* TV
channel within a five-hundred-mile radius of the
plane's location. The channel was reserved for one
thing only: when the President of the United States
wanted to address the people whose TV sets had been
commandeered below.

Now it had clicked on. A blinking amber light, right
in the middle of the pilots' control board, indicated a
message was coming through.

"What the hell is this?" the copilot, Clancy, asked. "There's nothing like this scheduled tonight—is there?"

The plane's CO, Captain Dow, checked their mission log. "No freaking way," he said. "We'd get at least a week's notice on something like this."

Dow turned the plane over to Clancy, then followed the rest of his crew back to the TV area. The White Screen was a 55-inch HD TV set, surrounded by a myriad of buttons and dials. At the moment, it was filled with snow static. The number *30* had appeared in the upper right-hand corner. It began counting down: *29 . . . 28 . . . 27 . . .*

This meant a broadcast was soon to begin. At 10 seconds, a blue bulb on the set itself blinked on. This was a voice communications channel; it allowed the crew to talk to people on the other end of the connection. Dow pushed the button below the blue light and opened the channel, at the same time flipping another switch that would allow the entire crew to hear.

Finally the countdown reached zero and the screen cleared. The image of a man sitting behind an ornate mahogany desk came into view.

But this was not the President. This was a little man with a red nose and huge ears. He began speaking in a southern drawl, listing a number of passwords and code sequences to let the crew know that he was indeed someone with a very high security clearance. He also apologized for "not being the President" but added this was a matter whose urgency would be evident in the near future. All this took about thirty seconds, but Dow and the DJs were quickly convinced that the little man was higher than God on the country's security clearance ladder.

Finally, Dow just asked him: "What can we do for you?"

The man hesitated, but just for a moment. Then he said: "I need you boys to go off your flight plan. Some people require your help."

"Do you mean a rescue operation?" Dow asked him, still amazed this was happening on the White Screen.

"No—not really," was the reply. "Just some fellow Americans who need your expertise—and quick."

It was strange, because the little man looked no more special than a next-door neighbor or the guy who ran the hardware store. Yet his voice, his mannerisms, the way he came across, even in a few spoken words, made you want to trust him.

Dow looked over at the rest of the crew; they all just shrugged. He decided to take the hard line. After all, this might be some kind of security drill. Or a trick by the Iranians or someone.

"We have our orders," Dow said. "And we can't break them for any reason."

But then came a surprise. The little man paused again but then said: "Well, I'm truly sorry, boys. But like it or not, I think you've just been drafted."

With that, the strange broadcast abruptly ended.

A moment later the plane's little-used air defense suite began whining. Located up in the cockpit, it was indicating that an unidentified aircraft was streaking toward the ship. Suddenly a pair of navigation lights appeared off the plane's left wing. An instant later, a second pair of lights appeared off its right wing.

"Who the fuck are these guys?" Clancy exclaimed.

The rest of the crew rushed to the windows. Though

it was still hard to see in the waning darkness, it was clear two very strange airplanes had come up on them. They looked dented, ragged, patched up. Real shit boxes with wings. But they were loaded with weapons and were very sinister looking.

"Are those F-14s?" someone finally cried out.

"If they are," came the reply, "they're the worst-kept F-14s I've ever seen."

The planes weren't carrying any military insignia. In fact, they weren't carrying insignia at all. Just blotches of black paint where the country markings usually would be.

Very strange.

Suddenly the big fighters began blinking their navigation lights. In the universal language of flight, this meant one thing: "Follow us—or else . . ."

Dow hurried back up to the cockpit and took over the plane again. He told Clancy to open the emergency radio channel back to their home base. Clancy did so but found the signal was being blocked with interference. A quick check of all their communication options revealed the same thing. They'd suddenly been struck dumb.

They rode along in this tense formation for about thirty seconds. The two ragged F-14s drifted even closer to the big EC-130; soon they were dangerously close. There was no way the EC-130 could outrun them. And fighting them was out of the question.

Dow looked over at Clancy, who just shrugged.

"Anyone want to argue with these guys?" Dow asked the crew.

A chorus of, "No!" came back in reply.

Dow almost laughed. He'd had a premonition that he

and his crew would be seeing some kind of action soon—
but he sure hadn't expected anything as weird as this.

Finally he just blinked the big plane's navigation
lights three times in reply.

"OK, guys," he said. "Lead on. . . ."

Chapter 12

All the tales about Khrash were true. Everything that was bad about the Muslim religion could be found here. Hate schools. Bomb-making schools. Weapons schools. Schools for young terrorists. This was a place where women were used for just two things: rape and servitude. A place where children were molested, then disposed of like soiled tissues. A place where torture chambers and opium factories could be found inside the city mosques.

That was a lot of wickedness to fit inside just 1.4 square miles. Sometimes it seemed Khrash was bulging at the seams with evil.

Just about everything within the city limits was built of clay and stone, although a few taller apartment buildings in the center of town were constructed of steel and cement. The Farāh River bordered the city on the south, then cut around it up to the north. There was just one major road leading in and out of the place. Highway 212 went through the middle of the city, turned west, and went over the Habeeb Bridge. From there it narrowed into a mountain pass that led up and into Iran.

Like many cities in Afghanistan, Khrash had a front gate. It was 22 feet high, made of wood and scrap metal. It anchored a wall, made of similar materials, that encompassed about two-thirds of the city, known as the Old Quarter. The rest of Khrash, the newer areas, was made up of blocks of warehouses, repair barns, and scattered housing. All of it was surrounded by wadis, manmade trenches that doubled as sanitation ditches and public latrines.

The main gate was guarded by members of the city's religious police. They manned two machine-gun posts atop the gate itself, as well as an ancient but still effective 75mm cannon left over from the days of the Soviet occupation.

There were 12 guards on duty this foggy early morning; all of them were on edge. There'd been some unseen tension in the city the day before, and this bad vibe had not diminished with the coming of night. Plus, most of them had spent hours the previous day searching Khrash for videotape cassettes. Old ones, new ones, anything that could be used. Their Chief needed a videotape badly. Incredibly, though, there were none to be found.

Electricity was usually at a premium in Khrash, so at night huge bonfires were built in metal pots located atop the city gate. Even on the darkest, dreariest nights, the light from these fires could be seen for miles. They lit a good portion of Highway 212 as it came up and over the nearby hill and into the city.

It was on this bumpy, potholed highway that the guards first saw the stumbling, bleeding ghost.

Or at least that's what he looked like. He came out of nowhere, naked, moaning loudly, leaving a trail of blood in his wake.

The guards almost shot him—that was their first reaction. But because there was the slightest chance this thing was invoking the mercy of Allah and the Great Mullah—demons had souls, too—to shoot someone under those circumstances could bring horrible bad luck. So the guards held off, and instead two were ordered off the wall to meet the phantasm before it reached the gate.

These two men did so, but only reluctantly. Carrying their weapons, cocked and ready, they went out the gate and approached the figure as he closed within one hundred feet of the city.

Again, it was a foggy, dark morning, and so it took a few moments for the guards to realize that this was not just a man, bloody and near death; it was actually someone they knew. One finally shone his flashlight in his eyes; only then did they realize it was the *kardiss* named Harbosi.

The guards stopped dead in their tracks. There was something very wrong here. Unclothed, Harbosi was smeared with blood. His hands were heavily bandaged and those bandages, too, were soaked through with blood. Blood was also gushing from his mouth. Most disturbing, though, a bloody bag had been tied around his neck.

What had happened to him?

The two guards finally stopped Harbosi and ordered him to raise his hands. But he had no hands to raise. They'd been cut off. Then the man opened his mouth to speak, but no words came. His tongue has been cut out as well.

All he had was the bag, and a note, written in ink on his chest, that read: *Take Me to the Chief*.

The guards knew where to find him.

The Chief lived in a palatial apartment on the bottom floor of one of the Holy Towers. Located in the city's center, this was where most of Khrash's privileged officials lived, especially higher-ups in the religious police. At 11 stories each, the two towers were among the tallest buildings in the city, and that included the trio of minarets.

Carrying Harbosi in the back of their pickup truck, the two guards pulled up to the Chief's door and knocked for five long minutes before they heard some kind of movement inside. The door finally opened and a teenage boy stumbled out onto the street. He looked almost as bad as Harbosi. Beaten up, bloody, certainly dazed. The guards simply pushed him on his way—they knew of the Chief's sexual peccadilloes. They all had them. This was not the reason they were here to see him.

The Chief himself came to the door. He was in his fifties, a large, terrifying man with a bald head and scars running along both cheeks. Nobody really knew where the Chief came from. He wasn't too sure himself. There were some indications, though, that he was from Chechnya, the Muslim republic in Central Asia that was once part of the old Soviet Union.

That made him tougher than even the toughest Afghanis. In addition to being the most powerful man in Khrash, he was also widely known as a sadist. And at the moment, he was furious with the two guards for interrupting his tryst. Even a glance at the bleeding Harbosi in the back of the truck didn't dispel his anger.

"What is *he* doing here, like this?" the Chief demanded of the guards. "I sent him out looking for videotapes hours ago."

The Chief was big enough to beat both guards to death at the same time. They were trembling as he took two giant steps out into the alley.

"Your *kurdiss* is near death," one told him. "And he says he has very important information for you before he leaves us. That is the only reason we brought him here like this."

This got some of the Chief's attention. He walked to the back of the truck and yanked Harbosi out onto the pavement. Then the Chief looked down at his flunky. The massive blood loss was something the Chief had seen before. He, too, had been a commander in the Taliban army before the Americans arrived.

"This man can no longer speak," the Chief said. "And he has no hands, so he can't write, either. How am I going to get this 'important information' from him?"

That's when the guards retrieved the bloody bag.

"Are those videotapes?" the Chief asked them.

Neither guard replied. Instead they just handed the bag to him, jumped back into the truck, and drove away.

The Chief climbed the stairs eleven stories up to the top floor of the Holy Tower.

He did it in two minutes, an accomplishment for a man of his size. But he was in a bit of a hurry. And not for a good reason.

Once on the top floor, he knocked on the only door up there. It led to a large apartment that many called the Penthouse, though such a thing didn't really exist in Khrash. The door opened and the Chief was looking in at a man who was nearly double his own substantial girth. This was Saheeb the Syrian, one of Al Qaeda's chief bodyguards. He was someone the Chief disliked greatly. Saheeb looked recently awakened.

"I have to see him," the Chief told him directly.

"He's asleep," the bodyguard growled. He started to close the door.

The Chief couldn't waste time. He pulled his handgun out and placed it against Saheeb's temple.

"I said I have to see him," the Chief repeated. *"Now."*

The bodyguard relented. The Chief pushed past him and into the dark and filthy living room. There was a bedroom off to one side; the sound of loud snoring was coming from it. The chief went toward it.

The bedroom was just as disgusting as the rest of the apartment. Here he found another large man asleep on a bed of very matted straw; it was obvious that Saheeb had been lying next to him just seconds before. The Chief lit a candle and gave the sleeping man a shake. The figure barely stirred but then fluttered his eyelids. The Chief winced. The man on the mat had only one good eye. The other was an empty, bloody socket.

It was Jabal Ben-Wabi. The infamous Al Qaeda hatchet man better known as the Patch.

Still half-asleep, Ben-Wabi's first conscious act was to pull his patch back on from the top of his bald head. Then he looked up at the police chief.

"Why are you here? Why are you disturbing me like this?"

"One of my *kardisses* just stumbled back to the city, beaten and bloody," the Chief reported. "I had sent him out to the fringes looking for videotapes—as you had asked."

Jabal's one good eye opened wider. "And he found some for me?" Getting a videotape was very important to him.

The Chief shook his head. "No—but he did come upon some very disturbing news."

Jabal finally sat up. "Other than we are still without videotapes, what disturbing news could he possibly have??"

The Chief handed Jabal the bloody bag Harbosi had been carrying around his neck.

Jabal blindly reached inside. He came out with Harbosi's two bloody hands, hacked off but still tied together with cord. Jabal turned white. There was something still clutched in the cold, dead fingers. It was a badge, taken off the shoulder of a uniform. It showed a drawing of the Twin Towers of New York City, with the letters *NYPD* and *FDNY* floating nearby and an American flag in the background. Beneath were the words *We Will Never Forget*.

Jabal dropped the pair of bloody hands to the floor.

"Praise Allah!" he cried. "The Crazy Americans . . . they are here?"

"That's the message," the Chief replied. "And this is the proof. They let him live only so he could bring these to you."

Jabal looked about to faint. The Chief studied him. He knew Jabal to be one of the most ruthless men in the jihad movement. He'd personally seen Jabal behead women and children—and certainly more than a dozen hostages captured by Muslim terrorists in Iraq. Jabal had had no qualms about chopping . . . chopping . . . chopping away at some struggling, screaming victim's neck and dealing with all the gore something like that

entailed. But now, at the mere mention of the Crazy
Americans, for the first time the Chief actually saw Jabal look frightened.

Saheeb the Syrian now spoke. He addressed Jabal
directly.

"My sheikh," he began. "There is no real reason for
concern. Even if these unbalanced Americans are in the
area, we know their numbers are few. We have never
heard of them being more than a few dozen people. On
the other hand, we have a whole city here, filled with
loyal mujahideens. These crackpots might be able to do
their magic tricks when they catch one of our unfortu-
nate brothers out on his own. But we are strong here together. They have little chance of hurting us."

But the Patch wasn't buying it. Having the Crazy
Americans on his trail was his worst nightmare come true.

"You don't know them," he spewed back at the bodyguard. "They can do things others cannot. They're
demons. Even their own people call them Ghosts."

Saheeb frowned. It was his job to not only protect the
Patch but also provide all of his comforts, including
calming him down when needed. He said: "Again, my
sheikh, this is probably just a bluff, by the CIA, because,
well . . . you know. It was a long shot by them, a wild
guess that at best this message would get to you. These
Ghosts probably don't even know we are here. . . ."

No sooner were these words out of Saheeb's mouth
when the entire apartment building began to shake. A
deep rumbling suddenly filled the room, getting louder
by the second.

"What is this?" Jabal cried out.

In the next second, a huge airplane roared by the
apartment window. It just missed hitting the building it-

self, not 10 feet away from its wingtip. It was moving incredibly fast.

Jabal and Saheeb hit the floor. Only the Chief remained upright. He was able to catch a fleeting glimpse of the aircraft as it went by. It was the craziest-looking airplane he'd ever seen. And the noise was incredible. The apartment house was literally trembling in its wake.

"See?" Jabal screamed at Saheeb from the floor. *"They are right on top of us!"*

The Syrian pulled Jabal to his feet and in an instant both were out of the Penthouse and running down the stairs, hell-bent on getting out of the concrete structure before it came down around them. The Chief followed, but not so much in a panic.

All three reached the street at the same time. They found many of their *jihad* associates already out here, some having been disturbed in the middle of perverted activities. They were scrambling around, looking up at the sky, trying to follow the trail of exhaust left by the big airplane as it buzzed the city.

"They were taking pictures of us!" someone screamed, his voice almost lost in the growing chaos. "I could see the cameras!"

More people were pouring into the street now and many had weapons with them. Religious policemen and Taliban types, they started firing into the air, only adding to the confusion. The chief screamed at them to stop, but they couldn't hear him over their own gunfire.

That's when things started rumbling again.

Amid the gunfire and the growing racket, someone else screamed: "Praise Allah! It's coming back!"

An instant later, the huge airplane roared over once again, this time even lower and trailing even more of an earsplitting noise behind it. Everyone got to see it for a few seconds this time. It was big and black and had lots of strange things growing out of it. It resembled a cargo-type plane that the Americans in the eastern part of the country always flew, but that bore just a passing resemblance to this thing.

And yes, they *all* saw the cameras this time. Not only a huge lens in a bubble located on the belly of the aircraft—next to a big white ball—but also people in black uniforms were seen aboard the aircraft, hanging out open windows, taking pictures with hand cameras.

The Chief started screaming at his men again—this time to resume shooting at the airplane. But it was already too late. The plane was gone, heading back from where it came, the mountains to the north, the rumbling fading like distant thunder.

Suddenly everything was quiet again. Many people were just standing around, dazed or in shock. Nothing like this had ever happened in Khrash before. They were protected here. Or at least they thought they were. But it had transpired so quickly, so unexpectedly, it had scared them. Wailing could soon be heard coming from nearby homes.

The Patch finally lost it. He collapsed to the ground, hitting the dirty pavement like a ton of bricks. He had fainted dead away.

It took both the Chief and Saheeb the Syrian more than a minute to bring the Patch back around, slapping his face and pushing on his big stomach to make him breathe.

When Jabal finally woke up, his face had completely drained of color.

"Allah, have mercy on my soul," he gasped. "The Crazy Americans . . . they *are* coming to get me. . . ."

Chapter 13

The helicopter landed almost silently. The only hint of its arrival was the small maelstrom of snow and dirt its rotors kicked up as it touched down. This was quickly blown away by the high winds sweeping over the top of the huge mountain. So, too, was the noise of the engines carried away by the gale.

This was Mount Zabul. It was nearly three miles high, covered with snow, and located about twenty-five miles northeast of Obo Field and some forty miles from Khrash.

It was still dark up here, as the mountain was so high and they had landed on the western face, away from the sun. There was a village up here whose inhabitants were not ruled by a subwarlord under the thumb of Kundez Sharif. These people were also known as the Zabul. Mountain dwellers who eked out a living three miles high, eating pinecones and mountain goats, they had a long history of fierce independence.

They'd fought the Russians with as much verve as

they'd fought their decades-old civil war with the authorities in Kabul. Their oral history was replete with stories of both great bravery and cold cowardice. Most of the other parties in the area, from government troops, to the Americans, to the forces of the warlord Sharif, pretty much left the Zabul, known as much for their irascibility as for their nationalistic pride, alone.

The two people in the helicopter waited for the engines to wind down and then stepped out into the wind and snow. One was Major Fox of the DSA contingent of the Ghost Team. The other was Ryder.

They were here on Murphy's advice, hoping to make some friends. That's why there were virtually unarmed.

Adjusting their night-vision goggles, they moved very carefully toward the snowbound village about one hundred yards away. Fox was carrying a hand-drawn map detailing each stone hut within the settlement. There were no armed men or guards watching over the village this windy night. The Zabul lived so far up in the clouds, sentries just weren't necessary.

Ryder and Fox found the stone hut specified on the map. It seemed larger than the rest, was circular, not rectangular, maybe 15 feet around. Fox checked its dimensions against the drawing, then handed it to Ryder. He did the same thing and whispered: "This must be the place."

They went in the back door, which was actually a series of thick leather hides hanging in place. There was a single candle burning within. Once their NVG vision adapted to the very low light, they found a figure sleeping inside, huddled under wool blankets near a still-smoldering wood stove.

Fox looked at Ryder, who just shrugged in reply.

"Be my guest," Ryder told him.

Fox moved over to the sleeping figure, unstrapped his .45 automatic, and very slowly put its barrel up against the person's head. Then Fox shook him awake.

It was a little old man—but when he woke up and saw the pistol barrel he started fighting furiously with Fox. Luckily the DSA officer had managed to put his hand over the man's mouth, so he could not cry out. But he gave Fox such a battle, Ryder had to come over and help keep the man down.

Then Fox started whispering urgently in the old man's ear: "Murphy . . . Murphy . . . Murphy. We're friends of *Bobby Murphy*."

Eventually the old man stopped fighting. Still they let a full minute go by before Fox took his hand from the old man's mouth. Finally they let him stand up and brushed him off.

He was no more than five feet tall, with a brown, leathery face, a shock of white hair, and a long white beard. He was stooped over but able to stand without a cane. He was covered by a garment that looked more like a house curtain than a robe; his hands and face were dirty. Yet there was something regal about him.

His name was Tarik Aboo. He was the eldest elder of the Zabul tribe. Why did the Ghosts care about him? A couple hundred strong, the Zabul were just as religious as the people who controlled the Qimruz. But the Zabul also believed Sharif and the people in Khrash to be heathens, a disgrace in the eyes of Allah. Because there was a well-known adage in the Islamic world—*my enemy's enemy is my friend*—the Ghosts were here looking for help.

After his rude awakening, Tarik agreed to talk, only because they'd spoken the magic words: *Bobby Murphy*.

They all sat down next to the wood stove. Tarik
crossed his legs, pulling his garment tight around him.
He lit up a long black cigarette to calm his nerves.

"Bobby Murphy is an old friend of mine," he began
in thick English. "He is also friends to my brother and
my cousin and my cousin's cousin. When we fought the
Russians many years ago, I felt Bobby Murphy was here
with us, pulling his trigger as I pulled mine. He arranged
for us to get weapons. Rockets, missiles, bombs. He got
us medicine and food. He helped us throw the Russians
out. We owe him many favors. *That* is the only reason I
don't kill you both right now."

Fox and Ryder rolled their eyes. The old guy was
feisty; they gave him that.

He took another long drag of his cigarette. "So,
then," he began again, "I recognize the emblem on your
shoulder. I know you are the infamous Ghosts and what
you have done in your fight against the sheikh bin
Laden. But why are you *here?* We are very far away
from any battlefields these days."

"We are after a man named Jabal Ben-Wabi," Fox explained. "He's a high-up Al Qaeda operative. We believe
he's living in Khrash."

Tarik almost went pale. "The Patch? You're here to
capture him?"

Fox just shook his head. "Nope—we're here to kill
him."

Tarik just stared back at them. These men were talking nonsense. "But, as you say yourselves, the Patch is
in Khrash. And Khrash is a fortress, with many weapons
and people with guns everywhere. Fifteen thousand of
them at least. How do you intend to get him?"

Fox glanced at Ryder, who just shrugged. "We're still working on that," he replied.

The old man still didn't understand. "Are you saying you are the vanguard of some great army? Are there a million more of you just over the hill?"

"No," Fox replied. "There's only a few of us."

Tarik looked like he didn't know whether to laugh or cry. He chose to laugh. "So what they say is true," he cackled. "You Americans *are* crazy. Catching the Patch with 'only a few' of you? Forget it. Didn't you hear me? There are *thousands* of armed people in Khrash. And they are all demons who will protect the Patch no matter what. They are loyal—it will be impossible for you to bribe anyone in the city to help you. And if you fly your helicopters in, they'll point those thousands of weapons up into the sky. Just like the day you tried to snatch Aidid.

"No, the Patch is not only hiding; he's hiding in the right place. You must know the U.S. military won't even bomb Khrash. They won't send troops in because it would only mean a huge fight and they don't want it spilling over into Iran. The swine behind the walls of that city are in a very powerful position. They hold all the cards, as you say."

Fox shrugged again. "We are still going to try. And we could use some help from people like you. Just name your price."

Tarik stopped cackling and turned very serious. "You Westerners are all the same," he said, shaking his head. "You come here, to this country, and you think you know it. The British. The Russians. Now, you, the Americans. You think you're so smart, and that you have

so many clever ideas. And that money can buy you anything at any time. And what happens? You're always
wrong. The British. The Russians. And now, you. You're
wrong because you *don't* know this place. And you will
never know it. And you will get tired of *trying* to know it
until eventually you will go away, too, just like everyone
else."

Tarik was working himself into a state.

"Now, as a man of God do you think I approve of what
is going on in that city?" he asked them. "I will tell you
that I have questioned God's very existence on the premise that he would never make such an evil place as that.
As a priest, it is my duty to try to change things for the
better. . . ."

He sniffled a bit, then lowered his head. "But as you
Americans say, you're missing the big picture. Even if I
wanted to, I can't help you—for one big reason."

"And that is?" Fox asked him.

"Kundez Sharif," Tarik replied, his lips trembling
when speaking the name.

"And who is he?"

"He is the god on Earth here in the Qimruz," Tarik
said. "The warlord. *The landlord*. This is his territory.
His turf. He allows what goes on in Khrash because the
people there pay him tribute. And because they pay him
tribute, they know that if anyone goes against them,
Sharif will exact revenge on the offending party. That's
their deal.

"Sharif is ex-Taliban. He's also a slave trafficker and
an opium baron. Very powerful. Very rich. And the man
has absolutely no conscience, no regard for human life.
If the Patch is in Khrash, you can be sure Sharif will do
everything to protect him."

Tears were actually rolling down Tarik's face now. His cigarette had gone out.

"So while I would love to be the dreamers that you are," he went on, "and while I would heartily desire to rid my homeland of this sin and idolatry, you must understand why I cannot. For if I helped you, whatever it is you decide to do, Sharif would cut me to pieces. Me, my family. My people. He lets us exist up here only for his own amusement, I think. He would be even happier if he had an excuse to finally wipe us out."

The Americans listened quietly. Tarik was tough, rugged. He'd obviously lived a hard life, filled with bloodshed and murder. And despite his age, it was clear few things frightened him. But this guy, Sharif, did. To the point of tears.

"Where does Sharif live?" Ryder asked Tarik, speaking for the first time. "Inside Khrash itself?"

Tarik shook his head no. "He would not dirty himself like that," he said. "He has a compound, maybe ten miles from the city. But this place he calls home, it is as formidable as the city is. Heavily fortified. An army of guards on hand at all times. It sits up high while everything else sits down low. His people can shoot at anyone within five miles of the place. It is here he keeps his weapons. His gold. His opium. On Thursdays, he has a bus of women and girls come up from Khrash and he has his way with them, all against their will of course.

"Be sure you understand this: Sharif is the protector of Khrash. But he lets the religious police and the Al Qaeda Arabs run the place from the inside, along with their Taliban cousins. Again, that's the deal made between devils. That's why the place is such a pool of sin."

Fox and Ryder had a short, whispered conversation. Then Fox relit the old man's cigarette.

"Wait here," he said to Tarik. "We'll be back. . . ."

Kundez Sharif's compound was a palace by another name. It was a collection of two-and three-story white-washed buildings, rambling by Afghani standards, a half-dozen in all. The buildings were made of simple hand-shorn brick, but there were many ornamental touches on their exteriors. Islamic designs of circles within circles, squares, and triangles along the gutters, fountains and trickling waterfalls around the front door. And palm trees planted everywhere. Add in its white-pebble walkways and high ornamental gates, and this place would have been comfortably at home in the Arizona desert.

It was located on a high hill, which was bordered all round by snow-covered mountains. The vantage point gave a clear view of the surrounding countryside and all of its approaches. And on a clear night, the glow from Khrash could be seen on the southern horizon not a dozen miles away.

The compound even had its own minaret, though it was never used. Like many powerful people in Afghanistan and throughout the Middle East, Sharif used his Muslim religion only as an excuse to maim and frighten and kill. He wasn't even sure which way Mecca was.

One of the smaller buildings, stuffed in the corner out back, was a barracks for Warlord Sharif's elite company of bodyguards. Heavily armed with Russian weapons, including AK-47s and RPG launchers, these fighters were the cream of the crop of Afghanistan's warrior class. They were also among the highest-paid people of their ilk in Afghanistan.

In addition to their assault rifles and grenade launchers, the bodyguards were also armed with 75mm cannons. These ex–Soviet Army weapons had great range and accuracy. There were four of them, one at each corner of the place. The way they were positioned, they could hit just about any target in the valley surrounding the compound's hill.

The compound was also protected by a quartet of 88mm antiaircraft guns, also of Russian manufacture. These weapons were highly accurate. They could hit a target as far as three miles up if operated properly. On a clear day, any target flying closer than that could be picked off almost at leisure.

For these reasons and because of Warlord Sharif's mystique, this place had enjoyed a reputation for years as being under the protection of God himself.

Until today. . . .

Sharif's guards heard them before they saw them, the far-off roar of aircraft engines churning up the cold Afghan air. For any kind of aircraft to go over this part of the country was rare. As the airspace was so mixed up with the border of Iran, few wanted to chance it, especially if the pilots knew the territory below belonged to Kundez Sharif and that he owned antiaircraft weapons.

And usually, when it did happen, the source of any aircraft engine noise could be seen right away, sometimes by the contrails, indicating whatever was going over was flying way up there, where the air was really cold. But now, this morning, the noise wasn't up around the ice crystals. It was right down here, near the rocks and trees.

About half of Sharif's five dozen bodyguards were on duty when it happened. It was just before seven in the morning, and their boss was still asleep. He'd been up late the night before, counting the gold in the compound's very elaborate safe room. This was how Sharif spent many of his evenings, at least the ones when he wasn't fouling girls from nearby Khrash.

The three helicopters suddenly roared out of the valley, rising up out of the early-morning fog. They went over the compound in a flash, one behind the other, flying impossibly low and impossibly fast. Some of the bodyguards scrambled to man their antiaircraft weapons. A few went running to wake the boss. Others went to wake their off-duty comrades as well. But really there was no time for any of these things. The helicopters had come in so quickly, most of the guards could do little else but watch as one of the aircraft dropped an enormous bomb it had been carrying under its fuselage.

The bomb tumbled down, landing directly on top of the compound's main building. The explosion was tremendous. Vivid flames of orange and red shot up into the dawn, causing the surrounding mountains to quake in response. Those guards not killed outright by the blast were blown off their feet by the bomb's shock wave. A tiny mushroom cloud quickly rose into the air, but just as quickly the high mountain winds blew it away. The smoke cleared to find the compound's main house had simply been vaporized, the result of two thousand pounds of impact-fused high explosives hitting it dead on.

The helicopters went into a noisy 180-degree turn to escape the explosion but were back over the target seconds later, this time three abreast. They opened up with rockets, their fiery tails once again lighting up the misty dawn. One barrage hit the guards' barracks in back; another slammed into the compound's drying house where Sharif's personal stash of opium was stored. A third took out the compound's generating station. All three buildings went up in balls of fire and ash.

The helicopters turned and came back a third time. All three opened up with their nose cannons, obliterating much of the guards' weaponry marshaled in each corner of the compound. This time over, men could also be seen in the copters' cargo bays firing bullets, grenades, and even shotgun blasts at the stunned guards below. They mowed the guards down like grass.

A fourth pass targeted the last buildings attached to the palace, a pump house and a covered swimming pool. Once more, the helicopters were firing their nose cannons with the soldiers crammed in the back firing at anything that moved below.

It was so frightening because it was happening so quickly. In just 45 seconds, nearly three-quarters of the compound had been destroyed and almost all the army of elite bodyguards had been killed.

Still the attack went on. On the next pass, the two lead helicopters raked the grounds again with cannon fire. But the third copter dropped another two-thousand-pound bomb right into the center of the flames coming from the main house. A bomb this size was not only able to penetrate the thick concrete cap put over Sharif's basement money safe; it was also able to crash through the top of the safe itself. The bomb exploded with tremendous force, destroying

Sharif's fortune of gold and paper money in less than a heartbeat.

Only then did the helicopters go away, exiting to the north, the last huge bomb hit being their exclamation mark on what they'd just done. When the remaining smoke eventually cleared, those who'd witnessed the attack saw that Sharif's compound hadn't simply been flattened.

It had been turned to dust.

10 minutes later

On top of a mountain about a half-mile away, Fox and Tarik Aboo were standing near one of the recently landed Blackhawk helicopters. They'd watched the attack from here. Ryder had piloted one of the copters during the assault and had landed here shortly afterward. He was now waiting to fly them off.

As intended, the strike on the compound had been quite a show. Tarik's jaw fell open at the first explosion and had yet to close shut. In fact, he was still having trouble speaking. That's how shocked and awed he was.

He'd fought the Russians and the Taliban; he'd fought rival tribes. He'd *seen* war, combat, killing. But he'd never seen anything like this. What the helicopters had done to Sharif's palace was astonishing simply by the brazenness of it all. It was clear no one in the palace survived—the strange Americans had stamped out Sharif as if they were crushing a bug with their boot. Such boldness went a long way in Afghanistan.

"You have opened up the earth," Tarik finally managed to say. "And Sharif has fallen down into it. He is gone, but it's like a dream. A stain, so suddenly removed."

Fox shrugged. "You had a problem; we made it go away," he said. "That's what we do. So, I'll ask you again: Will you help us?"

Tarik smiled broadly now. These Americans *were* different. They actually did what they said. By that alone Tarik had gained tremendous respect for them.

"Yes," he declared finally. "I will help you."

And he'd come prepared. Tarik reached inside his robes and retrieved a cloth that he opened like a handkerchief. On it were hand-drawn pictures of heavy weapons such as tracked guns, tanks, rocket launchers.

"This being Afghanistan," he explained, "you can get weapons just about anywhere. You can buy them or you can rent them. You can even rent whole armies. My cousin, next valley over, has two hundred men at your disposal. Another cousin has some artillery. Still another has some tanks. This and more is available."

Fox asked for more details. Tarik's first cousin had two Russian-built T-72 tanks; he'd been using them as tractors to plow his poppy fields. Tarik's second cousin owned a platoon of 125mm guns, fairly long-range artillery. A third cousin ran his own personal army the next mountain over. Again Tarik assured Fox these cousins would do just about anything for their kinsman. Fox asked Tarik to intercede on his behalf and the tribal leader agreed. They shook hands and then kissed cheeks, sealing the deal.

Then Tarik turned back to the ruins again. Nothing over a foot tall had been left standing. Sharif's compound looked like a small atomic bomb had hit it. "I have one more question," Tarik said.

Fox replied: "Go ahead."

"Why are you *really* doing this?" he asked unexpectedly. "I mean, what is your true reason for going after
the Patch? I've dealt with the CIA before. I've dealt with
the American military before. But you people—you are
not like them. You are like characters in a book. You are
going up against an entire city, just to get one man?
What military person would do that? I suspect this
might be more of a matter of the heart."

"The Patch was in on 9/11," Fox told him. "He killed
three-thousand Americans."

But Tarik was a smart old bird; he shook his head and
slowly wagged his finger at Fox. "The American Army
came to Afghanistan to avenge that September day and
they're still here. But even your brothers in Kabul are
not willing to come to Khrash, simply because it's not a
militarily prudent thing to do. That's how I know something else is happening here."

He turned and pointed to Ryder sitting in the cockpit,
about ten feet away.

"There was a look in that man's eyes," Tarik said. "I
saw it when you first visited me this morning. And it's
in your eyes as well. It's what we call *kapak*. You call it
revenge."

Fox shifted uneasily. He didn't want to get into this,
but the old guy was persistent. Finally Fox said: "OK—
the Patch also killed a good friend of ours recently."

Tarik's eyes went wide again. He was obviously fas-
cinated by this. "So, you're really here because *one* person died?"

"She was killed," Fox corrected him coldly. "Murdered, here, by Jabal Ben-Wabi."

The old man just shook his head. "Sir, the soil of this

country is filled with people who have been murdered. They're buried everywhere. It is our history—and we live with it. But you—you are really doing all this, whatever it is going to be, for a woman?"

Fox just nodded again but remained silent.

Tarik thought about this for a long time, then looked over at Ryder again.

"Your friend," he said to Fox. "With the revenge really burning in his eyes. I get the feeling all this is about a loved one of his. Is it about his wife, perhaps?"

This time Fox just shook his head.

"Something like that," was all he said.

Chapter 14

The studios of Al-Qazzaza TV were located in Umm al Qaywayn, United Arab Emirates, built right on the sparkling waters of the lower Persian Gulf.

The upstart of all-Arab TV, indeed the Muslim world's first superstation, Al-Qazzaza had moved into its new digs just a few months before. The building was impressive. Very modern in appearance, it looked like a flying saucer, with the station's large transmitting antenna soaring high above resembling the mast of some futuristic man-of-war. Dozens of bright blue satellite dishes surrounded the saucer, with hundreds of smaller, more conventional radio antennae surrounding them.

Al-Qazzaza was he go-to place for Islamic terrorists these days—that is, if they wanted to get free airtime for their videos of beheadings, roadside bombings, and other mayhem being committed in the name of Allah. Like rock musicians trying to get their latest song played on MTV, the terrorists clamored to get on Al-

Qazzaza as often as possible. Their couriers could be seen entering and leaving the studios on a regular basis.

No surprise, then, the place was under constant surveillance by many intelligence services, including, today, the Mossad, Israel's premier spy service. Three of its agents were ensconced in a hotel room across the street from the seaside studios, cameras and eavesdropping equipment in hand. But these men weren't simply voyeurs. They were also assassins. They had a computer-generated list of terror suspects who, should they appear at the studio, were to be taken out.

This mission was typical duty for the Mossad, as several of their number-one marks were known to be in the area. So far it had been a dry hole, though. The team had been in place for three days and there had been neither hide nor hair of any potential victims.

This all changed early this morning. Just before 7:00 A.M., a well-known Islamic bagman named Ishtar Abdula was spotted climbing out of an unmarked white van in the studio's parking lot. It was only a fleeting glimpse—but that was OK with the Israeli agents. They were videotaping everything.

Ishtar was on their hit list as he'd been observed previously moving tapes and other communications between Israel's most hated enemy—Hezbollah—and the various Arab TV outlets. But while he was ducking through the back door of the studios, the Mossad agents noticed something unusual about the man. Because he was a courier for several different Islamic terror groups—Al Qaeda, Hamas, Hezbollah—he would have been expected to arrive at the studio with a suitcase full of videotapes. Yet this morning he was not carrying anything with him, not even a coat.

What's more, Ishtar was only inside the Al-Qazzaza building for a few minutes before he reemerged carrying a white canvas bag. By this time, two of the Mossad agents were down in the street, huddled inside their disguised taxicab. Ishtar climbed back into the same van that had dropped him off. When it sped away, the Mossad agents followed in silent pursuit.

They weren't surprised when the van turned back toward the nearby harbor. This fit Ishtar's pattern. No matter who his clients were, the terrorist delivery boy always moved in and out of Iran, as this was the easiest country in the area for someone like him to transit through. Indeed Iran was the only country willing to give him a passport.

From the nearby port it was just a short trip across the narrowest part of the Persian Gulf to landfall on Persia's western shore. If Ishtar made it onto his waiting boat, it would be impossible for the Mossad or anyone else to get him until he popped up again, somewhere else.

Ishtar's van pulled up to a small dock where a French-built yacht was waiting for him. The Mossad agents pulled in right behind him. Moving very calmly and naturally, one agent walked up to the passenger side of the van and pumped three bullets into Ishtar's head. The van driver, a local terrorist confederate, got three in the hat as well, courtesy of the second agent.

Now the Israelis knew they had mere seconds to search Ishtar before the local police showed up. So, while one agent watched the road leading to the isolated dock, the other frisked Ishtar's bleeding body. He found nothing.

Then he checked the canvas bag the man had been carrying, this as the second agent joined him. In the bag they found only a six-pack of high-grade, broadcast-quality blank videotapes, along with Ishtar's Iranian passport.

Attached to the passport was a small map of Afghanistan and Iran. In the lower right-hand corner, circled in red pen where the borders of the two countries met, was Ishtar's apparent destination: the city of Khrash.

Chapter 15

The *Ocean Voyager* stole its way into the Persian Gulf under the same early-morning fog that would have given cover to Ishtar Abdula had he made it out of the port at Umm al Qaywayn.

The ship had sailed on afterburner speed since leaving the Suez Canal. Now that it was in the Gulf, its purpose was to provide as much support as it could for the strike force, up in the Afghan mountains, several hundred miles away.

Murphy was still living inside the Captain's Room, going over every piece of information and communication the Ghosts had sent him. He'd just received the message that his old friends the Zabul were on board. And he'd previously arranged for the recon plane that the team needed. And after the buzzing of Khrash earlier that morning, the mooks certainly knew by now that the Crazy Americans were in the area.

But the hard part still lay ahead. Using the results of the *Psyclops* plane's noisy photo mission, the images of which had been immediately relayed to the *Ocean Voyager,* and bottles and books and pieces of wood, Murphy had constructed a mock-up of the city of Khrash on the floor of his cabin. Thanks to the strange airplane's spying capabilities, he'd been able to see not just up-to-date images of the terrorist city but also, through heat analysis of those images, where people were congregated, where weapons were stored, and other valuable pieces of intelligence.

From all this, the pictures and the mock-up, Murphy had been able to uncover some very curious, if disturbing, things about Khrash. For instance, he'd determined that the Taliban were concentrated in one part of the city, Al Qaeda fighters in another. How did he know this? Because the Taliban traditionally slept in large groups, sometimes taking over entire apartment buildings in order to house their fighters. There was a huge cluster of two- and three-story apartment buildings on the east side of Khrash, a slum by another name, with a lot of military equipment parked nearby. The Al Qaeda fighters, on the other hand, being higher up on the food chain than the Taliban, had taken up residence in more comfortable one-family houses on the west side, this after expelling the owners of course. The terrorists had no real equipment other than rifles and sidearms. Their location was closest to Iran, however, a shorter distance for them to flee should the roof fall in.

The other force in the city—the religious police— was scattered everywhere in between. Their main weapons were pickup trucks bearing large-caliber weapons. Known as technicals, these speedy hit-and-run gun platforms served to terrorize those lowly civilians unlucky enough to still live in Khrash. But the police also had some large ex-Soviet weapons at the main gate and at various points around the city.

The *Psyclops* plane also detected a very large mobile SAM weapon—a massive Russian-made SA-6—capable of firing a one-hundred red-pound warhead to heights exceeding 12 miles. This was such a dangerous, if one-shot, weapon, it appeared the religious police constantly moved it around the city so it wouldn't present so tempting a target should regular U.S. forces ever decide to move in.

But Murphy noticed something even more disturbing: A certain part of the city seemed completely off-limits to everyone, Al Qaeda, Taliban, religious police—everyone. This was the southern part of the city, nearest to the Farāh River, where few people lived and many warehouses and repair shops were located. According to the *Psyclop*'s recon photos, nothing was moving in this area, except several heavily guarded trucks making what looked to be food deliveries to huge buildings that looked otherwise unoccupied.

He was baffled by this.

Sometime during the long night's trip here to the Gulf, Murphy slowly became convinced that the strike team's only hope for success was what he called the third option.

There were several reasons for this. His preliminary needs had turned out well: They needed recon, so they got the *Psyclops* plane. They needed military help, so they got his old friends the Zabul on board. They'd needed to put a scare into the mooks, so they'd buzzed the city and made sure everyone knew these were the

Crazy Americans above them, people who had yet to show any mercy to anyone of the terrorist ilk, as the late warlord Sharif had just found out.

Then there was the makeup of the strike team itself. The State Department Security guys were very, very stealthy, cool but cruel. The Delta guys were great land warriors. The SEALs were good at guarding the flanks. Even the Marine mechanics and the regular Navy guys accompanying the strike force were seasoned shock troops, having participated in previous missions. The pilots who actually flew the helicopters, Air Force special operations guys, had also had some down and dirty combat experience, as did the DSA guys, Fox and Ozzi.

Murphy also knew that perceptions were important. There was a reason the World War Two flag raising on Iwo Jima, long before the battle itself was ever decided, had been a crucial factor in the eventual American victory. Every American soldier on the war-torn Pacific island was able to see the Stars and Stripes flying from the highest point of land, and they, too, were uplifted. In the same vein, every Japanese soldier who saw it was plunged into despair. There was power in Old Glory. Murphy would have to remember that, too.

So they had some things going in their favor, including the sky-high revenge-motive factor. But there was no getting around the fact that Khrash was a city crowded with terrorist fighters. And somewhere in the middle of them was Jabal Ben-Wabi.

How the hell were they going to get him?

During the night, all of the principals left aboard the *Ocean Voyager* stopped in and communed with Murphy for a while. The Spooks. Bingo. Even the Delta Thunder guys. They all studied the mock-up. They all prayed over the pictures. They offered advice. They answered questions, trying to visualize what the future might hold.

But in the end, the decision came down to Murphy alone.

The third option. Was it as impossible as it seemed? The Ghost Team had put together a strike force in an insanely short amount of time and then armed and fueled themselves. But it was a shoestring operation at best. Three helicopters, two shit-box F-14s, three dozen American soldiers, and what would probably amount to a few more dozen local fighters and their near-antique equipment.

And what lay ahead would be both mind-bogglingly dangerous and extremely complex. A city could change quickly during battle. Streets filled with rubble. Wrecked buildings became ideal hiding places for weapons. Fifteen thousand very pissed-off people running around with AK-47s and RPGs? That was Mogadishu times ten. The numbers didn't lie.

But Murphy knew on several occasions in the last decade, during uprisings and wars in Africa, small mercenary groups numbering less than 100 fighters had defeated insurgency groups that had numbered in the thousands. It had happened in Angola; it had happened in Sierra Leone. Smaller, better-trained forces defeating overwhelmingly superior numbers. And at least some of that fighting had taken place in cities.

So it wasn't going to be easy. But it could be done.

Besides, with time slipping away, they had to move quickly.

That's why Murphy decided, just before dawn, that

the only way they were going to get Jabal Ben-Wabi was to go with the third option.

The Ghosts would invade the city.

All 36 of them.

Or at least that was the plan.

Chapter 16

The people who ran Khrash had a plan too.

It had come courtesy of the Iranian military, at the urging of the Iranian intelligence community, should the city someday be attacked by enemies of Kundez Sharif or by a refurbished Afghani army or even the U.S. military. This plan laid out several different ways to defend the city. It was based on tactics used in Iraq by Al Qaeda insurgents battling U.S. forces. The Iranians were helping these people, too, if just to bring even more instability to the region.

It was in Iran's interest to keep Khrash as wild and woolly as possible. There were two ends to any pipeline. Just as Khrash served as a conduit for Al Qaeda fighters who needed to cool their heels in Iran, the dirty little city also served Iran as a pathway for its agents to move into not only Afghanistan but also the countries of Pakistan, Uzbekistan, Tajikistan, and beyond. Next to oil, Iran's main export was Islamic terror.

Having a way station right over the border helped them vastly in this enterprise.

Plus, should the American military ever come to the region in force, the plan set up Khrash just like the Iraqi insurgents set up Fallujah, except in a mirror image. Fallujah was a large city with a small percentage of terrorists; Khrash was a small city with a large percentage of terrorists—more than 80 percent in fact—and again, they were hard-core. If properly implemented, any attempt on the city would be long, slow, and bloody for the Americans. And the Iranians just couldn't pass up seeing something like that. Thus the blueprint for a bloodbath in Khrash.

Having a plan was one thing, though. Getting it to work was another. That Khrash was filled with more than 15,000 seasoned Islamic fighters was not in dispute. But they were from many different groups, with no one leader.

One man then would be in charge of implementing the defense plan.

The man they called the Chief.

It said something about him that after the *Psyclops* plane buzzed the city, breaking nearly every window in its path, the Chief simply shed his clothes and went back to bed.

Just because Jabal Ben-Wabi had wet his pants at the first sign of the Crazy Americans, that didn't mean the Chief had to. Quite the opposite, the Chief saw the Ghosts' hurling of the gauntlet as an opportunity to get rid of them, to put an end to the mystique of the Crazy Americans once and for all. If the Chief did this, it would make him a big hero of the terrorist underworld. With that would come many benefits.

He went back to sleep thinking that to accomplish this he had to get into the heads of the Crazy Americans, just as they had gotten into the head of Jabal Ben-Wabi. The Chief was certain the Crazy Americans would try *something* in Khrash—the question was how could he turn it around on them and finally kill them all off for good?

He was not so dumb as to underestimate his enemy, not by much anyway. The message of the bloody hands had been very clever, as it operated on two levels. The Americans had sent the *kardiss* to him knowing that he would run the horrible message right to the highest Al Qaeda poobah in town. In this case, Jabal Ben-Wabi, the Patch.

And the anticipated effect happened. Jabal had turned into bee jelly. It was disturbing to see how the big, bad Patch reacted when he learned these nutty Americans were out to get him. It caused Jabal to go right down the Rabbit Hole, and frankly, the Chief was glad to be rid of him. Already on his way to becoming a mental basket case, the Patch would have proved nothing but a burden should any real fighting erupt.

But the Crazy Americans' grisly message had proved one thing: they were here because the Patch was here. But *why* had they come for him? What had the Patch done to make the crazies fly to the ends of the earth to find him? To a place where even the rest of the U.S. military feared to tread?

The answer was easy. It was because of the girl, of course. It was the only explanation.

This made the Chief feel very confident. The Americans were going to war for the worst reason possible:

love. Wars of love had been waged many times over the centuries. One side steals a woman. One side kills a woman. One side insults a woman. The other side seeks revenge. Wars of love. They always turned out bad for the avengers, as the Greeks eventually found out after Troy.

The Chief knew languages, too. The Chinese character for *crisis* had two images. One stood for "chaos," but the other stood for "opportunity." If the Americans were stupid enough to come to Khrash over a woman, then the Chief was smart enough to make them pay.

Besides, how scary could these Ghosts be?

While most people were still walking around in shock caused by the American plane's surprise appearance over the city earlier in the day, when the Chief finally awoke, sometime past noon, he barely thought about the incident. In his world, it was already so five minutes ago.

He ate his first of many meals in the day, climbed into the same old, ratty clothes he'd been wearing for a month, and made three phone calls. One was to the highest officer found among the Taliban forces on the east side of town. Another was to the top Al Qaeda military commander on the west side of the city. The third was to the Chief's own command staff. The message to all three was the same: There was a good chance that some kind of American strike was coming to Khrash, most probably limited in nature, most probably after daybreak the following morning. The Chief was implementing the Iranians' defense plan, specifically part one, but laying the groundwork for parts two and three as well. The Al Qaeda and Taliban officers were aware of the Iranian plan; the Chief always made a point of briefing the top Al Qaeda or Taliban commander whenever he came to town. So these two men understood what the Chief was going to do. He was confident he would be able to handle what he believed the Americans were about to throw at them. All he asked of his Islamic brothers was that they send him reinforcements should he need them at some point. They both promised they would.

As for the Chief's own men—he had nearly 1,000 under his command—they'd already begun putting the first part of the Iranian plan into action.

It was midafternoon when the Chief finally emerged from his quarters at the Holy Towers. His driver was waiting for him in his heavily armored Land Rover. Along with an escort of technicals, they began speeding around the city, making sure that preparations were being properly made for the impending American action.

People in Khrash were already fearing some kind of American strike—word had spread everywhere by now. But the Chief was not nervous at all. He'd been chewing qat since waking up, as most of the Islamic fighters in town had been, and the mildly hallucinogenic leaf was finally having some effect on him. Besides, he'd contacted close friends in Kabul, people who were inside the government, and they insisted that no one in Kabul had any idea what was happening in Khrash. So how big of a strike could it be if the regular U.S. military was not involved? As far as he could tell, it was just this bunch of crazies, lovesick and looking for revenge. In the past, they rarely numbered above 50. The Chief was estimating the next morning's battle would be over by noon.

His tour of the city began well. Many of the defense positions needed had already been built. This was espe-

cially true around the city's main gate and the wall that
encompassed the Old Quarter. The clutter of buildings
and high points in this district was an intricate part of
the plan.

The Chief was convinced that any American raid
would come by air. It was the only thing that made
sense. In their previous successes, the Crazy Americans
always rode in aboard helicopters; they would have to
come looking for the Patch the same way. That's why
the Chief had stationed armed men on every roof in the
Old Quarter and throughout the most of the city as well.
When the Americans appeared, there would be many,
many weapons pointing up at them.

And these were not only the hundreds of AK-47s the
religious police had on hand, again courtesy of the Iranian military; there was also more than 200 RPG launchers in this part of the city. The Chief even had a couple
antiaircraft guns—40mm double-barreled antiques,
leftover from the Soviet invasion—stationed at the far
end of the quarter, nearing the center of town.

And if all else failed, they also had one very big SAM.

The Chief visited the city's trio of mosques next, one of
which was located in the Old Quarter. These buildings
were another key part of the defense plan. It was well-
known throughout the Muslim world that the American
military *never* fired on mosques. In fact, they always
went to great lengths to avoid even going near a mosque
during military action. It was a stupid policy. Whether it
was Fallujah, Sadr City, or Khrash, every Muslim
fighter involved in such things knew that because of the
Americans' obsession with political correctness, by not
firing on mosques the United States was handing them

safe haven in the middle of a war. This was why all of Khrash's extra ammunition, weapons, explosives, and fuel was kept in the city's mosques.

The Chief's driver finally brought him to the place known as Kibosh. It was an old blockhouse located on the western edge of town, about a dozen blocks away from the center of the city.

This was the Chief's office. This was where the Chief's top lieutenants could usually be found; it was also where his own substantial bodyguard force was barracked. The Chief maintained separate living quarters here as well, away from his wife and kids. There were torture chambers and a small jail here, as well as a rape room.

The Chief arrived to a flurry of handshaking and ass kissing by his officers. They had much to report to him, but he demanded a cup of tea and for someone to light him a hashish cigarette first. He dealt with several small matters first: The moving of two more field pieces up to the city's front gate. An increase in the ration of the hallucinogenic *qat* to be dispensed to his fighters starting with their evening meal. The testing of the city's half-dozen huge bells, located in the minarets as well as atop the Holy Towers. These bells would be rung as the signal for the visiting Muslim fighters in the city—the Taliban and Al Qaeda—that they would be needed after all in the defense of the city.

The Chief then heard a report on the city's pride and joy—the huge SA-6 SAM. He wanted to make sure that the batteries inside the big missile's launcher were fully charged—this weapon had to be ready at all times. He was assured that everything was hot within the missile and that the backup batteries were also fully charged.

These things done, the Chief sat atop an old, moldy rug and called on each of his cohorts to give his latest report.

First to appear before the Chief was a group of mullahs. They were essentially his department's secret police. They reported something the Chief already knew: that rumors were going through Khrash that the city was about to be attacked by the Americans, possibly even a strike by B-52 bombers—a very frightening thought. The mullahs had a warning for the Chief: They were sure that those civilians who could would attempt to escape the city before whatever was coming finally arrived. And the mullahs said, just as certainly, if such a trickle began, it would soon turn into a torrent.

The Chief knew this was a problem. One part of the Iranian defense plan called for civilians to be used as human shields. Just as they were reluctant to fire on religious places, the Americans rarely opened fire if there were civilians around. Again, this gave a huge advantage to the Islamic fighters. In this regard, the lowly citizens of Khrash were one of its most valuable commodities at the moment.

The Chief moved quickly. He told one of his commanders to take a squadron of technicals out to the western edge of Khrash and stop the first group of civilians they encountered who were trying to leave the city. These civilians would then be brought back to the city square located next to the Holy Towers. Their time up, the mullahs kissed his hand and quickly departed.

The next officer to step before the Chief was his arms master, the man in charge of the city's weaponry. He reported that he was expecting a huge arms shipment to arrive in Khrash sometime tonight. More RPGs, more

AK-47s, and ammunition for both were due to be delivered. But more important, several tons of TNT and HE were coming as well. These explosives had been slated to go into the terrorists' schools to make booby traps and improvised roadside bombs for Iraq but could be made available to the Chief's police force at his request.

The shipment was scheduled to arrive around midnight, via a river caravan, coming up the Farāh from the Iranian border town of Rimut fifty miles downstream. The exact time of delivery was unknown, though. The Chief waved away the man's apologies for the imprecise timetable. He just wanted to know one thing: Would the arms shipment be here before sunrise the next day? The arms master replied in the affirmative.

"Then all will be well," the Chief declared.

The arms master departed to be replaced by one of the religious police's lowest deputy officers. This man was visibly shaking when he knelt before the Chief.

"We have come up empty on our search," the man said, eyes glued to the floor.

The Chief just stared back at him—what was this man talking about?

"The search for what?" the Chief asked.

"Videotapes, sir," the man replied, certain a hatchet of some kind was about to come down on his head.

"You? You're the one in charge of looking for videotapes?"

"I am, sir," the deputy said.

"And still you can't find any? Not a one—in this entire city?"

The man shook his head slowly. "No, sir."

The Chief felt his shoulders slump a bit. What a pain this was! TV sets, batteries, cell phones—even fax machines. These things could be had at just about any shop in Khrash as well as throughout the Qimruz But not a single usable videotape? Anywhere? Who was going to tell the Patch?

The Chief stuffed his mouth with more strands of qat, but suddenly he wasn't feeling as good as he was just moments before. He dismissed the deputy but told him to continue his search. That's when one of the Chief's field commanders burst into the room. The Chief's bodyguards were right on the man's tail, but seeing the look on his face, the Chief beckoned him forward. The man was highly upsct.

"Very bad news, sir," was how he started his report.

"What could it be?" the Chief asked with a snort. "The city is tight. Security is high and we are dispelling any rumors. So, what bad news could you possibly give me?"

The man gulped. "Kundez Sharif's compound has been destroyed," he said.

The Chief stared back at him in disbelief. "What did you say?"

"I saw it myself," thc commander reported. "It has been turned to dust. There is nothing left."

To emphasize the point, the commander pointed out the room's only window facing north. There was still a distinct red glow on the horizon.

"That could be a simple brush fire," the Chief said. "Or some fool burning his manure pile."

One of his top lieutenants intervened. "Sir—it is coming from the same direction as Sharif's compound," he said. "Perhaps you should call him."

The Chief nodded brusquely to the lieutenant. This man dialed Sharif's private cell phone and handed the phone to the Chief. The phone rang and rang. There was no answer.

Now the Chief's face creased with worry. He did not want to even think about an existence without the protection of the almighty Kundez Sharif.

"The sheikh has many escape routes in his palace," the Chief suddenly told those assembled. "He would have managed to get out of any kind of bandit attack."

But the field commander just shook his head. "This wasn't just a bandit attack," he insisted. "Sharif's compound was *bombed* from the air. There is nothing left but dust, and even that is still burning."

"Bombed from the air?" the Chief roared. "By who? Certainly not the Americans. We have a deal with Kabul. . . ."

"They might not have been sent by Kabul," the man reported meekly.

At this point, another of the Chief's officers burst in unannounced. He was the man the Chief had sent out to look for any civilians attempting to escape. He reported that his men had corralled two dozen civilians—women and children mostly—who'd been attempting to leave Khrash via the northwest wadi. They had been brought to the city square as the Chief had ordered.

In a foul mood now, the Chief demanded to be taken to them.

It was now late afternoon and the sun was beginning to sink over the mountains to the west when the Chief arrived back in Khrash's main square.

The civilians who'd been caught trying to escape were huddled next to a wall of the Holy Towers. There were 26 of them, and indeed most were women and children. They were all carrying hastily packed bags and suitcases. Besides these and the rags on their backs, they had little else. Many of them were crying.

The Chief had his men round up as many locals as they could find, and a crowd of several hundred was soon gathered in the square. The Chief stood atop his Land Rover with a battery-powered megaphone and made an announcement: Anyone caught trying to leave the city in this crucial time would be considered an enemy of Allah and dealt with accordingly.

Then the Chief had his men line the escapees up against the Holy Towers wall. It took some time to get them to obey; some had to be whipped or beaten. The wailing and panic grew. The Chief waited impatiently, chewing qat and fanning himself in the seat of his truck. If only he'd found a damn videotape, he was thinking. Then everything would have had a positive face on it.

Finally, the 26 people were in place. Eighteen of the Chief's men lined up in ragged fashion, each holding an AK-47. The Chief gave a signal and each man raised his weapon. Stunned silence enveloped those looking on. The Chief returned to the hood of his Land Rover, again with his electronic megaphone, and recited his speech a second time: Anyone caught leaving Khrash would be shot.

Then he gave the order for his men to fire.

But just before they could pull their triggers, the air above the city started rumbling again.

They came in low, wingtip to wingtip, two airplanes so loaded down with bombs, they looked like they were carrying pianos.

The noise was horrific, the sound wave that arrived was so intense. The men in the firing squad saw the planes first, coming in right over the city's main gate, with barely a shot thrown up in response from the gate guards. The planes seemed huge to these men; they quickly broke and ran.

The Chief's bodyguards saw the planes a split second later—their reaction was just about the same. They instantly fled, though two of them managed to put the Chief back into his Land Rover before they ran away. That's when the intended execution victims scattered as well. The Chief was furious.

This was not the way things were supposed to go.

The two planes arrived over the square a moment later. They were the F-14s, crudely converted into Bombcats. Each was weighed down with 12 five-hundred-pound bombs, way over the expected safe load of the F-14, especially shit boxes like these two. To add to the stability of this very risky attack, both planes were flying with their movable wings extended fully, as if they were landing. Between the weight, the swept-out wings, and the generally bad condition of both planes, they were moving very slowly.

To the surprise of just about everybody on the ground, a siren began blasting away across the city. Then two searchlights stabbed into the early-evening darkness. Suddenly the sky above Khrash looked more like World War Two Dresden or Berlin. There were streaks of tracer fire coming up to meet the two planes. So-called golden BBs were being sprayed over the sky.

The two planes turned almost painfully to the south. They were so low, they both nearly clipped the tops of the Holy Towers as they banked left. It took a while, but finally the F-14s went level again. Straight ahead, about a half mile away, was the city's Grand Mosque.

The two jets went down even lower, if that was possible; they reduced their airspeed, too. Now just a few blocks away from the huge ornate mosque, both planes put their noses up sharply and dropped four bombs each. This slow-motion lobbing technique resulted in all eight bombs—two tons of explosives—hitting the mosque squarely on its minaret.

The impact caused an explosion that turned night into day. An instant after that, there was another explosion, just as grand, just as bright. Then came another, and another. . . .

The bombs had found the huge stockpile of weapons and explosives hidden in the basement of the mosque by the Chief's men. Things started lighting off in a big way, this as the two planes rode right through the massive fireballs, turning this time to the east. The noise was incredible. The flames rising so high and being so concentrated, they created a mini–mushroom cloud.

When the smoke was blown away a few seconds later, not only was the Grand Mosque gone—every building within two blocks of it was gone, too.

Now the two planes, weighing slightly less, headed for the minor mosque located in the city's Old Quarter. This structure known as the Easter Moon Mosque was more than 300 years old; it was also filled with explosives and weapons, especially RPGs. The holy building received the same treatment as the first—four bombs from each slow-moving plane, two tons of explosives slamming into a dozen tons of the same inside. Another great explosion, another bright flash of light. Another mushroom cloud streaming up into the night. Another gust of wind, another peek at the destruction. As before, more than six blocks of buildings, including the three-century-old mosque, had been turned to searing rubble.

Still locked in the searchlights, the planes turned back to the west. The Red Star Mosque, also known as the poor people's mosque, was located in this part of the New Quarter of the city. It was here that the religious police had stored hundreds of gallons of gasoline and diesel fuel.

There was a storm of antiaircraft fire coming up at the two raiders now. What had looked like Dresden a few minutes before now looked like Baghdad, January 1991. The two planes pressed on, though, throwing four more bombs each into this third mosque, igniting all that fuel and creating a flash brighter than the two previous ones combined. This time there was a fireball that didn't dissipate. Fueled by all the gasoline and diesel, it spread a burning, napalmlike substance all over this western neighborhood, creating a small firestorm. As most of the buildings down here were made of wood, rather than stone—it was the poor section—the fire was quickly raging out of control.

Only then did the two planes, now free of their ordnance, finally accelerate and disappear over the mountains in the north, leaving the stunned people inside the city to assess the damage.

Three parts of Khrash were on fire. More than half the city's ammunition, explosives, and fuel was gone. Many of the top religious police commanders, caught inside the mosques, were dead.

All in less than three minutes.

Even to the most uneducated on the ground, it was quickly apparent this had not been done by typical Americans.

And that was *very* scary.

Chapter 17

Red Curry was one of the bravest men Ryder Long had ever met.

Though Curry had flown jet aircraft before he joined USAF Special Operations as a copter pilot, he'd never piloted an aircraft like an F-14 before. First, he was Air Force and the F-14 was a Navy jet. Second, it was big and old. Third, these Iranian versions were big and old *and* just barely airworthy. It was all Ryder could do to keep his own beast in the air, and he'd had thousands of hours in jets. He didn't know how Curry was able to do it.

They were now circling Obo Field, draining off speed before coming in for a landing. The surprise bombing-raid run on Khrash, it being the first step in the team's final option plan, had been a success. But not without a price. The pair of Tomcats had been so overloaded with bombs, the strain on their engines, already in bad condition, had been close to catastrophic for both of them.

Just taking off from Obo proved to be a nightmare.

At thirty-five hundred feet, the runway held just the bare minimum of roll distance for an F-14 that *wasn't* carrying any bombs. As it was, both jets used every inch of the bumpy airstrip just to fling themselves off the Obo ridge and out into the turbulent air between the mountains beyond, praying all the way for some wind beneath their wings. It made taking off from a carrier seem like kid's stuff. Again, it had been a puckering adventure for Ryder—he couldn't imagine what it was like for Curry.

Somehow they made the liftoff, though, went over Khrash, dropped their pianos, and made it back alive. But now here was the hard part. Landing again, on the portable arresting wire setup that no one at Obo was really sure had been installed correctly. And it was Curry who was going to try to land first.

The problem was that while they had stolen the mobile arresting gear fairly easily, the damn thing didn't come with an instruction book. They had no idea how taut to pull the wire that would catch the jet's arrestor hook. The Spooks had tried to help, suggesting tension data they'd gleaned from the Internet, but it was all relative to stopping planes at sea, on carriers, not a few miles up, in Arctic-like conditions.

The first time they'd banged in at Obo, the cable had been pulled too tight—the Ghosts had guessed at the needed tension, and it had been too much. It nearly ripped the arrestor hooks from both Tomcats. Some of the tension had been relieved from the wire for their second landing, after hijacking the *Psyclops* plane, but it was still a guess on the right amount and it wound up being too slack. Both Ryder and Curry nearly wound up at the bottom of the next mountain over. Now they had put a new tension setting on it. But again, too much and the plane would tear itself apart. Not enough and the plane would go over the cliff.

That's why Curry volunteered to land first, on the premise that as Ryder was the better pilot and the team's CO, he would be more needed should anything go wrong with the cable. This was a fatalistic decision if there ever was one—but that's how the Ghosts were operating these days. Most, if not all, believed that their days were numbered. In fact, some of the team members were so hardened by now, going out in a blaze of glory was not all that objectionable to them. This was just another occupational hazard, part of the price of being thought of as "America's terrorists."

Besides, as corny and melodramatic and clichéd as it sounded, this one *was* personal. And to a degree, everyone in the team shared it. It was ironic that Li never thought of herself as one of them. Even the guys who'd only known her for the few days they'd all spent on the ship considered her as much a part of the Ghosts as Murphy. For the slime of Al Qaeda to take away such a beautiful creature was a crime against nature itself. That's why they were here, on the moon, ready to take back the pound of flesh.

That's why they knew if one, two, or all of them cashed in during this, their last mission, it would have at least been in pursuit of a very noble cause.

There weren't many better ways to go.

It took Curry three tries, but he finally managed to put his F-14 on the ground. The noise the portable cable setup made when his Tomcat's hook caught was so loud, Ryder heard it plainly even though he was flying several hundred feet above and riding on top of two very noisy engines. Bouncing around his crash helmet, it was the most horrible grinding sound.

It was amazing the damn wire didn't snap, which actually would have meant big trouble for both of them. But the cable held and Curry was down, and even now the Ghosts were pushing his F-14 off the runway. With the horrible noise still echoing in his ears, Ryder put the nose of his own Tomcat to the ground and started his landing approach.

Again, this was his third time banging in at Obo, and as the first two had been a bitch, he couldn't help but wonder if this time something really would go wrong. But the good thing about such thoughts, like landing on aircraft carriers or at a shoestring base like this, was that everything was happening so fast that by the time you started worrying about it, it was over.

That's what happened now as Ryder fell out of the sky and slammed onto the broken runway, snagging the arrestor cable on the first try. The god-awful sound echoed again, and he was yanked to a stop from 120 mph—all in two seconds. Like having sex in a car wreck was how someone had once described tail-hook landings. For Ryder, this one featured only the car wreck.

But he was down and he was stopped and that's all that mattered. The Ghosts came out of the support buildings and pushed his plane off to the side as they had just done with Curry's.

But Ryder and Curry wouldn't be staying long this time, only until the last of the bombs were put on their planes and the last of their allotted fuel put into their tanks. Then they would be heading back to Khrash—there would be no attacking-at-dawn shit for them.

Everyone around Ryder was moving fast. People

were running everywhere. They'd all been briefed on the plan, the ominous-sounding final option. Three dozen people invading a whole city, with very little help? Would it work? Could it work? No one knew. And again, at the moment, no one really cared. They were going to do it, win or lose, for Li.

Ryder rolled up to the second support building. Curry's plane was already inside. Ryder jumped from his 'Cat and immediately began helping the Marine mechanics load more bombs onto Curry's dilapidated F-14, this while Curry himself was up in the cockpit hot-wiring his auxiliary oxygen system, which had taken a large-caliber round square on during their surprise attack on Khrash.

The miracle was that either F-14 was flying at all. Again, the Tomcat was the Navy's premier fighter-interceptor. Its job was to protect America's supercarriers from incoming aerial threats, be they enemy airplanes or missiles. But the team had done a field modification that even the Navy was somewhat reluctant to do. Starting around the time of the first Gulf War, the Navy began flying F-14s in the expanded role of dropping bombs as well as carrying out fleet defense. Some results were mixed, but when it happened, the F-14 Tomcat went from being a purely defensive aircraft to one adapted for offense as well. The Tomcats became Bombcats.

The two Iranian shit boxes carried rudimentary equipment that would allow them to perform this offensive capability. But it was only the minimum setup: just two hard points on each plane on which to attach five-hundred-pound bombs. The Ghosts had stolen *two dozen* of the mud movers from the Iranians and wanted to drop them all, and not just two at a time. So prior to the Khrash raid, Ryder, Curry, and a gaggle of the Ma-

rine mechanics had jimmy-rigged a system that allowed
the F-14s to carry up to 12 of the five-hundred-pounders
each, hot-wiring a number of temporary hard points that
could each drop bombs separately. All these wires and
the Rube Goldberg devices that controlled them took
time and attention during the bombing run, hard to do
especially while getting shot at *and* trying to zero in on
the target. But Ryder and Curry's raid on the dirty little
city had gone surprisingly well and everything had
worked. So now they were back to get bombed up and
go again.

They were just hoisting the last two bombs onto
Curry's jet when the chief of the Marine mechanics
called Ryder out from under the F-14. He had some bad
news. He and his men had looked over both fighter jets,
and both were now unflyable.

"It's not the combat but the landings and the take-
offs," the chief mechanic told him. He explained that
their most recent departure, with both jets insanely
overloaded with bombs, had literally twisted the fuse-
lages on both planes out of whack, the torque had been
that severe. Rivets had popped near the tail section on
both planes, their fuel tanks had sprung leaks, and some
secondary interior wing systems were now all jammed
up. As for the landings, the runway at Obo was not really "soft" asphalt or the relatively flexible surface of a
Navy aircraft carrier. It was solid rock, with no give
when many tons of airplane slammed into it, going 120
mph. The jets' landing gear were the victims here, the
chief mechanic said. On both planes, there were cracks
from the wheel wells right up the hydraulic extension
and into the retracting gears. Any shock-absorbing

properties contained in the undercarriage were now nonexistent.

In the chief mehanic's opinion, the two Bombcats might be able to weather one more takeoff. But neither the gear nor the twisted fuselage would survive another arrestor hook landing.

Ryder heard him out but then just smiled. The guy was being sincere as hell, but he was missing part of the picture here.

"Don't worry about it, Chief," Ryder finally told him. "Once we take off from here this time, we won't be coming back. . . ."

That the big *Psyclops* aircraft fit inside the third support building at Obo was just one more minor miracle of the operation.

Actually, the wingtips scraped the sides of the building's door going in, but a couple scratches on the paint job were the only result. This was where the big plane was hidden after its earsplitting low-level flight over Khrash. This was where it was now, as night was falling again.

J. C. Dow, Clancy, and the rest of the crew were huddled within the interior of the airplane, waiting, just like everyone else. They were more than 24 hours overdue returning to their home base at Abok, in eastern Afghanistan, and they were sure, officially at least, their airplane was considered "lost" by this time. Search planes had no doubt been dispatched to look for them— or their wreckage. But as their flight plan when they "disappeared" was more than 200 miles northwest of Obo, those search planes wouldn't start looking for them so far off-course down here in the Qimruz, for at least another 48 hours. Whatever was going to happen with Khrash would have transpired by then—and they were going to be in the thick of it, by their own choice. So if the United States had already contacted their families to report them as missing, then maybe it was just a case of bad news being premature.

The *Psyclops* crew was now part of the team. Just like other disparate groups the Ghosts had met along the way, they had joined up. It was just as soon as they'd landed at Obo after their in-flight kidnapping that the *Psyclops* crew found out the mysterious special ops team had been their abductors. They knew well the achievements of the Ghosts—as all Americans did by now. At Hormuz and Singapore and within the United States itself, the Ghosts had been carrying on their own war against Al Qaeda while the majority of the U.S. military was up to other things.

For this reason, and after having the situation explained to them about Khrash, the Patch, and the girl named Li Cho, to a man the *Psyclops* crew agreed to stay on and help the Ghosts see it through. They'd been briefed about the final option and were getting ready for the adventure of their lives.

One of the most unusual cargoes the *Psyclops* plane carried was a large box filled with American flags. Made of a tough fiberglass substance that actually looked and felt like cloth, each flag was five feet by three feet and could be folded up and stored away in no space at all. The plane carried the flags as another part of its psychological operations. Whenever they made a propaganda leaflet drop on a targeted village, something that took place a couple times a month, they would drop a smaller box containing some of the American flags as well, hoping those same people would display them as part of the ongoing hearts and minds program. But now, as part of the final option plan, they had been asked to give all the flags to the team's shock troops, several hundred in all, for use somewhere down the line.

One of Dow's guys had just returned to the plane from delivering the flags when the White Screen blinked on again. This time was just as much a surprise as the first. The light filled the cabin, and when the screen cleared of static they saw it was Murphy again. He wanted to have a private meeting with the EC-130's crew, out of sight and earshot of the other team members.

The crew gathered around the screen now. They felt like they'd known Murphy all their lives, a common reaction by those who'd met him. He said hc had something to ask them and it was a bit complicated.

"That igloo thing you have attached to the bottom of your plane," Murphy said, "can it do what I think it can do?"

The question caught the *Psyclops* crew off-guard. In their initial mission for the Ghosts the *Psyclops* had served as a very loud, very intimidating photo plane. They had performed what was asked with perfection, but in reality taking pictures was one of the most pedestrian things their big plane could do. Breaking into radio broadcasts, commandeering TV stations, speaking through amplifiers that intentionally made them sound like the Almighty, these things the civilian crew could do with ease.

But now Murphy was asking about the Snowball. That was something different entirely. That was *ultra*-top secret.

In times like this, only Dow could speak for the crew.

"I know better than to give you the standard denial about it," he told Murphy evenly. "But you, above all, have to be sensitive to something like this. That thing is so top-secret, we're not sure the President even knows it exists. At least that's what we've been told.

"We are here with you today because we believe in what you guys are trying to do. But who knows what will happen tomorrow—if any of us is still around? You know how the military is. Things can flip in the blink of an eye. I'd hate to be the reason that we all get court-martialed and thrown in Leavenworth for life at hard labor, just because I started blabbing about the Snowball."

Murphy understood and told them so. "Believe me, I know what it's like to give up secrets that might come back to haunt you," he said. "And I don't want you guys to put yourselves or any of us in jail. I just want to make sure we can make use of all our options in what's coming up, should things start to go that way."

There was a long silence. Dow didn't know what to say. They'd all taken a security oath not to talk about the Snowball and what it could do—but just by being here, in the Obo, with the Ghosts, it seemed like national security laws didn't matter that much anymore.

No one was talking, so Murphy asked the question again.

And finally, after an approving glance around to his crew, Dow nodded yes. "Let me put it this way: Just by asking the question as to what it can do, you've probably guessed right."

But he quickly added this caveat: "And I want to say that we appreciate what you guys are trying to do out here, and we're proud that you've let us help. But I have to tell you that as far as employing the Snowball, I can only do it as a very last resort. . . ."

They saw Murphy smile slightly.

Then he saluted them and said: "Thanks, men. That's all I have to know."

30 minutes later

Ryder was back in the cockpit again. His plane was moving very slowly, heading toward the runway one last time. He could almost imagine the tips of the variable-wing fighter scraping the ground, so many bombs were hanging underneath him.

The small strike force was laid out before him, lined up on the short taxiway leading to Obo's bumpy airstrip. Again because of the lack of communications between them—the jets' radios simply didn't work—they were going through a series of hand signals to get everyone on the same page for takeoff.

They weren't all going, though. Two of the Marine mechanics would be staying behind at Obo. One aspect of the operation included a possibility that one of the Blackhawks might come back to take on the very last of the fuel and any ammunition that might remain. Leaving someone at Obo was insurance that if the copter needed two more warm bodies aboard, they'd be available. But if the two Marines, volunteers both, were unable to get on the copter at that time or if the copter never came back, they were to make their way to friendly lines in eastern Afghanistan, with help from the Zabul. If they made it to Kabul, then at least someone would be able to tell the world someday what had happened here.

As for everyone else, they were anxious to go. Before they'd all climbed into their respective aircraft—the shock troops into the helicopters, the *Psyclops* guys into their weird aircraft, Curry and Ryder into the Bombcats—Ryder had gathered the team around him. Did everybody understand the part they had to play in the upcoming operation? he asked them first. Did everyone know the final option plan by heart? The reply came back unanimous: Yes, everyone did.

His second question was a little more difficult. Did anyone want to jump ship right now, with absolutely no shame attached?

Again, the response was unanimous: No one wanted to back out. They were all going. Together.

This was what Ryder was thinking about now, sitting in his cockpit, doing a final check of the few working instruments he had left. The team was standing firm, new guys and old, committed to what lay ahead. But why was *he* here? The team was out here to kill mooks and to avenge the loss of one of the team. But what was his motive? His *real* motive? It was a strange question, especially since he was the CO of the mission, yet he'd been asking it of himself since leaving the *Ocean Voyager*. These and other thoughts, haunting him for days, were coming from so deep down in his soul that he couldn't understand them, at least, not at first.

He started fiddling with his wedding ring as the rest of the team finished moving into position. He hadn't taken the ring off since the day his wife died. He'd vowed then that he'd never take it off again. But looking at it now unleashed a flood of emotion. Again, what was he *really* doing here? Whose ghost *was* he chasing? By avenging Li's death, was he forgetting about his wife? How could that be? How could he ever forget her?

It was all very confusing, and unsettling, and very unlike him. It was changing him, just like taking over the team had changed him, but this change he didn't like. He felt like a hypocrite, but he didn't know why.

These thoughts were broken by the sound of someone banging on his canopy. He looked left to see one of the young Marine mechanics had pushed a ladder against the F-14 and climbed up beside him. He had the yellow cell phone with him, the only secure communication line the team had with the outside world. Ryder had carried it on his person every moment since Murphy gave it to him. But shortly before the team got ready to depart this time, it was decided that it would be best to leave the cell phone at Obo. After all, Murphy had told them it was the most secure line in the world. Putting it on one of the aircraft risked it being compromised should that plane get shot down. And no one wanted that. So, it was being left with the two mechanics who were staying behind. This kid banging on Ryder's canopy was one of them.

But why was he bringing the phone to him? Ryder had just had a last conversation with Murphy before he climbed back into the plane. That conversation had been brief: Murphy just wanting to know if they had crossed every T and dotted every I for what lay ahead and Ryder telling him they had. They wished each other good luck and thanked each other for all they had accomplished and that was it.

So what was this about?

Ryder lifted his canopy and the kid handed the phone to him. It was indeed Murphy.

"I didn't know whether to make this call or not," Murphy told Ryder. His voice sounded very somber and far away. "But I thought I owed it to you at least."

Ryder really didn't know what he was talking about.

"It just arrived," Murphy told him. "Li's execution video. We just dragged it down from the Al-Qazzaza tele-link."

Ryder felt his chest cave in. His ears began burning. His eyes filled up. He'd been waiting for this inevitable piece of bad news ever since they'd left the *Ocean Voyager*. He'd been steeling himself, expecting the crushing blow he knew it would bring. Now that it was here, it was almost too much for him to take.

"I just thought you'd want to know," Murphy went on. "The thing was time-stamped. It was filmed four days ago. So, at least she went quick."

Ryder choked up. Li had been dead for only four days? It seemed like four years.

"Bates has the footage now, down in the White Rooms," Murphy concluded. "He volunteered to watch it. God knows I could never do so. But he'll study it, see if we can come up with something that might help us, in the future. If there is a future. But again, I just thought you should know."

Ryder thanked him, hung up, and gave the phone back to the mechanic, who promptly disappeared.

He breathed deep from his oxygen mask. And that's when he finally had his answer. He would have liked to think that they would still be doing this if it had been himself or Fox or Ozzi or Curry or any of the team members, right down to one of the *Ocean Voyager*'s sailors or the Marine mechanics who had been kidnapped by The Patch and executed. That they would come here and kill those who had killed them.

But this *was* different, because it was her. Li . . .

This beautiful girl . . . now gone.

He took another deep breath, and got back into himself again.

Between his legs was the bag of money Murphy had given him back on the ship. He'd kept it with him this entire time as well. Now, he threw the bag back into the unoccupied space behind his seat. Then he revved up his engines and started moving again.

Once last look around told him they were all as ready as they were ever going to be. Ryder would be the first to take off. The others would follow. He was about to hit his throttle and pop his brakes when he caught himself looking down at his wedding ring again. He closed his eyes and it was Li's face he saw, waving to him as she left aboard the CIA helicopter, the last time they would ever see each other.

He opened his eyes again, and wiped them. He thought a moment . . . then slowly, with shaking fingers, he removed the wedding ring and put it in his pocket.

Then he popped his throttles and took off, climbing steeply and quickly becoming lost in the stars.

PART THREE
One Bad Night over Khrash

Chapter 18

The first copter touched down on the eastern edge of Khrash just two minutes before midnight.

The landing spot was close to the place where the city's three main drainage culverts converged into one. On the team's final option plan, this area was called Weak Point East.

Ten heavily armed soldiers jumped off the helicopter, quickly taking up positions on one side of the cracked concrete culvert. These were all Delta guys; their squad had been designated 1st Delta for this operation. The squad god was one of the original Ghosts, Sergeant Dave Hunn. What they did in the next sixty minutes would determine whether this long-shot battle would be won or lost.

The copter took off immediately after dropping Hunn and 1st Delta. It rose almost straight up into the sky, parking itself about one thousand-feet above the joining of culverts. Hunn did a head count; everyone had made it to the ground OK.

He trained his night scope goggles in toward the city. They were about three-quarters of a mile from the center of Khrash, just a few hundred feet from the edge of a dead-end street. It was lined with clay and wooden houses for several blocks before the edge of the city proper began. This was the cluster of slum buildings where the city's Taliban fighters had settled.

Hunn could see lights in most of these hovels; he could also see armed men milling around outside some of them. The Superhawk copter that had dropped them here was nearly silent, but all it would take was for one sharp-eyed mook to look up into the sky and see the thing hovering up there and the game would be up.

Hunn checked his watch. One minute to go. He scanned the Taliban neighborhood again; if anything, even more armed men seemed to be moving around inside the dilapidated buildings.

Don't these guys ever sleep? he thought to himself.

The seconds passed like hours. If they were caught here, in the trench, and suddenly thrown on the defensive, it would get real nasty real quick.

Thirty seconds . . .

Hunn checked his weapon and attached his bayonet, the team's trademark. He passed word on down the line that everyone else should do the same.

Twenty seconds . . .

He pinched the tiny gold cross he always wore around his neck—it had belonged to his kid sister, at 18 one of the youngest victims of 9/11. Just like every time before he went into battle, he now whispered five solemn words: "This one's for you, Maggie."

Ten seconds . . .

Another sweep of the slum neighborhood. Small

armies of Taliban could be see on the buildings' roofs now. They looked particularly dangerous in the green glow of the NV goggles.

"Five seconds . . . four," Hunn said aloud. "C'mon, guys, don't let us down now. . . ."

Three seconds . . .

Two . . .

One . . .

Zero . . .

Nothing.

One of his men turned to Hunn and started to say: "Wouldn't we hear them by now?"

But suddenly he couldn't be heard anymore. A tremendous noise had washed over them.

The sound of many, many jet engines. The roar of jet fuel being burned and hundreds of tons of metal speeding through the cold air. Many of the Delta guys caught themselves looking up into the clear night sky, as if they would actually find contrails up there.

Then came the sound of bombs. Bigger than the two they'd dropped on Sharif's compound, these bombs made a whistling sound as they fell from a couple miles up. First dozens, then hundreds of them. The sirens in the city suddenly came alive. Antiaircraft fire began to paint the sky. The noise got even louder. By all indications, a B-52 strike was about to rain down on Khrash.

Or at least, that's what it sounded like.

Now Hunn could see the mooks in his NV goggles start looking and pointing skyward, too. They'd heard it, too.

The noise grew to monstrous proportions, earsplitting—but at the same time it was different. Sure, it was so loud. But the ground wasn't moving beneath their feet.

Finally one of the Delta guys cried out.

"Here they come!"

The whole squad looked behind them. But what they saw was not a fleet of B-52 heavy bombers approaching. It was the *Psyclops* plane, going right over their heads, broadcasting the *sounds* of a B-52 strike via their God's Ear external speakers.

On Hunn's signal, every man in the squad applied a piece of cotton to his ears, this as the plane began dispensing incredibly bright flares above the slum. Between the noise and extreme light, it was like the most bombastic fireworks display they'd ever seen, times 10.

"OK, that's our cue!" Hunn screamed. "Let's go!"

The 10 soldiers jumped out of the culvert and began rushing right into the heart of the enemy encampment, weapons blazing.

The Battle of Khrash had begun.

The next two minutes unfolded like a dream for Hunn. It was always like that for him in combat. But this—this was particularly surreal.

They hit the edge of the slum just 10 seconds out of the trench. They were all firing their weapons, from the hip, as they were running, adding even more to the substantial confusion. Because Hunn kept his NV goggles down, to him, it looked like they were running into a green hell.

The Blackhawk helicopter that had dropped them off now reappeared and laid a barrage of .50-caliber machine-gun fire into the first house in a row of buildings. Despite the racket being made by the now-circling *Psyclops* plane, and his blocked ears, Hunn could hear people screaming inside.

He and his men reached the first apartment building a few seconds later. There were many Taliban inside who were trying to jump out of the windows after dodging the copter's bullets and still thinking that B-52 bombs were about to pulverize them. Hunn's guys opened up on them; at least 12 mooks died in this initial fusillade.

Hunn hit the house's front door running. It exploded in a storm of wooden splinters. Two Taliban fighters were in the hallway, bent over, hands covering their ears, trying to block out the horrendous sounds coming from above. Hunn shot both of them in the head.

His men poured into the building after him. They began a split-second clearing operation. The place was full of Taliban, but like the first two, most were in shock or were jumping out the windows. Those who remained were shot, stabbed, and kicked to death. The first and second floors were cleared inside a minute. Somehow a fire had started in the kitchen.

Hunn and his guys headed for the roof. Up here they found another knot of Taliban who, incredibly, were in the process of pouring a barrel of rainwater through a hole in the roof onto the kitchen fire below. Seemingly unaware of what was happening, five of these six men died in a hail of bullets. One was spared intentionally.

The *Psyclops* plane went overhead again, the roar from its loudspeakers now mimicking strings of bombs hitting the ground. The plane was also shooting out an incredible number of flares now. It was as bright as day in the slum. Even through their blocked ears the men of

1st Delta could hear the commotion; without any protection, it was deafening.

Still, Hunn was able to yell down through the hole in the ceiling, telling his men below to verbalize the securing of the building. Five shouts back confirmed the building was clear and under their control. Their Blackhawk helicopter went over again, firing at mooks in the next apartment building over. Suddenly half that structure was on fire. Hunn turned to his guys up on the roof and said: "Get the rope."

They took the surviving Taliban fighter, so frightened he had soiled himself, and pulled a noose over his head. Then they dropped him over the side of the building. His scream pierced the chaos of the night—caught short only by his windpipe collapsing, his neck breaking. He was dead in a second. Then the Delta soldiers unfurled one of the dozens of American flags they'd carried into Khrash and draped it over the still-twitching body.

Then they ran out of the house and back onto the street, this as the Blackhawk resumed firing into the next apartment house they intended to seize.

Hunn stopped for a moment and looked up at the first smoking building, the dead body, and the flag waving above it all.

"That's one . . . ," he said.

No sooner had Rich Kennedy's feet hit the ground when the great blast of light arrived, knocking him on his ass. Two bombs went over his head. One hit the side of the tin and plywood wall approximately fifty feet away from Kennedy's current location, obliterating a fifty-foot section of it. The second bomb landed somewhere on the other side.

It began raining dirt and pebbles and flaming debris. Huddled beneath this cloud of sparks, Kennedy, another original member of the team, and nine other Delta operators kept their noses in the ground. For the night, they were 2nd Delta. They'd just been dropped off by one of the team's other Blackhawks; the aircraft was climbing above them somewhere, vanishing into the dark.

Ryder's F-14 streaked overhead a moment later. It had dropped the pair of five-hundred-pound bombs, one on a section of Khrash's wall identified in the plan as Weak Point North, the other into a neighborhood a few feet beyond. His F-14 was so low, Kennedy and his men could actually feel the heat of its exhaust as it passed over them. At the moment, it was the best feeling in the world.

Ryder's Bombcat went right through the fireball it had created, adding a burst of nose cannon shells to the fiery chaos. Then it stood on its tail, went completely over, and disappeared to the west. All this happened in about five seconds.

Through the newly created hole in the wall Kennedy saw streets of whitewashed buildings with neatly packed dirt sidewalks, and even a few trees lining the roadway.

This was Khrash's Old Quarter, the ancient part of town. Because of Ryder's dead-on one-two punch, though, the wall had been breached and the first block of buildings had been leveled. This is what usually happened to something on the wrong end of a five-hundred-pound bomb.

While this was going on, the noise being generated by the *Psyclops* plane was also washing over them. The bizarre-looking plane was now circling directly above. They were well hidden in a berm not a stone's throw

away from the blasted-out wall. Still they were finding it
just about impossible not to keep their heads in the
ground when their ears were telling them that tons of
explosives were dropping all around them. It sounded
that real.

Still, Kennedy managed to get all of their attention.

"Bayonets, on?" he yelled to his men.

They replied, as one, with a massive grunt.

"Cotton, in?"

Each man put the cotton pieces in his ears. Now raising their hands meant they were ready.

"OK!" Kennedy screamed, trying to yell loud enough
for them to hear him. "Let's rock and roll!"

A second later they began pouring through the hole
in the wall.

At the same moment, their guardian angel Blackhawk went into action. Moving incredibly fast, it threw
a few missiles into the buildings just ahead of 2nd Delta,
then peeled off and opened up with its nose-mounted
cannons on other buildings farther up the street.

While the copter was here to cover Kennedy's attack
team, its primary job was to clear the nearby rooftops of
the city religious police. Many of them were stationed
up here by way of their chief's defense plan. But they'd
been expecting to shoot their RPGs at American helicopters that were either moving slow or even stopped in
a hover. They weren't prepared to shoot at helicopters
going very fast, with missiles firing and soldiers stuffed
into the open cargo bay shooting back at them.

Kennedy's men could almost feel the panic in the air
as the Islamic fighters realized that with the sounds of
huge B-52 bombs falling all around them, the blinding
flash of the flares, real bombs hitting buildings around

them, and streets that suddenly seemed to be filled with hundreds of Americans—well, a rooftop was just not the place to be.

But whenever the fighters would flee a building, inevitably the Blackhawk would be waiting for them, shooting them down as they came out. Inside a minute, the streets in this part of the Old Quarter began filling up with bodies.

Kennedy's men pressed on. In the air were even more sounds now. Explosions, people shouting. People killing. People getting killed. The real sound track of war.

They went house to house, arriving just moments after the speeding copter had strafed it. They found religious policemen trying to jump out windows or cowering in closets or corners. All of them met the bullets of Kennedy's guys coming in. Loki Soto had been perfect training for this. Fighting in confined spaces was now another specialty of the Ghosts' Delta members. In less than five minutes they'd cleared five buildings and claimed them by displaying their American flags and hanging a mook or two.

There were no heroes among the religious police who managed to escape all this.

They began fleeing for their lives.

Finally 2nd Delta reached the area where the three-hundred-year old Eastern Moon Mosque had once stood. They couldn't believe what they saw. Even in the midst of the chaos and confusion, with the *Psyclops* plane roaring overhead and the Blackhawk helicopter flitting back and forth and the sound of the two F-14s up there somewhere as well, Kennedy's men found themselves stopped in their tracks, awestruck by the destruction caused by the bombing of the Muslim temple.

It was utter devastation for six blocks. Many buildings flattened. A few still on fire. A huge smoking hole in the ground where the former holy place had been. It really did look like a small atom bomb had hit it. No wonder resistance in the Old Quarter was scattered at best.

Kennedy got his men moving again; he had to. This operation wasn't so much about seizing and holding territory as it was about scaring the hell out of the mooks and getting them to retreat in disarray toward the western part of the city.

Delta took over another series of buildings on the other side of the blast zone, all of them abandoned by fleeing mooks. Kennedy was able to look back and see more than a dozen American flags fluttering in the breeze now. What's more, about a quarter-mile away to the east he could see more buildings with more flags flying above them. This was Hunn and 1st Delta doing their work in the Taliban slum.

So far, so good, Kennedy thought.

Then he and his men turned the next corner and found themselves at the first intersection they'd come to. That's when a rain of shells and bullets came down on them from every direction.

In seconds they were pinned down.

Kennedy kept his cool. This wasn't totally unexpected. He made sure his men were under good cover; then he took out his flare gun and fired two large green flares into the air.

That was the signal.

They needed a tank up here.

The DSA officer named Ozzi was leading the third attack squad.

Unlike the first two, which were made up of Delta operators, Ozzi's team, designated 3rd IF, for Irregular Forces, was comprised entirely of Zabul tribesmen. They'd been dropped about a quarter-mile south of Hunn's position, more than 20 Zabul, plus Ozzi, crammed inside the third Blackhawk helicopter.

Their objective was to clear a four-block area known as Kuhada Circle. It was a lightly populated area of Khrash, but there were several utilities' centers here, including the city's electrical power plant, its waterworks, and the telephone exchange. Destroying them would mean lights-out for the city, with no water to fight fire and no phones to call for help, demoralizing aspects for the people living here. It was the art of psychological warfare again. No matter what was happening in combat, it always seemed twice as bad if it was happening in the dark. The confusion the Americans were sowing now, in the opening minutes of the attack, would only be compounded when the lights went out. And the whole idea was to keep that confusion up for as long as possible.

But Ozzi's squad also had a secondary mission down here. Utilities used underground tunnels, and tunnels offered perfect hiding places to set up ambushes. Gunmen could pop up through a manhole, fire away, and then disappear again. Many of the city's utility tunnels began and ended here at Kuhada Circle. If the mooks were going to use them for dirty work, they'd probably try to either enter the tunnels here or use them as their means of escape.

Taking out the utility buildings could have been done by an air strike. But because the manhole covers were scattered all over the circle, it would have been almost

impossible for aerial bombs to get them all. That's why
Ozzi's 1st IF was sent in.

Ozzi was armed with his short-stock M16; his
Afghani allies were carrying AK-47s. The Zabul elders,
the cousin of Tarik Aboo had assured them, were the
tribe's equivalent of Special Forces; that's why Ozzi
would be the only Ghost Team member accompanying
them. It seemed like a good match. He could speak a
little Arabic—not a year ago he was a systems analyst
sitting in the smallest office in the Pentagon—and a
couple of the Zabul fighters could speak English. Before jumping off, they'd also agreed on hand signals to
be used in combat.

They blew up a half-dozen manholes in the first two
minutes. It didn't have to be pretty: Two hand grenades
down the spout usually did it, as the tunnels were old
and for the most part were made of dirt. A few times his
fighters wanted to go down into the tunnels and look for
the defenders of Khrash, but each time Ozzi managed to
diplomatically talk them out of it. There really was no
need to be tunnel rats here, like in 'Nam. All they had to
do was seal the tunnels from this end. That might be
enough to trap a whole lot of mooks inside.

Another ten manholes were taken out before they
reached Kuhada Circle itself. The first building they
faced was the waterworks. It was a two-story squarish
structure; built of typical red bricks, it looked like something built in the nineteenth century. It was unoccupied.
There was a massive pipe and a huge control wheel running right next to the building. It seemed as simple an
act as turning this wheel would shut off all water in the
city. Ozzi instructed his Zabul friends to prepare four

explosive charges. Two would go on the pipe; two would go beside the building itself.

It took five minutes of skulking around, wrapping sticks of dynamite and laying fuse wire, but the building and the water pipe went up in a grand explosion. The *Psyclops* plane flew overhead just as the four blasts were going off and had to bank violently to the right to avoid getting caught in the fireball. Ozzi watched the plane go over, nearly lose its flight envelope, and then recover again, only to fly away. He didn't know whether to laugh or cry. Through the whole thing, the plane had continued broadcasting the earsplitting mimicry of a huge B-52 raid.

The telephone exchange building was just a few hundred feet on the opposite side of the circle. It was surrounded by a forest of telephone poles and wires. This, too, looked simple. Take out the poles, the poles rip down the telephone lines. End of phone service in Khrash.

Ozzi signaled for more explosives. The blast packs were prepared; Ozzi and the Zabul CO hustled them over themselves. Stretch out the fuse wire, connect the battery, and *bang!* The poles went down like redwoods, causing a series of miniexplosions on top of each pole leading right up into the city. It was like a string of firecrackers going off.

This brought a great cheer from his Zabul friends. The CO said to Ozzi: "Whole city. Busy signal now. . . ."

"Exactly," Ozzi replied.

Two down, one to go.

They regrouped and made their way toward the last major building in the circle, the Khrash Electric Plant.

They were ready to give it the same treatment when suddenly long streams of tracer bullets cut through the chaotic night. Ozzi and the Zabul hit the dirt immediately. The stream of gunfire was not aimed at them. Rather, it was going across a marsh—and right into the neighborhood fifteen hundred feet away where Ozzi knew Hunn and his men were doing their thing.

Damn. . . .

Ozzi didn't even think about it. He crawled as close as he could to the electric building and clicked down his NVG gear. The building was a three-story clay structure, almost tent shaped, surrounded by gaggles of wires and transmission poles. The strange thing was, Ozzi could see people moving around inside the building— carrying candles. *Candles?* he thought. *In an electric plant?*

It was obvious these people could see and hear Hunn's assault about a quarter-mile away. There was a .50 caliber machine gun set up on the third floor of the electric plant—it was the one doing all the firing. But Ozzi also observed other mooks setting up more weapons on the first and second floors. These firing positions were also aiming at Hunn's attack.

This was all Ozzi had to see. He told the Zabul to stay in place and keep low. Then he pulled out the other weapon he was carrying in addition to his M16. It was a 25.4mm Czech-built naval-load flare gun.

He loaded one of his huge cartridges into the gun, aimed, and pulled the trigger. The cartridge exploded from the barrel, rode a short arc, and landed practically on the back door of the electric plant building. Everyone inside the building saw the bright green glare, and after much rushing about, a number of those weapons previously pointing north at Hunn were now pointing at Ozzi and his troop.

The mooks quickly opened fire on them, but Ozzi kept shouting to his guys to stay down, stay cool, and hold their fire. And they waited. Thirty long seconds while the flare burned and the men in the power plant continued shooting at them.

Then came the noise they'd been waiting for. The rumble of rotor blades, the high whine of its supercharged engines.

It was one of the three Blackhawk helicopters. And it came in shooting.

One of the precious Hellfire missiles went right over Ozzi's head. It went through the back door of the power plant and detonated somewhere inside. The building went up like it was made of matchsticks. A huge ball of flame, followed by a tremendous explosion. Ozzi yelled for his guys to still keep their heads down, as they were soon pummeled by a rain of flaming debris.

The helicopter banked hard, came back around, and opened up with its forward-pointing cannons. They tore into the rubble for five long seconds before the copter once again pulled up hard and then fluttered away into the night.

Ozzi then stood up and yelled, "Let's go!" The Zabul leaped from their positions and charged the power plant, guns blazing.

Their attack was ferocious and loud, as it was supposed to be. But it lasted only as long as it took Ozzi and his men to reach the building. When the smoke cleared, they realized there was nothing left of it but a pile of sizzling rubble.

Ozzi yelled to the Zabul to stop firing. The destruction of the power plant was so complete, there was no way anyone inside could have survived.

Ozzi turned to his two lieutenants and shook hands with them.

"Get the flag," he told them. "That was easy."

Ryder had 8 bombs left.

He'd taken off from Obo with 12 under his wings. Two of them helped Kennedy's guys get into the Old Quarter. One had hit a blockhouse on the edge of the same neighborhood—a place Murphy had tagged as a police interrogation headquarters. Another smashed into an ancient bell tower, just a few blocks from the center of the city. There must have been more than bells inside, though, as it went up like a box of matches.

All this happened during his first 5 minutes over Khrash. Now the battle was nearly 10 minutes old and already approaching a sort of critical mass. Ryder had spent the last few minutes buzzing the city, holding on to his bombs until needed and using his cannon sparingly. At the moment, his part of the plan called for him to fly low and create as much noise as possible to add to the substantial commotion the *Psyclops* plane was already making. He would do this by climbing very high over the city, then putting the Bombcat into a heart-stopping dive, kicking in the afterburner and breaking the sound barrier on his way down. Each time he did this, he had to use all his muscles to pull the plane back to level, rocketing over the center of the city, usually cracking the sound barrier once again. The pair of sonic booms, traveling at approximately the same speed, arrived at approximately the same time, shaking the ancient city right down to its last bloody nail.

At one point, he flew in formation with the strange *Psyclops* plane, going right over the center of the city and watching the mooks scatter below. But what the EC-130 was putting out over its loudspeakers was so intense, Ryder found the sound waves actually rattling the rivets in his beat-up F-14. It got so bad, he had to peel off and get away from the racket.

He then returned to his own buzzing spree, on several occasions flying down the wider streets of the dirty little city no more than 50 feet off the ground. He was flying so low, some unusually brave mooks still stuck up on the roofs by the Chief's defense plan were *shooting down* at him.

So far it seemed that the Americans' plan was working. The confusion throughout the city was huge. Traffic jams, people running through the streets, antiaircraft fire being shot off wildly, causing tons of spent shells to fall back onto the city and sometimes onto the gunners who had just fired them. It was all so persuasive Ryder himself had to resist the temptation to glance upward every once in a while just to make sure a flight of B-52s wasn't up there somewhere.

He could see many fires below him, much smoke, and a real beautiful sight: many small American flags flying from buildings in the eastern part of the city. The flags were Murphy's idea, and it was a good one. It looked like a wave of America's red, white, and blue was slowly engulfing the city.

So this was how they were going to do it. What was

the best way to get Jabal Ben-Wabi? By killing every mook in Khrash and hoping he was among them.

They still had a way to go, though. And it was inevitable that someone in Khrash would figure out that a massive bombing raid wasn't coming. What would happen then was anyone's guess. But so far, so good.

All of this excitement was doing something else, too. It was preventing Ryder from thinking about the Ghosts of Li and his wife, and all the personal stuff that had been tearing him apart ever since this mission began. It was all still there. All the flying and strafing and buzzing and bombing was just a diversion from these disturbing thoughts. And like everything that was repressed, he knew he'd have to deal with it sooner or later. But in this case, it would be preferably later.

It was on one of his buzzing runs that Ryder noticed somehow a flash of light out of the corner of his eye. It wasn't coming for a weapon of any kind. It was more like the light for an acetylene torch.

The strange part was that he'd spotted it in the southern part of the city, a place where absolutely nothing was happening at the moment. No fighting, no confusion. Nothing.

Very weird.

He swung out extra wide this time and rocketed over where he'd spotted the light. It was actually coming from an unblocked window in one warehouse that sat among a sea of warehouses.

It was strictly on instinct or maybe a whim, but he turned again and laid one of the five-hundred-pound bombs right through the window of the place. It went up like a fireworks factory. In seconds a huge fireball was rising in the sky above the southern part of the city.

"Damn," he whispered to himself. "I wonder what that was?"

There were a dozen intersections leading to the center of Khrash. Crowded with shops, bazaars, and apartment buildings, these crowded crossroads possibly made the most perfect defensive position an army could want in an urban combat setting.

By their very nature, intersections offered fields of interlocking fire. Two weapons were all that was needed to cover four streets. Double that number, with a gun at every corner, and passing in any direction became impossible. Plus, an observer stationed in any building on the four corners could see attackers approaching from any of four directions.

There was a particularly wide intersection in the Old Quarter, just down from where the Eastern Moon Mosque had been destroyed. At the moment, this intersection was bristling with weapons; many of the fighters that Kennedy's 2nd Delta had chased out of the mosque's neighborhood had regrouped here, and indeed they had set up heavy weapons on every corner.

That's why Kennedy had signaled for the strike force's one and only pair of tanks. Within five minutes of his making the call, the two T-72 monsters smashed through the wadi and came rumbling through the hole in the Old Quarter's wall.

Both were now heading for the intersection.

The man they called the Chief was sweating bullets. He, too, was at the intersection, huddled behind some of the flimsiest barricades imaginable, several dozen of his fighters on hand and psyched that he was in their midst.

This was no place for him to be, though. He was much too important to actually *see* combat. Never mind risking getting wounded—or worse.

Yet here he was . . . and not by choice.

After he'd recovered from the surprise of the air raid by the two Bombcats earlier in the evening, the first place the Chief wanted to go was the area around the Eastern Moon Mosque. All indications were that the holy building might have been one of their targets, and he had to see for himself the destruction the two shit-box airplanes had caused, if any. There was so much equipment, ammunition, and rifles stored inside the mosque that if the building was damaged, which at first he'd doubted, his intention was to gather as many of his men in that area as possible and recover anything of value they could find. Up to that point he, too, had been fooled into thinking the Americans would never directly bomb a mosque.

It had been a grave mistake, for once he arrived on the scene, he saw that not only was the mosque and everything in it gone, but the six blocks of houses and several secondary weapons storage places around it were gone, too. The Chief couldn't believe it.

Moments later, he found himself talking to lieutenants he'd sent out to check on the city's other two mosques and realized the news was the same. Both had been demolished as well, as had their neighborhoods, and everything within was lost. Just like that, more than half the city's storage of weapons and ammunition and explosives and fuel was gone. *Ballsy* was the American word for it. *Insane* was what the Chief thought of it. But it was the first time the Chief thought that maybe Jabal Ben-Wabi had a reason to pee his pants anytime the no-tion of the Crazy Americans was brought up.

This did not deter the Chief, though. Not completely, anyway. There was still a fight to be had here—and it would best be coordinated back at the Holy Towers. That's why after hearing that all three mosques had been destroyed, the Chief ordered his bodyguards to get him back to his main headquarters right away.

And this they were doing, preparing to rush him back, when they first heard the sounds of B-52s dropping bombs.

The Chief's convoy made it exactly a half-block when he ordered his driver to stop and took cover along with everyone else. The distinct racket made by B-52 engines and their bombs was known to anyone who'd fought with the Taliban. They knew the only hope of survival was to get down at the first sound of a bomb whistling through the air and stay there until the mighty airplanes passed over or blew you to bits.

So they hid in a tea shop. Huddled on the floor, hands pressed against their ears, the Chief and his bodyguards waited for the final blow. When it did not come, though the racket and chaotic sounds of a massive air raid continued, they crawled back out onto the street, saw the light glowing from the eastern edge of town, and assumed the Strato-fortresses had dumped their loads over there first. Which meant that they would be back, usually very, very soon.

Again the Chief wanted to convoy back to the Holy Towers, but no sooner had he and his bodyguards started out a second time when they heard two more tremendous explosions in their vicinity. Looking just down the street, they saw a huge hole had been blown in the Old Quarter's wall not 200 yards away and that sev-

eral more buildings had been blown away even closer to
their position.

Again they thought these were bombs from B-52s—
it was only when one of the ugly jet fighters that had
leveled the mosque suddenly streaked over their heads
that they realized that at least one of the mosque
bombers was back and that it had just delivered the one-
two blow a few blocks away.

Seconds later they saw the black-uniformed soldiers
start pouring through the hole in the wall. Not the Chief
nor any of his men stayed around long enough to count
exactly how many Americans were rushing through the
breach. Instead, they finally got aboard their vehicles
and squealed away in retreat.

But for a third time, they didn't get very far. They
reached the intersection a few blocks up from where the
mosque used to be and found it crowded with religious
fighters fleeing what they perceived to be a massive
American ground attack through the hole in the wall.
Explosions, jets in the air, the *chop-chop* of helicopters
added in. The sounds of their comrades being slaughtered just down the street only confirmed the reason for
their alarm.

In fact, there were so many fighters and their vehicles
in the intersection, there was no way the Chief and his
convoy were going to be able to get through.

Believing that the center of town may have been pul-
verized anyway, and due to the fact that when his fighters saw him they started shouting for joy because they
knew he would know what to do in their sudden crisis,
the Chief realized reluctantly that he had to make some
kind of a stand here—at the first intersection.

But what he really wanted to do first was get to a bell and start ringing it—so his Taliban and Al Qaeda brothers would know enough to join the fight. If that message didn't get out soon, he knew, they were looking at a catastrophe.

His cell phone was dead, killed by electronic interference. So he tried a phone in one of the shops bordering the intersection. He was calling his cadre back at the Holy Towers, located about a half-mile from his current position. If he could get through and the buildings were still standing, someone there would be able to start the bells ringing and get the reinforcements in gear.

But just as someone at the headquarters was picking up the phone, the line suddenly went dead, At almost the exact same time, they all heard another huge explosion go off to the east, in the vicinity of Kuhada Circle, the Chief knew.

It had been at that precise moment that Ozzi had blown up the city's telephone exchange, mere seconds before the Chief would have been able to put out the all-points signal to immediately bring hundreds of Al Qaeda and Taliban fighters into the fray.

It had been that close.

Once the Chief realized he was stuck here, at the intersection, he dug down into his bag of tricks. Obviously the Americans weren't coming the way he thought they would. There would be no Mogadishu here. So he screamed at his men to start erecting barriers across the west-facing street, the road that eventually led to the center of town—but he also ordered them that they should erect these barriers of the flimsiest materials they could find.

Then they were to fire at the soldiers accompanying the tanks for just about thirty seconds. Then they were to allow the tanks to bust through the barriers. . . .

It seemed like a suicidal order, allowing the tanks to essentially roll over them, but again, the Chief had fought in the streets before.

This was combat and there really was such a thing as the fog of war. Things happened fast but always seemed to the participants to be moving very slowly. There was also the tendency especially of tank commanders to run over or break through anything standing in their way. Now these two T-72s were heading for the intersection, their orders no doubt were to clear it of the Chief's fighters.

This was a piece of his own brand of psychological warfare. Why would the Chief instruct his men to erect barricades the flimsier the better? Because he wanted to actually *encourage* the armored vehicles to smash through them, which was their natural tendency to do. Doing so was a critical mistake, though, because once the tank hit the barricade, his fighters would simply let it go past them—then they would attack it from the rear. The key to this deceit was that no way could a tank turret turn fast enough to fire backward at these attackers. Two or three well-placed RPGs could disable just about any tank from the rear, thus trapping it in the middle of a swarm of fighters. When the crew sought to escape their burning tank, they could be slaughtered almost at leisure. When the Chief fought in Chechnya, this odd strategy had worked every time.

The tanks were now within five hundred feet of the intersection. The first in line fired one round as it was building up speed. The round landed not six feet in front of the first barricade. Curiously, it was not an explosive charge but actually a smoke round. It ignited on impact, and within seconds the entire intersection was obscured by thick white smoke.

The Chief's men ceased firing on cue and fell back, disappearing behind the barricades as ordered. The Chief knew what was going to happen next. The tank would burst through the intentionally weak barriers, apparently triumphant. But then his fighters hiding nearby would emerge quickly and attack the tank from the rear. That was the trick.

Sure enough, the first tank went through the barricade with ease—just as the Chief wanted it. The smoke obscuring the scene made it hard to get a complete handle on it, but very quickly the bravest of his men ran out and prepared to fire their RPGs at the tank's vulnerable hindquarters. But just after the second tank went through, a sudden storm of tracer fire erupted, coming from many directions, bullets pinging and bouncing off things everywhere. A moment after that, the worst of the smoke bomb blew away . . . and finally the Chief and his bodyguards, under cover about fifty feet away, could see what was happening. Both tanks had indeed burst through the barriers. But they had done so with their turrets *already* turned backward. The two machine guns on the top of the swivel as well as the huge tank gun itself opened up in a fantastic display of pyrotechnics and fiery lead.

The Chief saw thirty, forty of his fighters cut down before his eyes. The brutality was incredible. Tank shells exploding and simply vaporizing five or six of his best men at a time. The others chopped in half by the huge .50-caliber rounds. It was unexpected and it was madness. The Americans knew the trick. They had beaten the Chief at his own game. He came very close to peeing his pants.

As this, he got up, turned on his heel, and started running as fast as he could in the opposite direction.

Behind him, all his bodyguards and most of his remaining fighters were doing the same thing.

Curry had watched all the action from afar. He was still carrying all his bombs; his cannon was still fully loaded. He was loitering over the western edge of Khrash, across the Farāh River, above the small slice of Afghanistan that quickly turned into Iran after one went over a steep two-lane mountain pass.

He was cruising at five thousand feet, barely making 150 mph, close to stall speed for an F-14 in flight. He was going in circles, trying to save fuel. When he put his NV goggles down he could clearly see what was happening over Khrash. Copters buzzing around, providing air support for the ground troops when needed, hitting targets of opportunity whenever possible. Above them, the *Psyclops* plane flying in even larger circles than he was, broadcasting both the sounds of a horrific land battle and noises mimicking a second B-52 raid.

And every once in a while he caught glimpses of Ryder doing his sonic-boom nosedives. Curry had wondered more than once whether Ryder was just brave or committed or, maybe, was a candidate for *being* committed. On the other hand, though he knew Ryder well, Curry had not walked a mile in his shoes. So it was not his place to judge. But the way the guy was flying and acting and bringing it to the mooks, scaring them to death as opposed to blowing them up, simply put, Curry had never seen anyone fly like that—even in the best of weather, during the daytime. Doing it at night, in very smoky skies, with antiaircraft fire all around him, the guy was flirting with disaster. But maybe that's exactly what he wanted to do.

These thoughts were suddenly distracted by a glint of light below, picked up by Curry's NV goggles. It turned out to be a single headlight, the only one working on a small red truck that had just pulled onto the Farāh River bridge from Highway 212 and was now making its way across.

It was exactly what Curry was looking for.

The red truck was actually the first of three. Curry sank a little lower, down to twenty-five hundred feet. Thanks to the NV goggles he could see each vehicle had at least six people jammed into it. Each vehicle also had bags or satchels tied to the roof or stuffed in the back.

Curry clenched his fist in triumph. This was the best thing he could have ever seen. It meant that their plan was probably working. Not only was it clear these people were making a hasty retreat out of Khrash and across to Iran, but he also could tell by the fact that they had motor vehicles that they were probably Al Qaeda types. And they weren't staying to fight.

Because there were only a few dozen of them, the Ghosts' bold idea was to create enough confusion and panic within Khrash that any Islamic fighters reluctant to meet Allah this particular day would naturally start moving west, get on the bridge, and get out of town. These three were trying it. And Curry knew there would probably be more to come.

Now flying too high to be heard over the commotion over the city, he waited for the three small trucks to get to the opposite end of the bridge. Then he swooped down and with very economical bursts from his nose cannon blew them off the road.

Then he went back up high again—into the smoke and darkness—and waited for his next victims to show up.

Nothing was routine in combat. But what Dave Hunn and the guys in 1st Delta squad had been doing for the past twenty minutes came very close.

They'd moved steadily out from their jump-off point, Weak Point East, and been methodically chasing the city's religious police fighters and leftover Taliban out of their slummy buildings, pushing them west, toward the center of town and ultimately the Farāh River.

They had already cleared three blocks beyond the slum, this after being on the ground not even 30 minutes. What they were doing quickly fell into a pattern. They came to a building and more often than not, especially in the past 15 minutes, these buildings were either empty or holding a few die-hards or mooks wounded and left behind by their comrades. If that was the case, instead of wasting time and going inside, Delta would riddle the structure with their heavy weapons, hurl in a few hand grenades, or fire an enemy RPG they had captured during their miniblitzkrieg. There would be explosions, bright flashes of light, and a minor quaking of the earth; sometimes part of the building would come down. The Delta guys would spray the rubble with gunfire and pepper it with more grenades. No screams from those trapped under the tons of rock would confirm that the leftover bad guys had been killed. Delta would then mark the building by planting an American flag somewhere nearby and move on. If they thought there were still people alive and unbroken beneath the rubble, they would leave the house unmarked—as a signal, for those following in their path.

This was the second wave, coming in behind 1st Delta, made up entirely of the Zabul tribe foot soldiers, essentially mountain men with weapons. Their role was nasty but necessary. They would come to a house that wasn't flying an American flag. They would first yell into the house, "Akbah! Salama-La-kin?" Roughly translated: "Brothers! How are you?"

If they received any reply, they would douse the rubble with something flammable and set it ablaze, finishing off those Muslim fighters still alive inside. Once the screams died down, then the Zabul would raise an American flag. And then they, too, would move on.

And coming right behind them was a third wave of invaders: hundreds of regular Zabul villagers who had created a small army of organized looters and were now spread over the liberated part of Khrash, robbing the bodies of the dead.

When Hunn and company did come upon a house that held a lot of living, breathing mooks, the ones that actually shot back at them, they would attack it full force. Heavy weapons, grenades, kick the door down, and go in blazing. They found bad guys everywhere in these buildings. They were in the closets, in the bedrooms, hiding in the ceiling. They were so crazy, so fanatical, or so doped up on qat, they would frequently reveal themselves too early by letting out a tongue-lapping scream and plunging at the invading Americans with their fists or knives, their heavier weapon unprepared. At such close-range fighting, the Delta guys used their bayonets more than their triggers. The larger, better-trained, stone-cold sober Americans won every battle, causing the wooden and clay floors to run thick with blood.

On the particularly hard-fought structures, the Delta guys would keep one mook alive, bring him to the roof, hang him over the side, and then raise the American flag themselves. Anytime the guys in 1st Delta looked behind them, all they saw was flames and smoke and dozens of American flags, whipping in the breeze.

Only when they got to a really hard target would they call in one of the choppers. Two flares would usually bring one calling; another flare shot at the target would bring the wrath of Hellfires or nose cannons. On those occasions, there was rarely anything to hang a flag on or a mook from, not after the copter was done with it.

By the 30-minute mark, 1st Delta had cleared eight blocks and sent dozens of Islamic fighters running. Just how far they would run before they realized this was really a grand hoax—or at least the B-52 strike was—no one knew. The hope was they'd keep running right into the river.

They left a large residential part of town and came to one that was more industrial. A bunch of repair shops, opium-processing plants, and gas stations. They took a few incoming rounds, but when the entire squad fired back en masse, on this strange night, that was usually enough to scatter whoever was shooting at them.

Hunn and his guys began the clearing process. No one was home in the repair shops or the gas stations. Just before they busted their way into the opium factory, the *Psyclops* plane flew over again; it was now simulating the sounds of a great land battle, explosions, the noise of tanks moving, and lots of gunfire. Even the Delta guys found themselves ducking; that's how real it sounded.

They cleared the opium business, set fire to the bins of poppies, and as a joke each trooper took a long, deep, noisy sniff of the resulting smoke.

Then Hunn and three other troopers went out the back door and it was here that they found the propane tank.

It was probably used in the poppy processing, Hunn theorized to his men. A lot of heat was needed to get the weeds to turn into the product from which they would eventually make heroin, slated for Europe's streets. Propane burned high. The tank looked to hold several hundred gallons. But when Hunn knocked on the side of it, it seemed empty.

This was a slight problem. Hunn just couldn't leave this thing sitting here, empty or not. Even if it contained just a few vapors, as he suspected, it was too much potential explosive material to leave in their wake—and God only knew what the follow-up Zabul troops would do with it.

So Hunn, never shy to make a little noise, took matters into his own hands.

He had his men step back about twenty feet. The tank was now about fifty feet away. Hunn raised his weapon, and before his men could say anything he fired a burst from his M16 directly into the tank.

That's when he discovered that the tank, as it was under pressure, was not empty but actually full.

Hunn saw the bright white light first. He never heard the sound, never really saw the flames. It was just the bright white light and the sensation that he was floating through the air. His first thought was one of amazement: *I must be dead. . . .*

Actually he was flying through the air—and three of his troops were up here with him. The force of the blast literally blew them right out of the alley and onto a major thoroughfare, nearly a half-block away.

One of his men crashed through the window of a scarf shop, landing out in the sidewalk. Two more came down on top of a *kaffee* cart. Hunn himself, all 250 pounds of him, just missed smashing into a wrecked and burning car and came down in a relatively soft mud hole instead.

He landed facedown, the bright white light replaced by the very dark brown mud. He sat up immediately. He couldn't believe he was still alive. More incredibly, the other three troopers thrown by the explosion were alive and unhurt, too.

The rest of his men came barreling around the corner moments later. They helped Hunn back to his feet and checked the three others. Cuts and bruises were the worst of their injuries.

Meanwhile, the repair shop, the gas station, and the opium factory were all now reduced to flaming embers, this as the small mushroom cloud the propane explosion had created was still going straight up into the night sky. One of the copter pilots flew over, more curious than anything else. Its rotor blades neatly cut the mushroom in half. Every window within a quarter mile had burst in the explosion.

Except those in the storefront next to the mud puddle Hunn had found himself in. Once he cleared the crap from his eyes, he took a long look into this shop and realized that they had just hit pay dirt.

It was a store that sold cell phones.

Hunn immediately led four men into the store. The one thing the American strike team lacked was communications with one another. In that respect, they had hit a gold mine—or so they had thought.

They found the clerk cowering behind the counter of the very cluttered store. The Americans looked down at him. He was shaking all over.

"Where are all the fucking phones?" Hunn screamed at him in English.

The man looked up at him in terror. "No more! No more!" he screamed.

And it seemed true. The shelves were empty, at least of cell phones.

Then, still terrified, the clerk added: "I don't have any videotapes, either. . . ."

Lieutenant Ozzi's attack squad had also made good time.

After leaving the utilities circle, they'd continued on to clear two more blocks of houses, both sides of the street, in just twenty minutes. As before, the opposition had been stiff at first. But whenever Ozzi and his Zabul friends returned fire in volume, those terrorist fighters they didn't kill quickly ran away.

Again, it was hard to believe that just a year before the diminutive Ozzi was riding a desk in the basement of the Pentagon. He'd never received any combat training beyond what was needed to qualify for his commission at Annapolis. But being a part of the Ghost Team was training enough. It was like going through Parris Island, Airborne training, and survival school all at once. He had such faith in Murphy, this didn't seem so strange for him to be doing. And luckily, the Afghani fighters he was leading were brave and hard fighters. At least, they weren't running in the other direction any time an explosion went off.

Ozzi and his team continued moving, way beyond what the plan called for. They eventually reached a large deserted intersection, a broad meeting of roadways. On one corner sat a good-sized building that had once been a hotel. There was an enemy machine-gun position sticking out of a building on the opposite corner. The gunners were inexperienced, sending off a few bursts as soon as Ozzi's team came around the corner.

This was probably the worst thing to do. Ozzi's guys took cover, and Ozzi fired the flare gun in the general direction of the gun position. The green phosphorescent light was like a siren. Suddenly one of the F-14s swooped down from nowhere and laid a five-hundred-pound bomb right on top of the machine-gun nest and then streaked away. The bomb blew not just the gun but the entire building sky-high, setting off a number of secondary explosions farther down the block.

Ozzi's guys immediately ran across the street and into the entrance of the hotel. The rush of the battle was flowing through them like hard liquor now. It was chaos, but it was also combat and, as always, everything, though happening fast, was actually unfolding in slow motion for them. The adrenaline rush, plus the complete lack of casualties among Ozzi's team, had him feeling higher than a kite.

That's when he stepped in the front door and found the bodies, and he felt everything drain out of him.

There were eight of them. Women and children, they'd all had their hands bound and their throats slit. They must have been stopped trying to escape in the opening minutes of the attack and executed by the city's religious police. Whatever happened, their deaths served no military value. It was just murder, plain and simple.

Ozzi was furious—and his Zabul allies stunned. No sooner had they tripped over the corpses when they started taking fire from the second floor of the hotel lobby. A spiral staircase led to this second level. There were about a half-dozen terrorist fighters up there, firing down on them.

Even though the bullets were splattering all around them, Ozzi let out a scream, something in the approximation of, "Let's go!," to his Zabul squad and up the stairs he went, firing his M16 wildly in front of him.

He took the steps two at a time, dodging bullets, screaming to his men behind him, suddenly reenergized with adrenaline and rage. The mooks were shooting down at him, even throwing Molotov cocktail–type bombs at him. But this did not slow Ozzi's ascent. He was firing nonstop and screaming at the top of his lungs. He was acting so crazy, the mooks began pulling back, running away from this madman.

Up to the second floor he went. He sprayed the stairs up to the third level with gunfire and continued climbing, still screaming nonsense and in Arabic urging his Zabul fighters onward. A burning bottle of gasoline came down on him, thrown by one of the retreating mooks. It hit Ozzi on the shoulder. He picked it up and threw it back at them, while never losing a step. It exploded above him, nailing two of the fighters. They both went over the railing in flames, screaming all the way down.

Still Ozzi charged on. He shot three more of the retreating mooks in the back. His M16 ran out of ammunition, but this was no problem. He simply shouldered his weapon, picked up an AK-47 dropped by one of the fleeing mooks, and kept on firing, hardly losing a second in the transition. All the while he was shouting at his men to be careful on the stairs, to zigzag, to move around, to not give the enemy a good target.

He reached the third level. Now all that was left was a ladder that led up to the roof. He shot the last mook going up this ladder in the rear end and flanks; he fell backward with a crash, mortally wounded.

Ozzi reached the bottom of the ladder, still yelling at his men. He looked up the hole in the roof and incomprehensibly saw a gas stove coming down at him. He dodged it at the last possible moment, yelling for his men to "*watch out!*" while he fired his gun over his head, in hopes of hitting the people who'd hurled this thing down at him.

Finally he reached the top of the ladder to find the two remaining mooks standing on the edge of the building, holding empty weapons, staring back at him. He didn't hesitate a moment. They didn't need prisoners; plus he was sure these were the people who'd killed the innocents they'd found below.

He put a half-dozen bullets in each of them. Both men pitched off the roof to the street below.

Only then did Ozzi stop to catch his breath and stop his heart from beating out of his chest. Then he turned around to address his men, to give them congratulations

for clearing the building . . . and for the first time realized that he was alone.

No one was behind him. No one was inside the hotel. The charge up the stairs? It had been a one-man
performance.

He started laughing. It was hilarious and absurd at
the same time.

But then he looked over the side of the roof and saw
that the street behind the hotel was filled with terrorist
fighters. Not just on foot but with three pickup trucks
armed with huge 75mm weapons.

Technicals. . . .

He looked over the other side and saw even more
fighters, a small army of them, and they were carrying
heavy machine guns. Behind them, on the next street
over, more trucks, more large weapons. Without knowing it, Ozzi and his men had walked right into a hornet's
nest not of Khrash's religious police but of hardened Al
Qaeda fighters.

Ozzi dashed back to the hole in the roof and looked
down at the third floor. Still he could not see his men—
they'd simply vanished. But he could see, down in the
hotel lobby three floors below, the Al Qaeda fighters
streaming in, carrying their heavy weapons with them.
There was no way Ozzi was going down that way.

In other words, he was surrounded, without much
ammunition, with no flares left and no real idea where
the hell he was.

It was now 0040 hours.

Forty minutes into the battle, Ryder still had six
bombs left. The last one he'd dropped, in support of

Ozzi's attack squad, had been a direct hit. Ryder had followed it up with a strafing attack right through the middle of the city, once again scattering Islamic fighters who had foolishly gathered in the central square, weakly firing up at him as he bore down on them, no more than 50 feet off the ground.

But after this, his latest low-altitude supersonic buzzing run, he put the F-14 on its tail, turned completely over, and found his nose pointing south again.

It was strange—there were now smoke and flames rising over more than half of the city. The Old Quarter was almost completely obscured by the results of the battle as Kennedy's 2nd Delta team continued to clear the ancient neighborhood with help from the Zabul tanks. The fire in the east-side slum that had housed a lot of the Taliban fighters had already burned itself out. The city's utilities centers were still aflame, as was its midsection as the twin prongs of Hunn's and Ozzi's attacks continued marching westward.

But in the southern part of the city, down by all those warehouses, nothing was going on except the fire Ryder himself set off about ten minutes before. This part of the city was almost completely dark. No headlights. No streetlights. No one in the streets at all.

Ryder knew that the relative inactivity in this part of town had baffled Murphy from the beginning. More out of curiosity than anything else, Ryder streaked in that direction again, wondering if he could get another eyeball on the place and find a clue as to why it was so quiet there while the rest of the city was going through a little bit of hell.

First he circled the warehouse he'd set ablaze. The

fire was slowly dying away, and none of the structures on either side of it had been affected. The smoke was still too dense, though, for him to see inside and determine exactly what it was that he had hit. He widened his circle and stayed at about one thousand feet. One thought that came to him was that the city's massive SAM weapon might actually be hidden down here, thus all the secrecy. If that was the case, though, he was certainly providing them with a fat target. Yet he saw nothing that would indicate any kind of SAM activity below. Plus why would a couple dozen blocks of the city be virtually blacked out just to hide one weapon?

Ryder checked his watch. The operation was just 42 minutes old, and so far things seemed to be going well. But there were several more aspects that had to go their way, or the tide could turn very fast. Plus fuel and ammo would soon become a concern for all of them, especially the air assets.

But then again, Ryder did have some extra bombs, one at least that was expendable. Though in a way he knew he was just looking for trouble, he turned the Bombcat over on its back, picked out an anonymous warehouse below, and dived on it.

A flick of his cannon opened a hole in its roof—he could see dim light inside. He released the bomb at about the same time, Stuka-fashion. It slammed into the roof almost where he'd opened the hole. He banked hard right and felt the explosion over his left shoulder. He turned up and out and saw that just like the first warehouse he'd hit, this one had a couple secondary explosions as well, indicating that something within was not just flammable but also explosive. But again, the flames were so intense and the smoke so thick, it was impossible for him to determine exactly what it was he'd hit.

At that moment, he saw two green flares rise up over the central part of the city. Someone needed another five-hundred-pound bomb, probably Kennedy's crew.

Ryder turned in that direction and streaked away, leaving the warehouse to burn behind him.

Somehow the Chief made it back to the middle of the city. He'd run from the carnage at the intersection, commandeering a technical several blocks away. The first thing he did after climbing aboard was ask the driver if the middle of the city was still there, or had it been hit by the B-52s as well?

The driver didn't know, so it was a surprise for both of them that even though they had to drive through a lot of smoke and flames, they found the city square virtually intact. Upon seeing this, the Chief thought the B-52s must have hit the southern part of the city then, down near the warehouses. There was almost a dark amusement about this. How strange would it be if the south end got flattened and the middle of Khrash was saved? Would that mean that Allah had a cosmic sense of humor?

The Chief shook away these thoughts and stuffed another wad of qat into his mouth. If it was a miracle that the city square and the Holy Towers were still standing, then he was going to take advantage of it. But still, it was utter confusion here, in the center of town, with dozens of his fighters running around, shooting in the air, shooting at anything that moved, not hitting anything but one another. Many others were not armed at all.

The Chief knew he'd screwed up thinking that this

was just going to be a smash-and-grab raid for the Americans. He'd also guessed wrong that the Americans would attack at dawn. Obviously the Americans were coming both on the ground and in the air, and not just with helicopters, either. He saw the beat-up jet fighters, too, and above it all heard the terrible noise of the B-52s doing their work.

He jumped out of the technical and ran into the first open shop he could find. He retrieved the owner's AM radio and tried to tune in the three stations that broadcast in Khrash. But two were being blocked out by interference and the third had a man's voice the Chief did not recognize speaking in Arabic, telling people in the countryside to stay away from Khrash, as it was being bombed by the U.S. Air Force *and* was being invaded by the U.S. 4th Army. *Damn,* the Chief thought. Did this mean the whole Crazy Americans thing had been a ruse all along?

Now he had to think. Just before the rout at the intersection, he'd sent out two of his most trusted lieutenants to find the Taliban and Al Qaeda commanders. Their message: that the situation was getting desperate, as if they didn't already know, and that their off-duty fighters were needed. He'd also sent out two more miniconvoys to get to the two other bells in the city and start ringing them like crazy. Ringing the bells would also signal their *jihad* brethren that they needed help.

If and when the bells started ringing or his messages got through, the plan changed from one of protecting against a small attack to one that was an all-out defense of the city. It called for many of the Al Qaeda fighters to flood the area and perform their particular specialty: laying Improvised Explosive Devices along the major streets surrounding the center of the city. These were the hated IEDs, killers of so many American soldiers fighting in Iraq. The Al Qaeda recipe for building an IED was deviously simple: take an unexploded artillery shell, bury it in the dirt of the street, and attach a cell phone as the fusing device. Call the cell phone and the bomb explodes. (That's why there weren't many cell phones to be had in the city, either.)

There was also a piece of the plan that had to do with the main roadway through Khrash. It was a multilane boulevard that was always crowded with dozens of yellow striped taxis. Per the plan, these cabs would be parked very haphazardly all over the road leading into the center of the city. Not only would these cars provide firing spots for ambushes, but many would also hold powerful bombs that could be detonated by the city's defending forces.

The plan also had provisions for some secret weapons. Very low-tech ones. The Chief was to round up several dozen of his lowest police officers and *kardisses* and the Al Qaeda experts would turn them into instant martyrs. Men who would have explosives strapped to their bodies, then be stuffed with qat, given civilian clothes, and released into the battle to detonate themselves as close as possible to the invading troops. Because it would be a waste to give these people real weapons, they were to be given wooden poles with knives attached to them instead.

If the American 4th Army was coming, then these things and more had to be done. But by all indications none of them had happened yet. Even above the roar of the battle, the Chief couldn't hear any bells ringing. Nor had any of his messengers returned after finding the Taliban and Al Qaeda commanders.

This was not good for the *jihad* side.

He finally got to his headquarters, located on the first floor of the second Holy Tower. All of the windows had been shattered by the repeated sonic booms. The furniture had been turned over, and his papers were everywhere. But it made no difference. He was still king of the court.

He sent for all his officers; his bodyguards scrambled about the building to find whoever was left. His arms master was the first one to stumble though the office door. The river-borne shipment of arms and ammunition, at one time destined to simply add to the city's already burgeoning stockpiles, was suddenly very important. The massive arms losses resulting from the Americans' unexpected bombing of the three mosques had left the city on the verge of being defenseless.

Incredibly, the arms master told the Chief that the arms shipment was not only still on, but it had been spotted already coming up the west side of the Farāh River, moving in the shadows of the overhanging trees covering the Iranian side. Rifles, ammunition, RPGs, high explosives, fuel, and one box of videotapes, all courtesy of the Iranian secret police. This was very good news. Heartened again, the Chief told the arms master to do whatever was needed to get those weapons safely ashore.

The arms master departed, but he was not gone two seconds when the assistant police chief bounded in. The Chief told him about the arms shipment, but the assistant remarked that they might have more rifles than people to shoot them. The Chief didn't know what the assistant was talking about at first. Then it dawned on the Chief. Making sure no citizens were leaving the city was one thing—but what would he do if his own fighters started deserting?

That's what the assistant chief was telling him: Many of the Chief's fighters *were* fleeing, toward Iran, some trying to catch rides with Al Qaeda fighters who were also leaving. The Chief was infuriated. The assistant had caught 10 of his policemen trying to leave the city by running across the Habeeb Bridge. He'd had these men gunned down by their own comrades and their bloody bodies left on the span as a warning to others. But there was no indication this act had stemmed the tide.

That's when the Chief knew he had to take matters into his own hands. To his mind now, the most important thing was to get some bells ringing. In some ways, it might be their last hope. And if he couldn't entrust the job of ringing them to someone else, he would have to ring them himself.

As it turned out, the closest bell was right on top of the Holy Tower itself. It was the loudest in the city. Still, the Chief was not sure if it alone would be loud enough to be heard over the commotion caused by the huge American invasion and the seemingly never-ending B-52 strikes.

But he had to give it a try.

He climbed the stairs to the roof, his five bodyguards walking out ahead of him, indicating that it was clear.

The Chief put his hands over his ears before emerging onto the flat surface. He was expecting the noise to be deafening up here. He was also tempted to put his hands over his eyes, because if he didn't, he expected to see more than half the city leveled, the result of the Americans' brutal carpet bombing.

But as it turned out, he didn't have to do either. It wasn't half as noisy up here as he would have thought. In fact, the sound of the wind was the biggest racket. And looking out now over the city from 11 stories up, he was astonished to see that Khrash was still standing. There were many individual fires here and there. And he could see muzzle flashes and hear gunfire down on the streets.

But what looked and seemed and sounded like a massive invasion, massive bombing, and massive rout of his forces on the ground appeared a lot different up here.

Over in the Old Quarter, the place he'd run from, he could clearly see the fighting was still going on. But there were not dozens of tanks roaming the streets of the ancient neighborhood. He counted exactly two. And in the midsection of the city, down near the Taliban slum and the utilities circle, he wasn't looking at a re-creation of the Normandy beachhead, with thousands of troops and guns and vehicles. In fact, he could just barely make out small packs of American soldiers being followed by the accursed Zabul fighters, chasing what seemed to be a tidal wave of his fighters back into the city square and the Farāh River beyond.

What the hell was going on here?

Where was the American 4th Army? Where were the B-52s?

If he had to guess, the Chief would have said he saw

fewer than 30 Americans, maybe a hundred or so Zabul, a couple helicopters, and two jet fighters at the most—and no damage that looked like it might have been caused by the heavy bombers.

Then it hit him. It was a farce. From the ground it looked like a wave of hell was heading their way. From one hundred feet up, nothing of the sort. The Chief clenched his teeth hard. They'd fallen for it; even now he could see streams of his fighters running through the city square and not stopping, so convinced were they that an American horde was right behind them. Instead it was just a handful of magicians and a couple tanks.

They'd been tricked.

Fooled . . .

By the Crazy Americans.

All the more reason that he wanted to ring the bell now. Maybe they could turn this thing around yet.

The Chief had brought a hammer with him. He walked over to the huge very old bell, drew back, and was about to swing at it when . . .

Suddenly the American helicopter arrived. It was so close that the Chief could see the eyes of the pilot and the six gunmen jammed into the open cargo bay looking back at him. They stared at each other like this for what seemed like the longest time. And the americans did look like monsters! Then the Chief saw the patch for the first time actually attached to something other than Harbosi's severed hands. The Chief felt something go *snap!* in his head when he saw it.

Then the men in the helicopter opened up.

Again, there were five bodyguards up here on the roof with him. None of them had seen the copter approach—in fact, they didn't know if it had come up behind them or had being flying at such a low altitude it had risen straight up after spotting them. In any case, the fusillade that came out of the copter was devastating. Four of the Chief's bodyguards were literally torn in half. His fifth guard had his head blown off. The Chief himself felt a great weight hit him at the same time the barrage from the helicopter did. He was thrown on his back, what seemed like molten steel washing over his body.

But somehow he saw the helicopter depart; the men were still shooting at him as it sped away. That's the only reason the Chief knew he was not dead, not yet anyway. He looked down at his chest and saw that he'd been hit not by bullets but by pieces of the bell that had been shattered in the fusillade. It was now in a million fragments—yet somehow he was still in one piece.

And right then and there, the Chief lost it. He felt an ice-cold shiver go up and down his spine and back again. He'd been through combat. He'd murdered innocent people in the name of bloodlust and Allah. He'd seen and felt and smelled and even tasted the worst aspects of war.

But he'd never felt anything like this.

Just like with the Patch, the Crazy Americans were now after *him*. And it was the worst feeling in the world.

He looked out on the city again, this time from a horizontal position, as he could barely move. There were more fires and more smoke and more noise and more gunshots—but suddenly these things weren't forefront in his mind anymore. Suddenly it was his own neck he was thinking about, always a priority but now even more so. They got under your skin; that's what everyone said. First you ignore them. Then you laugh at them. Then you fight them. And then they beat you. *The Crazy Americans.* One close encounter with them was all it took. They got into your bloodstream, and after that it was only a matter of time before they hunted you down and sliced you up.

Who wanted such a horrible way to go?

It was at that moment that the Chief began making plans for his own escape.

Chapter 19

Gil Bates was not looking forward to what came next. He was sitting alone in one of the White Rooms at the bottom of the ship. The video captured from a feed by Al-Qazzaza TV and taken down by accessing the ship's Echelon system had just completed loading onto his hard drive—it contained a zillion megabytes. Once it was done, he would have to watch the beheading of Li Cho, one of the bravest, most beautiful women he'd ever met.

As he was head of the Spooks, this would not be the first Islamic execution tape Bates had ever seen. Nick Berg. Eugene Armstrong. Jack Hensley, Daniel Pearl—Bates had watched them all. It was part of his job as the senior intelligence person on the ship, even though he was barely into his twenties, the result of his being a child prodigy and graduating from MIT at the age of 17. Bates *had* to watch Li's execution video because it most likely contained clues about the people who had killed her, the people whom Ryder and the rest of the team were in the process of stomping, on this, the Ghosts' last mission. Bates also wanted to see the video in its original form before the CIA got ahold of it and doctored it, as they would surely do, seeing as they were responsible for Li's death in the first place.

The signal from Echelon finally completed the endless downloading. Bates immediately made a backup copy and then ended the connection to Echelon. Then he took a deep breath—and pushed the video to play.

The first image was the Al-Qazzaza TV station identification slide. Then it switched to two news anchors jabbering about what was to come. Both men seemed positively orgasmic in announcing that a new execution video had been received.

There was a burst of static and electronic snow. This cleared up in a few seconds, and then Li's image came on the screen. Bates gulped hard; he hit the pause button. These beheadings were always brutal, gory stuff. His hands began to shake. He wasn't sure he was going to be able to handle this.

The ship began rocking sideways; they were in the Gulf and it was a rainy, windy afternoon and the water was getting rough. The sudden lurch brought Bates back to reality. He studied the frozen frame. Li was kneeling before a large handmade black and green flag with Islamic scribbling all over it. There were people kneeling on either side of her. Bates recognized them as Filipino laborers kidnapped by an Al Qaeda group in Iraq in the last two weeks. Standing directly behind them were five men in black uniforms, wearing black ski masks. One was holding an enormous razor-sharp machete.

The tape was very grainy, the sound almost indecipherable, but Bates knew what was going on. The man with the knife was reading from a prepared statement. He was saying each person in front of him had been convicted of crimes against Islam and that he was about to carry out their death sentence, all in Allah's name, of course.

The man with the knife folded his statement, then went to his right. He grabbed the first Filipino laborer and began chopping at the man's exposed neck. The victim screamed so loud, it blotted out all other sound being picked up by the camera's microphone. He struggled fiercely but to no avail, as his hands were tied behind his back. The blood came first in spurts, then in a gush as tendons, cartilage, and bones were destroyed by the heavy-bladed knife. When the machete hit the man's jugular, the blood began spraying out of him like water from a garden hose. The victim continued fighting, but life was draining out of him. Finally, with one last chop, his head was severed. In a grisly coda, the man's body continued struggling for a few more seconds before it finally went limp. The blood and the gore were massive. Some of it fell on Li.

There was an abrupt stop in the tape, more static, more electronic snow. When the image returned, the man in the mask was reciting another statement. Li had been moved closer to the center and was now shoulder to shoulder with the remaining Filipino. She was blindfolded, as was he, but Bates believed he could see a look of determination, not fear, on her face. At least he thought it best to remember her that way.

His statement concluded, the executioner raised his knife again and with one forceful blow hit not Li but the other Filipino square on the jugular. The man was surprised; he hardly moved as the blade went through the first half of his neck. The executioner withdrew the machete, then, holding the man's head steady, swung again and completed the job. It had happened so strangely and quickly, the man who'd done the cutting held the man's head up and started laughing through his ski mask. The look on the dead man's face was a mixture of horror and complete, absolute surprise. Again, the gore was unbelievable.

The tape stopped again. When it started a third time, Li alone was sitting before the five men in ski masks. The man started reading his statement. They were the same words every time, so Bates knew it would take exactly 23 seconds for the man to recite them—and then the killing would be done.

This was the moment of truth for the young Bates. He was just a supergeek employed to be a spy. He wasn't blood-and-guts like Ryder and Curry were and Gallant and Phelan used to be, before they died. Bates had fought this war against Al Qaeda from a place so devoid of all of that, they called it the White Room.

But this—what he was about to see? This wasn't going to be so clean. This was going to be rough.

But in a strange way, he felt he owed it to Li to watch it. He knew that after being introduced by Al-Qazzaza, the tape would be shown on TVs all around the globe and downloaded on people's computers and e-mailed everywhere to be laughed at in the slums of Karachi and Delhi and a hundred other places. For her spirit to be defiled like that, Bates thought it would help somehow if a friend saw it first.

The seconds counted down. The executioner was more than halfway through his spiel. He began pulling the machete from his waistband. The men on either side of him braced themselves for what they knew was about to come.

Ten seconds . . .

Bates's finger hovered over the pause button. Could he do it?

Seven seconds . . .

The guy was folding the paper; he knew the last few sentences by heart.

Five seconds . . .

He raised the machete over Li's neck.

Four seconds . . .

Bates nearly hit the stop button, he so didn't want to see this, but he knew he had to.

Three seconds . . .

Sorry, Li. . . .

Two . . .

One . . .

Bobby Murphy was standing at the big window in his cabin, looking out on the dark blue water of the night-time Persian Gulf. He was praying. For Li. For himself. For all of them. For the whole goddamn world and all the disheartened souls out there, the victims in this war, which Murphy felt would claim more lives than all of the other American wars combined—that it would be the first real nuclear war if Al Qaeda wasn't stopped.

He was praying and extremely bummed out, feeling his soul in his shoes, when suddenly the door to his cabin burst open and Gil Bates, their top Spook, rushed in.

Though Murphy had seen him excitable in the past, he'd never seen Bates quite like this.

He was crying, almost hysterically—and in that first instant this was such a shock to Murphy, because he knew Bates had been downstairs watching the execution tape and he was sure that the young genius had lost his mind. What he'd seen had been that horrible.

But the strange thing was, Bates was also laughing, just as hysterically. And these two things were coming in waves. Murphy thought he was looking into the eyes of a madman—and in a way, he was.

The young Spook reached the other end of the table and nearly collapsed. He was holding a disk.

"Put this in," he was saying to Murphy between catching his breath—he'd run up 10 levels to get here.

Murphy just stared at him. He really didn't want to watch Li's murder. His body language alone was screaming that. But Bates was insisting.

Murphy finally relented. He took the disk, put it in his laptop, and started it running.

Bates was beside him by this time. He reached over Murphy's hand and fast-forwarded through the two grisly slayings of the hapless Filipino workers.

Bates stopped the video just as the executioner was hovering over Li, the machete already out of his waistband.

"You have to see this!" Bates insisted.

Bates put it in slow motion. Murphy watched, horrified, as the knife was raised over Li's head, as the executioner began his swing down—and then suddenly a burst of static, followed by a series of scratch lines across the screen.

Then among the electronic snow Murphy could see the ghostly figures of the five men again. The tape became jumpy, and still full of static. But it was clear enough to see the men were discussing something; they seemed stumped by something. The knife was now back at the man's side, and Li was still unhurt.

More static—then the men changed positions abruptly. It was as if they were starting the execution all over again. But then more static, more scratch lines, and more fuzzy scenes of the men, once again discussing something, being stumped by something.

The very last scene showed the man with the knife literally throwing up his hands in frustration.

Then the video finally ended for good.

Murphy just turned to Bates. The young Spook was now laughing more than he was crying but still doing a lot of both.

"Don't you get it?" he asked Murphy excitedly. "All that static and scratching things at the end is them twisting it backward and going over it, again and again. Three times total. There were trying to get some use out of the last few inches of it. But they couldn't, because there's not enough of it."

"*Enough of what?*" Murphy finally asked him.

Now Bates was just laughing. He was happy. "*Video-tape,*" he replied simply, boisterously. "They *ran out* of videotape. . . ."

Murphy just stared back at him. He had to let this sink in. "They ran out of tape?" he asked, looking back at the blank screen.

"Yes," Bates replied. "They're rewinding it, thinking they can tape over it—but they can't, not without erasing the tape of the Filipino guys getting it. But you can't rewind cassettes by hand like that."

Murphy just shook his head. "*They ran out of video-tape?*" he repeated Bates's words back to him.

Murphy was suddenly a ball of motion. He started punching numbers into his laptop. He quickly retrieved a short report they'd received from Obo Field in the minutes following the strike team's arrival. The Delta guys had caught a mook looking down at them. He was a messenger of some sort from Khrash, and they had sent him back minus his hands as a message to the people inside the city. But before they cut him up, this flunky had told them that he was out in the wilderness looking for videotapes. Murphy had thought this was very strange at the time.

But then he began typing madly again. He stopped on a file they'd dragged down just the day before. It was the details of an Israeli hit team that had killed a well-known terrorist courier, someone who was thought to be heading for Khrash. Usually a guy like this might be carrying terrorist money or bombs or bomb parts. But as it turned out, the dead man was carrying just one thing: videotapes.

Murphy just looked up at Bates.

"Goddamn," he swore. "Could this mean what I think it could mean?"

"I think it might," Bates replied.

Murphy had his yellow phone up in a flash.

"We've got to call Obo right now!"

Obo Field

The yellow cell phone rang twice before one of the Marine mechanics answered it.

The Marine recognized Murphy's voice right away.

But the Big Boss sounded extremely excited and anxious, not typical for the little man from Texas.

He was almost yelling into the phone. "Can you stop
them? Can you?"

The Marine was confused. "Stop who, sir?"

"The guys!" Murphy yelled in reply. "The strike
team. Can you stop them? We have some very important
information. Something they have to know before they
level that place and kill everyone in it."

But the Marine just found himself shaking his head
no. "Sorry, sir," he told Murphy. "But they left a long
time ago."

No sooner had Murphy hung up when the two Marines
heard the sound of an aircraft approaching. They
grabbed their weapons, but by this time the aircraft was
already coming in for a landing. It was the so-called
Scramble copter, the team's third Blackhawk, coming
back to pick up the last of the ammunition—and the two
Marines. This meant another aspect of the plan was
about to take place. Which must have meant things were
going well in the battle.

Fox was riding in the back of the Scramble chopper.
He'd been surfing the air currents above Khrash ever
since the attack began. The copter had been providing
air support for Hunn's attack team mostly, though between Hunn's own highly destructive tendencies and the
follow-up troops of friendly Zabul fighters, there really
wasn't much the Scramble ship had to do except watch
as the wave of American flags whipping in the breeze
got larger and larger, sweeping east to west across the
midsection of the city.

It was clear to Fox early on that it wasn't really a battle he was watching below him. It was something else. A grand hoax. A ruse on the already panicking defenders of Khrash and their R and R guests. The smartest thing the Ghosts could have done was send the message early on that the Crazy Americans were in town. That alone obviously put the dirty little city on edge. Add in the surprise attacks on the mosques, the middle of the night "mini-invasion," and all the psych-out stuff the *Psyclops* plane could blanket the city with—no, it wasn't a battle, at least not yet.

But whatever it was, now they were back at Obo to start Round Two.

"Frankly, sir," one of the mechanics told Fox as he climbed off the copter, "we never thought we'd see you again."

Then the mechanics told Fox about the call they'd just received from Murphy.

Fox couldn't believe it. . . .

"Li's alive?" he asked them over and over.

"That's what Murphy thinks," was their reply. "Something to do with videotapes, the bad guys not having them."

By this time the copter crew had loaded all the bombs and ammo on board and they'd filled the tanks with the last bit of gas. Then Fox told the two Marines to jump aboard and the Scramble ship took off.

The Marines were extremely happy to get out of the Obo for good. That is, until they traveled up and over the mountains and saw the fires of the city of Khrash on the horizon. They were lighting up the night for miles around.

That's when one Marine leaned over to the other and said to him drily: "And we didn't want to miss *this*?"

As for Fox, he got Murphy on the yellow phone and had him repeat the news about Li. And it was great news—except they didn't really know if she was still alive, and if she was, they didn't know where she was at the moment, other than she was most likely in the city that they were in the process of severely fucking up.

Fox went pale at the thought of this. Was there a chance she'd survived because the mooks had run out of videotape only to be killed in the Ghosts' unorthodox attack?

And if that had happened, who the hell was ever going to tell Ryder?

The trouble was, Fox and the Scramble copter had another mission to fulfill.

Murphy's plan called for an airborne assault on the center of the city if by the 50-minute mark everything was still going well for the Ghosts. The Scramble copter was to lead that assault. Fox was to be the CO.

The idea was to attempt a thrust at the heart of Khrash, a direct attack on the building that Murphy and the Spooks believed was the headquarters of the city's notorious religious police. They had deemed it both a military and a morale-busting target. To that end, all of the team's air assets were to head for the center of the city at exactly the 50-minute mark and provide cover for what was to come.

The target was the Holy Towers buildings, the tallest structures in Khrash.

. . .

When the Scramble copter arrived over the target, the two other Blackhawk copters were already waiting for it. Ryder's F-14 was also in the vicinity, while Curry stayed out west, continuing to attack anything that moved over the Habeeb Bridge toward Iran. He'd been very busy doing this for the past 15 minutes, as indeed the trickle of fighters trying to escape had turned into a torrent, just as the Ghosts had hoped.

The pair of Blackhawks and Ryder's F-14 each performed several strafing runs up and down the designated building, preparing the way for the Scramble copter to land on the roof, this while the *Psyclops* plane cruised farther overhead, still blaring the deafening sounds of battle to the ground below. More than once, as Fox saw Ryder's F-14 streak back and forth, he wondered how the hell, in the heat of this miniwar, they could get a message to him about Li. Of them all, this guy had the most right to know. But because of the lack of any communications among the Ghosts—their gravest weakness—there was no way Fox could think of to do it.

And again, he had to concentrate on the matter at hand.

The pilot of the Scramble copter waited for the other air assets to exit the area; then he slammed the Blackhawk down on top of one of the two Holy Towers. The troopers on board quickly jumped out to take on any opposition, but the rooftop was empty, except for the five dead mooks shot earlier by one of the other Blackhawks.

This was perfect for the Scramble crew. As the Delta troopers set up a defensive perimeter around the rooftop, Fox and the two Marine mechanics started working on the real reason they'd come here.

They unfurled another American flag, this one also given to them by the crew of the *Psyclops* plane. Unlike the other flags being thrown up on every building the Ghosts captured, this one was huge, six feet by ten feet. They had brought a staff with them. Now hooking the flag to the staff, they carried it to the southern edge of the tower's roof. By this time the Delta operators had gathered around them. On cue, several of these operators started shooting off flare guns—because they were on the highest buildings in the city, there was no doubt most people below, friend and foe alike, could see the sudden pyrotechnic display.

In fact, the display was so high and so bright, Fox and the others on the roof heard a distinct quieting of gunfire below. Knowing they'd gotten a lot of people's attention, they raised the huge flag up over the 11-story Holy Towers buildings for all to see.

It wasn't quite the flag raising over Iwo Jima—but it was damn close. And the intent was the same. The message: The battle continued, but American troops had made it this far. They could almost hear their comrades cheering down in the streets.

The hail of enemy gunfire came at them just a second later.

Fox first became aware of it when two bullets went zinging by his right ear. Suddenly the air was filled with enemy rounds, impacting on the roof, off the scramble copter, and even the flag staff itself.

But where was the enemy fire coming from?

Fox went down on his stomach, crawled to the edge

of the building and for the first time realized the enemy fire was coming from the almost identical tower next to the one he was on. This building looked like it was full of the city's defenders. These were the people who were shooting at them.

There was only a about a 10 foot separation between the two towers. As Fox and the others watched in horror, two mooks firing at them from the roof of the second tower began running towards them, as if to leap across the distance and land on the roof they currently occupied.

This was insanity, and Fox knew it. Why would these two want to jump over to their roof where they would be killed immediately . . . unless.

Fox instantly opened up on the two gunmen—everyone around him did too, as if they all figured it out at the same time. The two mooks both jumped off the first tower together. The American fusillade caught them in mid-air. Suddenly both mooks blew up in twin balls of flame and dust.

Then everything got quiet again. Fox felt all the air go out of him. These guys hadn't just been gunmen, they were suicide bombers.

And that was not good.

Somehow the crews of the other two Blackhawks figured out what was going on. They returned with a vengeance, strafing the second tower mercilessly, this as Fox and the others on the roof of the first building traded intense gunfire with enemy fighters in the other.

It went on like this for what seemed to be the longest time. It was almost like to great man of wars ships battling each other at close quarters on the open sea. Meanwhile, Fox could see other enemy fighters in what looked like full retreat, running through the city square, heading for the river and what they hoped would be sanctuary in Iran beyond.

Why then were the mooks defending the first Holy Tower so ferociously? Was it simply because they housed the headquarters of the religious police? Or that the big American flag was now flying up here? Or was it something else?

He had to find out.

Something told him the answer lay at the bottom of the building. He gathered eight of the Delta guys with him, plus the Marine mechanics and down they went.

It turned out to be almost a replay of the assault on the prison at Loki Sato in West Africa. With Fox taking the lead, he and the other troopers burst through the top door of the building and started making their way down. They made a head long dash down the stairs, cluttered by refuse, garbage and dead or dying Islamic fighters.

Meanwhile the Scramble copter took off, and began circling the building, firing at any enemy gunmen its could see. As it turned out, this first tower was virtually empty. Fox and his squad met only a few mooks on the way down and they looked to be so high on qat, they offered only token resistance before fleeing or dying.

It only took a couple minutes before Fox and company arrived on the ground floor. Sure enough here was the headquarters of the city's religious police. The place was empty and appeared ransacked. Enemy fighters were running right by the window, some armed, some not. But they weren't bothering to stop or do anything about the Americans suddenly in their midst.

It was at that moment that Fox and the others realized

why. A commotion was happening about a block away. Fox dared to stick his head out the door and saw a truly beautiful sight: it was Kennedy's 2nd Delta squad and the two Zabul tanks.

They had finally reached the center of Khrash.

Yet even as these reinforcements flooded into the city square firing and chasing the still retreating mooks, enemy gunmen in the second tower were still firing down at them.

Why would they be doing this? Fox wondered again. There was something else here; he knew it. But what?

Or who?

Once he was sure that Kennedy and his men had secured the front of the building, Fox turned to the Delta guys and asked: "Do you think this place has a basement?"

It took them five minutes to find the door to the lower level—it was hiding behind a false wall in the police chief's office—and another five minutes to actually get it open, but Fox and his squad finally gained entrance to the Tower's basement.

The first thing that hit them when they got the door open was the smell. It was horrendous. Body sweat, urine, death or near death.

They rushed down the stairs into a dark hallway. That's when they heard moaning, groaning, crying. The hallway was lined with plain white doors. Fox shot the lock off the first one and kicked it in. Within, they found two men, chained to the wall. Both were emaciated. Both showed signs of having been beaten and tortured. Both were wearing U.S. Air Force flight uniforms.

Next door down the Delta guys found two Afghani

Army officers, one dead, the other dying. In the room next to that, two Filipino women. On and on, 22 people in all. Hostages. POWs. Kidnap victims. All of them awaiting execution. An incredible discovery.

As one of the Delta guys said to Fox: "Everyone's here except Judge Crater and Jimmy Hoffa."

Fox just nodded.

"And Li . . . ," he whispered.

The Farāh River ran swiftly from north to south. Flowing out of the mountains in Afghanistan, it bordered Khrash on the west, at points defining the border with Iran.

The river had been a lifeline to Khrash for centuries. Where the river cargo years ago had been such exotic things as fresh fruit, figs, and cooking oil, these days it was almost always guns, ammunition, and explosives, along with some luxury items such as C-size batteries, Bic lighters, and blank cassette tapes, including videotapes.

The river caravan of seven boats had left the Iranian city fifty miles downstream just after sundown the day before. Because they had to sail against the current and the 30-foot boats were powered by small diesel engines, those fifty miles upstream could take as long as 10 hours.

But because the smugglers, who were actually members of the Iranian military police, knew there was a sudden desperate situation in Khrash, they'd traveled the night full out, in an effort to get the much-needed arms and ammunition to their Islamic brothers.

That's why they were now just a mile from Khrash, hidden under the overhanging trees on the Iranian side, looking into this city where nothing ever really happened and wondering whether World War Three had suddenly broken out there.

On the seven boats were tons of military supplies, especially guns and ammunition, a cargo too expensive by weight and too dangerous by origin to be driven over the mountains to Khrash. Usually these deliveries would be made with no muss, no fuss, on one of the many docking areas that could be found up near the Habeeb Bridge. But at the moment the Habeeb Bridge seemed to be on fire. The smuggled weapons would have to be dropped off at a more secure location farther downstream.

There were 21 Iranian military police scattered along the seven boats. The boats themselves were simple wooden carry-alls, long, flat rowboats that were supplemented by diesel engines. All of the cargo was stored up top. Wooden boxes carried the AK-47s and RPG rounds. Waterproofed plastic tubs held the ammunition, plus the batteries, the lighters, and the tape cassettes. The seven boats were lashed together to prevent their getting lost in the dark. They had no running lights and there was no radio communication among them. Wherever the first boat went, the others had to follow.

A man named Zbeg Kamani was riding in the last boat. He was an officer cadet in the regular Iranian Army, assigned to the military police's smuggling operations. This was his first ride up the Farāh River.

He'd been as surprised as anybody when they turned a bend and saw the unmistakable glow of combat coming from Khrash. He'd been expecting nothing more than a simple drop-off of the smuggled items and a guarantee that they would get into the hands of the right people. Now he could see helicopters firing on the buildings in the city and jet fighters diving on targets near the Habeeb Bridge and dangerously close to the south end of town. Above it all the strangest airplane he'd ever seen was circling like some mechanic bird, looking for a meal.

Praise Allah, he thought. *What have I gotten myself into?*

There were two other men on the boat with him. They, too, were cadets in the regular Iranian Army. This was their first trip as well.

Zbeg was riding down near the end of the boat. As soon as it was apparent something unusual was happening in Khrash, he started making his way up to the front of the craft; he wanted to talk to his two crewmates, to see if they had any idea what was going on.

They were standing at the front of the boat, looking at the glow of the burning city now just about three-quarters of a mile away. Before Zbeg could say anything, though, incredibly, two figures shot up out of the water and landed on their feet right in front of his two comrades. Zbeg couldn't believe it. These two beings were like something from a horror movie. They were slimy and had things sticking out of their ears and noses and mouths. Zbeg was frozen to the spot. He couldn't move; he couldn't speak. He watched helplessly as his two comrades, paralyzed themselves by the sudden appearance of these two creatures, offered no resistance as the monsters grabbed them around the shoulders and brutally slit their throats.

At just about the same moment, the boat in front of

them suddenly blew up, as did the boat in front of that.
These particular vessels were carrying the majority of
the high explosives in the shipment, so the twin blasts
were incredible. Zbeg found himself being thrown
through the air and the air was suddenly filled with fire
and smoke. Even before he hit the water, he saw other
water creatures moving quickly around the boats at the
head of the column. They were killing the people on
those boats as well and apparently blowing the boats
up, too.

Zbeg hit the water an instant later, this as the first five
boats of the caravan went up in a string of explosions.
He went deep under but somehow managed to fight his
way to the surface again. He came up gasping for air and
realizing that half his clothes had been burned away in
the blast.

Strangely, he saw some of the other people who'd
been in the caravan were in the water nearby. This made
his absolute panic die down a bit. At least he was not
alone! But as he started moving toward them he saw the
river creatures again, popping up like from a nightmare,
grabbing them, stabbing them repeatedly in their necks
and throats, only to disappear back into the black water
once their deed was done.

Zbeg was extremely frightened now. He started pad-
dling away from the horror, but he was not a good
swimmer and the current was running very fast. To his
surprise, he saw one of the cargo loads floating right up
to him. It was one of the plastic tubs. Zbeg grabbed
onto it for dear life, and it alone prevented him from
drowning.

He rode the plastic tub all the way to shore, blocking

his ears when he could so he wouldn't have to hear the terrified screams of his colleagues being killed by the water monsters.

The horror seemed unending. But finally Zbeg was able to push himself up onto dry land, the only survivor of the disaster in the river.

But a bigger surprise was yet to come, because no sooner did he get his wits about him when he heard a voice above him. He looked up to see two men in uniforms with rifles staring down at him. Their faces were highlighted by both twin glows of the riverboats still burning out on the water and the flames coming from Khrash itself not far away.

Zbeg remained frozen with fear as one of the men literally stepped on him to get to the plastic tub that had held just enough buoyancy to save his life. They seemed unconcerned about the seven boats in flames farther out on the river. The soldier ripped the top off the tub and reached inside. But instead of coming out with gobs of ammunition, he had a bunch of batteries and video cassettes in his hand.

"We've been waiting for you, *pasha*," one of the soldiers said to him. "And you have brought us just what we needed."

Only then did Zbeg realize these people weren't Americans—he recognized their uniforms. They were Iranian military, just as he was.

But what were they doing on this side of the river?

Captain Dow put the big EC-130 plane into a sharp bank and flew over the Farāh River. He and his crew had spotted the series of explosions about a mile south of Khrash and thought it was best that they take a look. Flying low, just above the flames, they saw the Ghost Team's SEAL contingent moving about the flaming bits of wreckage making sure they'd killed as many of the caravan's crew as possible.

Dow asked one of the DJs to briefly shine the plane's searchlight down on the SEALs. This was done and they clearly could see some of the SEALs giving them the thumbs-up. Their business had been done here—that, too, was clear by the number of bodies swiftly moving down the river, back toward Iran.

Turning the big plane around again, Dow steered back over Khrash, returning to his orbit station just a minute later. He asked the DJs tostart broadcasting a sound disk known simply as *More Confusing Sounds of War.* This done, they started circling the city once again.

It had been quite a night for the EC-130 crew. Never did they think they'd be putting their aerial psych-out machine to work like this. Their role in all this was to create confusion, something they were well equipped to do and something they'd been doing nonstop since taking off from Obo. But they had also caught glimpses every once in a while of the Ghosts' attack teams on the ground. It was like looking down on a war movie, something real but not, unfolding before their eyes. The damage that the Ghost Team had caused to the old city so far was just astonishing. But the chaos they'd created, with major help from the *Psyclops* crew, was the incredible part.

They could still see streams of Islamic fighters rushing toward the river and the Habeeb Bridge, at the same time they watched as Curry's F-14 continually strafing anything that went over the span, be it a truck, a car, or someone on a motorbike or on foot. It was almost too horrible for the *Psyclops* crew to watch. The bridge and the road beyond were literally soaked with blood. The carnage was sickening. The Ghosts were used to doing things like this. Not so much the civilian soldiers from Pennsylvania.

As Dow completed yet another loop around the city, the godlike speakers blaring the sound of tanks and big guns and explosions and gunfire, one of the DJs who doubled as an image analyst brought a bunch of photos up to the flight compartment. They showed a panorama of the city, and without a doubt, they could see the battle lines moving east to west, just the way the Ghosts' plan was supposed to go. The smoke and fire were intense—all except in the south end of the city.

This had been a mystery from the beginning. The city of Khrash was literally crawling with Islamic trash, terrorists, hardened fighters, suicide bombers. Yet why would none of them bother to venture to the southern end of the city? If even to hide from the shoestring American assault?

A thought came to Dow as they skirted the edge of the darkened part of the city. Maybe no one was going there because they'd been ordered not to. . . .

Suddenly a bright flash went through the cabin of the airplane. For a split second Dow thought they'd been hit by a SAM. But no warnings sounded, and the plane was still under their control. He looked over at Clancy, who just pointed to their control panel. An amber light right in the middle was blinking.

The White Screen. It had just snapped on. That's what had caused the bright flash.

Dow was out of his seat in a second, quickly making his way back to the rear of the plane.

Murphy was already on the screen when Dow arrived.

Murphy looked both happy and devastated at the same time. "Captain, you have to somehow find Colonel Long immediately," he said. "We have some very important news about Li. . . ."

It took a very long time for the heavily armed trucks surrounding the battered hotel to leave. Ozzi had spent the time looking down at them, counting them, trying to learn more about them, at the same time painfully aware of what would happen if they ever found him up here alone, with just a few bullets left in his magazine.

This was not a good place to be and he knew it. Whether he and his Zabul squad had moved a lot faster than anyone could have anticipated or they'd simply become lost and didn't know about it, something had gone wrong and now he was alone, in enemy territory, with no idea where he was or how he was going to get out.

Finally the technicals did drive away. He didn't see in which direction—and they could have just moved a bit farther down the street. The heavily armed Al Qaeda types drifted away as well. Ozzi knew this was his chance. Maybe the only one. He had to get off this roof. And he had to find someone friendly, and soon.

He slowly made his way back down to the third level. He looked around and saw nothing but dead mooks everywhere. He peered over the railing to the next two levels below. They, too, were clear. The hotel lobby was dark, another thing going in his favor. At least he could get out of the building without being seen.

He started down the stairs but suddenly felt a sharp

pain in his leg. He looked down at his right thigh and saw his pants leg was drenched in blood. He couldn't believe it. He'd been wounded all this time—without even knowing it. And this was no paper cut, either.

He hobbled down the stairs and made the lobby but was out of breath and suddenly very thirsty. He looked out onto the street. All of the lights had gone out by this time. The street was covered with bodies. Dead mooks and the dead women and children they'd first spotted when they got here. The building across the street, the one that Ryder had put a five-hundred-pound bomb into, was still aflame, and this provided the only illumination.

Ozzi checked his rifle once more—again just three bullets left. Then he left the hotel, stepping over the bodies, and began walking in the shadows, not really knowing which direction to go.

He stumbled along for a few blocks, realizing that he was losing blood and losing strength. Every once in a while the EC-130 would fly over, almost directly over his head. But it was flying too high and too fast to spot him. Sometimes he also heard the helicopters close by, but again, they didn't come close enough for him to signal them. And somewhere up there he could hear the F-14s, too.

He was dragging his leg now, the pain turning to numbness. He didn't want to stop because now he felt if he stopped he would die. One thing about the Ghosts. In all their bizarre and highly dangerous operations, their fatality rate had remained extremely low. They'd lost a handful of Delta guys and a pilot when they stopped the attack on the USS *Lincoln* in the Strait of Hormuz; they lost no one during their operations in Singapore and the Philippines. Another pilot died while they were tracking down the Al Qaeda terrorists who had smuggled Stinger missiles into the United States just a few months ago. This operation so far as Ozzi knew had been lucky, too—except of course they had lost Li. . . .

Ozzi had always thought of the Ghosts as being extremely lucky—and now, as he began to feel even weaker, he was wondering if that luck was starting to run out. At least for him.

He stopped at one corner of the street and looked it up and down. It was like he was standing in an Old West ghost town. The miniwar had passed this place by. He couldn't imagine anyone being within a mile of him.

That's why he was so surprised when he turned the next corner and one block down he saw his Zabul!

He couldn't believe it. . . . He actually wiped his eyes, just to make sure he wasn't hallucinating due to his sucking leg wound.

But he wasn't. There they were, the seven guys of the first squad—the guys who had run into the hotel with him and then disappeared sometime very soon after that. They were greeting a handful of civilians who had somehow survived the fighting and were now wailing with joy that they were still alive and that they'd been rescued by the Zabul.

Ozzi staggered to the middle of the street and called out to them. They spotted him and waved and smiled back.

Damn, I'm going to make it . . . , Ozzi thought.

At that same moment, one of the civilians, a middle-aged man, embraced the head Zabul officer. As he was doing this, he reached into his shirt and pulled the detonator on the belt of TNT he was wearing around his waist.

The bomb went off a split second later.

It was so powerful, it blew Ozzi back ten feet and landed him on his already painful right leg. When he looked up again, all he saw was bodies, some torn limb from limb, others looking like they were just asleep.

But they were all most certainly dead. All the Zabul. All the civilians and the suicide bomber himself.

And Ozzi was alone, lost and bleeding, once again.

The Chief had packed his bags hastily. He'd thrown some dirty clothes in one and as much money as he could grab in thirty seconds into the other. American dollars, some euros, a few gold pieces. He was worth a lot more, so he would be leaving a lot behind. But time was the important thing now. He'd been forced to move quickly.

All this happened just minutes after he'd been shot at on top of the Holy Towers roof and just minutes before the American had actually landed up there and hoisted their flag. Khrash was in flames around him. There were explosions going off every few seconds, and the tracer fire in the streets and the sky above was almost blinding. His men were in full retreat, just to get away from the chaos alone, and now the Chief didn't blame them. These Crazy Americans *were* devils and at last the Chief wanted nothing to do with them.

He knew Khrash would never be the same. No more privileges in the face of religious law, no more perverted sex trysts. Even if the Americans were somehow stopped this nightmarish night, the Chief did not want to live in rubble.

So he was getting out. Just he and his two bags of possessions. He was leaving a wife and 17 children behind.

His driver knew a secret way out of the city. It involved driving through the western part of Khrash,
along a road that hugged the river, to a rough trail that
ran to the southernmost point of the city limits. From
there, an even rougher trail would carry them 15 miles
to another bridge that was used only by the Iranian
military—the typical ones, anyway.

If the Chief reached this outpost, he would be safe.
Crossing this bridge and then going through a small
opening between two mountains beyond would put him
in the promised land of Iran by morning. It would be a
rough journey, but that didn't bother the Chief. Getting
out with his skin was the most important thing.

His driver was waiting for the Chief when he finally
ran out of his quarters to the debris-strewn street. The
Chief jumped inside the Land Rover, preferring the
backseat. His driver had one more thing of value with
him, taken from the Chief's blast-proof safe box at the
blockhouse, his unofficial HQ deep in the Old Quarter.
It was a package holding three CDs. On these CDs were
the names of every person in the Qimnuz, 22,517 in all,
with a notation beside each name measuring that person's loyalty to the religious police. About two-thirds
were considered loyal; the rest, less so.

The Chief knew this list was extremely valuable,
more so than his money and bling. Someday what was
happening in Khrash would be avenged—maybe a lot
sooner than people would think. That's just the way
things went in this part of the world. Eventually the
Americans would all be killed or go away and then old
scores would be settled. Those few thousand people
listed on the CDs as not considered loyal would be the
first ones to pay the price. At the very least, he knew the

Iranian secret police would appreciate the information he would be carrying with him. It would make his life in the country next door that much easier.

They'd set out just as the Scramble helicopter was landing atop the Holy Tower. They got about two blocks when one of the F-14s came right over them, at practically rooftop height, dropping a bomb on a gun position just off the main square while firing its nose cannon at a target several blocks away. The huge jet screamed so close to the Chief's vehicle, he could have reached out and touched it. Then just as quickly, the jet was gone— and off they went.

It took a few minutes of steering around all the debris in the streets, as well as the bodies and the retreating fighters, for them to find the road that would take them down to the river. From there they would get on the river way itself—and that would lead them to their escape point. They could be out of the fighting completely in just a matter of minutes.

And that's where they were now. But even this side road was littered with burning debris. Wrecked vehicles and military equipment, the victims of the nonstop air attacks. Buildings on either side of the road were aflame. And again, there were bodies everywhere. And the noise of explosions going off was absolutely deafening.

The dirt road nevertheless brought them through one last large section of the city that was totally engulfed in flames. Once past these structures, though, they found themselves driving by a burning field. But from here to the river there was no other traffic or anything blocking the road.

They did pass small groups of the city's defenders along the way. All of these men were dazed and con-

fused; many were injured and bleeding as well. They
were all leaderless, too, and at first sight of the Chief's
well-known Land Rover they cheered, thinking finally
someone was going to rally them to counterattack the
Crazy Americans. But each time the cheering was extremely abrupt as the Chief's car approached them at
high speed—and kept right on going. Not a wave, not a
salute. Not a toot of the horn. Nothing.

The Chief didn't have time for them. He was getting
out as fast as he could.

They finally made the river's edge and turned south.
This roadway really was no more than a glorified trail,
but the Land Rover had no problem negotiating it at
full-out speed.

Though it was a rough and bumpy ride, the Chief was
still able to look out on the river. To his great surprise,
many parts of the surface were aflame. He knew that the
ammunition and weapons boats had been expected in the
city sometime during the night. Now it was apparent that
these boats had been caught out in the open and sunk by
the Americans. It was a frightening sight, all the burning
water rushing by. No replacement weapons, no extra
ammunition? The Chief was glad he left when he did.

When they reached the southern point of the city a
few minutes later, unscathed, the Chief almost became
giddy. The mountains were right in front of them
now—just an hour or so from here and they would
make the small military bridge downstream. Most of
the fighting was behind them. Off to the left, the southern edge of the city, where the many warehouses were
located, was still dark and uninvolved.

The Chief no longer wanted any part of that, either.

He was already thinking about his new life. Single, wealthy, connected, and possessing valuable information. Things might be pretty good for him, living in a ground-level *boit* in Tehran. He was getting tired of Afghanistan anyway.

These sweet dreams would last but a few seconds, though. They went around a bend in the trail—and found a huge hovering helicopter suddenly blocking their path.

It was if the aircraft materialized out of nothingness. How could it have flown in here so stealthily? The Chief didn't want to believe it was there at first. Only after he blinked his eyes several times was he convinced this thing was real. And that meant real trouble.

This helicopter was definitely not of the same type as had been attacking the city relentlessly all night. This one had two huge rotors, one at each end; it resembled a nightmarish flying banana. There were heavily armed men jumping out of its access doors and heading right for the Land Rover.

The driver slammed on the brakes, which was probably the worst thing to do. It gave the hovering helicopter the time to finally set down on the trail, blocking any hope of speeding under it and getting away. The Chief now threw up, he was so scared. He screamed for his driver to open fire on the men. It was clear that this he did not want to do, but the Chief's screams caused him to take the AK-47 on the seat beside him and fire it out the open window at the black-uniformed soldiers.

At the moment this happened, the Chief bailed. He opened the door, grabbed his bags, and was out of the truck, this just as the first fusillade of return fire hit it. There was a storm of tracers, but also two pumped grenades came flying through the night. They hit simultaneously and the Land Rover went up in a ball of flame, taking the hapless driver with it. In that moment of smoke and chaos, the Chief rolled himself through the grass and into the river.

The black-uniformed soldiers saw him but did little in the way of pursuit. The Chief felt lucky—for about a second. That's when the current caught him. He didn't know how to swim. He lost the bags in a second; the CDs were ripped out of his pocket an instant later.

He was quickly caught in a whirlpool that sent him round and round for a few terrifying seconds, long enough for the black-uniformed troops to make it to the riverbank. They could clearly see him, but none of them bothered to shoot. It was obvious he was drowning.

Water soon began entering the Chief's mouth. He turned to see that he was actually heading for a wall of fire. The conflagration that was burning away on the water's surface had reached this far up the river and was about to engulf him.

By fire or water, he was soon going to die, and the Chief knew it. That's why it was so strange that his last thoughts were not about his family or a flashing of his life before his eyes.

They were about the soldiers who had just killed his driver and were now watching him drown. They were obviously American; he could tell by the uniforms and their huge builds.

But what was so odd was the soldiers themselves.

He could clearly see their faces in these last seconds of life, lit up by the approaching wave of liquid fire.

Every one of them was a black man.

. . .

It was Delta Thunder.

Somehow, someway, Murphy had arranged for a Chinook helicopter from the USS *Reagan,* which was also cruising the Gulf, to pick them up and deliver them to this weird fight. A hell-raising low-level high-speed flight followed, and suddenly here they were.

The only caveat was that the Navy guys flying the Chinook would not get involved in the fighting. That's why they'd been dropped so far from town.

They formed up again and started marching along the riverbank toward the city. It seemed to them that half of Khrash was in flames, which was not that far from the truth.

They knew very little about what was going on exactly. They knew what Murphy knew up to two hours ago, that the operation had started and from the scrambled reports coming from the *Psyclops* plane things seemed to be going OK—or at least it hadn't turned into a disaster yet. They knew nothing, though, about what had been seen—or more accurately *not seen*—on Li's execution tape.

They'd made it a half-mile up the river when they heard an aircraft approaching, a helicopter. They were sure it was one of the team's Blackhawks, but the squad took cover anyway. It was a good thing they did, for as it turned out, it *wasn't* one of the three Superhawks.

To the astonishment of the Thunder team, it was a Bell-72 military copter. But not just any Bell-72. This was the same French B-72 helicopter that had left them high and dry in the border clearing back in Africa. None of them would ever forget what it looked like.

It flew right over them, traveling along the nap of the

river. Instantly every man in the eight-man Thunder squad raised his weapon to shoot at it, a natural reaction. But they were so stunned upon seeing it, and were still stunned now, that it was out of range before they could fully snap out of it. Soon it disappeared in the darkness.

That's when they all just looked at one another, the same expression on each man's face.

Did we really just see that? Was that really the same helicopter?

If so, what the hell was it doing out here?

Dave Hunn finally reached the place called Al Sharim. One of the highest points in Khrash, it was a berm about 150 feet in elevation, located a half-mile from the center of town. A rare, flattened-out part of the city, the area had once featured a soccer field and a park nearby. The berm itself faced west.

This was Hunn's IP. The goal of his charge through the heart of the city. He could clearly see the huge American flag flying from the top of the Holy Tower. He could also see the fires out on the river, and he could hear the copters and at least one of the F-14s flying somewhere overhead. But Hunn knew the fighting wasn't over quite yet.

What faced him now on the other side of the berm was the neighborhood of Hasha. It was made up almost entirely of truck garages, old factories, and junkyards, the worst of Khrash's grimy industrial section. Beyond this metallic wasteland was the city's western edge, where hundreds of hard-core Al Qaeda fighters were still theoretically holed up.

The plan had called for Hunn to switch tactics should

he ever find himself here, at his goal point, atop the Al Sharim berm. Going up against a lot of Al Qaeda fighters, with a junkyard for a battlefield, was just asking for trouble. There was a good chance some of the hard-core mooks were already in Hasha, hiding among the wrecked cars and abandoned buildings or at the very least booby-trapping the place. If Hunn and his men ventured into the grubby trash-strewn area, it was likely they would never come out.

That's why they were going to let someone else do the dirty work for them.

Hunn had about a dozen flares left. He stood atop the berm and looked behind him, past the rolling hills on the other side of the city's main gate, to the mountains beyond. Up there, somewhere, was Tarik Aboo's second cousin—or was it his third? Whatever, the guy was in charge of six 188mm artillery pieces and plenty of ammunition. Tarik had arranged for a 20-minute bombardment. As the artillerymen already had the firing coordinates for the Hasha neighborhood, it was simply up to Hunn to signal them by shooting off three flares. If they saw another three flares from Hunn about five minutes into the bombardment, they would know that they'd destroyed the target. At that point, they would extend their range so their shells would fall onto the west side of the city itself, where the Al Qaeda fighters had been taking their vacations from murder.

If after 10 minutes or so the second target area was also destroyed, Hunn could fire off another series of flares, ordering a new area to be hit. The gunners would know by the direction these last flares traveled which way they should turn their guns.

Hunn fired off his three flares and the barrage started almost immediately, this after 1st Delta had safely dug itself into the east side of the berm. They watched as the large 125mm shells went over their heads, causing faint yellow streaks of light as they fell onto the grimy neighborhood beyond. The noise was so loud even the cotton in the troopers' ears didn't do them much good.

They kept their heads down like this for the full five minutes. Only then, after a break in the barrage, did Hunn dare to peek over the top of the berm. He was astonished by what he saw.

There was nothing left. What had been a crowded, overloaded section filled with everything from cement mixers to hundreds of wrecked cars now looked like the surface of the moon. It was as if the place had been hit by a *real* B-52 strike.

Hunn knew nothing could have survived the massive bombardment, so he sent up three more signal flares and told his guys to get down again. Within a minute, the shells were going over their heads once more, this time at a little longer distances. The noise was no less horrific, though. Nor was the new glow coming from the west. Once this segment of bombardment was over, Hunn took another peek and was heartened to see that the section of housing on the other side of the junkyard had been leveled, too. Were there still some Al Qaeda in those rat holes? Or had they already moved out or escaped? Either way, Hunn was sure they wouldn't be coming back anytime soon.

He checked his watch. He still had ten minutes of artillery to be used. But where to shoot it? Everything to the north of him still had friendly personnel operating in it. Straight ahead was nothing but the demolished west side and the burning waters of the Farāh River. So he turned his eyes left, to the darkened south end of the city. Except for the two hits Ryder had delivered earlier, the blocks of warehouses had stood mute during all of this.

Hunn just shrugged and start shooting off flares in that direction.

What the hell, he thought. *Maybe we can kill something interesting down there.*

Ryder was enjoying himself. He'd joined Curry over the western end of the Habeeb Bridge, the roadway that, up to an hour ago, had been an escape route to Iran. It was now covered with wrecked vehicles and slick with blood. Even the snow on either side of the road was bright crimson; that's how many people had been killed here.

Curry had been here the whole time, bombing and strafing the half-mile of dirt and asphalt that was filled with at first Al Qaeda fighters trying to escape, then left-over Taliban, then finally the city's religious police themselves.

Hundreds tried to flee by foot and by car and truck. None of them made it. Curry had shot up several vehicles just before the road rose up and over the mountain pass. This sealed off the roadway—and everything behind it just added to the traffic jam.

After that it really was like a shooting gallery. Some chose to hide in their cars and get shot up. Others tried to run for it. But there was really nowhere to go. Certainly not in the river. Certainly not into Iran. And certainly not back into the city.

This had happened before. February 1991, the first Gulf War. On the road out of Kuwait City back into Iraq, retreating Iraqi units were slaughtered by hordes of U.S. warplanes as they were trying to escape advancing Coalition forces. Formerly known as Route 6, it had been renamed the Highway of Death.

Something very similar was going on here. All the wreckage and bodies were stark proof that the Ghosts' bold plan had worked. Their efforts to sow confusion and chaos in Khrash had created a stampede of mooks. Cowards, really—as all terrorists were. This was where that stampede ended.

As fighting was winding down in the city itself, two of the Blackhawks crossed the river and joined in the destruction. Then Ryder showed up and began adding the last of his cannon shells and bomb load to the carnage. It was all brutal and without mercy, but no one involved ever considered bringing it to a halt. They knew if they let just one terrorist get away, that same mook might one day step on a plane with a bomb or smuggle a nuclear device into the United States and more American deaths would result. The Ghosts had a chance to kill as many terrorists as they could, here and now, and they were going to do it.

It was at the height of this mass murder that the *Psyclops* plane arrived.

It began flying so bizarrely above the ongoing attack that the pilots of the fighters and copters couldn't help but take notice. Then finally the big EC-130 brought itself almost level to Ryder's F-14. In a reverse of the first time they'd encountered each other, now it was the crew of the big four-engine plane trying to get the F-14's attention.

Finally, the *Psyclops* plane pulled up beside Ryder's fighter. Ryder looked over and saw Dow holding up a sign against the cockpit's oversize windows.

Written in thick black letters, it simply said: **Li Still Alive—maybe. Follow us. . . .**

Fox and the Scramble copter had landed atop the Al Sharim berm.

Hunn and 1st Delta were still up here, and the artillery bombardment of the southern end of the city was still going on.

Fox had told Hunn the news about Li and how there was a chance she was still alive or had been before the Ghosts descended on Khrash. The problem was, information Fox had just learned from the prisoners at the bottom of the Holy Towers had led him here, to try to stop Hunn's artillery barrage.

Their conversation was interrupted by two sounds. The dull roar of the *Psyclops* plane, for the first time not broadcasting any *faux* sounds of battle, and the high-pitched scream of an F-14's twin jet engines. A desperate three-way communication minutes before among Murphy, the guys on the *Psyclops* plane, and Fox on the yellow cell phone had resulted in the EC-130 crew bringing Ryder here. Other written messages to the fighter pilot on the way over indicated that the only way he was going to learn more about Li was for him to bail out nearby and make contact with the friendlies atop the windblown Al Sharim berm.

The *Psyclops* plane flew over now, leading the F-14 to this meeting point. The F-14, however, came in very low over the old soccer field nearby. Its engines sounded like they were about to fall off.

"What's that crazy bastard doing?" Fox cried. "Doesn't he know he supposed to bail out?"

"Jesuzz!" Hunn yelled. "I think he's trying to land. . . ."

Incredibly, the F-14 came down, wheels up, and hit the field hard. It began skidding madly, throwing up dust and sparks and leaving a trail of fire and smoke behind it.

Why the F-14 didn't go nose over and kill Ryder outright they didn't know. It took a long time, but finally the big battered fighter came to a screeching halt not 100 yards from the base of the berm.

The canopy popped open immediately and Ryder half jumped, half fell out. Some of the 1st Delta guys ran down the hill to help him, but Ryder was obviously operating on a different level by now. He bounded up the hill, out of breath, eyes wild.

"Li . . . ," he said, gasping. "Just tell me now."

Screaming to be heard over the still-falling artillery shells, Fox told Ryder everything he knew about the preempted execution tape. Ryder's face lit up; he smiled for the first time in what seemed like years.

But then Fox told Ryder his latest information, things he'd been told by the POWs found at the bottom of the Holy Towers.

"These guys we freed said they saw Li just before we came down on this place," the DSA officer told Ryder now. "But when the Patch disappeared, he took her with him. They said he was determined to go ahead with her execution and all they were waiting for was a goddamn videotape."

More artillery shells went over their heads.

"Here's the problem," Fox continued shouting to the wild-eyed fighter pilot. "These guys told me about a shit-bum TV studio here in the city where the Patch would bring his victims to execute them. The way they described this studio is exactly what Murphy saw on the execution video. And the POWs say it's inside a white building with a red stripe running across the door. So if Li is still alive, she's probably at this place with the Patch and God knows who else."

Ryder was just about shaking the DSA officer now. "So where the hell is this place?" he yelled at him.

That's when Fox's face fell a mile. He just pointed to the southern end of town, even as the rain of artillery shells continued pummeling the place.

"Take a guess," was all Fox said.

It took a moment for this to sink in—but then it hit. The south end of town. The place that was now being flattened. The place that Ryder himself had bombed on two occasions.

That's when he went crazy for real.

"I've got to get down there!" he yelled at Fox.

Ryder started down the berm, but Fox just managed to grab him. "Wait!" he said. "There's more you have to know. These POWs say that there's all kinds of strange stuff down there. Really *dangerous* stuff."

But it was obvious Ryder didn't care. He unhooked Fox's hand from his flight suit, then resumed barreling down the berm. Borrowing an M16 from one of the Delta guys, Ryder took off running, right into the storm of artillery shells still raining down on the south end of the city.

There was no way anyone was going to stop him.

"Well, that went well," Fox said in frustration.

Not knowing what else to do, Fox climbed back aboard the Scramble copter. He was heading up to the Zabul's mountain artillery emplacement to try to get

them to stop the bombardment. But he knew by the time
he reached them it would probably be too late.

"Next time we do something like this," the DSA officer told Hunn before leaving, "we've got to make sure
everyone can talk to each other. Doing it this way is just
fucking nuts!"

Inside five minutes, Ryder found himself approaching
the dark center of the south end of the city. The artillery
blasts were still going off all around him. He could
hardly hear them; that's how far around the bend he'd
gone. But strangely, the only other real light down here
was coming from the two fires Ryder had started during
his improvised air strikes.

It was like running through his own version of hell.
Dropping his bombs down here earlier had been purely
capricious, little more than a result of the desire to kill
even *more* mooks, a few of whom might be hiding in the
shadows.

But now the thought of it—that one of those bombs
might have killed Li after she had miraculously escaped
death at the hands of the Patch—was burning a hole in
both Ryder's heart and his soul.

You should never have taken the ring off, he kept
taunting himself, over and over, as he dodged the huge
125mm shells. *You should have shot yourself when you
had the chance.*

Somehow, someway, he reached one of the buildings
he'd bombed. This was the place that had attracted his
attention after he'd spotted the glow from an acetylene
torch. The fire was still hot, but at least now he was able
to see inside. And thankfully it wasn't painted white
with a red stripe going across its door.

He stopped at one corner of the wrecked warehouse and looked in. Incredibly the first thing he saw was an American Stealth fighter—an F-117 Nighthawk—in pieces, smoldering on the floor. It wasn't his bombs that had torn it apart. It had been in pieces before his attack and had obviously been in the process of being rebuilt.

How did a Stealth jet get into a warehouse in Afghanistan? Ryder had no idea. His only guess was that it had been shot down somewhere and the mooks or someone they were in cahoots with was trying to put it back together.

He moved on.

He began running again, wildly trying to find his way through pitch-black here, blazing light there, artillery shells still coming down all around him. Three blocks away, he found another building he'd hit. It was still totally engulfed in flame, but again, he could see somewhat clearly inside. Glass bottles—hundreds of them, some broken, some steaming—littered the warehouse floor. What were these things? He didn't know. They all had Arabic writing on them, but he had no idea what the words said. However, more than a few were carrying an image he did understand: the skull and crossbones. The universal symbol for toxins.

Dirty bombs were the first two words that came to his mind.

He ran around the front of the building and was once again relieved to see that it was not painted white with a red stripe going across it.

Two for two, he thought. Neither of which looked like a TV studio. At least, *he'd* not killed Li.

But maybe someone else had.

He started running again. Now he had to find the

building that the POW had described as the Patch's execution studio.

All white, with a red stripe running across the door. That was the clue. But now, as Ryder was skidding through the oily streets, he was wondering if anything down here would ever be white again. Khrash had had a permanent layer of dirt on it in the first place. Now with all the smoke and debris falling, it would be hard to find a building colored anything but grimy.

But then, like an angel from above, he saw the *Psyclops* aircraft pass directly overhead. How they were able to find him in this maze of warehouses and storage bins he would never know. But as it streaked over him, it started dispensing flares at a furious rate. Suddenly the sky was lit up as bright as day.

It immediately came to Ryder that the airplane was trying to get his attention. The pyrotechnic display would have been hard to miss. Maybe somehow with all their high-tech gear they had spotted the building he was looking for. The flares were falling about three blocks over. He turned a complete 180 and was soon running in that direction.

Following the glow of the flares, he turned another left, ran down an alley full of burning debris and on to the next street over.

At that moment, the *Psyclops* plane went over again, more flares shooting out of its fuselage. It was flying very low and wagging its wings as it went over.

Ryder followed the glow again, running down two more alleys, then emerging on a much wider street. He looked to his right. Nothing but old wooden buildings. He looked to his left and saw exactly what he was looking for: a line of warehouses, made not of wood but of aluminum and tin. They were painted bright white with a red racing stripe going right down the middle of each one. The whole street was filled with them.

Amazing . . . a few seconds ago he'd been lost. Now, suddenly, he was right where he was supposed to be.

But which building was it?

Two artillery shells came down dangerously close to him, reminding him that he really didn't have time for deep thought here. He ran over to the door of the first building and yanked it open.

It was dark inside, with extremely pungent odors drifting around. There was no electricity anywhere in the city, so there would be no lights to turn on in here. But his eye was directed to a small red bulb burning about six feet down from the open door. This might be a switch for emergency battery-powered lighting.

Ryder felt his way along the wall, finally reaching the tiny red light and pushing the switch below it. Sure enough, some very dull emergency bulbs clicked on. Ryder found himself looking at a warehouse full of one-thousand-pound aerial bombs.

But these weren't ordinary half-tons. Printed very clearly on their nose cones, among a lot of Arabic writing, was the skull and crossbones symbol again. But that wasn't all. Along with it was the national insignia of not Afghanistan or Iran but the armed forces of Iraq. The old armed forces, back in the Saddam days.

Son of a bitch . . . , Ryder thought, the ramifications not yet sinking in. *Good thing I didn't bomb this place. . . .*

He got out of the warehouse as quickly as he could and started running again.

He reached the next door seconds later, this as another pair of artillery shells came down nearby. Just his luck that Tarik's cousin was giving them some bonus bombardment.

This second door was unlocked as well. Ryder went in, gun first again, to find another darkened interior. He found the emergency lights again and snapped them on. And again he was confronted with a room full of bombs bearing the insignia of the "old" Iraq military. But these explosives weren't carrying the universal toxin symbol.

Instead they bore the very distinctive black triangle with the bright yellow cut-out circular icon inside.

The universal sign for radioactive materials.

And that's when it hit Ryder.

The missing WMD . . .

The reason for the war in Iraq.

Here it was.

But he didn't have time to think about this now. As globally significant as it was, Ryder had something even more important on his mind.

He still had to find her. . . .

He exited the building quickly and went toward the third door. But before he could reach it, the door opened on its own and two armed men walked out. They might have been guarding the entrance; he wasn't sure. Strangely, they were not dressed like typical mooks. They were wearing uniforms, helmets, boots. They both looked up into the sky nonchalantly, checking to see if the artillery was still coming down, as casually as someone checking on the rain.

Whoever they were, they were so surprised to see Ryder tearing down the street that he was able to kill both of them easily with a burst from his borrowed M16.

A third uniformed soldier stumbled from the door-way. Ryder nailed him with a bullet to his head. A fourth soldier stumbled over his comrade's body, losing his weapon while falling right at Ryder's feet.

He looked up at Ryder and screamed, "*Fatah!*" Mercy! . . . Ryder put a bullet through his throat.

A fifth soldier stood paralyzed at the open door to the warehouse. He shouted something in Arabic, cut short as Ryder's bayonet ran him through. This man's uniform he checked. It was standard issue, Iranian Revolutionary Army.

Again Ryder didn't have the luxury to contemplate the geopolitical significance of this. He burst into the warehouse itself.

Like the first two, it was dark inside here—except for one spot, in the corner the farthest away from him. Down there he could see bright lights, like movie lights, burning as if on fire. He could also see a man, holding a large video camera; he was inserting a tape cassette. Ryder could see wires and cables and large car-type batteries. There were other people around, too, technician types. But for whatever reason, they seemed so intent on their work, they hadn't heard the battle taking place just outside the door.

No doubt about it—he'd stumbled upon a barebones TV studio.

Ryder kept his cool and crept into the murk. The closer he got to the klieg lights, the more people he saw in the illuminated corner. At least a dozen or so, maybe more. Five were dressed in black robes and rags. They were standing in the light, in front of a black curtain that had been hung on the far wall. There was Arabic scribbling all over this backdrop. One of the men was holding a huge machete-style knife.

And on the floor in front of him, blindfolded and once again awaiting the fatal blow, was Li. The way the light was hitting her, she almost seemed aglow.

Now it really was like Ryder was in a dream, because the next thing he knew, he thought he was flying two feet off the floor. He began firing his weapon, single shots all, each round looking like it was laser guided, each bullet finding its mark among the people gathered near the camera. It was like being inside his own video game, flying toward the small army of mooks, killing each one with just one bullet apiece. At the same time, bullets were coming his way; some might have even been hitting him. But still, he kept advancing.

By this time, he'd attracted everybody's attention, but it was too late for anyone to do anything about it. He could hear people shouting in Arabic, words he somehow knew meant "Hurry up!" and "Proceed!" They were more intent on getting their camera rolling than they were on dealing with him.

So this is what it has come to, he thought darkly. A simple and deadly truth. The mooks might have been expecting an entire army to come through their door, not just him and his weapon. Yet they were still determined to kill Li anyway—on videotape, in hopes that somehow, someway, the gruesome footage would find its way to Al-Qazzaza.

More bullets went by him now, but Ryder didn't care. He was in among the camera crew in an instant. He shot four of the five men standing over Li; they were all armed, but in posing for the camera they'd had no time to take their weapons over their shoulders and fire back at him.

Then Ryder turned and put two bullets into the camera itself. It exploded in a thousand pieces. One more bullet for each of the huge klieg lamps. He destroyed two but only wounded the third. It stayed on and started swinging wildly, causing weird shadows to dance around the room. This made things even more eerie.

Only a handful of men now stood between Ryder and Li; she was now on the floor, hands over her head.

Ryder shot the man closest to her, catching him once in the chest. He fell over, dead before he hit the floor. Then Ryder dispatched the man behind the camera, this bullet going to the stomach. He went over with a scream.

Two more fighters appeared out of the dark. Ryder put two bullets into the first man's groin. The second man fired at the crazed pilot—and missed. Ryder turned his M16 toward the man and pulled the trigger.

But nothing happened.

Ryder was out of ammunition.

He fell forward in an instant, his bayonet catching the man in his ribs. The man fell over but grabbed onto the razorlike weapon, slicing off three of his fingers. The scream that came out of him was bloodcurdling. Ryder finally yanked the blade from his rib cage and quickly stabbed him again, this time the bayonet going right into the man's open, screaming mouth. There was another sickening crackling noise, and the man finally died. But in killing him Ryder discovered he'd snapped his bayonet in two, leaving half of it in the man's skull and rendering the other half useless.

That's when Ryder saw one more shadow rise up

from the floor. The last man, with the machete in his hand. He'd pulled the mask over his head and now Ryder was face-to-face with him. He looked like something from a horror movie. His hands and body were, for some reason, covered with blood. But it was his face. Gnarled and bloody, too. And he was wearing a patch.

He raised the hatchet—Ryder had no defense. No gun, no knife. Nothing. Everything froze—now he awaited the blow, supremely pissed that he'd made it this close to rescuing Li, only to be dispatched by this monster.

Ryder looked up at his executioner. The man was literally foaming at the mouth. He started to swing down with the gleaming hatchet. . . .

When suddenly he stopped. Just for a moment. His eyes looked to the right—it was almost as if someone was calling his name. At the exact same moment, the unmistakable rumbling of the *Psyclops* plane going over filled the empty warehouse. In all this took maybe two seconds, but it was all the time Ryder needed.

He hit the Patch with a rolling block. They both fell over; suddenly Ryder was on top of the terrorist. And suddenly the hatchet was in *Ryder's* hand.

He put it right to the terrorist's throat.

"Ryder Long," he spit at the man. "Colonel. United States of America. This is for all the people you killed on September 11th."

The Patch went white. He tried to say the Arabic word for "mercy"—but it never came out. Ryder pushed the hatchet into the Patch's throat, severing his jugular, his windpipe, and his vocal cords all at once.

The look of horror froze on his face. His one good

eye went to his right—almost as if he was looking at Li. Than he mouthed his final words: *All for that American bitch. . . .*

Then he died.

Ryder somehow got to his feet. He staggered over to Li, pushing debris and bodies out of the way. She heard the footsteps but did not look up. He stood over her, not really believing this was happening. He reached down and lifted her blindfold, then rubbed his fingers lightly across her cheek. Only then did she look up and open her eyes.

It was clear to him that she thought she was dead— and was experiencing something in the Afterlife. Because when their eyes met, she almost laughed at the absurdity of it all.

Ryder knew he had to say something to convince her this was all real. So he smiled and then whispered: "Time to go home."

That's when she leaped to her feet, threw her arms around him with such enthusiasm they both toppled to the floor. He felt his whole body turn to pins and needles. He went numb. She squeezed him so tight he thought his ribs would crack. She pulled him down to her and kissed him once, twice, three times, all over his face—finally on the lips, and that's when they both just fell into each other's arms. Laughing and crying at the same time.

"I can't believe it," she kept saying over and over. "I can't believe you came for me."

She never stopped hugging him. They kissed deeply—their first. Outside, the artillery shells were still exploding. The ground beneath them was shaking—or at least that's what Ryder thought it was. He couldn't quite believe it himself—that this quest, first for revenge and then as a rescue of this precious girl—he couldn't believe he'd actually done it.

He would learn later that two of the Superhawk copters were outside firing on groups of mooks who were trying to get to the warehouse. The building itself started to collapse all around them, but no matter. Ryder and Li remained there for the longest time, just holding on to each other.

That's when one strange thought went through Ryder's head. He'd done the impossible. Li was alive. He'd saved her. And now he knew that she was into him, in a very big way.

And as he added all this up in his head, just two words came to mind: "Now what?"

One mile away

Ozzi was having trouble walking now. He'd lost a lot of blood. He was disoriented. He was cold yet sweating profusely. Still stunned over seeing his Zabul allies blown away, he felt his own life start to drip out of him.

He'd stumbled into yet another alley somewhere in the middle of the city. The blood was pouring out of his leg and he had nothing with which to tie off the wound. He was too weak to rip some material off his own uniform, too weak to look for tourniquet material among the ruins all around him. If he didn't do something about the wound soon, though, he knew he would die here, in this dirty little city.

He fell facedown in the alley, and for the first time in his life he didn't want to get up. What was the point? He could stumble just a few more steps, for what? Only to fall again?

So he stayed down and closed his eyes and saw bits and pieces of his life flash before him. It was just like they said: a movie reel, from his first day in school to his first bicycle, his first girlfriend, his first cool car. High school, college, Annapolis. His tiny office in the Pentagon. An OK life. An ordinary life. No wife. No kids. Nothing to leave anybody, except some misery for his parents once they found out he was KIA.

There the movie reel stopped . . .

But only for a moment. When it started again, he began seeing flashes of his life since joining the Ghosts. The mooks he'd taken out. The lives he'd saved. The way that he'd made his country just a little bit safer, a little bit better. It was corny, but it was also true. He might have been an ordinary guy, but the Ghosts were certainly not an ordinary bunch. It was a very exclusive club. And suddenly it seemed very important that he stay a member of it.

So, with all his strength, he started crawling. Over broken glass and burning pieces of metal. Through garbage and muck and whatever other crap could be found lying around in this dirty Muslim city. And somehow the crawling got him to the end of the alley. And it was here that he looked up, into waning night sky—and saw an American flag flying atop the building right next to him. His heart started beating right out of his chest.

But then he collapsed and went facedown again. And this time he was sure he could not move. It had been a joke after all. God had given him the strength not to live but just to see the flag one more time.

But he laughed about it.

At least I can die happy, he thought.

That's when he heard the sound of someone walking toward him. He could barely open his eyes, but when he did he saw two boots not two inches away from his nose. They were American boots. *Schwarzkopf* boots. That meant American Airborne. Or someone damn close.

Two hands came down and gently rolled him over. Ozzi found himself looking up at the blackest yet sunniest face he'd ever seen.

"Hey, brother," the member of Delta Thunder said to him. "Looks like you need a friend."

No one really knew how Saheeb the Syrian survived the battle for Khrash. He wasn't so sure himself.

Being the Patch's bodyguard was supposed to be a 24-7 job, and for Saheeb it had been, until the bombs started falling for real. That's when his contract ended. When the bombardment of the south end of the city began, Saheeb simply deserted the Patch in the TV studio and tried to head back for the center of town. All of Saheeb's personal belongings were there; he had to get them—and then get the hell out of Khrash before it all came crashing down on him.

But getting back to the Holy Towers proved a lot harder than he'd hoped. At first he found himself running at top speed, not easy for such a large man as he, trying to avoid the rain of artillery shells falling all around him. He was wounded several times in this dash for freedom but somehow made it out of the impact zone. Once clear of the south end, he found himself battered and bleeding and wandering through Hasha, the neighborhood of junkyards and old factories that had also just been leveled by the fierce artillery barrage.

There were many fires still raging here, but among the junk and wreckage Saheeb also saw many bodies. Al Qaeda fighters, who to him appeared to have been in some kind of retreat when the artillery came down on them. Many had packed bags by their sides. Others had died with explosive devices—booby-trap material—still strapped on their persons. Saheeb thought about robbing some of the corpses he saw but decided against it because his hands had been cut up and it would have been too painful for him to steal.

When he finally did reach the city square he found the place crowded with Americans and Zabul fighters. Thinking he was just another bloodied citizen, the Zabul let him through the lines. He walked to his apartment next to the Holy Towers and discovered it was in shambles. All of his possessions had been either looted or destroyed. This was not the work of the Americans. They were too busy to bother with his meager collection of junk. He was sure that members of the religious police had been the actual culprits, leaving him with absolutely nothing at this point in his miserable life.

Suddenly enraged, he wanted revenge—again not on the Americans but on the religious police. *They'd stolen his stuff*. There certainly weren't any hanging around the city square at the moment, so Saheeb headed for the only other place he thought he could find them: the Chief's blockhouse on the edge of the Old Quarter. Saheeb vowed to kill anyone he encountered there.

Saheeb had to hide a few times along the way because there were still some Americans and Zabul moving about and they might not mistake him this time. Somehow he made it to the blockhouse, but only to get another surprise. This place that everyone had always thought was invulnerable to attack had proved otherwise. Most of it was in ruins, the victim of a direct hit by a five-hundred-pound aerial bomb.

But one attachment had survived the bombing, more or less. This was the building's garage, a place where any bodies leftover from the rape and torture sessions held inside the blockhouse were dumped for pickup later.

It was also one of the places where the religious police sometimes kept their most precious weapon: the huge SA-6 SAM.

Saheeb broke into the garage and indeed found within no bodies but the famous SAM itself, covered with dust and debris. He also discovered that the garage roof had been blown away in the bombing. When he looked up, he saw nothing but the clearing sky above.

He also stumbled upon something that in some ways was more valuable than the big missile: the late Chief's hidden supply of the hallucinogenic qat. Weary, hurt, and at the end of his rope, Saheeb plunked himself down beside the stash and started chewing it by the handful. He was high as a kite five minutes later.

Before he'd signed on to be the Patch's bodyguard, Saheeb had worked in the freak show of a traveling circus. Before that he'd been committed to a home for the insane. But before *that* he'd been in the Syrian military. In fact, he'd been assigned to the rocket defense forces. He'd worked around SA-6 SAMs for four long years and they all smelled the same. Grease and burned wires, combined with the stink of the rocket fuel.

He stuffed another handful of qat into his mouth and, getting even higher, started examining the controls to the missile's launcher. He was surprised to see it was one of the newer models, a Russian export version that took all the brain work out of launching the damn thing, a must when selling exotic weaponry to Third World countries. With this model, all it took was to snap on the control panel, put the radar on search, and then just wait for a target to fall into the weapon's electronic web. Once the fly was close to the net, with one push of a button the missile was off.

It was that simple.

Any idiot could do it.

Even him. . . .

He sat back and chewed some more qat and contemplated just how penniless he now was. But then he looked back over at the missile and thought of something. It was like a lightbulb turning on in his head.

Is Al Qaeda still paying rewards to anyone who shoots down an American aircraft? he wondered.

Chapter 20

An hour passed.

More flares shot in the air called all of the Americans and their Zabul allies to the Al Sharim berm. The artificial hill next to the old soccer field had become the Ghosts' regrouping point.

The Delta Thunder guys were among the first to arrive, accompanied by the SEALs and carrying Ozzi with them. The Thunder troopers told the others about leaving the *Ocean Voyager* and landing along the Farāh River just in time to prevent the Chief of the religious police from escaping. Eventually teaming up with the SEALs and after rescuing Ozzi, they came upon the one-sided battle in Khrash's city square—and at just the right time. Only they and the SEALs had anything left in the way of ammunition. Still, it was a strange introduction to what had been happening in the formerly terrorist city this very strange night.

Most of Kennedy's 2nd Delta and the rest of Hunn's 1st were also on hand at the berm, as were most of their

Zabul allies. Everyone got a drink of wine. Everyone got a chance to sleep. More than one member hoped they could wake up and find out the whole thing had been one big dream.

And still a few of the team were missing.

About 0930 hours, the morning quiet was broken by the sound of an aircraft approaching.

It came out of the south. A big Navy Chinook. It set down on the field not far from the burning *Psyclops* plane. Johnny Johnson, CO of Delta Thunder, called his men to him. This was their ride out.

Fox, Hunn, and the rest of the Ghost Team walked them down to the LZ. The Chinook crew looked out the aircraft windows, staring at the ragged, bearded, unkempt Ghosts like someone would look at visitors from another planet. The expressions on their faces said it all: *Who the hell are these guys?*

Just as this copter was settling down, a second Chinook flew overhead. The Ghosts looked up to see someone in it, looking down at them from the cockpit, giving them a bold salute. Then the aircraft increased speed and headed off in the direction of Mount Zabul.

The guys from Delta Thunder climbed aboard the waiting Chinook, this after shaking hands and embracing the Ghosts, now truly their brothers in arms.

Fox above all shook hands warmly with Johnson. "You know, usually after going through the wringer with us, people tend to join up," the DSA officer said to him. "I mean—look at this crew. We got all the flavors of the rainbow."

Johnson replied: "Your reputation is well-founded. And we could all do great things together. But we've got something else going on that at the moment is as important. We've got to get back to our place. A lot of problems back there. We have to do our part in trying to fix them. You understand, I'm sure?"

Fox did—but he hated to see them go. They all did. The Delta Thunder guys would have been a perfect fit for the Ghost Team.

"I hear you," Fox told him. "Maybe we'll hook up again then."

Johnson saluted him. "Count on it," he said.

Then he climbed aboard the Chinook and closed the door. The big copter rose into the air, turned, and headed southwest.

That's when Hunn came up beside Fox. "They have things 'as important' to do?" he asked the DSA officer. "Like what?"

Fox watched the copter disappear over the horizon. "Like trying to save an entire continent," he finally said.

The huge helicopter circled Mount Zabul once before setting down in a maelstrom of dust and snow.

A squad of armed Zabul fighters met the big aircraft. It was painted gray, had two huge rotors and the words USS *Ronald Reagan* painted on the side of its fuselage. That name was well-known, even up here at the top of the world.

Tarik Aboo appeared from his round stone hut and walked to the landing site. The door to the helicopter slid open and two armed crewmen stepped out. They took a look around, eyed the armed Zabul, but lowered their weapons, as did the mountain fighters.

Then the Navy crewmen helped out the copter's only passenger. He was wearing a borrowed flight deck win-ter suit, complete with hood and huge rubber boots. The outfit appeared to weigh more than the man did.

It was Bobby Murphy, here to thank an old friend for his help.

Tarik greeted him warmly, with much hugging and cheek kissing. Murphy took it all in good humor, then followed Tarik back to his hut.

They sat inside next to the small stove and Murphy accepted Tarik's offer of one of the huge black cigarettes, not quite realizing it was stuffed with both tobacco and hashish.

"We owe you more than before, my friend," Tarik told Murphy. "Your men have removed the blight of Warlord Sharif and have put an end to the sinful enterprises in Khrash."

Murphy just took a long drag of the Afghani blunt. "We had our own reasons, our own motives. But I'm glad you will benefit from it all."

"Our fighters will remain in the city for as long as they are needed," Tarik reported. "We will try to rebuild it. Try to make it a place where the innocent and the uninvolved can live in peace."

Murphy nodded solemnly. "That's how it should be," he said. "And you'll have a lot of ex-Iranian equipment at your disposal should anyone seek to disagree with you."

Tarik shook his head slowly, then waved the smoke out of the air. It was clear he did not want to talk about what had happened in Khrash's center square just after the Iranian brigade showed up. It was just too spooky for him.

"As for whatever is down in those warehouses," Murphy went on, "we'll have to leave that to the brains in Washington. If what I suspect about some of the stuff is true, I'm sure they'll be dying to announce they'd finally found what they've been looking for all these years. On the other hand, there's a good chance they'll want to keep the whole thing secret because they don't want to admit that anything went on in Khrash and with Iran and Al Qaeda because they'll never know what happened exactly. Could get confusing."

Tarik smiled. "Sometimes I'm happy I live high up in the mountains," he said. "And other times I'm not sure if I live high enough."

"But whatever happens, you must remember," Murphy went on, "the promise you made to me a long time ago. Peace and freedom for everyone in that city, in the entire Qimruz. If people want to sing or dance or fly a kite, they have to be able to. If they want to read a book, see a movie, praise Allah, or Jesus, or Yahweh—they have to have the freedom to do so."

Tarik was nodding in agreement. "The old times must pass," he replied. "I'm smart enough to know that."

Murphy took another drag and then raised his finger to make one more point. "And no beating of women," he told Tarik soberly. "Or children. Those things are the most important of all."

Tarik nodded again. "I understand and promise that to you, my friend."

"That's good," Murphy said. "Because I'll be watching. And if things go wrong, or if they start to go backward . . ." He nodded in the direction of Khrash. "Well . . . you know now what we can do."

Tarik smiled again, but maybe a bit nervously. "Of all your points you've made today," he told Murphy, "that one is the most clear."

They shook hands and then embraced.

"And spend all that money wisely," Murphy added. "You earned it."

Tarik looked back at him queerly. "What money?" he asked. "We didn't do this for money. We did this for the spoils of Khrash and to rid this part of our world from that *jihad* filth."

Murphy was stumped. "You mean you weren't paid, my friend?" he asked. "Two million dollars in American cash?"

Tarik just laughed and took another long drag on his cigarette.

"Two million dollars, American?" he said. "What would I do with that kind of money?"

The battle for Khrash was over.

For the first time in many hours, there were no sounds of gunfire or explosions. No clank of tank treads, or jet fighters roaring overhead. No B-52 strikes, real or imagined. Khrash was quiet. The only sound was that of many American flags whipping in the breeze.

The city square was still filling up with Ghosts. Some of 1st Delta were now here; so was Kennedy's entire 2nd attack squad. Many of the Zabul fighters were also on hand. The pair of tanks were here, too; they were guarding the two main approaches to the middle of town, guns locked and loaded. But no one was coming at them now. No one was left—at least not among the city's once visible defenders and visitors. They were all dead, out on either the bridge or the mountain pass road, or within the city itself. *That's* why it was so quiet.

How many terrorists had been killed? It really didn't make much difference to the Americans now lounging about the city square, many of them taking their first rest break of the night. If they'd gone through all this just to kill one Al Qaeda member, it would have been worth it. That was the measure of hatred the Ghosts had for the Islamic terrorist group. They had vowed to get them all, one by one, and all of the Ghosts truly believed that someday they would reach that goal. The fact that there were at least 10,000 dead mooks currently lying around and that many were hard-core Al Qaeda was just a small step in that direction.

Gradually the civilians started coming out of their hiding places. Many were wailing, twirling kerchiefs over their heads. Happy and sad at the same time, the subtitle of this story. Once they got over the initial shock of seeing Americans standing in their city square, they began thanking the Ghosts and the Zabul for what they'd just done. The triple plague of the Taliban, Al Qaeda, and the religious police was now gone. The people had their city back again. They could sing. They could dance. They could fly a kite. They could read a book. They were free.

They were also being frisked now for explosives before they were allowed to mingle among the liberators, offering them figs and much-appreciated cups of water.

The only problem now was how and when were the Ghosts going to get out of here?

Their work was done. It was time to go home.

As if in answer to that question, one of the team's helicopters appeared overhead, pulling up in a hover above the crowded city square. Many of the Ghosts started gathering up their equipment. This was the beginning of their transport line out; they were sure of it. It might take a while before they eventually made it back to the *Ocean Voyager*, but every happy journey has to start somewhere. . . .

But suddenly everyone beneath the helicopter sensed something was wrong. The aircraft was not moving; it was just floating above them, maybe three hundred feet up, its nose pointing south. Those on the ground could almost see the pilots squinting, as if trying to see something farther down in that part of the city.

Then one of the copter's crew leaned very far out of the cargo bay door and started yelling down to the troopers below. But he couldn't be heard over the sound of the rotors. He realized this—and in desperation started pointing wildly toward the south.

The first he shell smashed into the city square a second later.

With madness typical of this night, the shell blew up in the midst of the civilians who had gathered to thank the Ghosts for what they'd just done. The resulting fireball was tinged with blood—two dozen people, gone in a flash.

The Ghosts actually had time to scatter before the second shell came crashing down. It hit the bottom of the Holy Towers, exploding in a gush of fire and concrete. Two more shells came in. More civilians were killed. Two more and the top floor of the Holy Towers was suddenly blown away.

The Ghosts had no idea who was shooting at them— only that it was coming from the south. One of the Zabul tanks started to turn its gun turret in that direction. It was hit twice, simultaneously, before the turret got halfway around. The monstrous T-72 was lifted off the ground like a broken toy.

Now the shells started raining down two and three at a time. The Americans began fanning out from the square, some carrying their rifles, some not. And those who were holding their weapons were very low on ammunition. Whoever this unseen enemy was, the Ghosts wouldn't have very much to throw back at them once they came face-to-face. And they knew it was the same for their air assets. All three copters and both jet fighters had run low on ammunition a long time ago.

Finally they all heard the first real noise of their attackers approaching. It was the very distinct and frightening clanking sound made by only one weapon in the world: a tank.

And as crazy and unreal and unbelievable as it seemed, there were two dozen heavily armored battle tanks rumbling into the city square. They were big ones: T-80s, ironically a souped-up version of the Zabul T-72s. And they were all wearing the battle colors of the Islamic Republic of Iran.

There was never any doubt that Khrash was important to the twisted old men who ran Iran. It provided deniability on everything from WMD, to stolen aircraft, to hostages, to brand-new Russian weapons. That *was* the same French Bell-72 the Thunder guys had seen earlier in the night. It was dropping off the parcel of plutonium it had picked up in West Africa that it never disposed of. The Iranians were into nukes, too.

So, what was lurking in the warehouses at the southern end of Khrash all this time? As it turned out, just about everything that couldn't be found in Iraq— hostages, weapons, WMD—and a whole lot more. And to guard it all? An entire mechanized battalion of the *Kvak,* the Iranian Special Forces. Twenty-four tanks. Twenty-four armored personal carriers. Twelve mobile guns and more than 2,000 men. Very well hidden, from the Americans, even from the people who used to run Khrash. But now they were on the loose.

Someone somewhere had decided the Americans had seen too much in Khrash and that there would be too many tales to tell. So they'd dispatched this column to make sure there weren't any witnesses. And being just about out of bullets and bombs themselves, the Ghosts didn't stand a chance.

But that's when the EC-130 *Psyclops* plane arrived over the scene.

There was no CD they could blare through their God's Ear speakers to stop this. The Iranian Special Forces weren't going to fall for anything like that. They knew what had happened in Khrash, had watched it all. And they probably would have let it all go and never have revealed themselves if the Americans hadn't started poking their noses around the southern part of the city. But of course that's where they'd allowed the Patch to bring the Asian girl and to do his killings—and that had been a mistake. Thus the need to seal many lips permanently.

Still the EC-130 started buzzing the Iranian column, this as the lead tanks continued bombarding the area around the Holy Towers, sending the Ghosts and the Zabul scrambling for any bit of cover they could find.

The Iranians were quickly aware of the huge strange-looking plane. Soldiers began popping up on the tops of the tanks and APCs with heavy-caliber machine guns and shoulder-launched antiaircraft weapons. Any combination of these weapons could bring down the big propeller plane, especially since it was flying so low.

The whole thing was madness—on a night filled with madness. The Ghosts were looking at the prospect of of-

fering only a minor defense before being utterly wiped
out by this overwhelming superior force. And it wasn't
like they could really call in a B-52 strike or expect the
4th Army to come to their rescue.

The tanks continued firing even as the soldiers on top
were shooting up at the EC-130. The sky above the main
street was now crisscrossed with heavy tracer fire, yet
the EC-130 came back again, this time lower and
slower. What the hell was it doing? It wasn't going to
scare the Iranians away.

But as it turned out, its crew had something else in
mind.

What happened next would be a matter of debate for
some time to come. The *Psyclops* plane came back a
third time—and on this pass it was flying even lower and
even slower right over the top of the *Kvak* column. The
sky was absolutely thick with tracer fire now; the EC-
130 flew right through it, taking hits all along its wings
and underbelly. But it was at this moment that some
people who were there said they saw the igloo-shaped
object attached to the *Psyclops* plane's belly start glowing a very bright white. Then a noise like a very high-
pitched siren went through the air.

And just as suddenly the column of tanks and guns
ground to a halt. All firing stopped. The Ghosts peeked
out from behind their cover to see a very strange sight.
The Iranians were abandoning their vehicles en masse.

Here the stories would differ as well. Some on hand
said the Iranians stumbled out of their trucks holding
their ears. Others said they had their hands over their
eyes. Still others claimed that many of the Iranians appeared to be vomiting or bleeding from the nose and
mouth. Whatever happened, one thing everyone agreed

on was that when the Persians bailed out of their vehicles, they weren't carrying any of their personal weapons.

And that turned out to be the end for them. Because at that moment, the helicopter that had been hovering above the square all this time was joined by the other two Blackhawks and they started firing the last of their ammunition down at the admittedly hapless Iranians. At the same moment, the Iranians began taking fire from the rear of their column as well. This barrage was coming from the ground and from heavy-caliber weapons similar to those carried in the copters.

It took just three minutes for all the *Kvak* troops to be killed. By the helicopters in the air and, as it turned out, by a combined unit of Delta Thunder and the Ghosts' SEAL team moving up from the rear.

In that time, no one saw any of the Iranian soldiers fighting back.

Most people on hand attributed what happened to something done by the *Psyclops* plane. The many witnesses to claim that the Snowball attachment to the plane was acting curiously bolstered this belief. A secret weapon of some kind and of some unknown capability. . . .

That's why it was so ironic that in the strange encounter it was the *Psyclops* plane that wound up getting mortally wounded. It had taken dozens of hits from the Iranian column, this before whatever happened, happened and the *Kvak* soldiers were firing just about everything they had up at the electronics-packed plane. By the time the big plane turned back over the city square, fire had broken out on both of its wings and down around its complex tail section.

It was obvious to those on the ground, still dealing
with the strangeness of what had befallen the Iranian
column, that the EC-130 was in desperate straits. As it
tried to climb for some altitude directly over the center
of the city, its engines were heard coughing and cutting
out. It seemed like the plane was going through its death
throes, right in midair.

But the worst was yet to come.

The plane was beginning to turn over, very slowly. It
looked like a maneuver that the plane couldn't possibly
recover from. Suddenly a massive whooshing sound
was heard. A second after that, a huge missile rose up
from the Old Quarter and began streaking right toward
the severely wounded EC-130.

Khrash's most famous weapon, the SA-6 SAM, had
finally made its appearance—and it was heading right
for the *Psyclops* plane. If the SAM hit it, the EC-130
and everyone on board would be blown to a million
pieces.

But that isn't what happened.

Just as the missile was about to strike the ailing
plane, there came *another* streak of light flashing across
the sky. It managed to somehow get itself in between the
missile and the big plane.

It was Red Curry in his F-14.

The missile locked onto his jet, forgetting about the
Psyclops plane. The ghost pilot jinked one way as the
EC-130 went the other. The SAM hit two seconds later,
blowing the F-14 to smithereens. Those on the ground
were stunned.

Curry had taken the hit. And in the process, the *Psyclops* plane had been saved.

For a few seconds, anyway.

. . .

Captain J. C. Dow knew they were in big trouble. He was losing power in all four engines of the EC-130, and many of the electrical devices on the plane were blinking off or, worse, catching fire.

Either they set down somewhere very quickly or they were going to crash. Simple as that.

But where could they possibly land?

Dow knew of only one place: the field near the Al Sharim berm. The place where Ryder had plowed his jet into the ground. With all their strength, he and Clancy turned the big plane over Khrash once again and started to fly east.

The field they were aiming for was only about one thousand feet long. Once a soccer field, before the Taliban took over Afghanistan, it was overgrown with grass and a few small trees. But at least it was flat—somewhat—and some of 1st Delta were still in the area, should the *Psyclops* crew need help getting out of the wreckage. If anyone survived, that is.

The field was in sight just seconds later. The crew of the EC-130 prepared themselves for a very rough landing. Dow did everything he could to slow the plane's airspeed. Full flaps extended, wheels down, nose up. He even tried reversing two of his propellers, nearly impossible to do in midair. But the plane was burning on both wings and he could see the flames creeping closer to the engines. Hard bang-in or not, they had to get down on the ground in a hurry.

Dow yelled for the crew to come forward and strap in as best they could up front. As they looked out the oversize windshield, the soccer field got bigger and bigger the faster they fell. The cabin was quickly filling with smoke. Their number-one engine was about to burst into flames.

Still Dow and Clancy held the plane steady.

They slammed into the ground a moment later. The first thing that happened was the right-side landing gear carriage collapsed, digging that side of the plane into the hard surface. They went screeching along the field, past Ryder's wrecked F-14, decapitating trees and throwing great furrows of rocks and dirt into the air. The right side dragging actually helped slow them down. Still they skidded the entire one thousand feet before the huge plane finally began slowing. Then came a loud thump—the sound of the left side wheel carriage collapsing as well. It shook the plane from one end to the other. But then, finally, they came to a stop.

The crew stayed frozen in place, jammed as they were up in the flight compartment. None of them quite believed they were still alive. A couple of the DJs checked their pulses, just to make sure.

Then . . . someone just started laughing. It was strange at first, but someone else joined in, and they were joined by a third person and a fourth and before long they were *all* laughing wildly. It was *funny*. They'd made it. They *were* alive. And they had just had the adventure of their lives.

Then someone turned around and looked back into the cabin and saw that it was a total wreck. Transmitters, condensers, computer stations. The White Screen—all smashed, crashed, or starting to sizzle with flames. Hundreds of millions of dollars' worth of equipment damaged beyond any hope of repair. And they didn't have to be reminded that they had essentially landed right on top of the mysterious Snowball. That alone cost a couple *billion* dollars.

The crew stopped laughing as they looked at the damage.

Then Clancy said, in perfect deadpan, "Who the fuck is going to pay for all this?"

And the crew went back to laughing again.

That's how the guys from 1st Delta found them when they pried open the doors to the big plane and helped them out. Each man laughing like crazy.

The big plane looked just as bad from the outside as it did within. The fires on both wings had burned themselves out in the crash, but the plane was still a total wreck. The Delta guys led the civilian soldiers away from the smoldering aircraft and got them up the side of the berm where many of the team were now located.

Someone had found some wine in the city and now a couple bottles were passed to the *Psyclops* crew. It was not yet seven in the morning. Still they drank greedily.

Fox's Scramble copter had set down by this time. He'd seen what had just happened in the city square; in fact, he'd taken part in the strange massacre of Iranian soldiers.

He walked over to Dow now and sat beside him. "Would it help if I told you I have a Level Six security clearance?" he asked the National Guard pilot.

"Help how?" Dow replied.

"Help in letting you tell me what the hell went on back there," Fox said evenly. "I saw that igloo thing blinking as bright as day when you were flying above that Iranian column. Then I saw those soldiers just stop their trucks and take it. No one in their right mind would just sit there and allow themselves to be killed."

"So?"

"So—it gets me thinking those Iranian soldiers were suddenly *not* in their right minds . . . and as nuts as it is to say this, I think your plane and that cupcake you were carrying underneath it had something to do with that. Maybe ultrasensitive sound waves, interfering with brain function? Or microwaves that have the ability to short-circuit electric charges in the cerebral cortex?"

Dow just stared straight ahead for a long time, sipping from the breakfast wine bottle. Then he said: "We won here, right, Major?" Dow looked down on the city, with its hundreds of billowing American flags.

"I'd say that, yes . . ."

"And that might not have happened if the Iranian Special Forces hadn't been stopped?"

"Again, true . . . ," Fox acknowledged.

"So the situation was somewhat desperate?"

"For sure," Fox told him.

Dow took another long swig of wine and relaxed, if just a little.

"Then all I can say is, everything other than that is classified," Dow told him. "And if you ever bump up another couple steps in the security ratings, *then* maybe I'll be able to answer your question."

He looked directly at Fox. "Know what I mean?"

Fox nodded slowly, then looked back at the plane wreck and the pieces of the Snowball that were now scattered all over the ground.

"Jesuzz," he whispered—Dow had essentially answered his question. "Now, that's *damn* scary."

By nine in the morning, the majority of the Ghost Team
had assembled atop the Al Sharim berm.

All three copters were on the ground nearby. Their
crews were sacked out in the long grass, trying to catch
their first real sleep in nearly a week.

It was finally bright daylight. The city beyond looked
surreal, like something from a fantasy war movie or a
real-life video game. There were American flags flying
everywhere. Atop hundreds of buildings. Big and small,
wrecked and intact. Rising above the smoke and the
flames. Rippling in the early-morning breeze. One look
at all this and there was no doubt who'd won this war.

It was up here, on the grassy hill, where the Ghosts
waited for the last of the stragglers to emerge from the
city.

They finally came out in twos and threes. Members
of the strike team, some of their Zabul allies. More
civilians who had somehow managed to survive the
hellish night.

And they saw one last miracle up here. A man
emerged from the western part of the small city, dragging what looked to be a parachute behind him. Some of
the Delta guys ran down to meet him. Incredibly, it was
Red Curry.

"Jesuzz," Fox told Curry once he had been helped up
the hill, "you're taking this ghost thing a little too far,
don't you think?"

"What do you mean?" Curry asked, already stripped
down to his trademark Oakland Raiders T-shirt.

"Didn't you go in when you took the hit for the *Psy-*

clops plane?" Fox asked him. "That was a pretty big SAM. . . ."

Curry just laughed wearily. " 'Go in'?" he asked. "Like take the bullet? Be an instant hero? Not me. That's what ejection seats are for."

Indeed, he explained, his zero-motion ejection seat was caught in the fireball created by the SAM hit—and he wound up going down in the Farāh River, his chute opening not ten feet before he hit the surface.

"You don't know what cold is," he concluded, "til you take a swim in that river."

They waited all morning. By noon, everyone had been accounted for—except for two: Li and Ryder.

And this turned out to be the strangest thing of all, because people had seen the pair after the battle had ceased, so everyone knew they were alive. One of the Blackhawk pilots said they approached him just before dawn, after most of the shooting had stopped and before many people started congregating atop the Al Sharim berm. The copter pilot had set down near the city's main gate to check damage to his aircraft. Ryder and Li were driving what appeared to be the Patch's Range Rover.

They'd asked the copter pilot if he knew how they could get to the part of town where Ryder's F-14 wound up. The copter pilot gave them directions that would allow them to avoid the more devastated parts of the city. The pair thanked him and left in the direction of the crash-landed jet.

The second copter pilot saw them a few minutes later. He flew over them as he was heading for the city square. They seemed to be salvaging something out of Ryder's wrecked fighter, which was very close by. They both

waved and the copter pilot waved back in response, like
the first pilot, happy to see that both had made it through
the ordeal.

Then, by coincidence, the first copter pilot saw them
again, just minutes later, as he, too, was flying west.
They were still in the Range Rover, this time driving
back into the devastated city.

That was the last anyone saw of them.

It would take a while longer, but the rest of the
Ghosts would also learn that day that in addition to Ryder and Li being missing, the $2 million Murphy had
given Ryder was missing, too.

Epilogue

The news of the Battle of Khrash soon flashed around
the world.

Though the U.S. government at first tried to down-
play the event, describing it as a simple skirmish between warring Afghan tribes, once the media jumped
on the story it was soon clear that a huge firefight had
taken place and that a major blow had been dealt to Al
Qaeda. TV images showing American flags fluttering
over the corpse-laden terrorist city only confirmed
that.

And there was no doubt who had so decisively defeated the terrorists: It had been the Ghost Team, the
near-mythical anti-terrorism unit that had been battling
the perpetrators of 9/11 while the U.S. administration

was preoccupied with invading oil-rich countries overseas and lining the coffers of its political friends at home. The deeply secret special-ops team's fingerprints were all over the Khrash operation.

So it was strange then, that at the moment of their greatest triumph, true to their name, the Ghosts disappeared.

No victory parades. No medal ceremonies. No press conferences offering praise to Bobby Murphy and his crew. No sooner was the battle over than the mysterious black ops team simply vanished.

And though it tried very hard to find them in the next few weeks, the U.S. government never did figure out where they went.

Not exactly anyway.

Several months later, a tantalizing clue was found.

One night, very late, a stray short-wave radio transmission was picked up by several U.S. listening stations, outposts hidden in some of the most desolated areas of Southwest Asia and the Middle East. From far down the channel, a voice spoke in a very distinctive drawl with a perfectly American timbre. As if caught in the middle of a private conversation, the voice was heard to say: *"My friend Nietzsche once wrote: 'He who fights against monsters should see to it that he does not become a monster himself.'"*

That was all that was captured of the transmission before it faded back to static. When analyzed by audio experts from several U.S. intelligence agencies, however, the unanimous conclusion was that the voice belonged to Bobby Murphy.

Several months later, a curious entry found its way into a top-secret briefing paper being prepared for the National Security Council's Terrorism Task Force. It concerned more than a dozen reports of strange Caucasian men spotted during routine undercover surveillance entering and leaving prominent mosques in locations around Europe and the Middle East.

Observed in groups of twos and threes, some of these men looked to have had surgical procedures done recently to their faces; others appeared to have had the pigment in their skins actually darkened. And though all were poorly dressed and generally unclean, they were also seen carrying rolls of American dollars in their pockets. More intriguing, the number of different individuals observed totaled 55, the same number of soldiers thought to be in the Ghost Team.

But these strangers were not infiltrating the mosques to do them harm. This fact was confirmed by informers the United States already had imbedded inside the Muslim temples. Rather, these individuals had been seen taking part in hours of solemn prayer, attending brutally long religious education classes, and participating in intense discussions about the teachings of Allah.

In other words, they were learning to *become* Muslims.

By the time the NSC thought to act on this report and track down the strangers and question them, the 55 men had completed their religious training and had dissolved into the ever-murky world of the Persian Gulf.

If these people *were* the Ghosts, they had disappeared again.

This turn of events only became more baffling when six months to the day after the Battle of Khrash ended, another faint radio signal was heard around the Middle East. Like the one months before, this transmission was ethereal, barely audible from the loneliest end of the shortwave radio dial. And like the first, its point of origin was unknown. It could have come from a transmitter located deep in the mountains of West Pakistan, or a radio house aboard one of thousands of container-ships at sea, or a solitary aircraft flying very high over the troubled region.

But it was the same voice, that same drawl as on the first message. And the words were just as enigmatic, if not chilling:

"This problem of Muslim terrorism," the voice had said, *"with all the hate and destruction and misery that goes with it is, in the end, a Muslim problem. Even with all its might and resources and manpower and bravery, it just cannot be fixed by Americans.*

"Muslim terrorism can only be fixed by Muslims themselves."

END OF SERIES ONE